# PLEBE SUMMER

**A NOVEL**

# HANK TUROWSKI

Paradigm Press

Duces Virum

C/O Paradigm Press
4912 Parkview Dr.
St. Cloud, FL. 34771
paradigmpress.com
(206) 595-1907

## AUTHOR'S NOTE

The United States Naval Academy at Annapolis is an institution entrusted with the training and motivation of the future leaders of our military and our nation. Every year more than one thousand new candidates enter Annapolis. They have been selected from more than 12,000 applicants. These are the plebes, and they come from every state in the union and from several foreign nations. They are the best that America's high schools produce, and they are outstanding young men and women. But they bring with them varied family backgrounds, multiple cultural roots, and often extreme differences in outlook and temperament. The duty of the Annapolis system is to indoctrinate the newcomers, and teach them to use these differences in background, personality, and talent to best advantage and in such a way that reflects the highest standards of moral and professional conduct.

The service academies have had their share of scandals and negative publicity, and it sometimes feels like something has gone wrong with the system. But this book examines subtlety whether these negative events are a failure of the system, or whether they are a sign that the self-policing honor system - in effect for more than one hundred years - still works.

The Plebe Trilogy tells the fictitious story of Plebe Year - the great crucible that separates the 'candidates' from the midshipmen. Specifically it is the story of one unusual group of first year midshipmen as they progress through Plebe Year in the late 1960s. It was a time when the social turmoil was mostly external, and young men and women were less inhibited by social and political correctness, and when each graduate considered mortality as a direct consequence of their career choice. The three novels that make up the trilogy develop the concepts of "*Plebe Summer*'" when the plebe group bonds as a unit through the painful reality of their new lives; "*The Brigade*", when the plebes become part of a much great whole and fight to be accepted; and "*The Hundredth Night*", when they must put into practice the lessons they have hopefully learned. The novels are available individually or as a trilogy set.

I acknowledge the fantastic support of my wife Elaine, who is my partner in this process, and who urged me on and who helped patiently through the rewrites.

Finally, there's Hank Jr., the mathematician, computer scientist, and my wunderkind, who helped develop and market the books.

ISBN 9781535021197 AND Library of Congress Numbers pending.

Published in 2016 by Paradigm Press, 4912 Parkview Dr. St. Cloud, FL. 34771. To order - Call (206) 595-1907 or E-Mail paradigmpress.com.

# PLEBE SUMMER

## KEVIN O'REILLY'S STORY

THE CLASS CREST OF THE CLASS OF 1971

Every graduating class at Annapolis designs its own crest, which is included on the class ring on the side opposite the Academy seal. The ring is worn on the left hand and the crest side is turned outward following graduation.

# *PLEBE SUMMER*

## PROLOGUE

June Week at Annapolis. Smiling parents. Joyous graduates. New careers. Celebrations of life and love! The city and the Academy campus reveled in the warm June sunshine. Not so the Herndon Monument. The obelisk was a mess. The sun that peeked through the branches of the enormous tulip poplar trees on either side dappled the gray marble in a rhythmic sway of shadow and brightness. Its shiny sides were coated with a mixture of various slimes -- both manufactured and human. Streak and smear marks traversed the mess at odd angles, along with an assortment of deeply embedded finger trails. The pointed top held the shredded remnants of material -- part of a midshipman's hat -- glued in place that morning, but ripped away moments before. In an odd way, Herndon looked exhausted. Me too, I suppose.

I was standing in what looked like a battle scene. The meticulously groomed lawn was chewed into unrecognizable trauma and transformed into a mud patch. The mud was littered with gym shirts -- some ripped into shreds. A solitary gym shoe stood toe-first in the middle of the muck, looking like a miniature obelisk. Blood stained the monument ten feet up where someone had broken a nose in their haste to climb. A vomit puddle steamed at my feet. This was a remnant from one of my more athletic classmates who had hurled himself into the mass of young humanity plastered against the obelisk, only to be crushed by the ensuing swelter.

A nearby enlisted medical crew worked on a newly promoted plebe who had fainted in the crush. The corpsmen laughed amongst themselves. I knew they thought we were crazy to have performed a ritual so inane and fraught with minor perils. I smiled. They would never understand. Climbing the Monument was a holy act, a messy First Communion that signified the official end of Plebe Year - for me and a thousand of my classmates.

My hands were grubby and slime-covered like everything else nearby, but they held a treasure unlike anything I had ever possessed: a hat. A filthy midshipman's cloth dixie cup. But this was not just any hat. It was *the* hat. The one that had mocked the plebe class from its perch atop the monument. The one that had been ripped away by one of my companymates. Of course my company had gained the prize. We were the *Tigers*!

The company of companies.  The ones every other midshipman hated -- and secretly envied.

I lifted the hat into the air and held it aloft.  I could feel a tear tracking down my cheek.  Where had that come from?  I laughed, startling the corpsmen, who stared at me as if I were a lunatic.  Maybe I was.  I didn't care.  It was finally over.  No more plebe insanity.  No more pushups till my arms gave out.  No more running and vomiting and running some more.  No more "How's the cow?" No more chopping in the passageways.  No more square meals.  No more chow calls.  No more bracing up.  It was finished! And I had survived.

 Minutes earlier my classmates had raced to Bancroft Hall to clean up for liberty and brief summer vacations.  The visitors and parents who had witnessed our triumph had also dispersed - some to wait for their sons at the statue of Tecumseh, others to wander the campus.  I was alone - almost.

 Across the street in front of the Chapel a familiar figure stared at me.  I hadn't noticed him, and I was startled.   The gold bars signifying his rank as a fresh Second Lieutenant sparkled in the sun.  He wore a brilliant white Marine Corps officer's uniform complete with choker collar, sword, and white gloves.  He smiled at me, but I only stared in return.  I could never be as elegant and poised as he was.  At one time I hated him with a passion.  Now - I wasn't so sure.

I lowered the hat, feeling silly for my euphoria.  The Lieutenant's smile broadened, then he snapped his right hand to the brim of his cap in a perfect salute.  The kind reserved for senior officers, dignitaries, and pretty females.  I had never been saluted before.  I felt suddenly powerful.  I knew I wasn't supposed to salute dressed as I was; but I couldn't *not* do this.  I raised my own hand in a less perfect version of his, then snapped it to my side.  He dropped his in return, spun smartly, and strode away, no doubt anxious to be off to Quantico and finally to some steamy jungle battleground.  God help the enemy he faced.

I watched him depart, proud that I had known him.  Immediately I caught myself.  Was I actually proud of Rockwell Stone and his *Tiger* mentality?  What had happened to me?  Had I changed so much in the last year that my bearings had shifted by some personal tectonics?  Looking down at the hat I considered this incongruity.  But I could find no shame in admiring Stone, and no self-mutiny in being proud of my own new-found status.  Maybe I had changed, and maybe that was a good thing.  Maybe Stone was okay, and maybe I could accept his philosophies.  Maybe, I realized -- with a little fear -- I had become what the system wanted me to be after all.  I was a midshipman and a naval officer -- even if pinning on the Ensign shoulder boards was three long years away.  I was amazed that I had gotten to this momentous point in just a fleeting year.

CHAPTER 1

## *FAREWELLS*

The first days of academy life were a confusing blur of intense physical pain, severe mental pressure, and unbelievable emotional turmoil. I suppose the overwhelming flood of new experiences caused a temporary sensory and psychic overload. It's funny how quickly we adapted. At least most of us did. Years later, when I tried to remember the details, I felt the specifics reluctantly emerge from the subconscious niches where I had stuffed them in the confusion. The safe perspective of more than twenty-five years convinced me that nothing could have prepared me for the bewilderment and chaos of Plebe Year at Annapolis.

Of course it wasn't just any Plebe Year. It was 1967 - not a good year to be a military school initiate. Camelot had recently crumbled, and residual bitterness hung like a dirty cloud around us. The country was embroiled in a confusing and messy war that we seemed to have no intention of winning. Young American men died before our horrified eyes every evening on national television. Anti-war protests raged while civil rights fervor and violent response swept the nation. America seemed lost -- without manifest destiny -- for the first time in its history. Yet, all the furious energies of the universe faded into obscurity on the morning of June 7, 1967.

I stood in the warm June sun beside the passenger door of our old green Nash Rambler, one hand poised on the pitted chrome front door handle holding it open. My mother and young brother climbed from the cramped back seat. I wore a new dark blue sport coat, purchased for the occasion. Only half noticing my family, I gaped at the scene that confronted me. It was the first of many gapes during that and the succeeding summer days.

Dazzling white clouds drifted above the campus in a joyfully blue sky. The muddy green Severn River, a hundred yards south of where we had parked, was alive with stark white sails, billowed and straining to exploit the balmy breeze. Young men in brilliant white uniforms sat on a nearby rock seawall, dividing their time between the confusion in the parking lot and the gorgeous view to seaward. The parking lot was a constant, jockeying swirl of motion, as other cars arrived -- each loaded with a prospective Naval officer and several close relatives -- and still others departed, one confused passenger lighter.

Two cars away a young man approximately my age was entangled in a passionate embrace with a pretty young lady while embarrassed relatives looked away. Nearby a tall blond boy retrieved a suitcase and guitar from the trunk of his family Buick. Our eyes locked and I answered his confused entreaty with a smile and a shrug. He smiled in return, then his family swept him away.

The scene must have mesmerized me far longer than I realized. My family had long since exited. They stood near the trunk staring at me, like they were seeing me for the first -- or the last - time. Maybe their unspoken fear was that once I disappeared into the bowels of whatever awaited, I would emerge a far different person from the Kevin O'Reilly who entered. I was taken aback by the sudden notoriety and yet realized that a new phase in O'Reilly family relations had begun.

My Mom wore a nervous smile, and I could see tears glistening in her green eyes as she huddled my ten-year-old brother Sean to her side. Sean buried his tuft of bright orange hair against the soft warmth of her cotton blouse. I suddenly smelled the earthy flavor of Mom's fabric softener mixed with the aromas of family meals and just a hint of perfume. Her smells had always delighted me when I was Sean's age and still willing to cuddle in the evenings while I was reading a book before bed.

My father - also a Kevin - smiled awkwardly. Once a flaming redhead, the same as Sean and I, his own hair had dulled with the years. He held my scuffed leather suitcase at his side, its plastic handle swallowed by his massive fist. Despite his formidableness and muscular bulk, he seemed uncomfortable, and I became disconcerted.

I rarely saw Dad confused. In fact, he had always been a bigger-than-life hero to me. Everything seemed so effortless for him. He made friends easily, and people listened to him. He told jokes with natural grace. And he had a devilish smile that could light up a room. In short, he was much that I was not. But, as he told me a thousand times, I had talents in other areas. I could run like the wind, carry a tune, tinker with machines, and play a good game of chess. I also had a talent for math and science and was recruited by several colleges, including MIT.

The decision of which school's offer to accept was a tough one, but my father's advice carried the day. "Kevin," he said, "you can get a decent education at any one of those colleges, but I suspect the Naval Academy will give you far more than an education."

I accepted the appointment to Annapolis.

But now Dad stared at me as if he might have regretted his advice.

'What's with the big guy?' I thought. 'Did I make the right choice after all?' I hesitated.

Then Dad brightened, and that famous smile enveloped his face. He put a massive hand on my shoulder. "Son," he chuckled. "I envy you."

Everything was okay! I relaxed. Realizing that I had held the car door open far too long, I tried to regain my dignity. I closed the door, and Dad guided me, hand still on my shoulder, toward Sean and Mom.

"Ready?" Dad asked as I took the suitcase from him, intent on handling the situation on my own - at least as much as I was able.

"As I'll ever be!" I stared into the confusion that swirled near the entrance of the Field House. But as I watched, I realized that the confusion was in fact a pattern of registration, assignment, and circulation. It gave choreography to the seeming chaos.

As we neared the front of the building, Dad still clutching my shoulder with pride, and Mom and Sean flanking me on the opposite side, a man in a crisp white uniform approached. His chest was lined with ribbons, and two large gold stripes crossed his shoulder boards. He walked with a loose confidence that I instantly envied. His nametag indicated he was *Lieutenant Bill Large, USNA Staff*. We stopped and waited.

His eyes twinkled as he asked. "Do we have a new midshipman in the group?"

"Yes," I said before either of my parents could answer for me.

The man smiled at me. "Wonderful!"

Speaking to my family he continued. "Listen, your son is going to be busy for the next few hours. It would be best if you said a short goodbye here to let him get registered. At 1600," he looked at me, "that's four p.m. -- there will be a formal Oath of Office ceremony in Tecumseh Court. Afterward you'll have a few minutes to say a better farewell."

"Well," I said to the family, "I guess I'll see you at four . . . " I looked back to Bill Large and said, "I mean 1600."

He addressed Mom and Dad. "Don't worry," he said to them. "He'll do fine. I have a sense of these things." With that he strode smartly away to greet the next confused family.

Dad watched him leave.

Unsure what to do next; we huddled at the corner of the building. Then Dad grabbed me in an enormous bear hug that squashed the breath from me. His huge hands patted my back as we embraced. He kissed me on the cheek, and I felt the raspy stubble left from the morning's shave. When he drew away, all teeth and freckles, I saw tears welling up in his deep blue eyes. Dad hadn't kissed me for longer than I could remember, and I almost bawled in front of everybody. But one hug was all he had in him. He held out his hand, and crushed mine in a farewell grip. "Good luck, son," he whispered.

I turned toward my Mom and found her weeping silently. She dropped my brother's hand and walked with quiet dignity to where I stood. "Give me a hug, Kevin." As I embraced her, she whispered, "We're all so very proud of you."

"I know, Mom." She didn't seem willing to let go, and I allowed the hug to continue for several warm seconds. Then I noticed Sean. He was also crying, and I knew how much the tears meant because he always made a point of never being a crybaby.

I let Mom go, kissing her on the cheek as I did so. "Can I have a farewell hug, Sean?"

Sean glanced at his feet, and shifted his weight. His straight carrot-colored hair, which hung almost to the bottom of his eyes, swished as he shifted.

Then he flashed an enormous smile, a smile very much like my Dad's, and said, "I guess so - as long as you don't tell anyone."

"I promise." I walked three steps toward Sean. Kneeling, I opened my arms, and we held each other. I could feel him crying on my shoulder as we embraced, and through the sniffling he said, "I'm gonna miss you, big brother."

"Me too."

"Well," I said. "Time to go." I lifted my suitcase and turned toward the Field House.

Another family, headed away from the building, passed very near to us. It was impossible not to notice. Two agitated parents flanked a short, dark-haired boy about my age. The father was a dark, ruggedly handsome man who wore polished boots, a white cowboy hat, and jeans with a silver belt buckle.

10

"I told you! I'm not going through with it!" the boy shouted.

His mother was a very pretty and petite blonde woman who wore jeans and a plaid embroidered shirt. Her long hair hung loosely down her back, swaying from side to side as she ran to keep up.

"But you haven't even tried," his father implored in a deep Texas accent. "How do you know it's going to be so bad?"

"I've seen enough! It was your idea to do this. I'm not going and that's final!"

"But, son . . .," his mother began in a sweet drawl, "can't we talk this over?"

The boy stopped, almost colliding with his parents. He turned toward his mother and I could see a frightened and exasperated look on his face. "Look, Mamma. All my friends are going to be at UT next semester. I've got a scholarship, so it won't cost you anything. I never liked the military. And you know Carol Ann isn't going to wait for me if I'm here."

Before his father could protest, the boy continued, speaking directly to his father. "Besides, Dad, this place doesn't even have a decent football team." As if that was the final nail in the coffin, he hurried away. His parents exchanged exasperated looks then ran after him.

I looked at my family.

My mother shook her head. Her neatly coifed dark hair didn't move so much as an inch.

My father chuckled, and judging by the look on his face, also admired the way the woman filled out her jeans, (which wasn't bad for an older lady).

Then he looked at me. "You can leave any time you want to, Kevin."

"I know! But I think I'll give it more than a few minutes, okay? See you at 1600," I hefted the bag, turned the corner, and walked toward the registration area.


Twenty rectangular metal tables sat in front of the Field House. Each table was covered with a white tablecloth, which reached precisely to the concrete sidewalk. Seated behind the tables were young-to-middle-aged women who greeted the incoming plebes. Behind each woman stood a metal pedestal with a sign that designated letters of the alphabet. I selected the line "M – P" and stood behind three other young men. As I waited, I noticed for the first time a large blue banner that spanned the front of the Field House.  On it, in bright gold letters was the message.  *"WELCOME – USNA CLASS OF 1971."*

"Nice touch," I said to the boy in front of me.

"Huh?"  He noticed me for the first time.

I indicated the banner with a nod of my head.

"Oh, yeah."  He returned to whatever thoughts consumed him.

At the front of my line I encountered an elderly woman.  "M through P?" she asked.

"O'Reilly!  I guess that fits."

"It does."  She consulted a computer listing.  After a few seconds she looked up.  "Okay, Kevin.  Just a moment and I'll have you on your way."  She opened a folder with the letter "O" boldly lettered on its front, found my file, and handed it to me.

"This is general information for you to read, and your copy of *Reef Points*.  You've been assigned to the Twenty-third Company."  She pulled an index card from the folder.  "This lists your Company, room number, and identification code, all of which you should memorize immediately."  She pointed toward the oval track across the street.  Inside the oval, lines of young men waited in the sunshine, suitcases on the grass beside them.

"Go over there and find your Company.  Then wait.  Someone will be along to escort you to your Company area."  As I took the card and folder, she smiled.  "Good luck," she said.

"Thanks!"

It was sweltering as I hurried toward the track, and I felt a drip of perspiration run down my face, then another tracked my spine.  Then I noticed the enormous light stone building on the opposite side of the track. The empty windows seemed to stretch forever north and south.  I shivered.


Rope barricades in the middle of the oval delineated thirty-six precisely equal spaces. Long wooden poles with small dark blue pennants suspended at the top had been planted in metal stands in front of each area.  The flags were numbered consecutively from one to thirty-six.  I found the flag that indicated the twenty-third, and moved to the back of a short line of six other boys.  The boy at the end of my line turned as I put my suitcase on the grass.

"Hi," he said.  He had a slight accent that hinted of the south somewhere.  "The name's Jim Merritt.  What room are you assigned to?"

"5405," I replied, looking at my index card.

He spoke to the others.  "See!  It's like I told you.  We're reporting by room numbers."

He smiled.  "I got here early this morning, and I've spent the last hour watching the registration procedures.  Our welcoming letters told us to report at ten o'clock, and I'll bet yours did too.  I think they can only handle so many new faces each hour, and if our group goes the same as the last one, at ten thirty a man in uniform will be here to take us inside the dormitory.  We're going to be living four-to-a-room, for a while at least."

"What do y'all mean for a while?" asked a squat, massive boy at the front of the line.

Merritt replied.  "Well, it stands to reason.  This place has an incredibly high drop-out rate, so while we may start out with four roommates, I'll bet we don't end up that way."

I held out my hand.  "Kevin O'Reilly is my name."

"Great!" said Merritt.  "Let me introduce the gang, if I can remember them all."  He pointed to each in turn.  "Up front is Joe Ramsey," he began, but before he could say another word, "Joe" spoke up.

"Ah'm *Jubal* Hunter Ramsey," he said in the thickest accent I had ever heard.  "Jubal is short for 'Jubilation' which is an old family name. - Don't ask!"

"Jubal, it is," Merritt, laughed.  "Jubal's from High Point, Alabama.  His father was in the Army.  And he's here to play football."

"I should hope so," I said looking at Jubal.  While he was smaller than my own six feet three inches, he was built like a fireplug, and every inch of him solid.  He had a nose that bent in several directions, his light brown hair was short, almost crew-cut, and his ruddy complexion and thick bull neck seemed out of place in his coat and tie.  He was suffering in the hot sun.  Sweat ran down his face, and just looking at him made me wish I had on shorts and Tee-shirt.

Merritt continued, "Next we have one of your roomies, Rico Guevara, from Brooklyn."

Rico proved to be a quiet, darkly handsome boy. "I know I'm going to like it here," he said without a trace of an accent. "I arrived last night with my parents, and during a stroll around the town I met several nice young ladies. I have their numbers here." He patted his shirt pocket.

"Next," Merritt continued, "we have my roommate Jeffrey Polk from New Hampshire."

"You can call me Jeff," Polk said, but offering nothing further. Jeff was several inches shorter than I, and seemed to weigh no more than 150 pounds. He had a pleasant, friendly face and dark, curly brown hair.

"Go, Red Sox," I offered. "I'm from Boston."

"After Jeff is Donny Delmont, another of your roommates. Donny is from Idaho, and his father's a rancher."

Donny, a thin, dark-haired, nervous youth, smiled but said nothing.

"This bean pole next to me," Merritt continued, "is Anthony Grizwald. Anthony hails from San Jose, California. He's your roommate, and he's a musician."

Anthony stood an awkward and angular six and a half feet tall, but couldn't have weighed more than 160 pounds. He had longish blond hair and a toothy, lopsided smile.

"I play the oboe," he said proudly.

Merritt then indicated himself. "I'm James Wesley Merritt. You can call me Jim. I'm from Amarillo, Texas. I don't have a thick accent because my mother trained me to *enunciate.* I play a little football, and to tell the truth I'm excited as hell to be here."

He looked at his watch. "It's almost ten thirty, and someone will be along to pick us up soon." He scanned the area. "But we're still missing someone. There should be eight of us."

CHAPTER 2


## *NEW FRIENDS AND FOES*


We talked until uniformed men began emerging from various doorways in the enormous gray building. They were identically dressed in pressed white uniforms. Black vinyl hat brims and brass belt buckles sparkled in the sunlight as they approached. Each was military trim and walked with an arrogant swagger. Watching them approach, we quieted.

A midshipman stopped in front of each line. A tall, very thin, light-haired individual faced our group. He examined us curiously then smiled. "So this is the next batch of Twenty-third Company rejects?" His voice had a raspy nasal twang. "Jesus, where do they drag you guys up from?" He looked at each of us closely for a long moment, shook his head, and then began lecturing. "My name is Midshipman Second-class Maxwell, but you can call me, *sir*. I'll be one of your two squadleaders for the next two wonderful months. You'll meet Midshipman Battle soon enough."

Jubal reached a large hand toward Midshipman Maxwell. "Glad to meet you, sir!"

Maxwell stared at the beefy hand that reached toward him as if it were infected with some hideous disease. He drew back, stopped, looked at Jubal, then laughed.

"Nice try, douchebag, but I don't spoon anyone so easily."

Jim turned toward me. "Spoon?" he whispered.

I shrugged.

"You seem to be missing one of your classmates," Maxwell continued. "Does anyone know where he might be?" When no one answered, he shook his head. "That figures. Well, time and tide wait for no man. Let's shove off, shall we, ladies?"

I sensed a disturbance behind us and looked back at a slightly rotund boy, lugging a suitcase with both hands. He was an absolute mess. His sport coat was undone and flapped at his free side, and his thin black tie was askew. His hair was mussed, and he was flushed and out of breath from the jog across the street.  He seemed about to cry.  To complete the image, the shirt flap on the side away from his suitcase had pulled from his pants, and in manhandling the suitcase, his shoes had become covered with grass clippings and clumps of brown soil.

"Excuse me," he asked.  "Is this the Twenty-third Company?"

Maxwell looked him over with a glare of absolute disgust.  "One of my children, are you?  Are you sure you're in the right place?"

"Ah, I am if this is Twenty-third Company," the newcomer panted.

"It is!  Get in line and follow me."

The young man waddled to a place behind me.

I picked up my own suitcase and glanced back at him.  "Hi!  I'm Kevin O'Reilly."

"My name is Thomas Henry Poole.  Sorry I'm late.  My Dad had car trouble."

"Don't apologize to me," I said.  "I think it's the guy up front who really matters."

Maxwell shouted in a grumble we would soon dread hearing.  "Okay ladies, let's get started.  We have a lot to do today.  Follow me!  Stay in a single file if you can."  With that, Maxwell headed off toward the building that loomed in the foreground.

We followed, each moving in his own individual style and thinking his own private thoughts.


We accumulated information about whom we were and what was expected of us in a piecemeal manner over the next several months, so I'm jumping ahead of myself, but let me explain about that imposing structure we headed toward.

The building, Bancroft Hall, is named after an early Secretary of the Navy, George Bancroft, who founded the Naval Academy in 1845.  Bancroft Hall is constructed in eight approximately equal-sized wings, each with a thick light-colored granite facade and a verdigris copper-clad roof.  The wings are connected by broad corridors on each of the four floors and are oriented to the north around a beautiful rotunda and formal reception area.  The four northernmost wings almost totally encircle Tecumseh Court, the center of all official midshipman activity.  It is the largest dormitory building in the world, containing more than 4.8 miles of corridor, 33 acres of floor area, and living space for more than 4,000 students. The students are called "midshipmen," an archaic term borrowed from the days of wooden sailing ships when the junior most sub-officer would stand duty *amidships* doing whatever junior naval officers did in those days. The proper modern slang term for a prospective naval officer, we soon found out, is "mid." It's improper to call Naval Academy midshipmen "middies." As I read in my Reef Points, *"Middie is an odious term for midshipmen sometimes used by mothers and newspapers."*

But as I studied the stately and imposing building, I experienced a sudden feeling of dread. Hundreds of windows seemed to be watching, and the darkness behind the glass felt threatening. Even the bright sunshine couldn't dispel my discomfort.

Inside Bancroft Hall are the thirty-six company areas, separated by communal toilets and punctuated by Company offices and Wardrooms. The rooms are equipped with a sink and shower and are sized to fit two, three, or four individuals in Spartan comfort. I suppose the facilities compare favorably with most other colleges and universities. My only complaint - a significant one - was that the building had no air conditioning system. This was normally not a problem since midshipmen are seldom aboard in the summer months. But plebes are, and the summer of 1967 overwhelmed us with the most miserably hot months I could ever remember before or since.

At precisely 10:40, thirty-six groups of eight-man snakes headed toward various entrances of Bancroft Hall. Because of Poole's late arrival our group was the last of the snakes, and we moved at a hurried pace as Maxwell pushed us to catch up with the others. It was not to be, however. We hadn't gotten more than 50 yards when I heard a dull thump and an exasperated sigh behind me. I turned to see Poole sprawled across his oversized bag, which somehow had exploded open and spilled his considerable possessions across the asphalt parking area. I stopped, unable to decide whether to keep up with the group or to stop and help Poole. My snake group was now twenty yards ahead, and the gap was widening.

"Wait!" I yelled. "There's a problem."

Maxwell turned without slowing. Even at this distance I could see his face redden.

"God dammit!" he yelled. He followed that exclamation with a loud, "Squad halt!" That command told me two things. First, that our little snaky group was called a squad;

second, that Anthony Grizwald, who might well be the best oboe player in America, did not tune any motor skills during his years in marching band.

Grizwald bit the dust, unable to stop his long legs as he plowed into Donny Delmont from behind. Donny would also have gone down had it not been for Jeffrey Polk, who, sensing the impending chaos, dropped his suitcase, braced himself for a collision, and held Delmont in place by extending his arms outward and behind him. Jubal Ramsey, a participant in countless football drills, stopped on a dime and waited. Rico Guevarra, who had been strutting behind him, yelled something colorful in Spanish and avoided colliding with Ramsey by leaping to his right, still holding his bag. Only Jim Merritt and I were unscathed, but I had those 20 yards of open distance to use to my advantage. Merritt didn't miss a beat. He helped Grizwald to his feet.

I tried to stifle a laugh.

Maxwell, who was passing me at that exact instant, stopped. He glared at me. "Do you think this is funny?" he barked. His pale blue eyes held the promise of something unpleasant.

"Well, - yes, sir," I replied, choosing the worst of two possible answers. Apparently neither the humor of the situation nor the sincerity of my smile impressed him.

Maxwell took one giant step and stood exactly in my face. His brightly white shoes almost touched my own brown loafers. Though I was taller, he seemed to tower over me. His pale, slightly squinted, eyes locked on mine.

He spoke in a quiet sneer. "What's your name, sonny?"

I watched the nostrils on his thin nose flare, and noted that his two bottom front teeth were crooked. When he talked, he pursed his bottom lip so that the two crooked teeth protruded, making a very menacing appearance.

I was scared senseless. "Kevin O'Reilly," I answered. For a second I thought I was going to wet myself.

"Well, Kevin," he jeered. "Later today I'm going to wipe that silly-assed smile off that Howdy-Doody face of yours. Do you think you'll be smiling then?"

"I'm sure I won't be, sir," I stammered.

"You're damn right you won't. Now get over there and help your effeminate girlfriend pack her things, and do it quickly before I get really angry."

18

I hurried to help Poole.

Maxwell turned to the rest of the group. "Anybody else think this is funny?" No one answered. Apparently they were all smarter than I.

"Good," he said. He pointed to Ramsey. "How much can you bench press?"

"Three hundred pounds, sir!"

"Very impressive, scum bag," Maxwell observed. "Now get your fat ass back there and carry the girl's bag for her."

"Excuse me, sir?" Jubal sputtered.

"You heard me, fatso. Carry your friend's bag!"

"Yes, sir!" Ramsey trudged to the rear of the line and grabbed the handle of Poole's suitcase, which we had only just finished repacking. He glared at Poole, hefted the bag, and returned to his place at the front of the line.

"Is everyone ready?" asked Maxwell. "I'm not going too fast for you, am I, girls?" He didn't wait for an answer. Instead he raised a hand above his head.

"Forward . . . march!" he commanded, and with a downward sweep of his hand, we started off again.

I had no idea how he intended to punish me, but I was sure I wasn't going to like it.


We set an even faster pace as we entered the building complex. Soon I was lost. Bancroft Hall is enormous, and every section seemed like the others. We entered through a lower level door, moved past a huge laundry facility and several darkened maintenance offices, then scurried up a small circular staircase and emerged in the barracks proper. We made a hard right turn, passed a group of similar newcomers being led by their squad leader in the opposite direction, and traversed a long broad corridor past innumerable offices. None of them seemed occupied, but the sounds of our various shoes clapping on the tile floor, and the sight of the long row of thick, official-looking dark hardwood doors intimidated me. After the long passageway we emerged through a set of heavy metal double doors into the Academy rotunda. I could hear murmured exclamations from my squad mates as we glimpsed the tall ceiling and the ornate beauty.

Merritt spoke as we neared the center of the domed area. "Wow! This is great, huh?"

"Very nice," I answered. It wasn't that I couldn't appreciate the majesty and grandeur, but ever since our ignominious delay in the parking lot, I hadn't been able to get my mind off Maxwell's threat. 'What a way to start my life as a prospective naval officer,' I thought while the others oohed and aahed.

We traversed the rotunda, which was alive with groups of new recruits and with visitors, then turned left onto a broad stairway and climbed upward past the second and third floors to the fourth -- and final -- floor. Four floors are not so many, and by the end of that first summer I could sprint from the rotunda to my fourth floor room and not even break a sweat. But on that first day, the upward distance (30 steps per floor) seemed daunting.

Poole almost didn't make it. By the beginning of the third flight of stairs I heard him laboring behind me even though he didn't have a suitcase. He had placed a hand on the railing and was hauling himself upward. His face was red, and his breath came in labored gasps.

"Are you okay?" I asked.

His only answer was a strained nod of his head.

At the top of the fourth flight of stairs we turned left and passed through another set of double doors into a barracks area. Several of these rooms were occupied, and Merritt, checking the room numbers, which were stenciled on a brass plate in the center of each heavy wooden door, turned to me again. "This must be our area. I'm in room 5404." He pointed to a door to our left that had that number on it. "You're in 5405." He pointed to a room across the hall. As I found out repeatedly that year, James Wesley Merritt was seldom wrong.

Maxwell growled a "Squad, halt!" To our credit no one fell down this time, although Grizwald did brush against Delmont's backside with his right knee.

We stopped, mostly out of breath, and put our bags unbidden on the tiled corridor floor. Maxwell stood in front of the center of the squad. As he did, I noticed several fresh faces attached to shiny bald heads emerge from two nearby rooms. None of these faces were smiling.

Maxwell also spied the spectators. "Do you have all your gear put away?" he yelled. I heard a meek "No, sir!" from somewhere, and the shiny heads disappeared like coral polyps threatened by a predator.

Maxwell turned to us. "You have your cards with the room assignments?"

Merritt held his aloft.

"Go to your rooms, select a bunk, and get the toiletries and other personal items from your bags. Put those items on your racks. Do not unpack your civilian clothes." He smiled. "You won't be needing them for a long while. Next, close your bags and put them on top of your rack. Select a locker and a desk, and temporarily store your personal things. Once you are finished, return to the passageway and stand against the bulkhead until Midshipman Battle returns with the last batch of your classmates. Then I'll tell you what to do next. You may talk amongst yourselves, but there will be no horseplay or commotion. Am I understood?"

Everyone murmured assent. Then I noticed my hand rising almost of its own volition. Maxwell noticed me.

"What!" he snapped.

"Sir, you mentioned something about a rack?"

Maxwell laughed. "Yeah. Your bed. The other kind of rack you won't be seeing for a long time." His smile faded.

"Now get moving! And hurry up!"

I almost collided with Poole as I turned toward my room, eager to be the first to pick a bed and desk. Poole, still panting from the long hike, walked to where Ramsey had deposited his bag. Hefting it with two hands, he lumbered to his room.


I was first inside the room, and what I saw was not complicated. The room was a large one. Ahead, a wide double window framed a view of the enclosed area between the east and west wings of Bancroft Hall. Below I could see the roof of a building I was later to learn was the Dining Hall. Four gray metal desks clustered in the center of the room in sets of two positioned front-to-front. On the right was a sink with a mirror and medicine cabinet, and a small shower stall. On the left was a series of four small lockers recessed into the wall, each with a wooden sliding door. A small closet area for storage and

21

hanging coats was built into the far left corner.  Bunk beds stood against the walls on either side of the room.  I hurried to the right side of the room and claimed the lower bunk and a desk by the window.

Delmont followed me and took the top bed.

 Grizwald put his bag on the bottom bed across from us, but before he could begin unpacking, Guevarra stopped in front of him and said, "Tony, do you mind taking the top bunk. I'm afraid of heights."  He said it with such seriousness that at first I thought he was being honest.

"Oh, sure," Grizwald answered, removing his bag and oboe case from the lower bed and slinging it up onto the upper bunk.

"Thanks a lot," Guevarra said, turning toward Donny and me.  Hidden from Tony's view, his face lit up into an enormous smile.  I smiled in return and shook my head.

I didn't bring many personal items, a few science fiction books -- mostly Andre Nortons and Edgar Rice Burroughs -- a Red Sox pennant, a pair of soccer cleats, a baseball glove, and a picture of my last girlfriend.   I had recently broken up with her – or her with me - but I figured the picture would make me seem more like one of the guys.  For toiletries I had a toothbrush, a half tube of Colgate toothpaste, some Mennen stick deodorant, a small bottle of English Leather cologne, and a black comb.  A half-hour later I realized how vain that last item was.  It remained unused the entire year.  Within five minutes I had unpacked and prepared my things as Maxwell had recommended.

I walked to the doorway and peered outside.  Merritt stood against the far wall examining the corridor with curiosity.

He noticed me and smiled.  "Come on out, the water's fine."  I peered outside and, not seeing Maxwell, stepped into the corridor and stood quietly against the opposite wall.

Maxwell, who had been using the communal bathroom in the center of the hall, strode into view.  My heart sank.

"O'Reilly!" he yelled.  "Get your redheaded ass over here!"

I cursed to myself and ran toward him, wondering about the anatomical possibilities his order implied.  "Where is everyone?" he growled.  "I thought I said for you to hurry up?"

"I did, sir."  It was my second wrong answer of the morning.

"When I say *you*, asshole, I mean all of you.  When one of you is late, you're all late.  When one of you screws up, you all screw up.  Go hurry up your sissy classmates.  If you aren't ready when Battle arrives, *you* -- and I mean *all* of you -- will be very unhappy."

I sprinted to my room. "Hurry up," I shouted.  "Maxwell's gonna kill us."

"Tell Maxwell to calm down," Guevarra said, feigned concern apparent on his handsome face, "stress can lead to a heart attack."

I started a reply, but Guevarra broke into a devilish grin.  His white teeth flashed, and his eyes twinkled with mischief.  "Go tell the other rooms," he said.  "I'll get things organized here."

I ran across the hall..  Merritt and Polk were stuffing Poole's suitcase as I entered.  "We've got things under control here, Red," Merritt said.  "We'll be out in a second."

Soon all eight of us waited against the corridor walls.

Maxwell, emerging from a room near the center of the corridor, looked at us.  "Well, well," he said.  "I didn't think you fairies would be ready so quickly.  Maybe we should play some games while we're waiting."

I didn't like the sound of that, but luckily, at that moment the double doors burst open and a shiny-bald, much shorter squadleader emerged, followed by eight, identically-bald young men.  The group lugged canvas duffel bags crammed to overflowing with various gear.  The weight was substantial and I wondered how Poole was going to hold up.

Ramsey must have wondered the same thing because he glared at Poole.

As the new group approached, its leader shouted, "Squad, halt!"

The group stopped without incident and I was jealous.

The squadleader smiled at Maxwell, then laughed.  "Ain't they pretty?"

"I'll say!" Maxwell turned toward us.  "Get a good look at each other, gentlemen; then look at your classmates here.  This will be your new hairstyle for the next year, unless of course you're insane and want to be a Marine when you graduate like classmate Battle.  Then you might choose to wear this particular cut for the next four years, and ad nauseam thereafter."  Battle turned toward his group.  "All of you into my room right now," he growled.  "I'll show you how to stow your gear."  The group trotted down the hall.

23

Maxwell didn't wait for us to observe the newcomers. "Okay, ladies," he yelled. "Form a straight line behind me and hurry up!"

We raced to comply. I purposefully watched Tommy Poole to see where he would position himself, and I squeezed in several people behind him. I didn't want to take any chances with drawing attention to myself again. Maxwell made sure we were reasonably ready and barked out another, "Forward . . . march!"

We exited our company area through the double doors and hurried down the same stairs we had recently ascended. This time we didn't stop at the rotunda but instead descended another level into the basement and proceeded along a broad passageway past several offices and storage rooms until we came to a well-used section of the building. Hundreds of our classmates streamed in and out of the area or waited at various gear issuing stations.

Maxwell marched us to the far end of the corridor. We halted outside a massive barbershop. "Fall in behind that last group!"

A steady stream of 'customers' entered and left the barbershop. The entering recruits sported hairdos of varying lengths and styles. What exited was a line of mostly bald, mostly shocked, and mostly very unhappy young men. As each squad completed the hair cut phase, squadleaders assembled them and marched them off to the next hurdle.

We seemed to enter the shop too quickly. Inside were more than twenty chairs, each manned by a grinning civilian barber. The floor overflowed with hair clippings of various colors and textures. The haircuts themselves were little more than ten swipe affairs using the closest possible setting on the clippers. I timed one poor lad, who spent a total of 30 seconds in the chair, all the while staring at the cascades of luxuriant blond hair that drifted to the floor.

His barber removed the drape with a matador's flourish and flapped it in the air with a loud snap. "Next!" he announced with sadistic gusto.

I took a deep breath as my turn neared. "This won't be so bad," I thought. "After all, everyone is going to be in the same boat." Well, almost all. As I waited, a recruit from another squad sat and pointed to his head, which sported hair as long as any I had seen today. "I was in a motorcycle accident," he said. "I've got scabs on my head. Go easy, huh?"

"No problem," the barber replied.  Thirty seconds later my classmate was as bald as the next guy except for ten thick tufts of hair that marked the location of his scabs.  He looked like a refugee from a nuclear accident site.

The barber spun him around in the chair -- something I hadn't seen done with any other recruits, and the classmate gaped at the sight he had become.  Before he could protest, the barber took scissors and deftly trimmed the patches so that ten dark stubbly spots remained.

"Come back when the scabs fall off," the barber announced.  "Next!"

It was my unfortunate luck to be the next victim of that same barber.  He smiled as I approached.  "How do you want it cut?" he asked sarcastically.

"I like what you did to that last fellow!  But with a few more patches.  Maybe you could make my head into a checkerboard and my classmates and I could use it to entertain ourselves."

He considered the suggestion, looking closely at my head from several angles.  "Wouldn't work," he finally said.

"How come?"

"The pieces would fall off!"  He burst into a deep, belly laugh.  My cut took less than fifteen seconds, and if possible I was even balder than the rest of my classmates.

Outside in the corridor my squad mates stared at my head in amazement, which immediately blew my theory about being in the same boat.  All heads are not created equal, and while the lack of hair was actually becoming to some of us -- which of course included Merritt -- my ruddy complexion and wealth of freckles made my head look more like a dull apple with worms.  I was quite a sight.  But I wasn't the worst looking mug by far.

Poor Poole was a phrenologist's dream.  I had never seen or imagined that a skull could be so variously contoured and landscaped.  He looked like a relief map of the moon except that *his* lunar cranium had had a collision with some other celestial body which caused a deep indentation on one side, making his whole head appear nubby and off centered.

"Form up!" Maxwell yelled, clearly happy at our discomfort.  We headed into the crowd.

What awaited us was a series of gear-issuing stations.  First we received identical duffel bags, which we carried to the skivvies-issue station where we received five pairs of boxer shorts, five v-necked T-shirts, and five crew-necks -- all white.  Next came three pairs each of thin white and black socks, followed by shirts of various styles, pants and jumpers, and five pairs of shoes -- two black, one white, one brown, and a pair of hideous-looking high-topped tennis shoes.  We also added a grey metal lockable box, jock straps, three caps -- two combination caps and a sailor's "dixie cup" cap, white with a blue stripe at the top -- and a shaving kit with razor, toothbrush, comb, Kiwi shoe polishes (white, brown, and black), and generic spray deodorant.

By the time we arrived at the tailor shop, we had loaded our bags to capacity -- except for Poole.  He couldn't fit it all in, and carried several shoeboxes while dragging the bulging bag behind him.  Most of the others slung the bags across their backs by stretching the one thick strap over the neck and shoulder.  I had tried that, but the strap dug into my shoulder.  Instead I hoisted the bag up onto my shoulders behind my neck.  Holding the bag balanced with both hands, I trudged, bent over like a beast of burden.  Ramsey, living up to his bench pressing image, carried his bag in one hand.

In the tailor shop, the staff measured us.   So many hands touched my crotch that morning that I was never exactly sure what they were calibrating.  One elderly gentleman circled my chest with a tape and called out numbers that could not have been my girth at that location.  I looked at him skeptically.

"We have to allow a little for growth," he said.  Then he taped my waist and pulled the tape so tightly I almost groaned.  He looked at me again.  "We must also allow for contraction in certain areas," he said.

The entire process of haircut and gear issue took less than a half-hour, and soon we had formed up in the hall for the return trip to the company area.  Maxwell took stock of us before we left.  He paused when he came to Poole.  "Why isn't your gear inside the duffel bag, mister?"

"It wouldn't fit, sir," Poole replied.

"Sure, pal!  You have two minutes to make it fit!" Maxwell addressed the group.  "I'm becoming very tired of these delays.  You won't like me when I'm tired.  I get cranky."

I nudged Polk.  "Let's help Poole, before we all catch hell."

Polk looked at me and announced fiercely but quietly, "This is all bullshit, you know."

"Yeah! I know. But let's do one thing at a time and worry about the bullshit later."

We knelt beside Poole. Tommy tried to help, but Jeff waved him away. Soon we had his bag unpacked on the terrazzo floor and had placed everything inside. It all fit, and the entire operation took less than a minute.

Merritt, who had changed places with Guevarra so as to be in front of Poole, asked Tommy, "How are you doing? Can you make it back up the long staircase?"

"Not with this load," Poole answered. "I don't think so."

"Okay," Merritt said, "here's what we'll do. I'll sling my bag over my left shoulder and reach back with my right hand and hold the front of your bag. You carry the back end. That'll reduce your load by half."

"Not exactly."

"Huh?"

"Well," Poole replied. "This bag weighs about 120 pounds. I should be okay on level ground carrying 60 pounds, but once we start up the stairs, the center of gravity of the bag will shift to the rear. On a 45-degree slope that will mean that nearly three-quarters of the weight will be on my end. I'm not sure I can handle 90 pounds up those stairs."

Merritt stared at Poole for a moment. "You calculated that in your head?"

"Yes," Poole answered. "Estimated, really."

"Well, no problem, because Rico, Jeff, and Kevin will help, right guys?"

Jeff and I nodded.

Rico spoke. "Shit. I'd really like to help, but I just got over this hernia operation and the doctor told me to avoid any heavy lifting for a while. You know how it is."

Merritt said nothing.

Polk blurted skeptically. "You must have had a hell of a time with your physical?"

Rico smiled, then put his right index finger to his lips in a gesture of silence. "I know," he whispered. "I'm hoping the brass doesn't find out. They might drum me out."

"No problem," Merritt said. "We can handle it."

27

With Polk and I alternating on one side at the rear and Poole on the other, we handled the load.  Soon we burst triumphantly through the double doors to encounter another group of fresh classmates lining the corridor.  They looked at us as if we were bald alien monsters.

"Don't they look great?" Battle asked the group in the hall.  He seemed enthusiastic.  No one answered.

We halted in the middle of the corridor, and Maxwell examined the squad critically.

"Whoever's in *that* room," he said pointing to 5404, "raise your hand."

The four occupants raised their hands, and I was thankful that he hadn't picked 5403, although I didn't know why.

He looked the four of them over for the first time.  "Well, well," he said, "we have the lady and the palooka in the same room with a midget and a smack.  I think I call 5404 the *Goon Room*.  Any objections?"  None came to mind.

"Okay," he continued.  "I want all eight of you douchebags in Room 5404 immediately.  Let's see if I can teach you how to fold your underwear."  He started for 5404, but when we didn't react quickly enough, his face changed to deep rage.  "Get in there now, God dammit!"

We ran, dragging our bags.

Maxwell selected the nearest desk and grabbed the duffel bag from Ramsey's hands.  He plopped it on the floor and looked at Ramsey.  "Which is your rack?" he asked.

Ramsey indicated the lower one to the right.

Maxwell opened the bag and dumped the contents onto the bed.  Next he selected a pair of boxer shorts and held them up by the elastic band for all of us to see.  They were rather large.

"Jesus, Ramsey!"  Who else is going to live in these things with you?"  Ramsey was smart enough not to answer -- a trait I hoped I would soon develop.

"Before I begin my demonstration, let me say that I haven't the faintest idea why we fold and stow clothing the way we do here, and I don't care either.  I also don't care how your Mommies taught you to fold clothes, because the *only* way that's accepted from now on is the way I'm going to show you.  Do it exactly as I say and you *might* survive the million

28

locker inspections you're gonna have before the Brigade returns in September." He then looked at Poole. "Then again, you might not."

What followed was a 20-minute whirlwind demonstration of how to fold everything we now owned from skivvies to jock straps and how to put them in the locker space provided. Each item was folded with exact dimensions and distances being vital. I would not have believed it possible that a stack of underwear could look square, but they did when Maxwell folded them. It also amazed me that socks could be rolled and formed into precise blocks so that the inside sock showed its fabric rows in an exactly vertical direction through a neat rectangular opening in the outer sock. I watched Maxwell as his hands deftly manipulating form and fabric.

Midway through the procedure, Jeff Polk looked at me from across the room. He shook his head in disgust. He didn't seem to be getting into the spirit of the exercise.

I could understand what Jeff was implying by his disapproval. Here were eight, nearly-adult human beings observing a person nearly their own age fold a jock strap into an equilateral triangle. It was very stupid. But on the other hand, it was Academy stupid, and these were skills -- no matter how inane -- I would have to master. I returned to intent observation and realized I had missed the technique that made 45-degree angled corners appear in the sheets and blankets on the ends of the made-up beds. That seemed like an important piece of knowledge to me, so I vowed to watch as my roommates did their beds.

When he was finished, Maxwell straightened and smiled. "Okay," he said, "I want each of you to do exactly as I have done in your own rooms and lockers. Be finished in 30 minutes." He started for the door and we parted for him like the Red Sea for Moses. Midway to the door he halted, and with a devilish smile he turned. "Almost forgot," he said. Going to Ramsey's locker, he swept all his recent clothes-folding efforts in a heap on the floor, and pulled the sheets from the newly-made rack.

He smiled. "You wouldn't want an unfair advantage over your classmates would you?" "No, sir!" Ramsey answered smartly.

"Sure, pal," Maxwell turned to the rest of us. "Well, get to it!" He swept from the room.

I dragged my bag to my room and emptied the contents on my desk. Starting with the skivvy shirts, which I thought would be easy, I began a frenzy of folding and stowing. I did a very good job on the skivvies and the linen, but the sock fabric either lined up at an acute angle or had an opening that resembled Marilyn Monroe puckering up for a wet

29

one.  And I couldn't seem to get the bed corners straight even though I watched Rico make his bed into a perfect match of Maxwell's work.  I finished in time to help Grizwald -- who had just worked his way through the cotton underwear -- with his linen.  As I finished Tony's last washcloth, I heard the final group of bald recruits return.  I poked my head into the hall to watch as they meandered in a shiny-topped eight-man snake to a set of rooms farther down the hall.

No sooner had my head broken the plane between door and passageway, than I heard Maxwell yell.  "O'Reilly!"

"Yes, sir!" I answered, copying Ramsey's snappy style.

"Are you finished folding your things?" he asked.

I realized that this was a question with no good answer, and I paused.

Before I could say anything to embarrass or injure myself, Maxwell continued.  "You had better make sure everything is perfect, pal, because I'll inspect later today."

"Yes, sir!"  I darted inside my room, hustled for my rack, and plowed headlong into the intricacies of hospital corners.  Grizwald had worked his way up to the gym gear, and Delmont was making his rack.  Rico sat at his desk reading a book, his feet on the window sill.

I didn't waste any time wondering about Rico's calm, because, except for his marvelous-looking bed, his stuff sure seemed in need of further attention to me.  But that was his problem.

CHAPTER 3


## *CHOW – SORT OF*


Thirty minutes later, Maxwell and Battle, stood in the middle of the hall outside their room and yelled. "Form up for chow!"

Together they moved down opposite sides of the corridor yelling in each room. Lunch sounded like a great idea to me, but though I reacted quickly, Merritt beat me by several seconds. He smiled as I arrived beside him, and soon a tide of new faces joined us and jostled for position.

"Face the double doors!" yelled Battle, his beak-shaped nose snapping up and down with each command. We managed a confused turn.

"Poole!" yelled Maxwell, "what's eight times four?"

Poole answered, "Thirty-two, sir."

"How can we divide into three, nearly-equal squads?" Maxwell asked again.

Poole answered, "Eleven, eleven, and ten men each, sir."

"Very good, Poole," announced Maxwell. "That higher math sometimes confuses me."

"Okay, people," Battle announced. "You heard Poole. I want you to form yourselves into three squads of eleven, eleven, and ten men -- beginning here!" With a gleaming white shoe he indicated a point in front of him. We raced to comply, and after a bit of initial confusion, the lines formed.

Our efforts offended his sensibilities, because he grimaced when we had finished. "Now," he said, "arrange yourselves in descending order of height starting with the tallest man at this end of the line." This quickly became an exercise in confusion as many nearly-equal individuals struggled to estimate who was taller.

"Hurry up!" Maxwell yelled.

Eventually the lines evened with three squads of stair-step precision tapering off to the rear. Battle looked us over for a moment, was about to make a further adjustment, thought better of it, then turned toward the doors and shouted in a clipped bark, "Forward march!" We exited the area and again turned right and went down the rotunda stairs.

Instead of going into the basement, we crossed the rotunda at an angle, passed through a crowd of gaping onlookers, and descended another flight of stairs toward the rear of the facility. We emerged into the Academy Mess Hall.

I may seem to be repeating myself, but *big* is the operative word here also. The Academy Dining Hall -- also referred to as the "Chow Hall" or the "Mess Hall" -- is the largest such facility in the world. More than four thousand persons eat simultaneously three times a day.

My first view of the facility staggered me. The Mess Hall is constructed in a "T" shape with three equal-sized wings extending out to near infinity from a central hub. We emerged at the top of the hub and so had an immediate view of the officer's and guest's seating area in front of us. The ceiling was more than 20 feet high. Amazingly, no columns marred the broad vista. Tall windows extended ahead and to both sides of us along every outside wall. Each wing seemed to be more than 100 yards long. How long is the Mess Hall? - That's another story.

We didn't have time to enjoy the view. Battle marched us down a wide central aisle and stopped at a middle set of tables on the right-hand side of the middle wing. Double sets of large, thick, ten-man tables extended out from the walls on both sides of all three wings. In the middle was an aisle six yards in width. We were assigned tables in order of Company Number. The first through the thirteenth companies of plebes sat in the right-hand wing, we sat in the middle wing with companies fourteen through twenty-six, and twenty-seventh through thirty-sixth sat in the left-hand wing. Even with 1,300 new plebes eating together, the building seemed empty. It was hard to imagine what it would be like with 4,000 diners. Small blue and gold placards designated our three tables.

Maxwell barked. "Grab a seat at any chair except those at the bow and stern of the table!" We scurried. Seated, we craned our necks to appreciate the view. Maxwell chose a seat at the head (bow) of a table on the aisle side; Battle sat at the foot (stern) in the rear of a second table. The third table contained overflow plebes. I waited to choose my seat, hoping to get at the table without a squad leader, but my hesitation killed me.

32

"O'Reilly! Poole!" laughed Maxwell, "sit here next to me."  He indicated the seats to his right and left, which were already occupied by unfamiliar faces.

I groaned.

Maxwell looked at the plebes in those seats, the smile gone from his narrow features.  "Don't ever sit before you're told!"

The two classmates leapt to their feet.

"Find a chair somewhere else!"  They hastened away, no doubt relieved to depart the source of such commotion.

I moved to the seat on Maxwell's right and put my hands on the chair back.  Poole stood behind the left-hand seat.

The table was set with utilitarian flatware and Naval Academy plates -- white with blue and gold trim.  A dark blue milk carton stood at each end of the table next to a sweating aluminum pitcher filled with iced tea.  There were two plates of hot dinner rolls waiting as well as a bowl of tossed green salad topped with garnish and three bright red cherry tomatoes.  The tomatoes looked inviting, but my math skills are excellent.  I knew it would be a long time before I could taste one of those juicy babies.

Although we were subdued and cautious, most of us were also excited by the newness of the experience.  There was a great deal of shuffling, neck craning, and gaping.  This general commotion continued until all the companies had arrived and were settled at their places.

Dong! Dong!  A bell, clear and resonant, sounded four times from somewhere in the vicinity of the hub.  We craned to see what new thing the sound would bring.  Standing on a podium, a midshipman called the Mess Hall to attention and a chaplain said a short grace.  General announcements followed.  We learned that the barber shop and gear issue statlons would remain open until 1500 -- three in the afternoon -- and that we must be in our places in Tecumseh Court for the swearing-in ceremony at 1530.  The announcer then intoned a "Brigade . . . seats!"

Most of my classmates scurried to sit, Poole among them.  Hands reached for the rolls and salad.  Maxwell watched with an amused grin.

I held my place.

Maxwell shot a smile at me, the effort making his pinched face seem even thinner. But it was a genuine smile that had a you-catch-on-quick message attached, and I felt proud of myself for knowing who was the top dog at the table.

His smile was a brief one. He became stern as he addressed the other occupants of the table. "Stand up, all of you!" I could hear an identical message being delivered simultaneously, and in varying degrees of severity, at every table in the Mess Hall.

My and I classmates stood.

"You might as well get the eating procedures straight," Maxwell snarled. "In the Mess Hall, like everywhere else on the campus -- for the next year you are all less than scum. You will defer to every individual who is senior to you, no matter how superior you think you are. Every individual who is senior has already made it through a plebe year. They have earned the deference you will give them. Today's meals are going to be stress free, but tomorrow morning, plebe year starts, and you will be bracing up and eating square meals." He paused.

"In the Mess Hall, you will always remain standing at your chairs until the announcements are over and *"Brigade, seats"* is called. Then you will sit only after all the upperclass at your table have seated themselves or unless you are personally ordered to sit by the senior midshipman at the table. Food will not be touched by plebes except to pass it to all other midshipmen in descending order of seniority. In other words you will serve yourselves last -- and you had better leave enough of each item so that all of your classmates at the table get an equal share of what remains. If you want more of any item or if a more senior midshipman so demands, you will hold the appropriate tray or plate aloft until a steward comes to the table. Tell the steward what you want and he'll bring it."

"During the meal you will look straight ahead -- or, "keep your eyes *in the boat*." Do not look anywhere else unless you are directed to do so by an upperclassman. If I ask you a question, put down your utensils and swallow your food before answering, but keep your eyes in the boat. There will be no banter except to pass food or drink or unless I grant the table a privilege called *carry-on*.

"'Carry-on' means you can act almost as if you were home with Mommy and Daddy, and you don't have to brace up. We'll tell you all about bracing and chopping and square meals after lunch today."

34

"Okay, gentlemen. I'm hungry. Let's eat." We sat -- after Maxwell made himself comfortable, of course.

I yelled to the classmate on my left. "Pass the rolls and salad, please!" Soon I had handed Maxwell the nearest roll plate. As he took the roll plate from me and I handed him the salad, I saw Polk scowling at me from across the table. Our eyes locked briefly, and I looked at my plate, embarrassed for playing plebe so well.

Maxwell eyed the rolls as if there were an actual difference between the various specimens. He selected one, taking care not to touch the others in the process, and handed the roll plate to Poole. When the rolls came to me, what remained was a misshapen, shriveled affair that had not been fully baked. And not only did I not get a cherry tomato, but all that was left in the salad bowl were a few wilted and soggy leaf pieces, some celery chunks, and one small carrot slice. I was not disappointed with the remainder of the meal. The main course -- dinner steaks -- arrived before I could become despondent at the thought of soggy salad and a doughy roll.

Serving instantaneous meals for 4,000 hungry and growing young people is a coordinated affair. Large double doors opened along the walls facing the main part of Bancroft Hall in the crosspiece of the Mess Hall "T," revealing the interior of an enormous kitchen. Stainless steel carts raced into view from the kitchen, each one pushed by several Filipino stewards to its prearranged position in the center aisle. The stewards pulled trays of food from the racks on the carts, and moved up and down the aisles bringing the food to each table. My mother always hated it when I told them, but Annapolis meals were the best I have had anywhere, before and since.

For lunch that day we had steak, a common experience. The steaks were choice cuts of beef, and everyone -- even me, Maxwell's serving boy -- had a satisfactory portion. In addition to the steaks, the stewards brought steaming bowls of several vegetables. When I held aloft the roll tray, it was snatched from my grasp and replaced with another.

'I sure won't starve,' I mused as I enjoyed the meal, although Maxwell's enigmatic smile made me a bit uncomfortable.

Maxwell noticed my stare. "What are you looking at, O'Reilly?"

"Nothing, sir," I stammered. I had fallen into a classic plebe trap and again had given exactly the wrong answer.

35

"Are you calling me nothing, O'Reilly?"

"No, sir!" I answered, then added before he could jump on me further. "I was wondering why you were smiling, sir?"

He brightened. "Sure you were, pal. I know something you don't know, O'Reilly."

"What's that, sir?" I asked.

"Oh, you'll find out soon enough," he said. "I don't want to get too far ahead of myself. Eat up. There isn't much time."

"Yes, sir!" He was correct. I had just finished my steak when a team of stewards arrived and our plates were cleared, and large bowls of ice cream appeared on the table.

We weren't left any time to savor. My spoon had barely entered my mouth with the final bite of ice cream, when Maxwell, looked at Battle's table. Confirming that Battle was also ready, he announced. "Okay, ladies. Put down your spoons. Take a last swallow, and let's form up.

After we achieved a close approximation of the formation we had arrived in, Battle, ordered a "Company . . . Forward, march!" We returned to the Company area without incident.

CHAPTER 4

## *THE PROCESS OF PLEBE*

Arriving in the Company area, Battle announced, "Go to your rooms, wash up, and straighten your clothes. If you have to visit the *head*, hurry. Leave your sport coats and ties behind. In five minutes I want you back in this exact location. Dismissed!"

I was the first one to the sink. I soaped and dried my hands on one of the wash cloths from my locker. Next I took off my coat and tie, undid my pants, and tucked in my shirt. When I had finished, I went into the passageway and found my approximate place in the formation. Battle and Maxwell emerged from their room and marched to our position.

"Very good," Battle announced. He stood rigid, hands behind his back. "I want you all to back up to the far bulkhead and have a seat on the deck."

"Okay," Maxwell said, taking the lead after we were settled, "it's time to teach you who you are. What I'm going to say is very important, so listen carefully." He paced nervously in front of the group as he talked.

"I'm sure you already know that this is Annapolis, a military academy. If you don't suspect that what happens here is far different from your average university, you have no business being here. This is a very difficult program. Not only are the academics among the toughest in the nation, but we will make severe demands on you physically, mentally, and emotionally. Annapolis graduates are naval officers who are responsible for the lives of fellow human beings. You have to be better than your peers and your enemy if you are going to survive in combat, and this place will give you the edge you will need to survive." He looked down at us.

"Some of you will not be around to graduate." He continued pacing. "Some of you won't make it through the year. Many will drop before the summer is over. A few of you won't even take the oath today. That's what I want to talk about."

"The military is not a game, and Bancroft Hall is not a big fraternity house. We are involved in the serious business of preparing you for war, and for your early deaths, in combat or in training. Annapolis is a life's commitment, gentlemen. And it brings

37

challenges very few people can meet.  You got this far, so you're probably smart enough, but it takes more than brains to be a good officer.  You must take orders without question.  You must learn how to maintain yourself at a peak of physical conditioning and to function under severe pressure.  You've got to be familiar with your own leadership attributes and how to use them to your advantage.  None of this is easy.  As a matter of fact, it's damned difficult, and it's no disgrace to drop out if you decide this is not the life for you.  So if you know right this second that you absolutely do not want to be here, let us know within the next two hours and we can make appropriate arrangements.

"As of the instant you take that oath, however, you are committed to allowing yourself to become the lowest of the low.  You will be officially *plebes*.  Everyone and everything outranks you as a plebe, including our mascot Bill the Goat.  You will have to refer to all upperclass as *sir* and do everything they tell you to do.  Your rooms must be kept spotless.  You will have to run in the passageways and square your corners in Bancroft Hall.  You will also brace up and keep your eyes focused straight ahead.  At meals you will sit on the last three inches of your chairs and eat every single bite of food with exaggerated square motions.

"And Midshipman Maxwell and I are not going to be your best buddies for the next two months," Battle continued, his hands still folded neatly behind his back.  "We're here to prepare you for when the Brigade gets back from summer cruises.  Right now you plebes outnumber the squadleaders seventeen to one, but come September there will be three upperclass for every one of you, and the pressure will really be on.  We don't have a lot of time to prepare you for that ugly moment, so we're going to be somewhat testy over the next few weeks.  As a matter of fact, we're going to run and harass the hell out of you and enjoy every minute of it.  You are going to memorize stupid sayings and statistics and spout them off on command.  You are going to learn how to wear your uniforms with pride, and believe it or not, we're going to make marchers out of all of you."  He paused, then smiled.  "On the fun side you are going to learn how to shoot the rifle and pistol, how to sail, how to function on a naval vessel, and how to operate a computer.

"When Maxie and I are through with you -- hopefully just before the Brigade returns -- you are going to be different persons.  You may even like yourselves better for the effort.

"Poole and O'Reilly!" Maxwell shouted.  "Front and center!"

I was shocked out of a deep reverie by Maxwell's summons, but I jumped to my feet and hurried to the fore.  Poole had a bit more trouble getting up and moving.

"Tomorrow morning," Maxwell began, "you will be plebes."

I watched his face, and I could see that he believed in what he was saying. His voice and features held such a conviction that I found it difficult not be caught up in the fervor.

"That means," he continued, "you will have certain responsibilities and obligations to yourselves, your classmates, and to the Brigade. To begin with you will 'chop' with your eyes in the boat whenever you are out of your room in Bancroft Hall. Chopping is a short-stepped jog, which you will use as your primary means of transportation from now on. And when you chop, you will square your corners."

He looked at me. "Do you know what that means, Mr. O'Reilly?"

"No, sir!"

"It means that you will turn all corners at a 90-degree angle by planting and pivoting on the foot opposite the direction of turn. If you are going to turn port, pivot on your starboard foot, and vice versa." He turned to Poole. "Do you think you could demonstrate what I've just said?"

"Well," Poole began, "I've never tried it, and I'm not certain what you want, and . . . "

"Silence!" Maxwell screamed. He stared at Poole, then turned to the group and smiled. "I must have gotten ahead of myself a bit. Forgive me."

"When an upperclass asks you a question, there are only three acceptable answers, gentlemen. They are, "Yes, sir," "No, sir," and "I'll find out, sir." When he gives you an order, you say, "Aye, aye, sir." Is that understood?" he asked us.

In response there was a polite smattering of "yes, sirs."

Battle exploded forward. "Listen up, douchebags!" He jerked his sharp features at us. "When we ask you a question, your answer first had better be the right one, *and* second it had better make us deaf for a brief period. And for me that means loud, gentlemen, because I'm already hard of hearing."

"Now," he said. "Did you understand what midshipman Maxwell just said?"

We yelled a booming "Yes, sir!" in chorus.

I thought it was pretty loud, but before I could mentally congratulate us for the effort, Battle yelled again. "You call that loud? I couldn't hear you. Try again!" We did, louder this time. But it wasn't loud enough. We tried again, and again, and again, until Battle was satisfied with the decibel level, or maybe tired of the game.

Maxwell addressed me. "O'Reilly," he said, "demonstrate the 'chop' for us."

"Aye, aye, sir!" I had been reviewing the procedures since Maxwell first asked Poole to demonstrate. I headed off at a jog down the passageway toward the far wing.

"Always chop in the middle of the passageway!"

"A little faster!" yelled Battle.

"Okay," Maxwell said. "Now stop, turn around, and come back, and when you get to your room, turn and go inside. And yell "Beat Army" when you pivot."

"Aye, aye, sir!" Coming down the passageway I watched my classmates. They seemed impressed with my mastering of the chop, so I stuck out my chest a bit. But just as I came level with Battle, he started running with me.

 "Didn't we tell you to keep your eyes in the boat?"

"Yes, sir!" I answered.

"Then do it!"

I concentrated on the double doors at the end of the passageway and continued chopping until I came even with my room. Timing the pivot, I turned on my starboard foot, yelled a loud "Beat Army," and jogged into my room. Inside, I stopped and waited for a response.

After a moment, Maxwell announced, "Good job, O'Reilly. Now get your ass out here!"

I ran straight to the group.

"God dammit!" Battle yelled. "We just said plebes always chop in the passageway!"

"Yes, sir!" I answered.

"Then why didn't you?" he asked.

I thought quickly, then answered, "I'll find out, sir!"

Battle smiled, and his eyes crinkled in a friendly but measuring way. It was a look that told me that Battle could be a nice person, if he ever decided I measured up to his standards.

"Okay, ladies," Maxwell announced, "I want you all to practice chopping for the next few minutes. Chop up and down the passageway, keeping your eyes in the boat, and chop into and out of your rooms. No collisions please." With that both Maxwell and Battle stepped back and let us chop to our hearts content.

Soon the sounds of shuffling feet and a continuous chorus of "Beat Armys" echoed in the passageway. Several classmates -- Poole included -- had trouble deciding which foot to pivot on.

After ten minutes, Battle consulted his watch and bid us be seated again. This time Battle started the lecture. "Okay, you know how to chop and keep your eyes in the boat, but now comes the hard part. You also have to "brace up" whenever you are out of your room. Let's have Poole and O'Reilly front and center again."

Battle put his hands behind his back and began.

"To brace up you push your chin into your neck so far that it comes out the back side. At the same time you keep your head and shoulders straight and of course keep your eyes in the boat. You will brace up whenever an upperclassman enters your room and whenever you enter his. You will brace up while chopping and while eating meals. You do not brace up in your rooms, outside of Bancroft Hall, in class, or when an upper class says you can carry-on."

"O'Reilly! Brace up!"

I pulled my chin in, but my head sagged toward my chest.

"Get your forehead straight, you stupid shit!"

I did, but my chin popped out.

Battle grabbed me from the side and shoved my shoulders forward while at the same time pulling my forehead back so that it was vertical.

"Hold that position!" he commanded.

I did. Next he put two fingers on my chin and shoved it toward my neck. Out of the corner of my eyes I could see his dark eyes watching me with a fierce intensity.

"Forehead back!"

I rotated my forehead and held my chin against the pressure of his fingers. Satisfied, he let go. I stayed braced for several long seconds, looking at my astonished classmates.

"Good, O'Reilly." He touched my neck. "I count three chins, how about you Tom?"

"Three it is! All right. All of you brace up against the bulkhead."

Battle and Maxwell toured the line, yelling and pointing out mistakes.

Suddenly Maxwell roared. "Everyone come here and look at your classmate Ramsey!" I joined a group of astonished classmates surrounding Jubal.

Joe had sprouted six chins on his thick bull neck. Battle and Maxwell flanked him, counting chins in happy amazement.

"This," Battle indicated pridefully, "is what it means to brace up." We stared in awe at Jubal, and I could see classmates pulling their chins down and moving their fingers along the bumps of skin in a vain attempt to copy Joe.

Finally Maxwell consulted his watch. "Okay. Enough for now. Everybody sit." Maxwell went to his room and returned carrying a large dark blue book. On its cover in oversized golden letters was printed, *NAVY SONGS*.

Battle began. "Now comes the hardest part of today's training. It's hard for me because I'm tone deaf and hard for Maxie because he can sing." He turned to Maxwell.

"As part of the Oath of Office Ceremony," Maxwell began, "you will sing two famous Navy songs. The first is titled *The Navy Song*, and it's sung to the tune of *Anchors Aweigh.* You all know the tune, so repeat after me." He took us through *The Navy Song* until we had it memorized - although I can't vouch for the quality of our little songfest since I saw tone-deaf Battle flinch. Maxwell, however, actually had a sweet voice that did not match his raspy bellow. When he was satisfied, we practiced *The Navy Blue and Gold,* a slower, solemn piece, which was sung mostly after Navy football games.

Next we practiced the Oath of Office Ceremony and memorized the choreography that would get us to and from our assigned seats. Battle checked his watch.

"You have 15 minutes before we have to leave the company area for the ceremony. Go back to your rooms and wait. But be back in the passageway in 10 minutes in the clothes you arrived in. Wash your faces, straighten your ties -- and comb your hair." He looked us over, then turned to Maxwell. "This is a sorry-assed group. Do you think any of them will make it through the summer?"

42

"Some might. But for several there's not a chance in hell." Maxwell stared at Thomas Henry Poole as he made that announcement.


We had congregated in the passageway without too much confusion when Battle and Maxwell emerged from their rooms to inspect us. Satisfied, Battle led us through the double doors, down into the rotunda, through the huge metal double doors that mark the main entrance to the rotunda, and out into Tecumseh Court.

After so long indoors, I squinted at the bright sunlight.

Behind me, Rico moaned. "Christ! It's God-awful hot!"

Maxwell heard him. He laughed. "This is spring. Wait until August, pal!"

Tecumseh Court had been roped off to the statue of Tecumseh. The area behind the ropes teemed with excited families and visitors, many calling and waving as they recognized -- or thought they recognized -- their friend or family member. I could not see my family.

Ahead, a flight of broad granite stairs ended in a wide landing. On the end of the landing near the stairs, stood a podium and several chairs facing the Court. Below, at the bottom of the steps, two identical sections of metal folding chairs awaited us.

We descended to the left side on one of the broad curving ramps that flank the main steps. Midshipmen waited near the seats to ensure we entered the correct row. The chairs had been set up in 18 identical rows of 36 seats. A cardboard sign attached near the bottom of the first chair indicated the number of the Company. Companies 1 through 18 sat on the left side facing the steps, 19 through 36 sat on the right. Battle led us into our row. Maxwell brought up the rear.

When we were about halfway down the row, a loud voice shouted "Rico! Amigo!"

Rico stopped and waved both arms high in the air. Cheering erupted from the crowd.

When we had arrived at our seats, Battle called "Right face!" followed by "Seats!"


Dignitaries emerged from the rotunda. At the time I hadn't the faintest idea of rank and seniority, but I could tell from the carriage and demeanor that they were important persons.  Hats and shoulders overflowed with gold braid and fancy designs, and their chests were resplendent with multi-colored ribbons.  The dignitaries sat, and one of their number approached the podium.  What followed was an invocation by the head chaplain, and a welcoming speech by the Superintendent of the Naval Academy, Rear Admiral Jake Conrad.  He stressed the qualifications of our group. -- Fifty percent varsity athletes in at least two sports. Seventy percent National Merit Scholars.  Eighty percent presidents of their High School classes.  Sixty percent Eagle Scouts.  I fit only one of those categories, so I was impressed – and a little intimidated.

The ceremony lasted 30 minutes, concluding with the Oath of Office, where we pledged allegiance to God, the country, and the president, and sang our rendition of *Navy Blue and Gold*, which didn't sound at all bad.  At the conclusion of the ceremony we waited for the dignitaries to depart into the rotunda.  A midshipman approached the microphone.

"Liberty Call commences for the Class of 1971!  Assemble in prearranged areas at 1730."  We had been instructed not to leave Tecumseh Court.  Battle and Maxwell would rendezvous with us at our seats at exactly 1730, and on pain of death, we had better not be late.

We filed from our seats.  Once in the main section of Tecumseh Court, (T-Court) we merged with the crowd.  However, like a thousand other plebes, I had told my family I would meet them at the statue of the Indian, and I soon dismayed that I would find them in the milling crowd.

My Dad, always the hero, had thought up a solution.  As I approached the pandemonium, I saw Sean, hefted up onto Dad's shoulders, scanning the approaching plebes.

"Sean!" I yelled, waving an arm in the air.  He spotted me and his eyes widened.  I indicated with a wave that they should move clear of the crowd, under one of the enormous tulip poplar trees that lined the brick walkway.  I approached them cautiously, wondering what their reaction would be.

My horrified mother stared at my baldness. "Oh, my God!" She put a pale hand to her cheek.  Sean burst into a laugh and pointed.  "Get a load of that!"

My father chuckled, his eyes sparkling with humor.  "Well, Kevin, how is it so far?"

"So far I've had my foot in my mouth a dozen times, embarrassed myself in front of my peers, and only managed to piss off one of the upperclassmen. -- I'm doing great."

Mom became serious  "Are they treating you right, Kevin?"

"Rin," Dad cooed, "this is like a boot camp. They have to be hard on them. It's how they weed out the good from the bad." His eyes welled up with tears. Rather than speak, he turned his head to one side and stared at infinity.

Mom noticed his predicament. She smiled like a Madonna in a stained glass window. "Your father is so sentimental. He cried during the Oath too." She put a small hand on his large arm and patted it gently. "I'm sure Kevin will be fine, dear."

"I know." Dad recovered from his near sobbing. "I'm sure of it."

We found a spot where we could sit. I explained everything we had done thus far, and they told me about their adventures exploring the campus and the beautiful city of Annapolis. Sean wanted to see me brace up, so I pulled in my chin for the family.

While we were talking I noticed Jubal Ramsey approaching with his mother and siblings. I waved. His mother, a petite and attractive brunette, steered the group in our direction. I introduced my family. His mother, May, talked with a gentle and refined Southern accent as she named her children for us. While she talked, she kept one arm protectively locked around Jubal's arm. Each of Joe's siblings smiled and offered a hand to shake.

When Jubal shook hands with my Dad, they held their grips appraisingly. Jubal stared at the sheer mass of Big Kevin, then sized me up.

I laughed. "I must have missed out on the family "Hulk" genes."

"Couldn't your Dad make it today?" Sean asked.

Jubal blurted, "No, he couldn't." The strange way he said it, and the sad look his mother gave him in response, told me there was a story somewhere that Joe wasn't ready to reveal. We let the subject drop, and in a few minutes the Ramseys excused themselves.

We traded small talk for most of the hour and I promised I would write every day -- a promise I would break the next day.

I noticed a general movement in the direction of T-Court and stood. "Well," I said, "time to go. If I'm late, I'm dead."

We exchanged hugs and kisses, and I gave my Dad a firm handshake, but this time it was easier to let go than it had been at the Field House. I had taken a major step on the road toward maturity. At least that's what I believed as I basked in the glow of family admiration.

Maxwell and Battle waited as we assembled at our chairs.  One of our classmates stood to the side looking at his feet.  After they had counted the last of us, we formed into the three now-familiar squads.  Maxwell spoke quietly to the embarrassed classmate and pointed in the general direction of the main office.  The classmate nodded but did not look at us.

Maxwell spoke quietly.  "Was it sad saying goodbye to your families?"

Several subdued "Yes, sirs" came in reply.

"Well, I have some good and bad news for you."  His faked concern then turned to sadistic glee.  "The good news is that some of you will be seeing Mommy and Daddy sooner than you think."

"What's the bad news?" asked Battle in feigned sincerity.

Maxwell laughed.  "Those of you who don't see them are going to wish you could."  With that Battle started us toward the bowels of Mother Bancroft.  What followed was my last meal in civilian clothes in the Mess Hall for more than 25 years, and the last meal for several months that wasn't accompanied by harassment and grief.

CHAPTER 5

## *A BRACING EXPERIENCE*

We returned to the Company area just after 1800.  Battle halted us in the passageway, and Maxwell went into their room.

"Stand against the bulkhead!" Battle ordered.  We moved to obey.  Maxwell returned with a chair and several sets of uniform clothes.  He placed the clothes on the chair, then scanned the crowd.  I slunk into the nethermost regions of the group against the ugly dull-pink tiles that covered the bulkhead.  He caught sight of me, and he knew I was trying to hide.

"O'Reilly!" he bellowed.  "Front and center!"

I groaned and Battle pounced.  "What's the matter, O'Reilly, are we being pests?"

"No, sir!" I chopped to the front of the group and stopped beside Maxwell.

Battle shook his head and walked toward me.  He stopped so close I could smell the garlic sauce from our spaghetti dinner, still lingering on his breath like a death cloud.  He leaned in closer until his nose almost touched my chin.  His brown eyes locked on my own in a narrow, emotionless stare which he held for several seconds.  I was completely unprepared for his close proximity, and I drew away.

"What's the matter O'Reilly?  Do I have bad breath or body odor?"

An honest answer was not expected.  I sputtered, "No, sir!"

"Well, then.  When I talk to you from now on you will remain rigid no matter how close I come."  He put his index finger on my chest.  "I may even have a reason to touch you during the course of our training.  You can understand that, can't you?"

"Yes, sir!" I hesitated, unsure where the conversation was going.

"You wouldn't consider me a faggot if I touched you, would you, O'Reilly?"

47

I was very confused. The silence behind me was palpable. I could sense that every person in the passageway, Maxwell included, was waiting to find what Battle was getting at.

"No problem, Sir! I can't see as how you'd be interested in me that way."

This was not an answer Battle expected. He drew back and gave me a suspicious look. "Why is that, O'Reilly?"

"Well, you see, sir. I'm just an Irishman, and everybody knows we have these teeny tiny pencil dicks. So what would be the point, sir?"

Maxwell and Battle laughed, and the group behind joined in. The laughter went on for a minute. Finally Battle calmed enough to look at me then at the group at large. "All right, everyone! You've had your little laugh. Calm down." His attention returned to me. "It's a good thing I have a sense of humor, O'Reilly. And you don't need to worry about the homo-thing either. The only time I'm going to touch one of you douchebags is when I kick your ass."

He addressed the group. "Is that understood?" There was a loud reply.

"Now," Maxwell continued, "It's time to begin training. He picked up a jock strap and held it aloft. "This is a jock strap," he said. "I'm sure some of you have never seen one, so let me just say that the fat part goes in front." He looked at me. "To protect your pencil dicks."

He reached down and picked up a pair of navy blue gym shorts. "These are gym shorts," he said, transferring them to the same hand as the jock. He did the same with a white gym shirt, blue-stripped athletic socks, and the ugly gym shoes.

"Together they make up something called *gym gear*. O'Reilly, run to your room and put on your gym gear as quickly as possible, then return." I chopped for my room, and was back in less than five minutes

When I returned, Maxwell and Battle looked me over as critically as they could, but after all, I was in shorts and gym shirt, so creases, polish, and alignment were irrelevant.

Satisfied, Maxwell turned to the group. "Okay, ladies! You see how O'Reilly is dressed? I want you all back here in the identical outfit in five minutes. Get moving!"

The herd stampeded.

No sooner had the thunder of departing feet stopped reverberating in the passageway than Maxwell turned to me again. "Come here, O'Reilly." He held up a white jumper and matching cotton pants. "I want you to go back to your room and change into this uniform. Wear regulation underwear, black socks and shoes, and bring your dixie cup. Go!"

I chopped to the room, confused about the necessity for such an exercise. By the time I returned, Maxwell and Battle had the rest of my companymates standing against the bulkhead, and were inspecting their gym gear. I clomped into the hall in the strange uniform, squared my corners, and waited beside the chair.

Maxwell moved to the center of the passageway and stood next to me. "Okay," he said. "Believe it or not, there is a reason for this exercise. Tomorrow morning we are going to begin a regular exercise program to get you into shape. You will be dressed in gym gear and standing against the bulkhead outside your rooms at 0600. Mr. Battle and I are going to take you on a short three-mile run followed by 30 minutes of calisthenics. I don't want any confusion to delay the program; consequently you now know what to wear and how to wear it. After the morning exercise you will have thirty minutes to shower and change into white works."

He pointed to me. "This is *white works*. Study what your classmate is wearing. Notice he has on regulation undies, black shoes and socks, and he has his dixie cup in his hand. Now all of you go to your rooms and get on your white works. Five minutes. Move it!"

Again the herd thundered.

"Go stand against the bulkhead, O'Reilly."

It was five minutes to seven in the evening – 1900 hours. I was exhausted. I had never had a day so full of activity and new experiences. I yawned.

Battle noticed. "Tired, O'Reilly?" It seemed an honest question.

"Yes, sir!"

"Well too damn bad! This is not how I'd choose to spend an evening either. Nursemaid to a bunch of wimps. Believe me, I'd rather be out on liberty or back home with my girlfriend. So spare me your droopy eyes or I'll start your plebe year tonight with a hundred pushups."

"Aye, aye, sir!"

My classmates returned within three minutes, wearing various versions of the uniform I had on.  Some wore v-neck T-shirts.  Some had no T-shirts.  Some had no underwear. Some wore the wrong shoes -- or the wrong socks.  A few forgot the hat.  Battle and Maxwell reacted.

Thomas Poole was the final midshipman to arrive -- reluctantly.  He had put on his T-shirt inside out, a barely noticeable error considering that his pants had been incorrectly fitted. The trouser legs were too narrow for his ample thighs, the flared bottoms ended several inches above his ankle, and the pullover barely cleared his abundant middle.  I felt sorry for Tommy.

Like sharks draw by the scent of blood, the squadleaders attacked.  Although I learned the precise technical word later in the summer, that first day I knew instinctively that Thomas Henry Poole was a perfect "shit screen."

It took twenty minutes for Battle and Maxwell to satisfy themselves that the group could dress itself for the first day of plebedom.  Afterward, Maxwell yelled us into gym gear. Maxwell's voice, strained from the yelling and constant jabber of the day, cracked as he moved from room to room urging us to hurry.


A very tired group of proto-plebes reassembled.  The chair had been removed from the passageway, and Maxwell and Battle had changed from their white uniforms into casual attire.  Maxwell wore a pair of old civilian boxer shorts, bright red hearts emblazoned thereon.  He also had on a T-shirt that announced him to be a devoted fan of the Saint Louis Cardinals.  Over this he wore a bathrobe, not a standard purplish, Naval Academy issue model like we had been given centuries earlier that day but rather a dull gray affair with an unfamiliar crest on the chest pocket.  On his feet were rubber shower shoes affectionately called "clacks" because of the noise they made.  He kept his hands in his bathrobe pockets as he waited.

Battle wore a red and gold pair of Marine Corps athletic shorts and a T-shirt with a picture of a hungry buzzard perched on a dead tree limb and a caption that announced that it was a bad day when you can't kill anything.  He also had on a bathrobe, but this one was a very old and significantly faded Naval Academy robe, the back of which sported various letters and the number "39" in several places.  He also wore clacks, but with white gym socks.  He stood with hands folded behind his back, and since this was the first time I had seen him without his hat on, I saw that he was going prematurely bald in the back and front of his head.

50

"Okay, gentlemen. Listen up!" Maxwell began. "This will be the final lecture of the night. But this one may be the most important one you will receive the entire summer. We'll go very slowly, but what we are about to say is vital to your survival and to the survival of this institution and the nation."

Many of my classmates murmured disbelief, and Maxwell paused to let the idea sink in.

He pointed to a plebe in the front. "You," he asked. "What's your name?"

"Nikolas Papadopalas, sir," the short, swarthy classmate answered.

"Why are you here, Nicky?"

"To get a good education, sir."

Maxwell pointed to another new face. "You, same question."

This classmate, a lanky, light-haired individual, answered, "Robert Strong, sir. To fly jets. And maybe be an astronaut."

Maxwell selected the only black member of the company. He was a small, attractive boy, who spoke precise English with a hint of an 'islands' accent.

"My name is Wesley Roy Lamont, and I am here because my father served in the Navy during World War II and now runs a small fishing charter in the American Virgin Islands. I have spent a great deal of my life on or near the water. I love the sea and everything to do with it. Where else but Annapolis?"

Maxwell stared at Lamont for a second before selecting Jeffrey Polk.

"Jeff Polk, sir. I'm here because it seemed like a good idea at the time."

"Sure, pal!" Maxwell replied.

Maxwell turned to Battle. "I've heard enough, Tommy. Tell them why they're here."

Battle moved to the front of the group. He looked us up and down before beginning.

"Bullshit!" he yelled. "What I just heard is pure bullshit! You're not here to get an education, or to learn to fly, or sail the ocean blue. You're here to serve the country and to prepare yourselves to die for your fellow citizens. Nothing more or less is expected from you." He paused to let the point sink in. "You will, of course, have to study hard *and* work your asses off for the privilege of serving your nation, but *that's* why you're here."

"The Naval Academy was founded in 1848 to train officers to serve in the fleet.  Since that time only sixty thousand men have graduated from this institution.  That is not a large number, gentlemen.  This is a very elite school with traditions that are deeply rooted in duty, honor, and loyalty.  Thousands of our graduates have paid the ultimate price fulfilling the mission of this nation.  Very few schools can make that kind of claim."

Battle continued.  "In combat you will be expected to obey the commands of your superior officers.  Your life and the lives of your shipmates will depend on that.  That's why midshipman Maxwell and I will accept nothing less than instant obedience.  We will tell you to do things that seem senseless.  You will be forced to memorize inane banter.  Part of what we ask may even be personally humiliating.   Tough!  But we're not going to ask you to carry a rifle up a hill against an enemy position or drive a ship into hopeless battle, or fly an A-4 against a SAM site.  Our little drills may be stupid, but they won't kill you, and you will obey nonetheless because that's what expected. If you can't deal with that, quit now.  There's no disgrace in admitting the error -- one of your companymates has already departed.  If you are not sufficiently gifted to earn a commission from this institution, your decision to leave now may save the lives of men who would be depending on you in combat."

Battle loosened his posture and paced toward the double doors.  "Everyone be quiet and listen."  Immediately I became aware that we were not the only group of plebes being trained.  From down the passageway, around the corner, and drifting up from the decks below, I could hear noise from other companies.

"Even as we speak," Battle continued, "35 identical groups are being assaulted and berated by other squadleaders.  And I'm sure that more than one thousand pea-brained plebes just like you are this very minute wondering what the hell they are doing here."

"You know, you guys are lucky.  Maxie and I are pussycats compared to some of the other squadleaders on the summer detail.  But when the Brigade gets back in September, you are going to face the toughest group of first classmen in the entire Academy.  They are a bunch of assholes who call themselves the "Tigers," and they make even the staunchest of my classmates look like Sunday school teachers.  Life will not be easy for you poor pukes.  Hell, I hate them myself, and I can run rings around most of them."

"I happened to be talking to a classmate after dinner today.  He works as an assistant to the Commandant for the Plebe Summer period.  He told me that nearly a hundred of your classmates either elected not to show up today or to go home. That's almost a tenth of the group the first day. But that's not unusual. This is a special school, and we have special requirements for our students and graduates. Tonight, as you prepare for bed, I want each of you to decide whether you really want to be here. If you're not prepared to meet the ultimate challenge, leave now." He turned to Maxwell. "Did I explain things well enough?"

"Great job," Maxwell answered. "Give him a hand, gentlemen. Tommy here is a truly dedicated professional." We applauded until Maxwell held his hand up for attention.

"For my part of the final hour I will do two things. First I'm going to tell you about what it means to be a midshipman. Second I'm going to have one room of classmates introduce themselves and give us all a one minute talk on their background and what they expect from this experience. For the first evening's entertainment I have selected 5404, "The Goon Room." I want the four of you 'goons' to prepare for your presentations while I am talking."

Poole pushed a flabby arm into the air.

Maxwell acknowledged him. "The head goon wants to speak. Speak goon!"

"Sir, can we go back to our rooms for pencil and paper to outline our talks?"

"Very impressive, Poole. You want to do a good job on your first assignment. What do you think, Tom?"

"Shit no!" Battle answered. "What are you going to do in combat, Poole, jot down notes before the enemy attacks so you'll know what to do if you face the business end of a bayonet?"

"You heard the man," Maxwell said, "This will be impromptu." Maxwell cleared his throat with some small difficulty.

"There is one concept that forms the basis for everything a midshipman is. That is the Honor Code. I happen to be an Honor Committee Representative for the Company, so I am familiar with the Code and all its nuances. But I can summarize with the words you will find in your *Reef Points*. '*A midshipman does not lie, cheat, or steal.*'"

"It sounds too simple," he added. "It seems unnecessary. It may even insult your personal code of behavior. But I can assure you that the Honor Code is very serious to the Brigade of Midshipmen."

He paused. "We midshipmen police the Honor Policy ourselves and are wholly responsible for investigating and punishing violations. A few students are expelled for such violations every year."

"At Annapolis we have a Code that differs from the ones at West Point and at Air Force. Cadets at the "Point" must reveal to the authorities whatever they suspect. Cadets at Air Force are only responsible for their own behavior. Midshipmen, however, are allowed broad discretion in how they treat honor violations.

"This is an important distinction because it not only makes each of us responsible for the actions of the entire Brigade, but it also gives us the ability to apply reason and common sense to the Code. If I see you violate the Code, I can first talk to you, discover what it is I saw, and ask how you intended your action. If I'm convinced you acted inadvertently, I can let the matter drop, or I can lecture you and have you make appropriate retribution. If I am sure you violated the Code, I can request that you inform the Honor Committee yourself, or, if the action is severe, I can and will report to the Honor Committee myself."

Maxwell continued. "But a violation isn't always obvious. In the heat of a moment you may say something that was never intended to be a deception, or you may do something just plain stupid. The system will punish these simple errors in judgment with demerits, not dismissal. However, if there is no doubt in the Committee's mind that you have lied, cheated, or stolen, you will be dismissed in disgrace.

"Over the next several days I will entertain questions regarding Honor policy, and I will give you some horror stories about midshipmen who thought they were too smart for the system. By the end of the summer you will know what the Honor Code means to each of us."

He took a deep breath. "Now, Mister Battle and I will go to our rooms for chairs, and when we return the Goon Room will tell us all the sordid details of their past lives. Wait quietly, children. We'll be right back." Maxwell and Battle departed.

Jim Merritt stood and searched for his roommates. Who wants to go first?" Nobody answered. "Okay, I will. How about if you go second, Tommy, with Jeff third, and Jubal last?" He smiled at Joe. "I'm sure you have the best story anyway." Nobody objected.

Merritt continued, "I intend to talk about my family background, brothers and sisters, where I went to school, sports, and generally about my interests. I think we should keep it light. No religion or politics. Everyone agree?" Again there were no objections. Merritt sat down.

Maxwell and Battle returned carrying the lightweight metal desk chairs from their room. They sat them to one side.

"Okay," Maxwell said. "One at a time, goons. Who's first?"

Merritt moved to the front of the group. "I am, sir!" He spoke with an ease and natural flair that I instantly envied.

"My name is James Wesley Merritt," he began. "You can call me Jim. I was born in Amarillo, Texas. My father, John, is a manager with Gulf Oil Company. My mother, Martha, is a housewife. I am the oldest of five children. I have a brother Samuel who is fifteen, another brother Houston who is twelve, and sisters Monica and Merri who are ten and six.

"I attended Sam Houston High School in Amarillo, where I played three seasons of football and two of track. I was the reluctant president of my class. I like music and sports, and I have a sweet girlfriend back home named Lynda. I'm very excited to be here, and I want very much to be a Navy pilot and astronaut." He turned to the squadleaders. "Questions, sirs?"

Maxwell addressed the group. "Anybody have questions for classmate Merritt?" Nobody did. "Sit down, Merritt. Next!"

Tommy Poole stood, straightened his gym shirt over his belly, and walked to the front of the group. He looked at the squadleaders. Maxwell nodded his head. Poole turned toward the group. "My name is Thomas Henry Poole," he began nervously. "I was born in Flint, Michigan. My Dad works at the General Motors Plant in Flint. I attended St. Ursula's High School in Flint, and I was president of the Debate Society and the Physics Club. I was also a member of the Drama Club, Chess Club, and National Honor Society.

"I enjoy sports but I didn't letter except as manager of the hockey team. I also like music, especially the Beatles, and I can play piano a little. I'm looking forward to the Annapolis challenge." He smiled. "Questions?"

"Got any sisters?" asked Battle.

Maxwell looked at him as if he had sprouted a second head.

Battle spoke. "I'm thinking of dating a woman with brains instead of the usual big-titted babes that hang out in town. Maybe Poole has a likely prospect?"

The idea of Tommy Battle dating his fictional sister overwhelmed Tommy, who stammered a hasty, "No, sir. No sisters." Then Poole paused and tears came to his eyes. "I had an older brother who was killed in an accident several years ago."

"Sit down, Poole."

Jeff Polk moved quickly to the fore. He turned toward the group and spoke in a deep nervous voice. "Hi. I'm Jeffrey John Polk. I don't have much of a story. I grew up in Derry, New Hampshire. My Dad works at a paper mill. I have a younger brother. I play baseball and a little guitar. Any questions?"

"That's it?" Maxwell asked. "Your whole life in under ten seconds? Doesn't that make you feel a little sad, Polk?"

"No, sir," Jeff answered.

"Sit down, pal," Maxwell ordered, "because I don't know about you, Tom, but I'm more than anxious to hear from the human tree stump."

"Yeah," Battle answered, "me too!"

Jubal Ramsey stood. Because of his unusual size, classmates had to squeeze sideward to let him through. Joe took it all in stride. He sauntered to the front, faced the squadleaders, bowed gracefully, then turned toward us. "Hi," he said in that unbelievable accent. "Ah'm Jubal Hunter Ramsey, and ah'm from High Point, Alabama, which, in case you cain't guess, is deep in the heart of Dixie.

"I love the military. My Daddy went to West Point. I have a brother, Mason, two years younger, who's bigger than me. And two sisters, one Becky who is three years younger and almost bigger than me, and  Melinda, who is only ten and ain't fully grown yet."

"Why didn't you go to West Point?" Battle asked.

"Sir, my High School grades weren't up to snuff and I had to attend the University of Alabama. No West Point appointments were available when I reapplied. But ah'm sure I'll like it here. You fellas seem real nice."

"See how nice we are in the morning, pal," Maxwell observed. "Sit down."

Maxwell stood and moved to a place opposite the center of the group.

"Well," he said, "that concludes today's festivities.  You can return to your rooms, but be absolutely quiet.  Lights out at 2100.  Set your alarms for early, and do not fail to be ready at precisely 0600.  Any questions?"  I had so many I couldn't frame them all in time to respond.  I'm sure the rest of my classmates felt the same.

"Good night, ladies," Maxwell said, and with that he and Battle returned to their room.

I eased myself off the deck and stretched my arms over my head.  I looked at companymates who were also looking at each other as we headed toward our individual rooms.

CHAPTER 6

## *LIGHTS OUT – DAY ONE*

I prepared my gym clothes and white works for the morning. Afterward, I folded my civilian clothes and put them in my suitcase. Finally, I prepared to take a shower. While puttering, I noticed Donny Delmont sitting at his desk. He ignored my gaze, and hurried from the room.

Once he was gone, Rico looked at me and said. "He's not long for this place."

"What makes you think so?"

"He's got the look."

I wondered what 'the look' was.

"Wait and see," Rico said. With that prophecy, he returned to reading a book.

Grizwald emerged from the coat closet. "I suppose it's all right to go to the bathroom?"

"Sure, why not?"

He left the room.

"He'll be next," Rico said.

"What?" I asked.

"Grizwald will be the next to go," Rico stated.

"He's got the look, too?" I asked.

Rico nodded, then returned to his book.

"What about me?" I asked. "Am I destined to soon depart these hallowed halls?"

"No. You're what they call a *lifer*," he answered. I wasn't exactly sure what that meant, but at least from the standpoint of Rico's crystal ball I was safe for the time being. For some strange reason, it reassured me.

Grizwald returned quickly, but Delmont was gone a long time. I had finished my shower and put on my bathrobe when he finally came back to the room. He didn't look at any of us, but instead went straight to his locker and put away his things. I could see Rico watching him from across the room. Delmont undressed and climbed into the bunk above mine. He slid himself as far against the wall as he could, turned his body away from the room, and lay silently.

Rico winked at me knowingly.

For a moment I considered saying something to Delmont, but I was unsure what to say. Instead I walked to the doorway and peered outside. I wondered if I should inform the squadleaders. Across the passageway, I could see activity in Merritt's room. They appeared to be getting along. As I watched, Jim Merritt appeared in the doorway, smiled at me, and headed down the passageway toward the head facilities.

I hesitated for a second, then followed.

Navy communal facilities are called "heads" for some reason that was never explained to me. The heads in Bancroft Hall were clean and spacious. Against one wall was a bank of five white porcelain urinals, separated from a series of three equally white sinks by a splash partition. Across the room were four green metal stalls. I selected a urinal next to Merritt.

"You lied to Battle tonight, you know."

He said this in such a serious voice that my heart sank and I lost control of my aim. Visions of Honor Committees and dismissal in disgrace flooded my thoughts. "What?"

"You lied to Battle. You don't have a pencil dick." He grinned.

I was overcome with relief. "That was a terrible joke," I replied.

"What do you think of everything so far?" he asked.

"The jury's out," I answered. "Listen, my roommate Delmont is acting strangely. Rico thinks he's quitting. Should I do anything?"

Merritt thought for a moment. "He's gonna quit, huh?"

"It seems like it. He's sure acting strange, but I'm not sure what's 'strange' after today."

"If he quits, he quits," Merritt answered. "He's old enough to make decisions on his own. Maybe you could get Delmont to talk to Poole about leaving. I have a bad feeling about him. He doesn't seem suited to the environment, and his screw-ups are going to get all of us in trouble. There's already friction between him and Ramsey because of the suitcase. And Ramsey has made it very clear to us that the Navy is sub-par and that he would rather be at West Point. And Polk has a bad attitude about what he calls the 'Mickey Mouse' rules. I expect fist fights before too long. I'm not sure I want to be in the Goon Room. Want to change rooms?"

"Maybe I'll have to," I answered, "because Delmont's going to leave, and according to Rico, Grizwald will be next. Soon I may be alone. I don't think I could handle that."

Merritt considered. "Listen. You're a steady influence. You've got a good head on your shoulders. And you're funny. Why not act as the peacemaker for my room. Come visit. Draw the others out into conversation. Get them to reveal things and start depending on each other."

"Can't you do that?" I asked.

"Maybe. But if I try to assume a leadership role, they'll resent it and clam up even more. No, what we need here is an outsider. Someone they know, but not too well. You're perfect for the role." He looked at his watch. "There's still almost an hour before lights out. Come visit." With that he left the head and ambled toward his room.


Still considering what Merritt had asked, I returned to my room. Delmont remained pressed against the wall. I didn't think he was asleep. Grizwald was in the shower. Rico hadn't moved from his seat. He looked up when I returned. I winked at him, then went over to his desk, drew up Grizwald's chair, and sat down. He looked at me expectantly.

I started to speak, noticed something peculiar about the book he was reading, and reached over to examine it. It was the kind of book we used to pass around in the locker room at high school, one with passages guaranteed to excite young hormones. The title was Sex *Spy,* and the cover showed a scantily clad young lady wearing a heavy fur Russian military cap and lying on a polar bear skin rug, thick lips parted and leering seductively at the reader.

"You actually read this stuff?"

"It's a technical manual. You can never have enough ideas about the different ways to please a woman. I consider it research."

I laughed. "I'm going across the passageway to visit the goons. Want to come along?"

"Not tonight. I'm going to shower and hit the sack. Tomorrow will come very early."

"Okay," I said. "I won't be long."

He smiled. "I'll leave a light on for you."

First checking the passageway to make sure it was empty of squadleaders, I hurried across to Merritt's room. Inside there was considerable activity. Ramsey was in the shower. Polk was stacking laundry in his locker. Merritt was wiping down his desk top. And Poole was sitting at his desk trying to fold his skivvy shorts.

"You guys look busy."

Poole and Merritt smiled, and Polk nodded but did not smile. I went to one of the desks and sat on the smooth top. "Ready for tomorrow?"

"How could we be when nothing they do makes any sense?" asked Polk. "They'll probably have us digging and filling latrines and call it a strategic exercise. Or maybe we'll sing songs and march around campus to impress the tourists. And have any of you looked at that stupid *Reef Points* book? Wait until you hear some of the insanity they expect us to memorize."

Merritt looked at me.

"Well, Jeff," I said, "it seems to me all the nonsense has a purpose. It's like the initiation for a club -- something you have to do to pay the dues. Think of it as self-discipline."

Polk looked skeptical. His dark eyes narrowed. "It's still bullshit!"

"No doubt about it," I replied, "but all the complaining in the world isn't going to change it or make it any easier." I lowered my voice. "I've got two roommates who Rico Guevarra swears will be gone in a week. If that's true, then they don't seem to be willing to give the place a decent chance. That's what I'm going to do. I'll wait and see, maybe through the summer. If I don't like it, then I'll go to MIT or Georgia Tech."

Poole interrupted. "You had acceptance from MIT?"

"Conditional. My verbal scores weren't outstanding, and my math scores were in the low 700s. How about you, Tommy? What were your scores?"

Poole hesitated. "I had 800," he answered.

"Wow!" I said, "that's a perfect score. Was that math or verbal?"

"Both," he answered quietly.

Ramsey had just emerged from the shower. "You maxed out the SATs?"

Poole nodded.

"What the hell! Y'all don't belong in military school with us dumb-dumbs."

"I want to be here," he said. "Maxwell didn't ask me, but I came to serve my country."

"This place is gonna eat you up and spit you out, boy," Ramsey said. "Look at yo'self. I'll bet you cain't even do one push up. How you expect to keep up with us?"

"If I had known we were supposed to arrive in shape," Poole answered, "I would have prepared. I thought the purpose of the summer training was to get us into shape."

"My Daddy used to tell me stories about what it was like at the Point," Jubal replied. "I think y'all gonna get the lot of us in trouble."

Merritt looked at me again. I was beginning to resent acting as his sounding board. "Well," I said, "I suppose if we all act together, it'll be better than getting angry at one another. We're supposed to be a unit."

"Tell me that tomorrow!" replied Jubal.

I had no answer for that. I'd just have to wait and see.

"Well," I said, "I'm really bushed. I think I'll get some sleep. See you bright and early." I left the room, my first stint at peacemaking a seeming failure.


Rico was in bed. Grizwald was asleep and snoring loudly. Delmont was deathly silent. I took off my robe, hung it up, turned off the lights, and got into bed. For almost a minute I lay on my back considering the swirl of the day's events. For some reason, I found myself whispering the Oath of Office as my brain slowed its frantic pace. I had assumed an awesome responsibility and I hoped I could honor my part of the bargain with Uncle Sam. As the last words of the Oath vibrated in my brain, I fell into the deepest sleep of my life.

## THE OATH OF OFFICE

*"I, Kevin Patrick O'Reilly, having been appointed a Midshipman in the United States Navy, do solemnly swear that I will support and defend the Constitution of the United States against all enemies, foreign and domestic; that I will bear true faith and allegiance to the same; that I take this obligation freely, without any mental reservation or purpose of evasion; and that I will well and faithfully discharge the duties of the office on which I am about to enter; so help me, God.*

CHAPTER 7

## *THE MORNING RUN*

The lights flashed on. I had been sleeping on my back in exactly the same position as when I had fallen asleep just five minutes ago. Only it wasn't five minutes.

"Jesus, guys!" announced Merritt in a ferocious whisper from just inside the doorway. "It's 0545! You should have been up a half-hour ago. Move your asses or you'll be in big trouble!" He left the room, no doubt to check for other slackers and ne'er-do-wells.

I exploded out of bed, as did Rico and Tony. I had left my gym gear within easy reach.

"Donny!" Tony said loudly, "Hurry up!"

Delmont rolled over. There was something in his eyes that told me he was avoiding us, reluctant to speak. He fumbled for words.

"What's the matter? Don't you feel well?" I asked, giving him an out if he wanted it.

He looked at me gratefully. "Yes," he mumbled. "I don't feel well."

"I'll tell Maxwell if you want," I offered.

"Please do that." He watched us don the necessary items. I was dressed in two minutes. Rico in five. Anthony got shirt and shorts mixed up, and held his jock strap up, plainly considering what to do with the alien thing.

"The other end goes in front, Tony," Rico offered.

"Huh?" Tony slipped into the garment, his long bony legs tripping over the first strap in the process. Eventually he was ready, and we slipped quietly into the passageway. I turned out the lights, glancing back at Delmont, who watched from his top bunk perch. Something was definitely wrong with the guy. I winked and smiled. "Wish us luck," I said. He stayed quiet.

A single bank of lights illuminated the entry to the heads; the rest of the passageway was dark. But the corridor walls seemed alive with dark and shadowy figures. Across the passageway I saw the Goon Room occupants -- nervous and restless.

Merritt waved.

"Thanks," I whispered.

He nodded and checked his watch.

At 0605 the door to the squadleaders' room opened and Maxwell's disheveled head emerged. He looked up the passageway at his expectant charges, groaned, then disappeared inside. We plebes exchanged nervous giggles and waited.

Two minutes later they emerged, dressed in their own versions of gym gear. Battle was red-and-gold resplendent in a Marine Corps gym outfit. Maxwell wore old civilian YMCA shorts and a torn USNA T-shirt. Neither wore the Academy issue gym shoes. They looked us over as they walked toward the double doors, although, in the dark, the most they could do was count noses.

"Everybody here?" Battle asked.

"No, sir," I answered. "Donny Delmont doesn't feel well. He's still in the room."

"Check that out, would you Maxie?" Battle asked.

Maxwell, who still hadn't said a word or made a sound, soundlessly entered our room. He returned a minute later. "Midshipman Delmont won't be joining us," he announced.

"Okay, scum bags," Battle began as he windmilled his arms vigorously. "Let's start Plebe Year with a little morning run. Line up in exactly the same formation we used for chow." We scurried, but not fast enough to suit Battle. "I said hurry, douchebags. Now we'll have to speed up the running to make up those lost seconds."

"Follow me," Battle said, "and be quiet in the Rotunda." We exited through the double doors, descended the familiar broad ladder, and exited into Tecumseh Court. In the center of the Court Battle stopped us. No human beings moved on the main campus. It was quiet, almost reverent, and quite beautiful. I had always loved the early morning, although, truth be known, I rarely rose early enough to enjoy it. But now as I tasted the cool air and noticed the pinkening sky, I was moved. I inhaled deeply, exhilarated.

"What are you doing, O'Reilly?" Maxwell asked from a position just to my rear. How he had sneaked up on me unawares I had no idea.

"Admiring the morning, sir," I answered.

Maxwell looked out at the huge trees and the silhouettes of massive academic structures. He smiled wistfully. "It is beautiful, isn't it?"

"Yes, sir," I answered.

He snickered. "Do you think you'll feel that way after our little work out?" In truth I wasn't particularly afraid of a run and some exercise. I had been in excellent condition during basketball and track seasons, and running had never been a problem for me. For the last two weeks prior to reporting in I had also been doing my own exercising. I was as ready as I could be for the physical aspects of what awaited -- or so I thought.

"Maybe, sir." Wrong answer!

"Sure you will, pal," Maxwell chuckled. To Battle he said. "Tom, O'Reilly thinks this morning workout stuff is all a piece of cake."

"He does, does he? Well, let's get Mr. O'Reilly up front with the top performers so I can admire his prowess."

Maxwell looked at me. "He probably didn't say anything -- he's very modest, you know -- but Tom was captain of Navy's plebe cross country team, and a member of last season's varsity. He'll be anxious to have you challenge him. Up front, O'Reilly. Don't keep Mr. Battle waiting."

I walked to the front of the group, where Battle looked me over and found me lacking.

"Anybody else think they can keep up with me?" he asked.

"Yes, sir," came two replies. One challenge came from a fellow plebe I didn't know as yet. The other challenger was Merritt, who had said he was a distance runner for his track team.

"Come forward, by all means," Battle announced, "and let's see what you've got."

Soon I was flanked by Merritt and a smaller classmate named John Pirelli. Pirelli looked like a runner. He had that lean, graceful look and the hungry, cadaverous eyes. I decided I'd put my money on Pirelli, no matter what Battle's qualifications.

Battle and Maxwell checked the remainder of the squad for positioning.

Merritt turned to me. "I didn't know you were a runner?"

"I'm not," I replied quietly. "I ran a little track, but I never lettered; and besides, I was a sprinter not a distance man. This is all Maxwell's idea of a joke."

"I see," Merritt answered. "Well, good luck. He held out his hand to me. We shook, then did the same with Pirelli.

"Kick Battle's ass," I whispered to Pirelli. He nodded, deadly serious. I became concerned about my unsmiling classmate Pirelli. Zealots always scared me. Victory is fine but sometimes survival is sufficient.

For me, the morning runs came to represent a subtle military metaphor. Some midshipmen plodded along not doing the best they could, never reaching for the maximum. Those classmates didn't last very long. Others ran strongly but easily, keeping up with the pack, doing whatever was expected but never pulling ahead to break the tape -- that was me. Some few others ran every step intending to be the first. Jim Merritt fit into that category. He wore his destiny for all to see. He would be a success no matter what he tried.

But there were others, like Pirelli, for whom winning wasn't the final goal. Winning wasn't enough. Their goal was setting the record. Annapolis nurtures people like this. And if the big one ever goes down, I know that the fleet is manned by professionals who will do whatever it takes not only to win but also to annihilate whoever is unfortunate enough to be the enemy.

Satisfied, Battle put his hands behind his back, and said. "Today we're only going to run three miles. We'll start here, head along Bancroft Hall, and run on the field out to Hospital Point."

"On Hospital Point we'll stop, do some light exercises, then return to the fields below. The run out and the calisthenics will loosen us up, so don't overdo it. On the run back, however, I want to see what you've got. We'll run in formation on the way. Step to the pace I call out. Coming back, those of you who finish in the top third can carry-on. The rest will have additional exercises to do. By the end of the summer you will all be performing in the top third."

While I was trying to digest the logic of that remark, he spun, and with a "Forward . . . March!" started us toward the entry to T-Court and the famous glaring statue.

"Left, right, left, right." I found it easy to get the hang of marching.

When we emerged from the Court he ordered a "Right Turn, March!" and we turned toward the river. Turning as a group was the wrong thing to do in a "right turn" maneuver. Battle didn't care. Maxwell ran alongside and herded us back into proper ranks.

"Marching starts tomorrow," he groaned. "Just follow the man in front of you."

We *marched* down a flight of stairs along the first wing of Bancroft Hall and into a parking lot. Once we were all safely on the asphalt, Battle looked back and announced "Double Time... March!" With that he picked up the pace, and we began a slow trot out onto Dewey Field, an enormous open area that lay between the academic buildings and the Severn River.

Immediately the evolution began to deteriorate as classmates dropped behind. Maxwell yelled. I heard the name 'Poole' followed by profane expletives.

I kept up with the front rank. Keeping up was never a problem for me.

The jog out along the river face was nice. The sun had just peeked over the eastern horizon, and the lazy Severn River was quiet and creamy in warm morning haze. The summer air, floating gently in from the water, brought exotic smells and tastes. I breathed deeply, and Merritt, running steadily, nudged me and smiled. I winked in reply. As we ran effortlessly along the river, I noticed other groups of plebes and squadleaders running in other various strung-out formations along the water. Most seemed headed for the same place. We followed the contour of the Severn River for almost a half-mile until we came to a narrow wooden bridge. This was the bridge to Hospital Point.

The bridge and I would develop an intimate familiarity during the next three years, especially in the time before I could legally have an automobile, when the dating ritual required some out-of-the-way location for the opportunity to "go-the-distance," or in my case, to try desperately to go the distance but usually to end up far short of success, disturbed by intrusions or moans from other groping couples or by the occasional watch officer who got his jollies from coitus interruptus.

But so much for Hospital Point. We moved along the bridge, its wooden deck planks hummed dull reverberations. It was a tune that old bridge must have played countless times.

Once we crossed the bridge, we reformed into loose ranks and followed Battle to the opposite end of the 'Point.' There were several groups in place when we arrived; each engaged in vigorous exercises accompanied by equally vigorous verbal abuse.

"Squad, Quick Time March!" Battle yelled.

I braced myself as we slowed. As far as I could tell there were no collisions, but I think that was more because we had spaced ourselves during the run. I glanced back to observe our progress and saw an irate Maxwell herding the stragglers, Poole among them, more than 100 yards to the rear.

"Squad...Halt!" Battle glanced rearward. A look of absolute disgust played across his face as he watched the approaching mess. He looked at us. "Anybody tired?" I wasn't, Merritt wasn't, and Pirelli wouldn't admit it if he were about to have a heart attack. Behind us in the main body no one else said a word, although I could hear huffing and wheezing.

"Spread out in ranks of six facing the bridge," he said. I was in a front rank with Merritt and Pirelli. They seemed comfortable with the front rank notoriety; I definitely was not.

The others caught up with us and entered the back ranks. Poole wasn't the worst of the new arrivals, although he was nearly so. Immediately after stopping, one other very overweight and out of shape classmate bent over and began heaving on the grass.

Battle was disgusted. "Jumping Jacks! Begin!" He extended arms and legs in the classic sweeping and jumping motion and counted us through 50.

"Push-up position!" We reclined on recently-mowed grass. The smell of chlorophyll was heady. We assumed an arms-extended position I would soon learn was called 'leaning rest.'

"Straighten your backs! Look at me!" He counted us through 30, very slowly. On my own at home I could crank out 50 pushups with no problem. At the end of 30 slow ones, however, I was beginning to feel the strain. Merritt and Pirelli hadn't even broken a sweat.

"Get a partner! Sit-ups!" He looked around the group for a partner, and naturally his eyes focused on my bald, red noggin.

"O'Reilly! Get your ass over here!" I wiped grass clippings from my hands before I held his feet down. Knees bent and arms behind his head, he counted through 50 sit-ups. Many could not do 50, and Maxwell's voice rose as he moved within the body of the company.

Battle and I switched positions, and he counted for me. He didn't notice the ease with which I breezed through. His focus was on the rest of the group, particularly the falterers.

After sit-ups we did a torture named 'squat-thrusts.' We started, backs straight and hands-on-hips, then quickly dipped and placed our hands on the ground next to our legs. Next we thrust our legs out and back behind us so that we ended up in a leaning-rest position. Then we reversed motions, ending hands-on-hips again. After ten of these monsters I began to tire. At 20 I was ready to stop. Luckily, Battle stopped at 20.

"All right, ladies," Battle said, windmilling his arms and twisting his body. "Form up. We're going to run back to Bancroft Hall the same way we came. Stay in formation until we get out onto Dewey Field, then you can open it up if you want. We'll finish at the parking lot. Anyone who beats me," he added smiling, "can have carry-on at breakfast."

I didn't know at the time what *carry-on* was exactly, but it sounded like a great idea. I intended to beat Battle if I could. We formed up in a squad. Merritt and Pirelli looked loose and ready. Battle glanced at us and smiled. "Forward... March!"

Within ten yards we had begun a double-time jog, which we continued across the bridge. At the opposite side, I glanced rearward. The squad was strung out over a 100 yards.

Battle picked up the pace. The first four rows of plebes matched him.

Battle smiled. We raced in formation, our pace strong and steady and our feet slapping the ground in identical thrumps. I felt good. When we reached Dewey Field, 200 yards separated us from the finish. Battle picked up his pace to a near sprint, and from behind several classmates broke ranks and began to pull even with him. One lanky plebe pulled ahead. Merritt and Pirelli also stretched out their pace and evened with Battle. I moved to the very outside and matched Battle. I had no intention of outdoing any classmate except to top Battle -- if I could.

One hundred yards from the goal -- my high school sprint distance -- Battle opened up. I caught up and passed him. We gained rapidly on the plebe who sprinted past earlier and who was quickly running out of steam. Soon Pirelli pulled ahead. Battle smiled, which deflated my spirits somewhat. I wondered what he knew that I didn't.

Battle tried to pull ahead of me, but as I said, I had been a sprinter - not the best in a school district dominated by inner city black athletes -- but my times were respectable. Battle did not pass me, although a determined Pirelli continued to nose ahead. I could also hear the sound of several sets of feet pounding behind us. Some were gaining. I didn't care. I focused on Battle and smiled back.

Twenty yards from the finish, Battle began an all-out sprint, and we both passed the front-running classmate, but I kept Battle slightly in the rear even when his speed neared my limit. The end came quickly. We never caught Pirelli, but one other classmate passed me with a final burst of speed, and Merritt caught up to Battle at the wire.

But Battle didn't stop. The little tird continued to sprint. I kept going too. We soon passed Pirelli, who shouted and raced to catch up. Ten, twenty, thirty yards we continued. I wouldn't let him pass. Then I began to wonder if I wasn't carrying the exercise a bit too far. I slowed ever so slightly and at fifty yards Battle caught up to me. The bastard was still smiling. I let him pull ahead, and he pretended to break a finish tape. I copied his effort.

He slowed, threw his hands into the air in a mock victory signal, and rounded his finish, whooping and beaming at me.

I tried to look more exhausted than I was as he jogged toward the finish line. I turned and started back, but not as quickly. On the way we passed Pirelli, who was retching on the grass. He wore a 'that-wasn't-fair' expression. Battle laughed. I shrugged and continued my trudge.

Despite our extra sprint and slow return, more than a third of the squad still hadn't finished, although I did notice both Ramsey and Polk recovering. Some of my classmates were sick. Many others were bent over, hands-on knees, gasping for air.

Battle hardly seemed fazed. He looked at my classmates with a prideful disgust.

I was winded, but I had drawn deep breaths after finishing, so I didn't feel the need for any public display of my exhaustion.

Maxwell yelled loudly to the approaching final group of seven classmates, which included Poole and to my surprise also contained Grizwald. "Any of you who don't beat me will have hell to pay!" There was no way most of the final seven could finish without slowing to a near walk, much less beat Maxwell. He knew that. Only one of the group could muster a semi-sprint, but Maxwell would not let him win. The group finished in a bedraggled and pathetic mess.

I watched their agonized faces. These guys were not athletes, and beginning their new lives with a three-mile sprint was extreme. Poole surprised me. I saw in his eyes, perched behind the pain, a kind of grim determination. He wasn't the fastest of the group, but he wasn't the slowest either, and the fact that he had finished at all seemed a source of pride to him.

His pride was short-lived.

"None of you scum sucking bastards will last a week here!" Maxwell screamed. "You're pussies! You're worthless! You're a disgrace to this institution! Go home to your Mommies now before the training gets really tough!"

Battle ordered us into formation again.

"Who beat me to the finish?" he asked. Pirelli, Merritt, and one other plebe raised their hands. I also raised mine, but not so quickly. "You four, huh?" he asked. He looked at Pirelli. "You were number one, weren't you?"

"Yes, sir!" Pirelli answered.

"How come you quit so early, pussy?"

Pirelli started to answer, but Battle yelled. "Do you have something to say, asshole?"

Pirelli swallowed, then answered. "No, sir!"

"Good!" Battle looked at the group. "The only one who had the guts to go the distance with me was O'Reilly here. Right, Kevin?" He put a hand on my shoulder.

 "Yes, sir!" I yelled.

"That's pretty impressive for a scum bag like you," Maxwell added.

"Thank you, sir!" I bellowed. I had discovered instinctively that noise is the bastion of military discipline. From the first day onward, I always answered as loudly as I could. It seemed to satisfy some primal leadership need.

Battle gripped my shoulder tightly. "But who won the final sprint, O'Reilly?" He asked that so that everyone could hear.

73

"You kicked my ass, sir!" I screamed in a voice that carried all the way to Massachusetts.

"Damn right I did!" Battle answered. He dropped his hand and addressed the group. "The four douchebags who finished ahead of me today will be granted carry-on for the breakfast meal. O'Reilly here can have carry-on for noon meal too. We're going to play this carry-on game every day but not for every exercise and training period. Sometimes we will announce when the contest is on; sometimes we won't. When we don't, it's up to you to guess correctly." He turned toward. "Let's eat!" he announced, and we started back to Bancroft Hall.

CHAPTER 8


## *EYES IN THE BOAT*


We returned to our rooms and began showering and changing.  Delmont was not in his rack.

Rico shook my hand once we were inside.

"That was great, redhead" he said enviously.  "I came a scrot hair from beating him myself.  If this carry-on shit seems like a good deal, I may join the ranks of victors tomorrow."

"I wonder where Delmont is?" I asked.

"Probably in the head," a very tired looking Grizwald answered.

"We won't see him again," Rico stated.  He was right.

Grizwald looked troubled.  But we didn't have any time to worry.  Our immediate need was remembering how to dress in white works.


There are three meal-time perspectives for a plebe at Annapolis.  The first is the standard 'brace-up', 'end-of-your-chair', 'eyes-in-the-boat' experience that is just one small step away from living in hell.  The second, and far more desirable, mealtime is an almost human 'carry-on' meal, where most of the pressures are relaxed.  The third option -- plebe paradise -- is athletic training tables where plebes are insulated from the company and protected from harm by their fellow jocks.  I had a brief shot at paradise while I desperately tried to gain a spot on the plebe basketball team.  But I fell short of the Promised Land.

We marched to the Mess Hall following the same path we had yesterday.  After Battle dismissed us, I joined the general mad scramble to get a seat at the leaderless table.  I was not successful, but I did manage a seat near the far end of Maxwell's table.  He didn't ask for me.

Once we had selected chairs, Battle announced, "Plebes, Brace-up!"

I pulled my chin in and waited. We stood rigid during announcements. At the call of "Brigade Seats" Maxwell and Battle sat. We waited. They looked us over.

Finally Maxwell said, "Plebes. Seats!"

Battle paraded to each table, pontifically touched the select four on the shoulder, and intoned a solemn 'carry-on.'

I was the final honoree. I relaxed and looked around.

Maxwell smiled at me. One of my classmates also gave a curious glance, but Maxwell saw him. "What's your name, mister!"

"Steinway, sir," he answered, dipping his head and swallowing loudly. Ronald Steinway was a slight, pallid boy, no more than five feet four inches tall. He had pale blue eyes that darted as Maxwell accosted him. He also had the largest, most protruding Adam's apple I had ever seen.

"Steinway, do you know what it means to get your eyes in the boat?" Maxwell asked.

Ronald's answer was timid. "To stare straight ahead, sir."

"Then do it, damn it!"

Steinway centered his eyes, but his head vibrated in a spasm: wavering as if psychic pressures were forcing his view to wander. No way could he hold that pose.

"All right, everyone," Maxwell continued. "I want you all to begin by sitting on the last three inches of your chairs."

I scurried to comply.

"Not the dummies with carry-on," Maxwell continued looking at me. "But you lazy assholes better observe closely, because your turn is coming very soon."

I slid against the back of my chair and watched.

"Straighten your backs!" Maxwell yelled. "Eyes in the boat! Brace up, God-damn it!"

I watched my classmates strain. It takes a bit of coordination to complete a *braced* Annapolis plebe meal. Sitting on three inches of a chair is no easy matter.

"I said the last three inches, Poole!" Maxwell had selected Tommy to sit permanently on his left-hand side.

Poole slid farther toward the end of his chair.

"Three inches, not twelve!" He rose and came behind Poole. Putting a finger on the chair seat behind Poole's ample rear to indicate position. "Stand up, Poole!" Maxwell took a small ruler from his hat and measured the distance from the end of the chair to his finger.

"Four stinking inches, Poole. Try harder! All of you try harder! Straighten those backs!" Plebes wiggled precariously and firmed up their spines.

Maxwell came around the table, and jiggled the chairs.

Rico Guevarra toppled onto the floor when Maxwell moved his chair.

"What's your name?"

"Guevarra, sir!" Rico answered.

"Good job! Sit down, Guevarra. Repeat exactly what you just did." Maxwell faced the group. "That's what it means to sit on the last three inches, gentlemen. You should be so close to the edge that any motion knocks your ass on the deck. That's what I want to see. Now get out on those final three inches!" My classmates squirmed their bottoms to the brink of collapse.

Maxwell reseated himself, then looked around the table with sadistic satisfaction. His eyes locked on mine. He smiled. "God I love this," he said. To the table he yelled, "Brace up! Eyes in the Boat!"

"Now," he continued, "serve the food!"

Plebes reached for the bread and scrambled eggs, and passed it to Maxwell.

"You're going to have to be a lot faster than that, " he said. "If you want to eat, that is." He picked a roll and scooped eggs onto his plate, then he handed the plates to the plebe on his right. The plebe held the plates, unsure what to do.

Maxwell looked at him. "Have all the upperclass at this table been served?"

"Yes, sir!"

"Who eats after the upperclass?" Maxwell asked.

"Plebes, sir!"

"Are you a plebe?"

"Yes, sir."

"Then begin eating for Christ's sake, or we'll never get through the meal!"

My classmate selected a roll, passed the bowl, then dumped a load of eggs on his plate.

Maxwell became instantly angry.  He slammed his hands down on the tabletop, causing silverware to hop into the air and tinkle to rest.  He jumped up from his seat, and leaned across the table toward the classmate.  "You scum sucking pig!"

The startled plebe gaped in astonishment.

"How many of your classmates are there at this table?" Maxwell asked loudly.

The plebe started to look, reconsidered, then asked, "Request permission to count, sir."

"Go ahead, shit-for-brains, count."

The plebe turned his head, and added up the total.  "Nine, sir!" he announced.

"Look at your plate, mister," Maxwell continued.  "Do you remember how much egg was in the bowl when you served yourself?"

"Approximately, sir."

"Well," Maxwell said, "if everybody takes an egg portion as large as you just did, how much will remain for your classmates at the other end of the table?"

"Nothing, sir."

"You're god-damn right, nothing!  If there's one thing that will not be tolerated at any table -- and that goes for firsties, secondos, and youngsters too -- it's hogging more food than you deserve.  *Everybody* gets an equal portion.  You had better get used to figuring out exactly how much to take, because you'll get your young ass reamed if you ever do that again.  Is that understood?"

The plebe nodded.

"I didn't hear that answer, mister!"

"Yes, sir! I understand, sir!"

Maxwell looked at the rest of the occupants of the table. "Do all of you understand that?"

A chorus of "Yes, sirs," boomed in response.

"Sure, pal," Maxwell said. "Continue the meal."

Filipino stewards brought large stainless steel trays from the serving carts. The trays contained plates of bacon, potatoes, and pancakes. They presented them to the plebes at the sides of each table. Rico grabbed the plates one at a time and passed them toward Maxwell, and the process of pass-and-serve began again.

Soon the rolls and eggs reached me, and I put a portion on my plate. I did the same with the other food. No one had eaten as yet, afraid to make some ritualistic error. It was a good thing.

"Okay, douchebags," Maxwell said. "Look at me, but do not relax your posture." picked up his fork. "This is what it means to eat a *square meal*." He forked a small portion of his potato and looked at us. "When you eat, you will only eat small portions and you will use this motion. First you will lift the fork or spoon vertically until it is exactly even with your jaw." He demonstrated.

"Then you will square the corner and bring the utensil horizontally to your mouth." Again he demonstrated. "Put your utensil on your plate while you are chewing, but do not dawdle. Chew your food quickly, swallow, then get another bite." He paused. "And do all this braced, on the ends of your chairs, and eyes where, Poole?"

"In the boat, sir!" Poole answered.

"You got it, pal," Maxwell said. "You may begin eating."

Soon small elevator utensils were lifting tiny portions of egg and meat tentatively into the air. During plebe year, mealtime was a focus of concentrated tension and abject terror. I hated every braced moment at the Company tables.

After a minute, Maxwell put down his fork. "Steinway?"

I looked at Ronald. He had just ingested a bite of bacon. His fork was still in his mouth.

"Yes, sir!" His fork poised in the air, the food unchewed in his mouth, and he struggled to keep his eyes from leaping in the direction of the question.

"Damn it, Steinway," Maxwell said. "Didn't your mother tell you not to talk with your mouth full?"

Ronald took a moment to consider, then quickly began chewing his bacon.

"Three-chews-and-a-swallow, Steinway," Maxwell announced.

Ronald nodded, his jaws worked like crazy. After 15 chews, he swallowed vigorously. I watched his Adam's apple bob like a fishing float.

"Yes, sir?" he asked.

"Put your God-dammed fork down, Steinway!"

Ronald complied.

"Put your hands in your lap, Steinway. And when I say three chews and a swallow, that's exactly what I mean. You chew the food three times, and send whatever's left in your mouth on its way to your miserable stomach." Maxwell addressed the table. "That's how to properly answer an upper-class question during meals. Is that understood?" There followed a moment of intense action as the remaining 10 plebes rushed to swallow, put forks down, and place hands on laps.

 "Yes, sir!" came the chorus.

"Good," Maxwell said. "Begin eating. Steinway?"

"Yes, sir."

"How's the cow?"

Steinway's brow furrowed. "Excuse me, sir?"

"How's the cow, Steinway?" Maxwell repeated.

Steinway thought furiously. I could see a light of inspiration. "I'll find out, sir!"

"Good, Steinway. You do that! Before evening meal." He looked around. "All of you do that by evening meal."

"Aye, aye, sir!"

"Plebe on Steinway's right," Maxwell continued. "What's your name again?"

"Wesley Lamont, sir!" I loved that accent. It might have been because of the contrast with his dark complexion, or maybe it was genetic or some magic ingredient in the island diet -- hell, maybe his uncle was an orthodontist -- but whatever it was, Wesley Lamont had the straightest, whitest teeth I had ever seen. They sparkled when he talked.

But it wasn't only his teeth that were perfect. His face was as smooth as silk. There were no ravages of the usual teenage fight-to-the-death with acne. No moles, no blemishes, no unusual protrusions, or even the slightest disfigurement. It also didn't appear that he needed to shave, or if he did, the process didn't irritate his skin the way it did my sensitive epidermis. Even his hair - what there was of it, anyway - was perfectly centered and without irregularity. He was so perfect I envied him. I pictured him in a native loincloth loitering on a white shady beach in the shade of a tall palm. He was smiling with a dazzling display of dentition and several young lovely women rushed to please him. He accepted the attention. It probably was natural for him.

"Lamont," Maxwell asked, "What time is it?"

The Mess Hall had any number of clocks, and Maxwell wore a black-strapped diver's watch prominently on his left wrist. The question was obviously a trick.

Lamont smiled. "Sir," he said intoning in a lyrical voice which started me wondering if he could also sing. "I am greatly embarrassed and deeply humiliated that due to circumstances beyond my control, the inner workings and hidden mechanisms of my chronometer are in such inaccord with the great sidereal movement with which time is generally reckoned that I cannot with any degree of accuracy state the correct time, sir. But without fear of being too greatly in error, I will state that it is about 0721 and fifteen seconds, sir!"

What the hell was that about? His answer certainly wasn't on the approved-response list. Everyone at the table seemed flabbergasted.

Maxwell beamed. "Well done, Lamont! You did your homework." He paused. "Shit, Lamont, you can carry-on for the rest of this meal." Lamont grinned at me and relaxed.

Maxwell addressed the table. "What Lamont just did, gentlemen, was to show unusual initiative. He memorized one of the plebe rates without being told. I like that in a plebe. It's one of the traits you had all better develop damned quickly or else you'll be out on your sissy asses before you know it. And, Lamont?"

"Yes, sir!"

81

"Don't get cocky, pal.  There's a lot of Plebe Summer remaining."

Maxwell checked chins and eyes and chairs and backs with a quick sweep of his vision.  He chuckled as my classmates lifted and shoveled tiny morsels of food at ninety-degree angles into their waiting mouths.  It was a ridiculous sight.  Polk must be loving it.

Because of the three-chews-and-a-swallow rule, bites were infinitesimal.  A square meal therefore had to be a rapid one, and some of my classmates, Ramsey among them, moved food from plate to palate in a blur of motion.  Maxwell watched.  Satisfied that all was well, he diverted his attention to his own food.  Soon a general quiet descended over the table.

Except on Training Tables, there is no such thing as a leisurely meal at Annapolis.  From the time the staff announced 'Brigade Seats' to when the Mess Hall emptied usually encompassed a period of less than forty minutes.  Breakfast, the hastiest of the meals lasted 30 minutes.

Twenty minutes into the meal Rico reached across the table, picked up a plate that had previously held potatoes, and lifted it into the air.  No one had asked Rico to order seconds, and when I looked at his plate I noticed that he still had food waiting to be consumed.

"Guevarra, isn't it?" Maxwell asked.

"Yes, sir!"

"Why are you holding that plate up?"

"Sir, I thought you might like some more potatoes."

"How did you know I needed more potatoes?" Maxwell's voice narrowed slightly.  I could see where this was leading, and so could Rico.

"I assumed that since most of my classmates were finished, you would be too, sir."

Maxwell didn't buy it.  "Sure, pal."  He turned to Tommy.

"Poole," he said.  "Go down there and give Guevarra a punch on the arm."

"Excuse me, sir?"

"Go punch Guevarra on the arm.  Hurry up!" Maxwell ordered.

Poole moved to a position adjacent to Guevarra. He poked him slightly on the upper arm.

"Did that hurt, Guevarra?" Maxwell asked.

"No, sir!" Rico shouted.

"Hit him again, Poole! Harder!" Maxwell ordered.

Tommy hit Rico again, slightly harder. Rico rocked to one side in response.

"Did that hurt, Guevarra?" Maxwell asked.

"Yes, sir," Rico lied.

"From now on you better not order extra food unless you are still hungry. And don't ask for anything you can't eat, understood?"

We blurted out a general "Yes, sir!"

"As for taking care of me -- my friend Poole here . . ." He put a hand on Tommy's shoulder, "and whoever sits in the other chair," -- he indicated the chair on his right -- "will see that I eat properly and well. Right, Poole?"

"Yes, sir!" Tommy answered enthusiastically.

"Why did you hit Guevarra, Poole?"

Tommy was confused by this question. "Because you asked me to, sir."

"No, Poole, you weenie! You hit Guevarra because he bilged you. He tried to steal your job. It's your responsibility to keep me fed, Poole, and you have to show your classmates that you're willing to fight for that privilege."

Maxwell took his hand away from Tommy's shoulder. "Now, Poole, why did Guevarra ask for more food?"

Tommy looked at Maxwell's plate. "Because your plate is empty, sir?"

"You're god-damn right it is! How dare you let a classmate cover for you like that! You should be ashamed of yourself, you Mommy's puke. Apologize to Guevarra for hitting him!"

Tommy took a breath. "Sorry, Rico!"

Maxwell leaned toward Tommy. "You don't address your buddies by first name while you are braced, Poole!" Say 'classmate' in public."

"Aye, aye, sir!" Tommy responded. "Sorry, classmate!"

"Now, Poole, since you shirked your duties and let a classmate be punished for your error, I want you to get down on the floor between the tables and give me twenty pushups. Hurry up!" As Poole prepared for his latest torture, I could see Maxwell looking nervously at the head table. Maybe exercises weren't allowed on the Mess Hall floor?

Tommy knelt on the hard terrazzo floor. Sore from the morning exercises, he assumed leaning-rest and began.

"Count them out, Poole. I can't see you from here."

Tommy strained through a "One, sir," and a "Two, sir," and a "Three, sir" before faltering. Number four took several seconds.

"Four! That's all you can do? Four?"

By this time Poole had struggled through the next. "Five, sir!"

"Poole, you are the biggest pussy I have ever seen. Your effeminate body and your Mommy's boy attitude disgust me. Do you want to be a man someday, Poole?" Maxwell didn't wait for an answer. "Get back here and sit down."

Tommy rose to his knees. His eyes met mine then he quickly looked away ashamed.

"O'Reilly," Maxwell asked, noticing that Tommy and I had exchanged glances. "Aren't you disgusted by your classmate Poole?"

What a question! "No sir!"

"You're not!" Maxwell yelled. "You're a liar, O'Reilly! How can you not be disgusted? Poole is the saddest excuse for a human being I have ever seen. Give me 20 for lying, O'Reilly!"

"Aye, aye, sir!" I hurried into leaning-rest on the cold deck and began quickly cranking out pushups.

"One, sir!" I yelled especially loudly. "Two, sir! Three, sir!" Maxwell rose and come around to the aisle to watch. "Eight, sir! Nine, sir!"

"Not so loud, O'Reilly!" Maxwell glanced toward the head table.

"Aye, aye, sir!" I yelled even louder, then toned down the noise for the remainder of the pushups. At 20 I stopped. Maxwell still watched from the head of the aisle.

"One more to Beat Army!" he demanded.

"Aye, aye, sir! Beat Army, sir!"

"Okay, O'Reilly. Sit down." Maxwell returned to his seat. "Anybody else not disgusted by classmate Poole?"

Rico and John Pirelli blurted simultaneous "Me, sirs!" followed by Lamont.

Maxwell smiled wickedly. "Twenty! All three of you!" They did their pushups, including one to 'Beat Army.' Maxwell didn't watch.

A full twenty seconds passed. Most of us had returned to eating, when Steinway blurted out a tentative, "Me, sir."

Maxwell looked up from his ice cream. "What, Steinway?"

Ronald took a deep swallow. "I'm not disgusted by classmate Poole, sir."

"Are you shitting me, Steinway? Why the hell didn't you answer with the rest of your brave classmates?"

"Sorry, sir. I'll find out, sir"

"You, are an idiot, Steinway!" Maxwell blurted. "Poole's probably disgusted with you." Maxwell returned to his ice cream.

Soon Battle and his table passed beside us on their way to the center passageway.

Maxwell took a final scoop of ice cream and put down his spoon. "Time and tide wait for no man, gentlemen. Let's get moving." Battle rousted the remaining table.

Once we had formed, Battle looked us over. "Those of you who had seats on the leaderless table will sit at my table for noon meal and at Maxie's for evening meal."

"All except my friend Poole," Maxwell continued. "We've become such good buddies that I can't bear to be parted from him. Right, Poole?"

"Yes, sir!"

CHAPTER 9

## *MARCH ON*

When we returned to the Company area, Maxwell announced, "Your next evolution is a 0900 lecture by the Commandant of Midshipmen, Captain Mack Hallahan, in Mahan Hall. We will leave here at zero-eight-forty-five, and we will be marching, God help us." He looked at his watch. "You have precisely 20 minutes to clean up whatever messes you've made and return to this spot. Be here on time. Dismissed!"

The slip-slap sounds of our new black shoes shuffling on the tile deck, and the booming yells of 'Beat Army, sir' as we squared corners, echoed in the previously quiet passageway.

I paused just inside the door. Delmont's rack was devoid of bedding. His desk was bare. And I was certain that if we opened his locker, we would find it empty. Delmont was gone. None of us ever saw or heard from him again. I strained for a moment to remember what he looked like, or what he had said or done that first -- and last -- day, but it was all lost.

I spoke "Shit!"

"Do you think he's gone for good?" asked Grizwald.

"Of course," answered Rico sarcastically. "Do you think he decided on his own to move to another Company or maybe to a room down the hall?"

Tony stared at Rico. I could understand Tony's reluctance to admit that Donny had quit after one day. His departure was a blaring alarm. None of us were safe.

We straightened our things without speaking. I pondered my mortality. So far things were fine. I could handle the physical aspects of the training without too much trouble -- as long as I avoided those damn squat-thrusts -- and the emotional pressure hadn't been more than I had experienced on the basketball court or avoiding groups of marauding slummies on my way home from school or the movies. Of course, there were only two squadleaders now and more than 30 of us plebes to divert their attention, and guys like

Poole and Steinway took up a large portion of their focus. What would happen when the Brigade returned was another matter. But, hell, so far it wasn't so bad. Why would anyone quit? Did they have some foreknowledge I lacked?

I revived from my reverie and found myself staring out the window.

Rico was watching me from across the room. "No big deal!" he said firmly. When I looked at him, he added, "This Delmont thing. No big deal! He didn't like it here and decided to leave. Let him go. It's none of your concern. Worry about O'Reilly. I'm putting Guevarra first."

I returned to my cleanup and folded my skivvies to perfection.

"No need to do that," Rico offered. I had wondered why he was so cavalier.

"Why not?"

"This is a training exercise," he answered. "It doesn't matter a fart in a windstorm how good your locker looks. They're just gonna come around, call it crap, knock everything on the floor, and make you do it over. After a couple weeks they'll slack off. Then you can store the skivvies with the skid marks on the outside and they won't care. Once they finish their games I'll fold it all perfectly."

What Rico said made perfect sense to me, but I still devoted some extra attention to the creases in my undershirts. Maybe I'm stupid. Maybe I'm a closet perfectionist. Maybe I have an underwear fetish. Whatever the reason, I've always been orderly, and at Annapolis I enjoyed the neat perfection of a well-organized closet and the comfort of an organized life.


We chopped out into the passageway with two minutes to spare.

"Delmont is gone," I whispered to Merritt as I passed him. He nodded sagely.

A minute later Maxwell and Battle approached. Battle stood near the center of the Company, and, hands behind back, he announced, "It is with deep regret that I wish to inform you that your classmate Donald F. Delmont is now an ex-classmate. Mr. Delmont is one of more than 50 of your group that did not make it through the first twenty-four hours. Adding that to the 100 or so who quit yesterday or didn't show up, you can see that your class has been decimated. But don't worry," he added, with a smirk, "I guarantee that there are still many of you standing here that will not be here at the end of the summer. As a matter of fact, most of the future dropouts already know who they are."

"Classmate Maxwell and I would like to think that we will provide the impetus for many decisions to quit. It's our job this summer, and we're proud of what we do. But it's also a waste of our precious time, so for those of you on the fence about staying here, please save us the trouble of running you out. If you know you aren't suited to the lifestyle, quit now."

He paused, then he smiled. "Maxie and I made a list of ten of you who certainly won't make it through the year. Of course, it wouldn't be proper for us to tell you whose names are on the list, but I can say that the seven slackers from this morning who couldn't even run a mile without crying for their Mommies figured prominently in our discussion."

He reverted to his military pose. "Okay, gentlemen. We're going out in public, and that means that we'll be observed. It also means that any screw-ups will reflect badly on Maxie and me. So you're not going to screw up. Is that understood?"

"Yes, sir!"

"Good! Here's what I want." He turned toward the double doors and used his arm to point in theoretical directions. With each individual instruction he added emphasis with a wave or chop of his arm. "We're going to exit Bancroft Hall the same way we did this morning. Then we'll form up in T-Court facing the statue of Tecumseh. I will lead the group. We'll march in step straight down Stribling Walk toward Mahan Hall. Mr. Maxwell will count cadence. At the end of Stribling by the Macedonian Monument, we'll turn left. For that complicated maneuver," he added sarcastically, "I'll order a 'Left turn, March!'"

"I'll give the command on the left foot. In order to turn to port, we'll pivot on our right feet in two consecutive steps, just like squaring a corner. However," he said loudly, "for a left or right turn in formation *we do not all turn together*. Instead, the front-most rank will pivot on the first right foot after the command. All other ranks will continue straight ahead until it is their time to turn. The second rank will pivot on the next right foot after the first rank. The third rank will pivot on the third right foot and so on." He moved to the front of the formation.

"I want this first rank of midshipmen to turn around so that you face in the opposite direction," he said. I was in that rank. We turned. "Now I want you to walk forward 30 paces, stop, and turn to face me." We marched forward and turned as instructed.

"Good," he said when we had finished. "Now, when I give the order I want you to march forward until you come to me. When you get here I'll order a left turn, and you will do a two-step pivot, one after the other into this room."

"Remember, only one person pivots at a time." He looked at us, shook his head slightly, then barked, "Squad... Forward...March!"

We began well enough, heading straight toward the group. Maxwell sang out the "Left, right" cadence. As we approached Battle's position, he took a breath and barked, "Squad...Left turn...March!"

Chaos ensued.

Being tall and therefore near the front rank, I didn't see everything that happened, but I could hear the slap-skid sound of two classmates behind me turning early. How they decided to turn early was beyond me, but they weren't the only screw-ups. Anthony Grizwald tried to pivot on his left foot and almost fell over as he tried to compensate. He stumbled, recovered, and took two large steps to bring himself back into formation.

I had lost count of steps by the time my turn came. It didn't matter. Battle was furious. He had left his position at the front and run behind me to scream at one of my classmates. I glanced at the doorway, timed my pivot, and followed the plebe in front. We entered the room without any trouble. Grizwald had apparently kicked his left calf with his opposite foot during the confusion. He hobbled. We faced the door, waiting for the wrath of Battle to descend.

Maxwell came to the doorway after the final squad member had entered. He was smiling and looking down the passageway. Outside Battle screamed insanely. The invective was both creative and unprintable.

Rico Guevarra, who had followed me in, smiled. I raised my eyebrows in astonishment. He smiled again.

"Okay, douchebags," Maxwell said, jerking his thumb over his shoulder, "out in the passageway. Now!"

We chopped outside and returned to the formation. Battle had the two clumsy classmates braced against the bulkhead. His face was contorted. As he screamed, turning first one way then the other to confront the plebes, I could see tiny globs of spittle fly from his mouth. Several struck the unfortunate plebes, one of whom was Nikolas Papadopalas, in their fresh young faces. I cringed at the thought of this saliva shower. I could see Nick flinch as each ejaculated bubble-glob arched its way toward him. He was desperate to leap aside before the slobbery impacts, but discretion kept him firmly glued in place, albeit wetly.

Battle inserted Grizwald and the two smaller classmates into the middle rank of the Company on the theory that they would be protected from their own coordinational stupidity. He then patiently explained the theory of the 'Right Turn,' which was the mirror opposite of the 'Left Turn' maneuver. He used the far right rank to demonstrate, and either that group was far superior to mine, or fear of reprisal is a mighty powerful tool. They performed the maneuver.

So we could do the turning necessary to get to the lecture, but it was too late to worry if we couldn't. Battle marched us out of Bancroft Hall and into T-Court. Since there were many visitors gawking at us, he must have felt verbally restrained.

Before he started us forward on our way to destiny, Battle looked at us. He didn't say a word. He didn't give any demonstrative hand signs. He didn't even spit. He just looked, and every one of us knew that whoever screwed up on this march had better fling himself off the Chesapeake Bay Bridge. His chances of survival would be better in the Bay.

We started. I discovered immediately that Battle was a *hot dog* squad leader. He strutted, chest puffed out twice its normal size, with his head, beak nose and all, poised skyward. If it wasn't for the fact that Maxwell was watching us like a hawk, I might have laughed.


The straight-ahead part came off without a problem. As we marched down the broad, brick paved, tree-covered lane we were observed by several groups of tourists who ogled impressively at us. One group of three young ladies gave us 'the eye,' and I was elated. Although 1967 was supposed to be the very heart of the sexual revolution, and I had heard the motto of all red-blooded college students was 'Free love for all,' somehow the Age of Aquarius had bypassed the ethnic neighborhood where I grew up. Girls in South Boston didn't even allow groping on the first date -- sometimes never -- and sex was a fantasy that had altogether eluded my fervent grasp.

I found my own chest expanding as we passed the girls. They cheered us, and I felt special. But then again they also cheered every group of plebes that passed -- all thirty-six Companies. The test of the left and right turns passed without incident, although I watched Ramsey grab Grizwald and hold him in place until it was time to turn.

Soon we entered Mahan Hall and made our way to a row of seats prepared for us. Guess which row? Twenty-third of course. Sitting, I noticed an interesting contrast. I assume that every Company started with the same number of plebe novitiates; however, some of the Companies had significantly fewer members than we had. Several rows in front of us in what must have been fourteenth row, only twenty plebes sat. I didn't think I was the only one who noticed this.

At the beginning of the lecture, a midshipman yelled out an "Attention on Deck!" and the Commandant entered from stage left. The audience sprang to attention. The sight of a thousand recruits leaping to their feet almost in unison was very impressive.

The Commandant of Midshipmen, Captain Mack Hallahan, gave a speech. He was a personable speaker who talked to us almost as if he were our father. He seemed interested in our success and well-being. I liked that. He welcomed us aboard again and told us to be good boys.

Next a younger officer named Lieutenant Loiselle came to the podium and the lights dimmed. He briefed us on the academic merits of the institution. He said we were fortunate. Our class was the first Annapolis class that would graduate with accredited degrees. Previously graduates received a degree in general engineering, but in order to further their education at some other institution they would have to finish a year of undergraduate work. We would have degrees as good as those from any other school, and in many ways our degrees would be better.

According to Loiselle, the typical academic semester consisted of 16 or more credit hours. If these were solely devoted toward the major, the load would be heavy. But in addition to the academic load, midshipmen were expected to complete courses in seamanship, navigation, leadership, military history, weapons science, and tactics. And this would be in addition to the requirement for parade practices, evening lectures, and mandatory afternoon sports participation. And, he chuckled -- the first year (when the load was heaviest) would also be our Plebe Year -- the year from Hell. By graduation, the lecturer continued, the typical midshipman would accumulate more than 160 credit hours. The speaker intoned about each major and its requisites and explained the academic policy on changing majors. It was almost frightening.

The lecture ended with my having more questions than I had when it began. But I figured that all my questions would be answered eventually.

We filed from our seats -- by Company, naturally.  Maxwell must have been in a good mood that morning, or maybe the sight of the female pulchritude that lined the walk buoyed his spirits.  Whatever the reason, he suddenly burst into song.

"Around her neck she wore a yellow ribbon!" he sang, keeping the beat in time to our steps (and like I said earlier, he had a good voice.)  When he came to the last line, however, he changed the words to indicate that the woman waited for a *midshipman* who was 'far, far away.'

After he finished -- with a flourish that delighted the observing young ladies, he bellowed, "All together!" and on the next left foot we began to sing exactly what he had sung.  We started tentatively at first, then picked up the volume and intensity.  He led us through several verses.  By the time we entered T-Court, we had that song down pat.

In the passageway in our Company area, Maxwell moved down the ranks and stopped at the front of the formation.  "Okay, ladies, that wasn't bad for a first march.  This afternoon we'll have additional practice."  He looked us up and down.  "Who knows how to sing?"  One or two tentative hands -- including Ramsey's -- went into the air.  Maxwell looked at the singers.

"Good," he said.  "You people heard other Companies singing songs.  I want each of you to find out the lyrics of those other songs.  We may not be the best military marchers, but by God you ladies are going to be the best singers.  I want you each to be ready to demonstrate your songs for the group on Friday at the first 'P-rade' practice."

Battle spoke.  "Your next event is physical training in Macdonough Hall at 1100.  This week you will get an introduction to wrestling.  Next week is swimming evaluations.  The following week you get a chance to box, God help you.  Then gymnastics, followed by track and field, soccer, softball, and touch football.  In August you'll have golf, tennis, squash, fieldball, and basketball."

He smiled.  "That's quite a schedule, gentlemen.  No other college or university has anything like it.  Over the next four years -- assuming of course you make it that far -- you will also be exposed for much longer periods to the same sports opportunities.  You'll be tested on many of them.  And it won't be easy, take it from me.  I'm a terrible swimmer and I spent my plebe year on the sub-squad catching up to classmates like Maxie here, who can swim rings around me."  He looked at his watch.  "Be back in formation, in White Works Charlie in ten minutes.... Dismissed!"

We chopped to our rooms and began changing from one uniform -- White Works 'Bravo' which was the white jumpsuit with white undergarments and black military shoes -- into 'Charlie'-- white works with the complete gym outfit underneath.  This hysterical clothing on-and-off process was an integral part of Academy life.


I returned to the passageway within the allotted time.  Suddenly Tommy Poole bolted from ranks and raced into his room.  He had mistakenly put on his black uniform shoes.

"Poole!  What the hell are you doing?" yelled Maxwell.

"Sir!  I have on the wrong shoes.  I'm going back to change them!"

"Hit it for ten, Poole, you idiot!" Maxwell shouted.  "And make them ten good ones."

Tommy dropped to the deck.  "One, sir!  Two, sir!  Three, sir!" At five, he tired.

"Come on, Poole, you pussy.  Five more good ones!" Battle yelled.

Tommy tried, but there was no way he could do them.

"You are the most disgusting sack of shit I have ever seen, Poole!"

Battle glared at us.  "All of you look at poor Mr. Poole!"  Tommy had just gutted out a weary number six.  "This asshole, and several like him, are slowing up the group.  They will draw you all down, cause the group to falter, and make you look foolish in front of your superiors."

Tommy had paused in leaning-rest position.  His arms shook from the effort, his back sagged, and his ample middle drooped till it was almost touching the tile deck.

Battle emitted an exclamation of absolute disgust.  "Poole!  Stand up!"

"Aye, aye, sir!"

"In order to make up for the weak links in the chain, all of you have to be stronger gentlemen.  I want all of you on the deck this instant.  Every one of you give me ten good pushups for Mr. Poole.  Poole, watch as your classmates do what you were supposed to do."

Thirty-odd voices sang out numbers. Some of my companymates had as much trouble finishing as Tommy had.

Battle watched. Then he looked at Poole. "How does it make you feel, Poole, having your classmates do your work?" Tommy watched as the remaining plebes finished and struggled to their feet. He swallowed hard and the look of grim determination returned to his face.

"It makes me feel bad as heck, sir."

"Bad as *heck*!" Battle exploded. "Bad as heck?" Battle moved to one side of Tommy's head near his right ear. Maxwell moved to the left side.

"You shouldn't feel bad as *heck*, Poole, you miserable shit," Battle yelled. "You should feel like you want to crawl in a deep hole and bury yourself. You should want to die, Poole!"

"What the hell is wrong with you, Poole?" Maxwell screamed from the opposite side. "You are the most disgustingly screwed-up embarrassment I have ever seen. I'm supposed to be impersonal, but I'm beginning to hate you, Poole. I want you to quit this place right now. Get out of here. Save your classmates the pain of having you for a classmate. Do you hear me, Poole?"

Tommy swallowed hard again. "Yes, sir!" he yelled.

"Are you going to quit?" asked Maxwell.

"No, sir," Tommy replied timidly.

"Why the hell not, Poole? You don't belong here. Don't you understand that?"

Poole stared ahead. "I can do this, sir!"

Maxwell, his face contorted with emotion, screamed. "You *can't* do this, Poole, you stupid, miserable, mother..." Maxwell's language became more colorful as his anger increased.

I was shocked, not so much by the language, which, while colorful, was no worse than some of the stuff I heard in my hometown neighborhood. But vernacular notwithstanding, Maxwell was absolutely out-of-control enraged. That scared me.

Battle had calmed. He stared at Maxwell. Even he seemed concerned.

"Okay, Poole," he said slowly, "back in ranks. We'll deal with you later."

Tommy scurried to the relative safety of the formation. We stood far more rigidly than we had earlier. I wanted desperately to leave the Company area. I could sense that several other of my companymates were frightened by Maxwell's anger.

Battle looked us over. "Does everybody have the correct uniform?" No one responded in the negative. He turned toward the double doors, and in a calm voice, commanded, "Forward...March!"

We marched along the same brick path we had taken not three hours ago on the way to the morning run. Instead of continuing out onto Dewey Field, we turned to starboard and approached a huge old building that was connected to Bancroft Hall by a covered passageway. This was Macdonough Hall, a brick and steel structure constructed near the turn of the 20th century. The upper portion of the Hall served as a physical education area.

Gymnastics gear had been set up along one wall. Ropes and pulley arrangements hung from the ceiling like thick spider webs. Exercise machines stood against an opposite wall. A huge expanse of mats covered the floor. In the basement of the same Hall, was a swimming pool. I swallowed a great quantity of water in that pool, over which hung suspended the dreaded platform from which every midshipman must leap into the frigid water 40 feet below.

Some midshipmen swore to me that civilian work crews arrived poolside early each morning to dump truck loads of ice into the water to cool it down for our hot young bodies. Most mornings I believed the stories, as it seemed impossible that a body of water that large could maintain near freezing temperatures, particularly in the midst of a sweltering summer, (at least not without some external agency stealing the precious calories from the water molecules).

But today we headed topside to the matted area for instruction in wrestling. This week-long training was supposed to familiarize us with the basics so that, come the start of academic year, we could embrace the real wrestling classes with gusto.

We doffed our white works in neat piles and sat on the mats facing the small office. We were one of three Companies that had wrestling training the first week.

A trim civilian physical education instructor approached. He stopped in the center of the mats and faced us. He smiled. It was a real smile. It was refreshing. He seemed human. "How is everybody today?"

"Fine sir!" Three Companies responded simultaneously.

"Whoa, whoa." He laughed and held his hands over his ears. "There's no need for that plebe baloney here, understood?"

Did we ever. He looked us over. "Good, let's get started."

What followed was a week of intense wrestling training. It was easy. It was fun. But all too soon it was time to return to the insanity of Bancroft Hall.

CHAPTER 10

## *SHINE ON*

When we returned to the Company area, Battle held us in the passageway. "This period is company training time," he said. "Today's lesson is how to spit shine your shoes. If you think you already know how, forget it. I guarantee you don't do it good enough to satisfy Maxie and me. Everybody get your black shoes and your *black* shoe polish and return to the passageway." When he emphasized the word *black* he stared hard at Tommy Poole.

We chopped to our rooms. As I prepared to leave, Rico stopped me.

"What do you think of Maxwell's little act?" he asked.

"You mean with Poole?"

"Yeah," he replied. "What he did with Poole."

"I don't think it was an act," I said. "He seemed much out of control."

Rico stared. "Why was everybody so frightened? I could sense it."

"Jesus, Rico, do you want him to do that to you?"

"It's just words, Kevin. They can't hurt you."

"But what if he actually loses control? *That* could hurt you."

Rico shrugged. "Listen Kevin," he said. "No one is allowed to hurt us  All they can do is yell or make you do exercises or some stupid embarrassing act. They're not allowed to touch, push, kick, or punch; and if they do, they're fair game as far as I'm concerned."

"You'd start a fight if they hit you?" I asked.

Rico smiled. "Can you how much trouble they'd get into if they used physical punishment on a plebe? They won't do that. And I can handle psychological abuse. But if they push me past my physical limit and use violence -- stand by.  I can take care of myself."

I looked Rico over closely.  "I'll bet you can."


Maxwell carried two pairs of shoes.  Battle carried a chair, which he placed on the deck in front of the Company.  Maxwell sat.  One pair of shoes, inside chamois pockets, he put carefully on the floor beside him.  He was smiling.  Had he forgotten the Poole incident?

Maxwell held up the other pair of shoes so that we could see them.  They gleamed nicely in the fluorescent lighting.  "These are my *everyday* shoes," he said.  "Notice how they shine?"

He rotated the shoes so that they caught the light from all directions.  "I polish these shoes every day," he boasted.  "Now hold up your own shoes."

We did.  There was no comparison to the gleaming brightness he held.  But then we hadn't applied a single coat of polish to ours.

"This is how I want your shoes to look before Sunday evening," he continued.  "And they will if you follow my instructions."

What followed was a 15-minute lecture on the fine art of spit shining.  I learned that actual spit is involved.  There must be some special enzyme in saliva because, according to Maxwell, ordinary tap water will not do.  He also said that those of us whose mama's told us to avoid expectoration better kill their fears, because it usually took a gallon of slobber to bring out a proper gleam from the black unpolished leather.

Maxwell took out a can of black Kiwi polish.  A gleam of metal from the bottom of the can indicated that it had seen plenty of use.  The process of spit and dip and rub began.  The smell of polish filled the air, and soon he had coaxed a brighter shine from the shoes.  He held them up, smiling broadly.  They gleamed.

 "See what a little care and attention can do to a pair of shoes?"

I was impressed.

Then he carefully lifted one of the covered shoes.  He held it reverently on his lap, almost as if he were about to unveil a holy relic.  He slid the chamois wrapping from the shoe, being careful not to touch the shined top, then he held the shoe up for us to see.

"These are my good shoes, my 'grease' shoes," he said.  "I only wear them to evening meal and watch formations."

98

The term 'grease' refers to any item that is top-of-the-line or saved for special occasions. We were supposed to reserve separate shoes, hats, and uniforms, whose quality and appearance immediately announced their 'grease' function. Also, a midshipman might date several girls in town, but his girl-back-home is always his 'grease' girl.

The process by which midshipmen accumulate leadership points and the grades that rate how well they adapt and adopt the Academy system is also referred to as grease. So far so good, but a midshipman who mindlessly adopts the system, can sometimes be called a 'greaser,' which is not good. No one ever called me a greaser. I'm strangely proud of that.

Maxwell held up his grease shoe. I heard a collective gasp. A crown jewel exposed to public view. His sacred footwear shone in the light almost as if it emitted its own black rays. It dazzled as he rotated it slowly first right then left. It gleamed equally well in all directions.

I was covetous. I wanted that shoe with a passion, even if it didn't fit.

"By the end of the week," he said, slipping the holy shoe into its protective pouch, "your shoes had better look like this." He held one of the now ordinary shoes aloft. He looked at his watch. "Go to your rooms and start shining. Dismissed!"

I sat at my desk and opened the polish. I suddenly realized that no one had issued us a polishing cloth. Maxwell had used what seemed to be a piece of torn-off T-shirt. Should I do the same? I looked at Rico. He was reading his book again. I was beginning to hate that Russian bitch on the cover. I'll bet sex with her wasn't any good -- but then again, how would I know?

Anthony was about to dip the end of a bath towel into the polish. "Wait, Tony!"

He looked at me.

"Rico?" He put down his book and looked at me.

"What should we use to polish the shoes? They didn't issue any cloth for that."

Rico considered. "Maxie used a piece of T-shirt." What a guy -- he actually called the human terror by a nickname. Rico went to his locker, took one of his T-shirts, and ripped it down the middle.  He gave a strip to Grizwald, another to me, and kept the third for himself.

"I suppose I should at least try this polishing thing," he said, clearly disappointed to be divorcing himself from Olga or Ivana or whoever that communist sow was.  In the end his sense of duty compromised with his lust and he propped the book on his desk with his metal lock box while he absentmindedly worked polish into the hungry leather.

After ten minutes Rico held up his shoe to the light and frowned.  He held it toward me.  "What do you think?" he asked.  It looked like hell.  Smears and streaks crossed and crisscrossed the top of the shoe haphazardly.  "Think I used too much polish?"

"I have no idea.  Yours looks about the same as mine."  I turned to Anthony.  "How are you doing," I asked.  There was no response.  "Tony?"

He looked up.

"How are you doing, Anthony?"

The lights came on behind his eyes.  "Oh.  Pretty good.  What do you think?"  He held up the shoe he had been working on.  It gleamed in the light.

"Jesus, Anthony.  How the hell did you do that?"

He shrugged.  "I don't know.  It seems pretty easy."

"Anthony," Rico said, "I'll give you ten dollars to do my shoes like yours."

Ten bucks?  If I were Anthony I would have accepted in a second.

Anthony hesitated.

Rico smiled.  "Fifteen, and I'll fold your locker."

"Well, my locker already looks good."  That was the truth.  In his free moments he had molded and cajoled the items in his locker into a very orderly arrangement.

"I'll make your bed for you the rest of the week," Rico offered.

Anthony considered.  "Well, I guess I could."

"Great!" Rico retrieved his wallet from the lock box and removed 15 dollars from a very impressive stack of greenery.  He handed it to Anthony, along with his shoes, then went to Anthony's rack.  Within a minute, Anthony's rack looked as good as Rico's.

This wasn't good. My rack now stood out like a lumpy, bumpy, festering sore.

Rico smiled at me, then raised his eyebrows questioningly. The bastard wanted to get his 15 dollars back from me. No way! I groaned, and turned toward my bed. Kneeling on the floor I attacked the problem of rack tightness with a scientific vengeance. Soon I had nearly matched Rico's efforts. Of course, it took me five times as long and it still wasn't quite as good. I had to do better.

I returned to my shoes with the same concentration I had used on my rack, while Rico returned to imaginary escapades with the frigid Ruskie.

After a few minutes, Merritt poked his head into the room. "Time for chow."

I noticed that my hands were black from the polish, and I moved quickly to the sink.

Merritt shook his head. "You'd better move your asses. The uniform is white works."

I looked at myself. I had on white works already.

"Without gym gear underneath," he continued. Oh shit! He was right as always.

"Five minutes, guys!" He departed to warn the other rooms.

Torn between dirty hands and uniform dismantling I decided correctly that I had better have clean hands before I touched my 'white' works.

Anthony did not reason as well as I did. In blind panic, he grabbed the front of his blouse and smeared a black stain across the belly. He groaned and looked at me as if he were about to cry. Tears appeared in his eyes.

"Hurry, Anthony! Wash up!"

He looked at me thankfully. This man needed guidance.

I applied soap roughly to my hands. Grizwald worked beside me. Two minutes of scrubbing were not enough to remove the stains completely, but I didn't have any more time to waste. I gingerly exchanged gym gear for underwear, and donned the same clothing. Then I realized that black shoes were going to be a problem. I had diligently worked to smear the hell out of my right shoe, but the left one was still virginal dull. I couldn't wear those shoes.

We had been issued a second pair of black shoes, but I hadn't even laced them. Sensing doom, I dove into my locker for the second set of shoes. As I watched, Rico departed. I wasn't sure I would make it. I missed several of the lace holes, but the pants would cover that up.

Seconds remained and Anthony still wasn't dressed. He looked panicked and needed guidance again. Shit! My heart sank.

I'm not really a son of a bitch, but I sure felt like one; and I'm sure Anthony has never forgiven me to this day, but -- I gave him a final look, shrugged, then darted from the room. My reasoning was that even with my help he never would have made it to formation on time, and it was better -- at least as far as I was concerned -- if only one of us caught hell. Anthony's Bambi eyes pleaded. He was close to tears again. I felt like hell, but I was soon safely in formation.

To his credit, Anthony wasn't the only late person. He wasn't even the latest. But late is late. Battle and Maxwell, sensing a momentous screw-up in progress, approached the formation with a look of anticipatory glee. I heard rustling and shuffling in several rooms.

As the two squadleaders settled in front of us, Grizwald emerged, running like he was escaping a fire. He forgot to chop. He forgot to brace. He forgot to square his corners.

Maxwell pounced. "Hit it for a million, Grizwald!"

Anthony tried to stop but instead tripped over a shoelace. He fell forward in slow motion like a giant redwood toppled by a logging crew. I swear I could hear his bones creaking and I fought the urge to yell 'Timber!'

He thrust his hands out to slow his fall but his right arm struck the deck dead-on with a resounding 'crack.' He emitted a strange squeak as he continued to fall, then his forehead thumped the unforgiving floor.

Maxwell and Battle exchanged glances. Battle ran to Tony and bent over to help him up. Grizwald rose on unsteady legs.

"Are you okay?" Battle asked.

Grizwald was not okay. His right arm hung at an unusual angle and a large lump bloomed on his forehead.

Battle helped him to a place against the bulkhead. "Sit here!" he commanded.

Grizwald moaned and slid down the wall, holding his arm gingerly.

Battle turned. "Pirelli!" he yelled.

"Yes, sir!"

"Front and center!" Battle commanded.

John Pirelli ran to the front in a perfect chop.

Battle looked him over. "The main office is directly below us on the first deck. Run down there as fast as you can and tell the Watch Officer to call for an ambulance. Tell him we have a midshipman with a fractured arm and a possible concussion. We'll bring Grizwald down behind you. Return immediately! Go!"

Pirelli streaked away.

Another late classmate arrived.

Maxwell pounced even harder in an effort, I think, to impress us with the fact that the show must go on. "Give me 100 pushups!" he yelled.

The classmate dropped to the deck and began yelling out numbers in time with his motions.

"Who's still missing?" Battle asked

"Terry Patterson, sir."

"What room is Mister Patterson in?" asked Battle.

"5409, sir!"

Battle went to room 5409. He stood in the doorway. "Patterson!" he asked loudly, his voice becoming gruff, "are you joining us some time this century?"

"Yeah," came the tired and incorrect answer.

Battle exploded. "What do you mean, yeah?" he screamed, advancing into the room.

"I said, yeah!" the hidden classmate repeated. "You guys win! I quit! This place stinks! Leave me alone!"

Battle softened. "Come to lunch with us." He laughed. "You can even have carry-on."

"I'm not ready."

Battle turned to the formation. "Take your time. Come to the table whenever you're ready." "Ramsey, O'Reilly! Front and center!"

"Take your classmate to the Main Office and wait with him until the corpsmen arrive. Once he's on his way to the Hospital, come down to the Mess Hall."

With surprising softness Ramsey grabbed Grizwald under his good arm and hefted him into the air so that he stood, still groggy, against the wall.

Grizwald moaned as he leaned backward. "Is my arm broken?"

"Sho' looks it," Ramsey laughed. "Don't ya'll worry. We'll get you to the office -- no problem." Ramsey lifted Anthony's good arm so that it was around his broad shoulders. "Lean on me," he said, softly.

Grizwald held his broken arm, and Jubal turned toward the double doors just as the Company departed the area.

I ran ahead of the two of them and pushed open one of the heavy doors. I held it while they exited, then walked ahead of them down the ladder, clearing an imaginary path. I felt helpless, as well as guilty about my earlier desertion.

At the first landing I turned. "Anthony, I'm sorry about running out on you."

He looked at me as if he were seeing me for the first time. "What do you mean?"

"I mean about not helping you just before meal," I replied. "There was no time left."

"Don't worry about it," he said.

I returned to my leading duties. An ambulance arrived in Tecumseh Court as we reached the rotunda floor. Corpsmen rushed to us. They examined his head, wrapped it in a bandage, put the arm in an immobilizing sling, and whisked Anthony out the doors.

I turned to Jubal. "What will happen to him?"

Jubal pondered. "Nothing much," he replied. "A broke arm ain't nothing. I wonder how he's gonna finish plebe summer, though."

"According to Rico," I interjected, "he won't finish."

Jubal nodded several times. "I thought so. He ain't got what it takes. And neither does Poole. I hope he quits soon. Ah'm gittin mighty tired of pullin' his weight."

"Maybe if we all helped him more, he could make it," I offered. I didn't say anything about my own feelings in the matter.

Jubal snorted. "Not a chance! He's a complete waste. He's no military man."

We wandered into the Mess Hall, where announcements had just finished. Unfamiliar squadleaders stared menacingly as we passed down the passage.

At the Company tables Maxwell had saved adjacent seats for us next to him, which I didn't think was a fair reward for our humanitarian services. We sat. I was supposed to have carry-on, but I was afraid to push the issue. Jeff Polk stared at me, questioning whether I was going to stand up for my rights. I wasn't. I was a coward. Hadn't the episode with Grizwald just shown that? I stayed braced for the entire meal, and neither of the squadleaders said a word.

The meal was subdued. No one -- not even Poole -- got yelled at. I could imagine what Battle and Maxwell must have been thinking. Having to explain an injury to a plebe entrusted to them -- even if it was his own clumsy fault -- couldn't have made them comfortable.

That afternoon Battle led us to the west side of Bancroft Hall to another attached facility - Dahlgren Hall. I liked this interesting older building. It had class. It was used for group functions such as intramural basketball competition and tea dances because it had an open-bay nearly 50 yards in length and 20 wide, and an ornate cast iron ceiling more than 15 yards high.

Dim light filtered inside through a continuous row of tall dingy windows that circled the upper mezzanine. Flags lined the mezzanine. State flags. Military unit flags. National flags. Flags I couldn't recognize. They provided the only color in an otherwise lifeless interior.

But we weren't there to shoot hoops, dance, or admire the flags. Along the walls of the mezzanine, under the windows, stood weapons of war. Actually they were racks of ugly old M2 rifles -- firing pins removed.

We reported to a team of enlisted personnel who issued each of us a rifle and bayonet, noting the serial numbers of the rifles as they did so. Two days in uniform and I was armed!

We descended the ladders of Dahlgren Hall into the open area below and affixed the bayonets without anyone cutting or maiming himself. I was ready to assault the beach!

Farragut Field is nearly a half-mile long, and stretches flat, green, and lovely from near the Field House at the far western end of Academy grounds to the Severn River -- the far eastern boundary. Wings seven and eight of Bancroft Hall, the farthest parts from the rotunda, flanked the northern side of the field, while the Annapolis inlet of the Severn River lay to the south.

As our three clumsy ranks clumped toward Farragut, I felt apprehensive. I had never marched before. But how hard could it be?

Battle halted us on the edge of the field. "Company . . .. Left, face!" He didn't actually say those words. In fact, he didn't say any words. What he barked sounded more like "Comp'ny . . . Le'l houghaaa!" We shifted in a more or less leftward direction.

Battle groaned. "Oh, Jesus! Why me?"

Battle stood in front of Ronald Steinway. "Is that piece heavy?"

'Ah, ha!' I thought, 'piece equals rifle.' I filed that information away in whatever newly formed memory section of my brain stored Academy trivia. I hoped my brain would never reach nautical overload. At least not that year.

Steinway hesitated.

"Well, Steinway! Is it heavy or not?"

"No, sir," Steinway mumbled. "Well, yes, sir, sort of."

Battle snatched the rifle roughly from Steinway's shoulder.

Ronald winced but didn't protest. He was afraid. He looked terrified.

Battle shook his head in disgust. "You're a god-damn girl, Steinway! Do you know that? Never let anyone take your piece away." He looked around. "Go stand behind the Company and give me twenty pushups, Steinway! Hurry!"

Ronald scurried to the rear and began pushups without much enthusiasm. The noise of Steinway yelling numbers brought a smile to Battle's face. Until Steinway faltered at number 15.

Battle looked to heaven, then toward Maxwell. "Maxie, would you bring the young lady back?" he asked sweetly.

"Of course, classmate," Maxwell answered with equal sweetness. He walked to the rear of the formation, then yelled. "On your feet, douchebag! Get into formation!"

Steinway scrambled back into line, wiping grass and soil from his hands as he returned.

Battle demonstrated the entire standing-still repertoire of 'left face,' 'right face,' and 'about face.' For several minutes we practiced without incident. Afterward, we right-faced into marching readiness and Battle started us forward.

"Follow the beat of the drum with your left feet!" he commanded as we moved in unison toward the inner parts of the enormous grassy tract. Several other Companies also practiced on various parts of the field.

Until he said the word *drum* I had been unaware except in some vague subconscious way of any drum sounds. Out in the very center of Farragut Field, several hundred yards away, stood a lone enlisted drummer, a kettledrum strapped over his shoulder. He beat a steady and repeated *thrum-thrum-thrum-ta-ta-ta*. I wondered what kind of terrible duty that must have been, standing for hours in the hot summer sun, beating a never-changing tattoo on a heavy drum. Maybe it was a kind of musician's plebe year for enlisted troops. At any rate, it must have been horrible for the poor guy. *Thrum-thrum-thrum-ta-ta-ta*, over and over and over.

But compassionate thoughts were fleeting at best that summer, and soon Battle began barking marching commands in the same alien language he used earlier for the facing commands. We learned the right and left turns, which were easy; but then he dared to attempt a 'to-the-rear' movement, and I thought we would take casualties.

Some plebes turned on their right feet, some on the wrong feet, some pivoted to the left, some to the right. A few hesitated and continued forward into their turning classmates. A chaos of stumbling collisions, and incredible confusion followed, punctuated by the yelps of frightened young men, the flash of sunlight on bayonet, and the anger of the two squadleaders.

"All of you!" Battle yelled. "Give me 20!"

"Ah, Tom," Maxwell interjected. "Do you think that's wise?"

"I don't give a shit," Battle answered. "These pukes are the most pathetic bunch of screw ups I have ever seen, and I'm going to teach them how to march even if it kills them."

We fell to the ground and began the ordeal. I had done more pushups that day than ever in my life, and my chest and shoulders tired quickly. After five I began to feel sore. But the sound of Ramsey's accented voice rang out above all the others as he did his pushups in time with the beat of the drum. It heartened me. Soon others joined in the vocal rhythm, and by the time we finished ten, the entire group -- less the several who had to stop at ten -- were counting identically. The sounds of young male testosterone voiced in unity of purpose echoed across the huge field. Adrenaline coursed in my veins, and I found the soreness lessening as I tried to shout louder than my classmates.

Maxwell and Battle stopped their discussion and watched in amazement. Battle smiled. "Ramsey!" he yelled, "if you survive this year intact, I'm going to make a Marine out of you!"

Jubal answered with a loud "Aye, aye, sir!" between push-up cadence.

CHAPTER 11


## *THE RATES*


That evening after meal, Maxwell's lecture dealt with plebe 'rates.'  This jargon term, however, had nothing to do with rights or privileges.  'Rates' were the requirements of the plebe system.  To summarize -- we were slaves.  We must do -- within reason and short of violating public law, human morality, or placing our lives in danger -- anything an upper-class asked.  He also explained that plebes were not to be personal servants to any upper-class, but that we had better carefully consider before refusing favors or requests because the resulting discipline could be severe.  Then he explained the difference between discipline and *hazing* -- a thin and confusing distinction.  We could do pushups until our arms fell off and run back and forth in the passageway until we passed out or puked on the deck, and that was allowed because those were permissible exercises recognized by the Academy as discipline enhancers.  However, we were not supposed to do something called a 'dead horse' or be placed in the 'thinking position.'  At meals, 'rigging pitchers' and 'locking on' to the table were also forbidden.  Maxwell's thoughtful voice indicated he himself had been the target of these academy inducements, and that he truly didn't believe they would do us any harm.

"Christ, they make it easy on you pukes," he said.  "When I was a plebe . . ."

He then told us how miserable and painful his own plebe year had been, wistfully recounting all the horrible things that had happened to his classmates.  He said it with such reverence and nostalgia that it was obvious he wanted us to experience the same painful and manly training he had endured.  Symbolically at least, no 'dead horses' meant no plebe year, and that was a shame -- at least as far as he was concerned.  But the thought of dead horses made me nervous, and I decided I would be perfectly happy with the pushups, thank you.

Plebe Year stories -- next to tall tales about sexual prowess -- are the most often heard boasts at the meal table.  Plebe year is the Academy badge of courage.  It's the ticket -- the dues -- that separates the men from the boys, although what they do now that women attend I don't know.  Women at Annapolis!  It sure can't be Plebe Year like I knew it.  Why, when I was a plebe . . .

"O'Reilly!"  The sound of Maxwell's shout broke my reverie.  "We need someone to demonstrate the illegal exercises -- for informational purposes, you understand."

"Of course, sir."  I hastened to the front of the group.

Maxwell smiled in his somewhat evil fashion and turned to the group.  "Mr. O'Reilly is now going to demonstrate two of the illegal exercises so that you will know what not to do when the Brigade returns in September.  First you will see the classic but ever popular 'dead horse.'"  He turned to me.  "O'Reilly, lie on your back!"

So far so good.  The floor was a bit hard, but otherwise...

"Raise your arms straight into the air, O'Reilly!"

I did.  This wasn't bad!

"Good!  Now raise your legs the same way."

Uh oh!  I lifted my legs into the air, but flexibility not being my strongest asset, they only came up to a 60-degree angle, then stopped.

"All the way up, O'Reilly!"

I rotated my legs backward by lifting my lower back slightly off the ground.  My legs got closer to vertical but still fell short of a right angle, and I held this position.  It was uncomfortable.

"Can't you do any better than that?" asked Maxwell.

"No, sir!"

"Well, hold that sissy position, pal."  Maxwell turned.  "Can anyone do better?"

Merritt and Lamont raised their hands simultaneously, and I wondered about their sanity.

"You two get up here and show us," Maxwell said.

Confused, I watched them assume identically perfect dead horses.  I held my position stoically, strangely angry that their dead horses were better than mine.  So far holding the position had been no strain. I focused on the ceiling, and saw for the first time the metal ceiling grid and the lenses that covered the banks of fluorescent lights. The plastic lens covers had been manufactured with a raised diamond pattern that sparkled and flashed if I turned my head slightly. I experimented with the glittering while I waited. It seemed psychedelic, although never having had any experience with drugs -- mind altering or otherwise -- I guess I can't be sure.

"O'Reilly!" Maxwell yelled. "How are you doing?"

"My horse is dead, sir!" I figured a little humor couldn't hurt the situation.

"Yours is the worst looking dead horse I have ever seen," Battle chuckled.

"Thank you, sir!"

After half a minute, my legs began to sag -- along with my sense of humor. I straightened. Half a minute more and my legs lowered again. I strained to get them back up. My arms began to tire as well. Within another twenty seconds I could not get my legs back up. They drooped toward the floor. I hunched my shoulders to relieve some of the pressure. Shit, this was hard! I groaned as I tried to adjust position without success.

"What's the matter, O'Reilly? Getting a teensy bit difficult?" Maxwell asked.

"Yes, sir!"

"Do you find anything funny now, O'Reilly?" asked Battle.

"Not as funny as a minute ago, sir."

"Everyone stop!" Maxwell ordered. I lay on my back and watched the ceiling as I recovered. I didn't like the sparkling lenses anymore.

"O'Reilly! Roll over and lock your hands behind your head!" he demanded. "Now rotate you elbows inward until they are directly beside your head!"

I didn't like the direction this particular 'exercise' was going.

"Lift yourself so that your weight is resting on your elbows and toes!"

I lifted.

The linoleum tile used in the Academy decks is a creamy white with specks of brown and green imbedded in the color. The tiles themselves are standard eight inch squares set onto the under deck with black adhesive.  Years of wear, and the tromping of young feet, had worn shallow grooves into the tile beneath me.

The deck is also extremely hard.  My elbows dug painfully into the tile as I held myself aloft.  Sweat erupted from my forehead.  I tried to adjust my position and groaned.

"Painful, O'Reilly?" asked Maxwell.

"Extremely so, sir," I answered.

"Hold that for another minute, asshole, if you can," he said.  "I used to hold the thinking position for five minutes without tiring."

"That's remarkable, sir!"

"Shut-up, O'Reilly!" Battle ordered.

At that moment the double doors at the end of the passageway opened.  I saw an officer enter, accompanied by two plebes.  My body was shielded by Merritt's.  Without thinking I changed to a push-up position.  "One, sir!  Two, sir!  Three, sir!" I yelled.

"Attention on Deck!" Battle shouted.  We sprang to attention.  Maxwell watched me while the officer approached.  His eyes told me nothing.

I winked.

The officer smiled.  "Carry on, gentlemen!"

Battle snapped into a parade-rest position.  The rest of us relaxed.

The officer wore a freshly pressed tropical white uniform.  His shoulder boards indicated he was a lieutenant, a stratospheric difference in rank from Midshipman Fourth-class.  It was Lieutenant Large, the greeter at the Field House from a million years ago just yesterday.

"A little push-up training, I see."

"Yes, sir!" I answered for the group.  Maxwell looked at me again.

"How many can you do, plebe?"

"This morning, sir, I could do 50.  Now, I'm almost pushupped to death."

"Well," he chuckled, "by the time I finished my plebe year I could do more than 100 good ones. That'll give you all something to aim for."

"Aye, aye, sir!" Battle answered.

"Carry on!" Lieutenant Large continued down the passageway.

Battle and Maxwell exchanged a look. "Time to post road guards?" Battle asked.

Maxwell turned to the group. "You know that everything we do is for the good, right?"

We yelled "yes, sirs!"

"Good," he continued. "Sometimes the Academy doesn't understand the need to take the training beyond recommended levels -- for demonstration purposes of course." He looked at me. "In order to stay out of possible conflict with the authorities -- something I'm sure you can all understand -- we're going to establish a guard on some of the things we do." He pointed toward the double doors. "When we deem it necessary, one of you will stand at those doors, and another down there at the passageway intersection." He pointed in the opposite direction toward where the officer had recently turned on his way to visit other Companies.

"At any sign of an officer," he continued, "or any visitor you do not recognize, the guard will drop to the deck and begin yelling out his pushups. And I mean yelling."

Maxwell looked at me. "O'Reilly. Back into formation!"

Maxwell next explained about the duty plebe room, whose responsibility was to perform 'chow calls' for the Company. A chow call consisted -- so we were told -- of loud public announcements at ten, five, and two minutes prior to every meal, of a litany of information, including the meal's menu; the appropriate uniform; the Officers of the Watch; the movies currently playing at the local theaters; and finally the number of days remaining until the next vacation period, various other important events, and the Army-Navy game. Why these particular tidbits of information were vital I never learned. Probably a national security thing.

For a closing activity that evening, Room 5401 introduced themselves. Those classmates consisted of George Thomas Abbott from Tea Neck, New Jersey, whose father was an advertising agent and whose mother was a first grade teacher. George was a brawny, good-natured individual with very dark eyes, a pronounced shadow of beard on his face, and dark stubble already sprouting profusely on his head. George would have to shave twice or more every day of plebe year to avoid the wrath of upperclassmen. George was an only child who had been an All-State soccer defender at a Catholic High School, and his thick muscular legs identified him as a formidable kicker. He looked tough, but he spoke with a soft femininity that belied his physical capabilities. I certainly didn't want to meet George on the soccer field -- or any field for that matter.

Henry John Butkowski spoke next. Hank was the largest of my classmates, standing well over six feet four and weighing I would guess close to 250 pounds. He had laughing blue eyes and prominent facial bones that matched his large arms and legs. But despite his formidable size, he was plainly nervous, and he spoke haltingly. He came from Jeanette, Wisconsin, where he played football. Hank's father ran a local lumber company, and he had three older brothers and three sisters.

"Did Coach Snelling contact you about pre-season practices?" asked Maxwell.

"Ah, yes, sir," answered Butkowski. "They start next week in the afternoons."

"I guess that means we have to dismiss you from the marching and from the morning workouts?" asked Battle sarcastically.

Butkowski, unaware of the god-like status granted footballers, stammered, "I think so, sir, but I don't mind the extra workout. I could come along in the mornings."

Maxwell looked at Battle. "Sure! Come along, pal. We'll try not to run you too hard."

Next was Tim Butler from Modesto, California. Tim was a small, medium build, regular looking, nondescript, plain sort of person. I'm sure his hair, when it grew in, would be standard American mouse brown. He seemed to be the kind of individual who could inhabit a crowded room for hours, and invariably be forgotten. He might even forget himself. Tim spoke in an ordinary, unpretentious, unaccented voice about his parents, one of who was head librarian at the county library; the other was a homemaker. Tim had no siblings, or if he did he probably forgot.

Bill Allen was the last member of 5401 to introduce himself. I liked Bill. He smiled a lot, and had an extremely easy-going personality, and a smoothness that made it obvious he could get along in any situation. He stood about six feet tall, was moderately thin, and judging by his ample eyebrows, would be very blond when his hair grew back. His parents were both engineers. They ran their own consulting firm in Denver. Bill announced that he had two younger sisters, both of whom were eligible and very attractive. Bill was my instant buddy!

Inside the room I approached Rico. "What do you think about Anthony?" I asked.

Rico thought for a moment. "I think he'll use this as an opportunity to quit. It's a perfect out. But I'm more concerned about one other thing."

"What's that?"

"Is he going to shine my shoes, or do I get my money back?"

He was serious. I took out my shoes for polishing. The one with the polish looked horrible. I attacked both shoes with a vengeance, and at the end of thirty minutes I had polish smeared on both shoes. They looked like hell, but at least they matched. I began thinking that my spit lacked some critical enzyme. Maybe I needed a medical examination. I could go to Sick Bay in the morning -- if I could find out where that was -- and hock one for the doctors.

At 2130 I decided to go visiting. "Going to the Goon Room. Want to come along?"

Rico agreed. We glanced into the passageway. No squadleaders were in sight, and we hurried across the passageway.

Things were quiet in 5403. Too quiet! Each of the goons sat grimly at his desk polishing shoes. But I could sense tension. "Hi, guys! What's up?"

"This place sucks!" said Polk.

"I hate it too," added Tommy Poole. His shoes sat on the desk in front of him. They looked worse than mine, and that made me strangely satisfied.

"An Ah'm tah'rd of classmates who cain't pull their load," said Ramsey. Jubal had brought a nice shine up on his shoes. He was holding them up to the light. I was jealous.

Merritt looked at us. "And don't you just love my happy roommates." One finished shoe rested on the floor beside the desk. Naturally it looked perfect. He was just glossing his second shoe. I was livid with envy.

"I see you guys all have your shoes in better condition than mine," I observed. "How about one of you coming over and polishing mine so I can watch your technique?"

Poole looked up from his polishing. He held up one badly done shoe. "Yours are worse than these?" he asked incredulously.

115

"Orders of magnitude, my friend. How do you do it?"

Tommy looked at me, then at his shoe. "I don't know," he said, and continued polishing with renewed vigor.

Merritt nodded toward Ramsey. The task for this evening must be to soften up Jubal.

"Just how big *are* your sisters, Joe?" asked Rico.

Ramsey looked up, staring with narrowed eyes at Rico. "What kind a question is that?"

Rico laughed. "I'm serious," he said. "I've always had a thing for southern women. Are your sisters like, really big, or are they just a little chunky?"

Jubal considered the question, then laughed. "They're really big," he said. "They could have played be'sahd me on the High Point football team."

"That's too bad," Rico said seriously, "'cause I do love southern women."

"How do your arms and legs feel, Tommy," I asked. "You had a tough day."

"He's a sissy!" added Jubal showing unveiled antagonism.

"Hold on, Jubal," I said. "If you had done that many pushups, you'd be tired too."

Ramsey spoke to Tommy's back. "Maybe, but he still don't belong he'ah."

"Let the system decide that, Jubal. In the meantime we have to work together."

"You know," Jeff offered from the opposite side of the room, "what you say is okay, but the damn system doesn't make much sense. The physical workouts are okay, if all they do is exercise us, but I can see why they outlawed those tortures Maxwell had you demonstrate. You can hurt yourself doing those, and what's the sense in that? And what the hell does memorizing the answer to 'How's the cow?' or the names of the sorry-assed movies in town have to do with being a good naval officer?" He swiveled in his seat and faced the room. Everyone watched as he preached. "And assuming we all make it through the next four years, what's in store? There's a war going on you know? People are dying, and that includes graduates of this place. What are they dying for? I don't understand."

"Jesus, Jeff, make some sense," Jim Merritt answered. "That's government policy. We'll go where we're told. If you're afraid of dying, maybe this isn't the place for you."

Polk burst out. "I'm not a coward! I want to understand why I might have to die or why I might have to kill someone else."

Ramsey stood. "Listen, you bastard! We're in Vietnam because the president said so, and y'all are here because you joined the military. If you cain't follow orders, quit! There's too many good men puttin their lives in danger every day. I don't want to hear your complaints, especially about Vietnam. So shut up right now!"

Polk stood. "Make me, asshole!"

Ramsey moved from behind his desk and advanced on Polk. Merritt and I jumped between them and held Ramsey back. Rico grabbed Jeff's arm, and turned him away from Ramsey. Poole stared open-mouthed at the activity. I doubt he had ever seen anything like that on the chess team.

"What's the matter, Jubal?" asked Jim Merritt. "Why did you get so angry?"

"'Cause if I believe that bullshit, then everybody who died in Vietnam died for nothing. I won't have it! He better just keep quiet about it, that's all."

I watched Jubal's face as he talked. Beneath the anger was something else, and he was near tears when he finished. "Want to talk about it?" I asked sincerely.

He glared at me. "No, Yankee, I don't want to talk about it, so leave me alone!" He shook loose and hurriedly left the room. We stared at the empty doorway.

"Wow!" said Merritt. "I wonder what's with him?"

"I don't know, but something," I added.

"Whatever it is, he must think it's a good reason," added Rico. He still gripped Jeff's arm. "It would be a good idea if you didn't say anything anti-military," he said quietly.

Polk nodded, then added, "I wonder if I should do anything?"

"Maybe apologize," added Poole. We had forgotten about Tommy.

"Yeah," Jeff said after another moment, "maybe I should."

"Well, that's enough excitement for one night," said Rico. "This room sure seems to be the focus of controversy. I think I'll visit whenever I'm bored." He let go of Jeff's arm. "Sorry about that," he said, nodding his head at the finger marks still visible on Polk's upper arm.

117

Jeff looked down absentmindedly. "No problem. Thanks."

We scampered across the passageway, but not before Merritt admonished us to get up on time the next day. We laughed. There was no way I wanted to repeat this morning's near disaster.

I watched Rico as he set a small alarm clock for 0515. He sat the clock on the middle of his desk, then undressed and climbed into bed.

"I'll join you in just a minute," I said.

"No hurry," he replied. "I could sleep through anything."

I spent the remainder of my free time writing a single-page letter to my parents, bringing them up to date on my experiences. Obviously, I left a few million things out. I had just finished the most active, unusual, and physically and emotionally demanding two days of my life. A whole summer -- hell, a whole year -- of the same lay ahead. I already felt like a veteran of combat. In my letter I summed it up in one word -- incredible! That night as I lay in my rack counting my bruises and nursing my sore muscles, I prayed I had the mettle to finish. It was a bedtime prayer I would repeat every night for a very long time.

CHAPTER 12

## *CONFLICTS AND CONFUSION*

The lights flashed on in the room at 0545. "Jesus, guys!" Merritt said fiercely. "This is getting to be a very bad habit. Fifteen minutes. Hurry!"

"God-damn!" Rico yelled as he and I came instantly awake. With an angry groan, he leaped from his bed, grabbed the alarm clock from the desk, glared at it, then threw it out the window. I watched him for several long seconds.

He smiled, then added sheepishly. "It must have been broken."

I laughed. Four floors below the clock splintered on the red-tile walkway. "If it wasn't, it is now," I said.

We arrived into the passageway with two minutes to spare.

Merritt stared at us and shook his head, amazed.

"So we like sleeping in," I whispered.

He chuckled.

This morning everyone was prepared prior to the workout, and we departed without incident. I found myself in a cheerful mood. My legs felt fine. I was ready to win more carry-on. But there were no physical contests that morning or any of the next three. I was disappointed.

As I jogged effortlessly along the seawall, I observed what transpired. With only two squadleaders and 30 plebes, it seemed impossible for Max and Battleaxe to observe everyone all the time. In fact, during the runs, their attention was focused on the stragglers. Those of us at the front were free from scrutiny. And as we exercised, I could see classmates surreptitiously watch the squadleaders to see where their heads were pointed. Whenever attention was diverted, the quality of the exercise would slacken. Rico, I soon discovered, was an expert at faking it. He would watch for any opportunity and seize it. If the break came during pushups, he would rest his stomach on the grass,

119

smiling and shouting the numbers along with the rest of us. During sit-ups he would rest on his back. Once or twice he glanced at me during his rests. I would labor away, afraid to stop for fear of being caught. He would smile or wink. He loved playing the game.

But cheating on a few pushups didn't motivate me. In fact, as the days passed and my physical strength increased, I basked in the endorphins and relished the physical training. I was being turned into a machine, and I liked what was happening to my body.

At the same time, though, I felt my attitude toward my classmates change, and to resent that we could slacken at all. I wanted Mike Maxwell to urge me on to greater efforts, and I wanted to race Tommy Battle across the fields. I began to think that any deficiency in the training process was because of our more backward classmates. Poole and several others were 'shit-screens.' Some were so badly out of shape and so unused to discipline that they drew constant attention to themselves.

So long as the two squadleaders were yelling at other plebes, they left the rest of us alone. Therefore, I reasoned, it wasn't necessary to excel. Was that good? In a strange way guys like Rico owed Poole a debt and I decided to use that argument on Ramsey. Maybe it would soften him up. Although it seemed ironic that I might survive my Plebe Year, not because of the forward thrust of my own personality, but rather due to the backward drag of the non-achievers like Tommy Poole. I wondered if the Academy suspected as much.


Later the first week, Battle lectured us on the finer points of formations and inspections while Maxwell inspected our rooms. I listened to Max as he went from room to room, humming in time to the sounds of sheets being pulled up and various gear falling on the deck from our lockers. This was the evening for our room to introduce itself. Anthony was still a no-show, which seemed strange since all he had done was break his arm, so Rico and I talked.

"Hola," Rico began in a thick accent and I was suddenly observing a character from *West Side Story* rather than the articulate, educated person I knew him to be. "I'm Enrique Jose Guevarra from Brooklyn, New York. My parents, they come to this great nation from Puerto Rico. My padre, he's a grocer. He has a small store and cantina. My Momma, she helps with the sales. I haf two seesters, mucho pretty -- but not for sale." We laughed.

Maxwell looked at me, then at Rico. "Okay, Pancho, knock it off!"

"Si, senor." Before Max could react, he continued, changing his demeanor completely. "I attended Brooklyn Polytechnic High School. I played varsity baseball and basketball and was a member of the National Merit Society." He looked at his feet. "I was also president of my class."

I rose and rushed boldly forward. "Wow," I said turning to the group. "What a resume! Let's all give Rico a big hand and welcome him." I started clapping, and my classmates joined in, at first hesitatingly then with gusto. Cheers erupted. After several long seconds I raised my arms in the air to signify silence and the group quieted.

"Give me 20, O'Reilly!" Battle barked, in a not totally unfriendly fashion.

"Aye, aye, sir!" I yelled and dropped to the deck and began counting.

"O'Reilly!" interrupted Maxwell.

I stopped and rested my belly on the deck. "Yes, sir!" I answered.

"Since you seem to be such a clown, why don't you make your presentation in leaning-rest?" he said. "Maybe it won't be so funny then."

"Sir! Would it help to remind you that leaning-rest is a *forbidden* exercise?"

Maxwell laughed. "No, pal, it wouldn't," he answered.

"Aye, aye, sir!" I raised myself up off the ground and addressed my companymates. "My name is Kevin O'Reilly. I come from Boston, Massachusetts, where I played basketball and ran a little track for my high school. My Dad works on the Boston waterfront; my Mom hangs around the house and takes care of my younger brother." I paused. "I may not be as gung-ho as Jimmy Merritt or as formidable as Hank Butkowski or as entertaining as Rico Guevarra, but I want you all to love me anyway. After all, I'm your classmate."

"Okay, O'Reilly," Max said. "Take your place next to the wetback."

Battle brought out a pencil and paper "Gentlemen, I have a little contest going with the nineteenth through the twenty-fourth companies. I want your verbal and math Scholastic Aptitude Test results. Merritt, come here and jot them down, then calculate the average."

Jim took the pad from Battle.

"Let's begin," Battle said.  He pointed to each of us in turn and we sang out our scores.  I was surprised at the range.  There were two classmates with a single score in the 500 range, and several with double 600s.  Most had a combination of six and seven hundreds. Three classmates had 800 in one category.  Tommy Poole was the only one with double 800s.

Maxwell whistled.  "Double 800s. Wow!  Poole you're a certifiable genius!"

"Gotten the average yet, Merritt?" Battle asked.  "I'll bet Poole could do it faster.

From deep within the group Tommy Poole announced sheepishly, "1,346, sir."

"What, Poole?" asked Maxwell.

"The average, sir.  It's 1,346."

"Are you shitting me, Poole?" asked Battle.

 "No, sir.  Not if I heard the numbers correctly."

Battle looked at Merritt, "Well, Merritt?"

Jim had just finished.  He looked up.  "Classmate Poole is correct, sir.  1,346."

I was too busy that night to visit the Goons.


At nearly midnight, urgent rumbling signals from my nether regions awakened me.  Since I didn't know the rules about leaving the room after lights out, I crept cautiously down the passageway in the weak light.  Once in the head I avoided turning on the lights, and selected a dark stall.  God, it felt good.  Five minutes later someone entered the darkness. He stood uncertainly in the doorway, then went to the sink.  I could hear the sound of running water and something else -- faint sobbing.

I felt like an intruder.  The water sounds ceased after a minute, but the tears did not.  I froze in place and quieted my breathing, dreading the possibility that I would make a noise and announce my presence.  I waited until the sadness abated, but the visitor didn't depart immediately.  Instead he went to the wall, flipped on the lights, and hurried to the sinks again.

With the lights on I was afraid he would see my feet under the partition door.  I raised them.  But now I could also see a portion of his body in the crack between the stall door and the partition wall. I didn't recognize him at first because the space through which I could view was narrow. Then he leaned closer to the mirrors to check something on his face. John Pirelli! Pirelli the tough man -- Pirelli the machine -- Pirelli the invincible. 'Super-plebe' himself was crying in the dark. Jesus, did that shake my confidence. After he left I waited in the dark for a full five minutes, pondering that unexpected turn of events.

A not so quiet truce prevailed in the Goon Room the rest of that week. The morning workouts continued unabated, with Tommy Poole, Ronald Steinway, and two others suffering the greatest wrath. On Thursday, Rico and I returned to our room after the morning wrestling class to find that all traces of former classmate Anthony Grizwald vanished from the room.

I felt sad, but Rico was angry. "He stole my 15 bucks!" I supposed Rico would have to learn how to spit shine.

Thursday evening Room 5402 had their turn in the limelight. First up was a classmate named Charles 'Chuck' Chalmers. Chuck was a medium height, very thin individual who had suffered the ravages of acne recently, and his face was moderately scarred. He also had a case of nervous jitters and could not remain still while he talked. Chuck's father was a police detective in Cleveland. His mother a housewife. He had two older brothers, one of whom had graduated from Annapolis four years earlier. He didn't say anything about his other brother. Chuck had played tennis in High School.

The next speaker was Daniel Carl French from Chicago, Illinois. Danny was a short, attractive, outspoken son of a city councilman. His laughing blue eyes and devilish smile indicated a mischievous nature. He had an older sister who was already married, and a younger brother still in grammar school. He lived with his mother because his parents had divorced several years earlier and had decided to split custody. Danny, a wiry individual who could do pushups from morning until well after dark, had been an All-State wrestler.

Barton Hardesty was next. I took an immediate dislike to good old Barton. He was an average looking individual who came from Memphis, Tennessee, which was okay in itself, but he declared himself a rabid fan of Elvis Presley, which was not so good to a modern rocker like myself. Barton's father was a minister of some Protestant denomination I didn't recognize, something that sounded like 'The Friends of the Evangelical Church of

Almighty Light,' and he professed to all of us with fervency that he had been reborn recently -- which seemed inconsistent for an Elvis fanatic.

I looked at my classmates and I noticed several raised eyebrows. Barton was a tall, very thin person, much like Anthony Grizwald was. Was? I was already thinking about poor Anthony in terms of death. But Barton's eyes scared me. They seemed to shine with an inner light that could be either divine inspiration or near insanity. Troubled myself by questions about life and death and deities, I decided to say a few extra Hail Marys that night and avoid Barton's intensity whenever possible.

The final occupant of the room was Nikolas Papadopolas. I already knew that Nick was here to get an education. He had announced that plan the first evening. I also knew that Nick was a pretty fair athlete; he was solidly muscled and had played lacrosse in high school. He had also been my wrestling partner that morning and had pinned me twice. His parents operated a restaurant – Greek naturally. He loved the mountains and the seashore and had several siblings.


That evening Ronald Steinway sought me out after dismissal. He entered the room so quietly that if I hadn't looked up from my shoe shining -- which was not going well despite more than eight hours of spit-and-rub -- I might not have noticed. He seemed embarrassed.

"Hey, Ronald," I said brightly. "What brings you here?"

Ronald looked from me to Rico and back again. He sat in Donny's vacant chair. He folded his hands in an absentminded gesture of supplication, placed them in front of him on the desktop, and stared at me from across the two desks. His Adam's apple bobbed several times vigorously, and I stared fascinated at the undulations while I waited for him to speak.

"I want to talk to you about what's going on here," he said.

I was taken aback. What was going on here? "Sure, go ahead," I replied cautiously.

Rico straightened as Ronald prepared to speak. He was obviously listening. A smile played briefly across his face. He was enjoying my position as the great mediator.

"Well," Ronald began. "I don't like it here very much."

"No problem there, Ronald," I quickly interjected, "but nobody likes it here. Hell, you'd have to be crazy to like what we've been through so far."

"Yes, yes. I realize that. But it's more than that for me. You see, my parents are very proud of my getting into this place. They were immigrants from Russia just after World War II. I'm the first of the Steinways to get to college, and they are counting on my success. I can't quit. It would break their hearts." He paused. "But Maxwell and Battle won't let up on me. I never seem to have a moment's peace. I can't think straight. What should I do?"

His last few sentences came out in an excited rush. But his damned Adam's apple, which jumped up and down so much during his agitation, distracted me. I sat back in my chair. For an instant I was annoyed that he was even here. I wasn't anyone's father-confessor. I had my own misgivings. I paused, hoping something would intervene, but common sense and my sometimes-irritating benevolence won out.

"Look, Ronald," I said. "You're in an unenviable position, because you're behind the rest of us physically. You've become a target, and Max and Battle have good aim. They know exactly what to do to get to you. It would be damned near impossible for any of us to endure what you and Tommy have had to go through.

"But, the way I see it, they can't really do anything to you that you can't handle. They're not going to beat you up, or throw you in a cell, or hold back on your meals. It's just a matter of attitude. If you think they can win, they will. If you convince yourself they can't beat you, they won't." I paused a minute thinking about Pirelli.

"Believe me, "I continued, "this place affects even the staunchest of your classmates. I go to sleep every night wondering if I'll make it through the next day. In case you haven't noticed, my defense is humor. Once they deprive me of my ability to laugh, I'm lost. You need a defense. Try to ignore the harassment. Think happy thoughts. Say a prayer. Whatever it takes."

After a long moment, he looked at me, swallowed with an enormous bob, sighed, and said, "Thanks, Kevin. You've been a real help." He headed for the door. Before leaving, however, he turned toward me. "I can't let my parents down," he said. "I have to make it."

After he was gone Rico put down his book and looked at me.

"You should have been a priest," he said with a smile.

Rico noticed my grim expression as I continued musing. I have too many thoughts about sex to be a good priest. Besides, I wanted to run my own life, not be responsible for the lives of others. Maybe I wouldn't be a good Naval officer.

"What do you think about Steinway?" I asked.

"He needs help. He's a very troubled lad."

I could sense that something about Steinway bothered him.

"Who the hell is here because of their parents anyway?" he asked.

Recognizing the rhetorical nature of the question, I stayed quiet.

He continued. "Ronald's got to learn to be a man and lead his own life."

CHAPTER 13

## *TAKE YOUR MEDICINE*

Sick Bay is the Navy term for the medical clinic. During that first week every plebe received a base-line physical and too many immunization shots to count. I felt like a pin cushion.

Part of the testing included an eye examination. After a petty officer corpsman dilated all the plebe eyes in the Twenty-third Company, we waited in a darkened room for the medicine to take effect. Twenty minutes later we took turns in three examination chairs as doctors peered into our eyes through strange instruments that focused intense beams of light.

Having watched the procedure being performed on my classmates, I had an idea how long the 'look' should take. Mine took much longer. Eventually the doctor grunted, told me to sit still, and left the examination room. He returned with a more senior officer who introduced himself as the head optometrist. He also stared into my eyes for an extended period.

Finally he sat back on his stool. "Wait here," he said. "I'm going to get the head of the Department." Meanwhile my classmates were zipping through their own exams. Rico winked at me when his exam was finished. I smiled weakly, but I began to worry.

An older, white-haired gentleman came to my chair, escorted by the other doctors. He introduced himself, but I wasn't listening. The doctor conducted his own examination, and by that time I was bursting with curiosity. But he gave me no information, and he and the younger doctors disappeared for consultation. I waited, enduring the questioning stares of my classmates.

I shrugged to Jim Merritt who put a hand on my shoulder, and said, "You look worried. I'm sure everything will be fine."

I didn't feel at all sure.

After several minutes, the young doctor ushered me into the boss's office. The senior doctor asked me to sit, and I could tell by his tone that something was wrong.

"Son," he began, "we don't want to frighten you, but if what we fear is true, you may have a rare eye disease." He spouted out a Latin name, but I didn't really hear or listen at that point. "If you have this condition, unfortunately, you will end up partially blind in your right eye within a year." Holy shit! Talk about bedside manner!

I had no sense that there was anything wrong. My vision had always tested 20/20 or better, so I had the feeling their concern was much ado about nothing, but . . .

"Since we don't have the proper equipment at Sick Bay," he continued, "I'm going to recommend further examination at the main Naval Hospital. Good luck." With that I was ushered from the inner sanctum of Academy medicine.

Before I left the area the corpsman scheduled me for the test. He could see I was worried. "Hey," he said, "don't worry. They've sent more than a hundred persons for the same test this week. It's nothing. They just want to be sure."

"Then how come they didn't say that?" I asked him. He gave me a shrug that indicated that officers were another breed altogether. That morning I had to agree.


Racing, I joined my classmates as the last group was starting the hearing exam. I had never had a hearing test. I imagined it might be something like reading an eye chart, except you would stand at a certain distance from a tester and try to discern the whispers and noises he emitted. But Annapolis is very high-tech. We entered sound-insulated booths in groups of eight. It was a very strange feeling. Almost no noise came through the thick walls. The walls also dampened internal sounds. The corpsman in charge had us put on headphones and grip a small button device in our right hands.

"Whenever you hear a sound," he announced, "I want you to press the button. Let up on the button when you don't hear it anymore." He shut the heavy door behind him. He was in a hurry and we were his last group.

As I soon found out, hearing tests can be confusing. I still wasn't sure what to expect, but I held up the button, poised, and stared at the wall. I concentrated, and waited, and waited.

Even though it was a soundproof room and I wore headphones, I could hear things faintly. I heard rustling from a neighboring classmate, the tapping of a foot against the wall, coughs and throat clearing, and other unidentifiable faint noises. And still I waited. Eventually a tone, clear and sharp, sounded in my ears and I hurriedly pressed the button in response. I could hear the button click. Another tone quickly followed, a little less audible, and I pressed again. I could hear faint clicking sounds from the booths around me, not all of which seemed to coincide with mine. I began to worry, wondering if they were hearing the same tones I was. The sounds and the clicking continued.

Then there came a pause in the process. Either the tones had stopped or had reached a level I couldn't decipher -- kind of like when a dog responds to a whistle too high-pitched for humans to hear. I strained to listen.

Then I heard a creaking noise that sounded like one of my body joints rubbing, and I couldn't be sure this wasn't a new 'tone,' so I pushed my button. Instantly I decided that I shouldn't have done that. Christ, what if some abnormality in my knee joint just caused me to fail the hearing test? Hand poised, I strained harder to ensure I heard the correct noises.

In the vacuum of the moment my ears and mind were ready to pounce on every sound. Suddenly an entire universe of sounds began to rush at me. Plucked unintentionally from the surroundings and from the far off reaches of my head and body, I began to hear tones. Shrill whistles, faint squeaks, dull rumbles, and sharp pops all vied for my attention along with what I was sure were the valid tones. I hesitatingly pressed the button, my brain whirling at every noise to be sure what I heard wasn't indigestion or a neighbor's fart.

Soon I pressed in a frenzy as my brain madly tried to separate manufactured symphonies from the sounds of biology. I began to sweat, thinking that this couldn't really be what I was supposed to do -- but I couldn't stop either.

Finally the door to the booth opened and the technician came in. As I looked around I realized to my chagrin that the test had been over for several minutes, but a quick check with my senses indicated that the errant tones were still running rampant in my head. I put up the headphones and button, shook my head to clear it, turned on the stool, and waited.

"Everybody please come outside," the technician ordered. Then he looked at me. "Had a little trouble didn't you, number four?"

I moaned, realizing I had screwed up. Now for the consequences. "I did have some trouble with false sounds," I said timidly.

The technician looked at my worried features and smiled. "Well," he said. "I figured as much. You passed -- but barely. Next time don't panic. The tones are easy to hear if you stay calm."

He released the group to our next appointed encounter with naval medicine, an invidious probing that I instantly hoped I would never experience again. Four hours later, we trudged to our rooms. I was exhausted.

The next night the squadleaders' lecture concerned the wearing of the winter uniforms. We raced back and forth into our rooms for the better part of an hour changing into Service Dress Blues and Working Blues. Strangely, these 'blue' uniforms were a deep, very dark black. No way would a sane person call any of those things blue.

Room 5409 was featured next. After Patterson's hasty departure, three people remained in 5409. John Pirelli was the first speaker. He was short, dark haired, and fixed us with an intensity I found uncomfortable. As I watched him I felt powerful. I knew something about Pirelli no one else would ever suspect. He would never be a god-figure to me.

"My name is John Pirelli," he began confidently. "I was raised in Bangor, Maine. My father is a fisherman. He owns his own boat," he said proudly. It sounded fine to me.

"My mother is a supervisory bank clerk," he continued. "I ran cross country in high school. I was president of my class and a National Merit Scholar. I have three brothers, all younger."

Next up was a classmate I had not talked to as yet.

"I'm Patrick Mulvaney," he said in a very clear voice with a distinctive Midwestern drawl. Patrick was a medium build, dark haired individual -- one of the pack. "I grew up on a small farm in Dubuque, Iowa. My father is a farmer. We raise corn and soybeans and run a few head of cattle. My Mom helps around the farm and runs the business end of the operation.

"I didn't play any sports in high school, but I did act in several plays, and I was a state finalist in debate. I have six brothers and three sisters, and it would take all night to name them and give their ages. But none of the girls is eligible. My Mom makes the best cookies, especially chocolate chip, and I brought some with me. They're delicious. I'll share them later."

The final occupant of 5409 was Wesley Lamont. Wesley strode to the front, equally as confident as Pirelli. I could see that there would be competition in that room. I pitied poor Patrick, but maybe with that many siblings, he was used to competition.

"Ho, mon," Wesley began in his musical accent, smiling easily at the group. "Most of you know me already. I'm from the American Virgin Islands. My father runs a fishing and sightseeing charter, and my mother is the organist for the Baptist Church. I attended a private high school that did not offer American football, but I played soccer and gymnastics, mon. I was Islands men's' champion on the parallel bars for two years. I have a lovely younger sister who is presently fifteen, but hands off -- my father won't hear of her dating before she is seventeen. I also have an older brother who helps my father." He looked at Pirelli. "I guess that makes John and me fellow sailors."

Sounded to me like the gauntlet had been thrown.

Maxwell addressed the group. "Gentlemen," he said. "You have just completed your first week of training. You have many more to go before you are qualified to call yourselves midshipmen. Tomorrow we will exercise as usual, and all meals will be braced.

"However, since it's Saturday, there will be no training in the afternoon. That will be free time. You may visit quietly among yourselves, shine shoes, stow your things, or just relax. You may not sleep, however, except after lights out. You also may not explore the grounds -- you're not ready for that yet. And under no circumstances are you allowed to fraternize with any females until Parents' Weekend, and then only with your families."

"On Sunday," he continued, "you are required to attend the chapel of your choice. I have posted a list of times and assembly places on the bulletin board. On Sunday there will be no morning workout unless you do so on your own. If you do, exercise on the athletic fields only. Also on Sunday there will be no brace-up at morning and noon meals. Sunday evening, Plebe Year will return with a vengeance, so memorize your rates and the other ditties we requested."

"Since this is a weekend," he continued with an almost evil smile on his face. "Tom and I have alternate liberty. We will be exploring the evening's possibilities, or we may be resting. Playing nursemaid to a bunch of sissies is hard work. Do not disturb us unless an emergency arises; otherwise you will suffer a severe penalty."

His eyes regarded us with a mixture of contempt and mischief. "The time for play is finished, gentlemen. Over the weekend I want you each to think about what you really want to do with your lives. The Navy is a lifetime commitment, and Annapolis is not a civilian university. Up to now we've been slack. Come Sunday evening things are going to get tough. But I promise they won't be half as tough as September when the Brigade returns. Then you'll wish longingly for plebe summer and your old friends Maxie and Tom."

"Some of you do not belong here," he continued. "Don't make it too hard on yourselves. Quit now and save us the trouble of running you out.   Dismissed!"

That night I spent a half-hour polishing my shoes. Rico read another technical manual.


At twenty-one thirty I visited the Goons. Rico chose to remain behind. I think he was concerned about having to stand up and reveal where his thoughts had been.

The Goons were quiet. Poole was shining his shoes, and I'll be damned if his didn't look better than mine.

"Poole, you bastard. You'd better hide those shoes!"

"Huh? Why?"

"Because they look so good I'm liable to steal them when you're not looking."

"Thanks."

I posed a question. "Anybody want to sneak into town for some pizza?"

Everyone looked up at. Poole and Merritt were shocked. Ramsey and Polk were giving the idea serious consideration.

"Just kidding," I said quickly.

"It happens, you know," Ramsey said after a moment.

"What?" I asked.

"Sneaking into town. My Daddy talked about his days at West Point. He said you get so stir crazy that you need to get free for a while. Ah'm not ready yet to risk the wrath of Maxie and Battle, but soon, soon, ah think ah will be."

Plebe Summer                                                              Hank Turowskl

"Well, count me out," said Merritt immediately.

"Me too," Tommy added timidly. "I'm in enough trouble as it is. God, I ache!"

Ramsey looked at Polk, who stared back. "Maybe," Jeff replied.

Ramsey looked at me.

"Let me know when," I boasted. "I'll check my calendar."

"That's just what we need, you know," Ramsey said. "A little balls in the Company."

"There are balls in the Company, Jubal," Jim replied. "It's just that Max and the Battleaxe have a strong hold on them."

"We'll see." Ramsey was up to something.

Suddenly Jim Merritt jumped to his feet and braced up. "Attention on Deck!"

I had my back to the door, so I couldn't see what was happening. But I braced anyway. Battle walked into my field of vision. He was wearing civilian clothes -- very unstylish civilian clothes. He looked at me for a second and continued over to Ramsey and his six smiling chins. But Battle wasn't interested in Jubal's chins. He looked troubled. "Carry on, Ramsey."

Jubal unbraced -- but so did Tommy Poole. I don't know why.

Battle whirled on Poole. "Who told you to carry-on, Poole, you stupid smack?"

Tommy realized his mistake and rebraced. "Sorry, sir!" he yelled.

"You're goddamn right, you're sorry!" Battle yelled. "You are the sorriest-assed excuse for a human being I have ever seen. I'll to see that you either quit or die, Poole. Count on that!"

Tommy wisely didn't reply, but I could see his shoulders sag.

Battle then turned to Ramsey and stared at him for several long seconds. "I found out about your father just a few minutes ago, Ramsey. I am deeply sorry. You must be very proud of him -- and he of you. Come see me on the day the Brigade gets back, and our relationship will change. Until then I will treat you like any other plebe, understood?"

I could see Joe's face from where I stood nearby.

His face clouded. He stared at Battle. "I don't want special treatment. I had hoped no one would find out, sir."

Battle paused, then shook his head slowly. "I understand." He turned on the rest of us. "If any of you breathe so much as a word of this to anyone, I'll see that you suffer. Understand?"

I had no idea what he was talking about. "Yes, sir," I said in time with the others.

"Good." He departed.

We unbraced. We stared at Jubal. Ramsey remained quiet.

"Joe," I said when I realized he wasn't going to offer anything on his own, "if you don't tell us what it is we're supposed to be quiet about, we may say something inadvertently."

Jubal considered. He sat at his chair and took a deep breath. "Okay," he said. "I'll tell."

I sat on the edge of Merritt's desk.

"My Daddy was killed in Vietnam two years ago. Ah didn't want anyone to know."

"Jesus, Jubal, I'm really sorry," said Jeff Polk from across the room.

Ramsey took a breath. "It's okay. No problem."

Of course we were all quiet, and no one knew exactly what to say or do.

Jubal spoke angrily, "I said it's okay. Let it drop, ya hear?"

"How do you feel tonight, Tommy?" I asked, trying valiantly to change the subject.

Tommy took several seconds to pull out of his meditation. He looked at Jubal with sympathy. "I lost my brother a few years ago," he said, "I know how difficult it is."

"Damn it!" Jubal exploded. "I don't want sympathy. I don't want apologies. I don't want to be buddies. Just leave me alone, okay?" He got up from his chair, checked his watch, slipped on his tennis shoes, and departed without another word.

"Wow!" said Jeff Polk. "Boy, do I feel stupid."

"So that's what's put the chip on his shoulder," said Merritt. "It all makes sense now. The question is, what do we do about it?"

"What do you mean?" Jeff asked.

134

"Well," Jim began. "Even though he's troubled and says he wants to be left alone, we can't change our lives and tiptoe around the issues. He's going to have to accept the fact that his father's dead and get on with his own life. I propose we act as if nothing has happened. If he's offended, he can leave the room, or change the subject, or, better yet, join in the discussion and get the weight off his shoulders."

Jim Merritt: sensible as always.


On Saturday morning Tommy Poole beat both Ronald Steinway and Nathan Spielenberg to the finish line. That fact did not in the least decrease the number of pushups Tommy had to do. But he did make it to ten without stopping once.

Nathan Spielenberg was the next to go. Nathan was an interesting character. I did not for a second understand how 'Big Nate' got accepted into Annapolis. But someone must have called in a major marker.

Not only was he significantly shorter than the rest of us, he was also fat -- not chubby, or stout, or pleasingly plump. Nathan was fat. His flesh hung over his waist in a pink wave of grossness. His arms and legs jiggled, and he waddled grotesquely wherever he went.

Nathan could not complete the morning runs even halfway without stopping to wheeze, and as for exercises, he was totally inept. The first morning he struggled to finish even a single pushup, or sit-up. By the end of the week he hadn't improved, and the talk among the Company was that he wasn't trying. Needless to say, Big Nate was another shit screen. But I didn't feel much sympathy for him. He seemed to pretend when everyone else was straining.

But what eventually did him in was food. Nate was constantly hungry and complained to anyone who would listen that he was starving. When he brought this complaint to Battle, Tom explained in return him that his presence made him physically ill. He demanded that Nathan hide his grossness in his locker for an hour. According to his roommates, Big Nate continued to complain about his hunger even from the depths of his dark coat closet. Battle also made him pledge that he would stay out of his field of vision at all times or else risk having him vomit on his shoes -- Spielenberg's shoes polished up nicely, by the way. But Big Nate was hungry, and nothing was going to come between him and the next meal.

On Wednesday evening, Nathan Spielenberg sneaked down into the common area of the Rotunda and made a low-voiced phone call to his mother.  When she heard about his rough treatment, she was angry.  When she heard that he wasn't allowed to eat enough, however, she was incensed.  The next day Mrs. Spielenberg phoned her Congressman to report the ghastly treatment.  She demanded action.  The Congressman - constituent interest always a primary concern -- called the Secretary of the Navy, who promptly relayed this 'hot potato' down through the chain of command to the Commandant of the Brigade of Midshipmen, Captain Mack Hallahan.  Rumor had it that his reply was characteristically unprintable, but Academy wheels were set into motion nonetheless.

Thursday evening, in response to the Spielenberg 'hot potato,' Midshipman Second Class Battle gave Big Nate his first taste of carry-on and also ensured that he ate to his heart's content - to the detriment of his classmates, whose portions had been reduced to compensate for Big Nate's gluttony.  Big Nate didn't care.  He was ecstatic.  Near the end of the meal, seeing that Nate's plate was finally empty, Battle went to a neighboring table and returned with a bowl of food.

"I know you've still got room," Battle said.  Smiling, he stretched the front of Nate's uniform shirt forward, and spooned an entire bowl of steaming mashed potatoes into the opening.

Nathan was dumbfounded.  Tears welled up in his fleshy eyes.

Battle leaned over and whispered into Big Nate's chubby ear.  "Had enough?"  Without waiting for an answer he pressed a hand on Nathan's ample middle, smashing the potatoes.

"You may not have had enough, Spielenberg, you disgusting puke," Battle continued vengefully, "but I have.  From this day until the instant you waddle out the Rotunda door in civilian clothes, you are going to be my target.  And I promise to make your life miserable."

Tears rolled down Nathan's chubby cheeks.  His shoulders shook and his stomach quivered.

I watched, not feeling the least bit sorry for Nathan Spielenberg.  I must be a real fascist.

Battle became even angrier.  "Stop that baby-assed blubbering, you sissy.  Do you really think you could ever be a Naval Officer if you can't take a teeny bit of pressure without bawling."  Battle straightened and turned away from Spielenberg.  "You disgust me!"

Sitting, Battle addressed Nathan. "Look around! Your Mommy's not here in this Mess Hall, fatso. Nobody's going to save you."

Nathan sobbed louder.

Nathan survived Friday without being killed, although I'm sure he prayed for death several times. He also finished the Saturday run, sort of. We thought Nathan had learned his lesson.

On Saturday afternoon, Nathan Spielenberg packed his personal things, put on his civilian clothes, and waddled out the door of his room. His roommates asked what he was doing.

"I'm going out in town for something to eat," he replied. When asked why he needed a suitcase for a meal he replied, "I'm really hungry."

It was totally out of character for Big Nate to exhibit any semblance of humor, so the roommates initially, albeit skeptically, believed him. However, when he had not returned thirty minutes before the evening meal, Bob Strong called on the squadleaders. After doing 50 pushups for disturbing Maxwell's beauty sleep, he reported Spielenberg's absence. The entire remaining membership of Room 5413 had to do 50 extra pushups in formation before every meal for the next week for not speaking up sooner. Battle probably wanted to escort Big Nate to the door.

CHAPTER 14


*LIBERTY CALL*


I wish I could say that my first taste of semi-freedom that Saturday afternoon was spent in worthwhile activity, but actually I sat at my desk, bored to tears, trying to write a letter home for an hour.  Then I tried to read a science fiction novel I had brought.  Finally I took my evil shoes from the rear-most recesses of my locker, and I tried again to spit some success onto my shoes.

Rico had discovered a wide ledge and gutter that ran along the outside of our window.  He went out on the ledge just after noon meal, took off his shirt, and sunbathed with another technical manual.  I could see the heroic CIA spy happily blazing away at an enemy of our nation while a totally unclad and rather enormous young lady clung to his muscular arm.

Midway into the afternoon, Ronald Steinway entered the room.  He looked very unhappy.  He explained the departure of Spielenberg, and I indicated that the chances of our seeing Big Nate again were rather small.  Steinway agreed.  He was more concerned with his own survival.

He took a letter from his back pocket.  "Here," he said.  "Read this."

I opened the envelope, which had been folded over several times so that it would fit in his pocket without showing.  It contained a short letter from his father that was written on the afternoon of the Oath of Office Ceremony.


*"Dear Ronald,"* it began.  *"You don't know how proud it made your mother and me, seeing you recite the pledge today.  This is like my wildest dreams come true.  The neighbors back home are so envious.  You a midshipman!  No one's child has ever done so much.  I know you'll do well, you have good blood in your veins.  And I am counting on you.  Be safe.  I love you.  Papa"*

I returned it to him, waiting for a clue as to what he wanted from me.

"What am I going to do, Kevin?" he asked me. "I hate this place, but I can't quit. My parents would die."

I still wasn't sure what to say. I hesitated. "Your parents won't die, Ronald. In my opinion they're putting impossible expectations on you. It's your life. You're old enough to make your own decisions. Why stay if you're miserable? Write your father and tell him how bad it is here; and, believe me, it *is* bad. Keep doing that for a couple weeks, and maybe he'll accept the idea you'd be better off where you are happier. He might even ask you to come home."

Ronald stared at me, then looked down at his feet. "I don't think that would work."

"Then stay here, Ronald, if you have to," I said getting perturbed. "I'll say a prayer for you, but it doesn't seem like you've given yourself any middle ground on this issue."

Steinway turned away from me. "I just don't know what to do."

At that moment Rico crawled in from the ledge.

"Where have you been?" Ronald asked.

Rico looked at him as if he were stupid. "Well, Ronald," Rico said. "I've been out on the ledge contemplating the possibilities of a swan dive off the roof."

Ronald stared at Rico. "Oh, I don't think you should kill yourself."

Rico pretended to be shocked. "No shit, Ronald? Well thanks. I appreciate your help."

Ronald suddenly realized he had been the brunt of a joke. He laughed. Then he walked to the window and stuck his head out into the hot sunlight. He looked up and down the ledge f bringing his head back inside.

"That's pretty neat," he said. "A person could hide out there." He walked to the door just as an idea sprang into my head.

"Ronald? What size foot does Big Nate have?"

He looked at me like I had lost my mind. "I don't know, but they seemed pretty small."

"Would it be anywhere close to a size nine?" I asked hopefully.

"I doubt it. Nathan has tiny, but very wide feet. Why do you ask?"

139

"Never mind.  Just an idea."

Rico knew.  He chuckled.

Ronald stared at me for a puzzled moment, then departed.

"Shit, Kevin," Rico noted, picking up his book.  "You must be desperate if you're thinking about wearing Spielenberg's shoes."  He was right about that.


Saturday early evening eight of us asked Maxie for permission to play basketball on one of the outdoor courts.  Chuck Chalmers had brought a ball.  How he fit it inside his luggage I wasn't sure.  Maxie agreed, providing he could play too.  It didn't seem he could possibly be an athlete, and he certainly didn't have the physique for basketball, but we agreed.  What else could we do?

The outdoor courts were over by the Field House.  This was the first time we had been able to wander anywhere around the yard, and the long walk around the rear of Bancroft Hall in the warm, humid evening was enjoyable.  A slight breeze coming off the Bay brought smells of sea life and diesel fuel.  That same breeze pushed a variety of craft in toward Annapolis Harbor for the evening. Multi-colored sails flapped and motors chugged.  As we passed along the outside of the fifth and seventh wings we could hear Plebe Year ongoing.

Maxwell laughed at our discomfort.  "You guys didn't believe us when we said we were pussy cats, did you?  As you can hear, some of my classmates are true assholes."  He shook his head.  "And when we told you about the 'Tigers' we weren't kidding either. Those guys are insane. You guys are in for hell when the Brigade gets back."

The scrimmage was successful in that for an hour I did not think about Annapolis, the 'Tigers,' or about those unshiny shoes lurking in my locker.  I did rather well, and so did Chalmers.  Maxwell wasn't really too bad either.  Jubal Ramsey also was impressive, but I thought he played basketball too much like football, as my bruised ribs later indicated.

It was Maxwell who broke the game up.  It was his night for liberty.

We returned to the Company area in far better spirits than when we had left, and I found myself restless.  After taking a long shower, a luxury I hadn't had the entire week, I wandered from room to room.

I stopped for the longest time in 5413. Maybe I was worried about Ronald. Maybe I wanted to be social. Maybe I just wanted to get a glimpse at Fat Nathan's shoes to make sure they really wouldn't fit. Willy Simpson was playing his guitar and singing *Tom Dooley*. Appropriate, huh? He wasn't bad. I hummed along for a few songs. More classmates wandered in.

Then I noticed that Steinway had disappeared, and on a hunch I went to the window. Sure enough, Ronald sat outside staring into the now dark night.

"What's up, Ronald?"

"Just thinking."

Despite the dark I thought I could see a glisten of wet near his eyes. I patted his shoe.

"It'll be okay, Ron," I said. "Just hang in there."

"I wish I had your confidence, Kevin."

Then he turned away, and I left him to his thoughts.

I was still restless when I reached the Goon Room. Inside, the four happy roomies were going about their business silently.

"Hey," I said. "Simpson's got his guitar out and there's a songfest going on in 5413. You guys should go check it out." No one seemed in the mood. I noticed that Joe had gone into his closet and was putting on gym gear.

"Where you going?" I asked.

"You don't want to know?"

"Do I sense adventure?" I asked.

I am usually not an adventuresome person. I had gone through high school without once speeding my father's car. I was scared to death of sex. And I was absolutely convinced that even being in the near vicinity of a dangerous drug like marijuana would cause me to commit violent murder. But suddenly I was feeling brave. After all, I had just completed a week of plebe training. What else could life do to me?

"Come on, Joe?" I asked. "What's up?"

"Ah'm gonna reconnoiter, that's all. I want to see what it's like around here at night."

"Want some company?"

He looked at me for a minute. "We could get into trouble if we're caught."

"I beat Battle to the finish line," I offered. "Who's gonna catch *me*?"

Jubal laughed. "Okay, classmate. Put on sweatgear and meet me in the head in five minutes."

I arrived in the head exactly five minutes later. Jeffrey Polk was also there.

"Is this going to be a trio?" I asked smiling.

"Yeah," Polk answered, "but I never figured you for this sort of thing."

"Never be predictable, that's my motto."

Jubal looked us over. "Okay, ya'll, here's the ground rules," he said. "We go out together along Dewey Field in back of the academic buildings; at the wooden bridge to Hospital Point we cross into the main grounds and explore. Be careful. If we get spotted, run like hell. If anybody gets caught, we don't turn the others in. Agreed?"

"Sure," we both said.

"Okay," Jubal continued. "Follow me, and be quiet 'til we're out of Bancroft Hall."


We made our cautious way deeper into the recesses of Bancroft Hall, stopping occasionally in communal heads or descending ladders whenever activity made passage difficult. It was an eerie process of lurking and skulking with classmates and upperclassmen mere feet away. It took some time, but we managed to slink unnoticed through the plebe indoctrination portions of the Hall into the darkness of unoccupied areas.

Eventually we passed through a set of fire doors into the humid darkness outside. Ahead of us was Macdonough Hall, and farther off the Severn River cut a black swath from south to north. Clouds obscured the moon, and the night air smelled of electricity, and in the distance I watched a thunderstorm hammer against the Chesapeake Bay Bridge.

Jubal wedged a small wooden doorstop under the door to prevent it from locking us out, then he straightened and we checked the surrounding area.

We had emerged from a side door of the seventh wing. With Jubal in the lead, we crept northward along Bancroft Hall. We paused where the construction of new academic buildings Michelson and Chauvenet Halls was underway, and peered westward toward T-Court. In the vicinity of Tecumseh, second class squadleaders and their dates met and departed for town. We raced across the darkened open space to the construction site and followed the dirt walkway behind Chauvenet and Michelson Halls toward Hospital Point.

As we turned west toward the officers' quarters, we noticed two couples strolling a block away. In keeping with the Academy regulations forbidding public displays of affection, the midshipmen and their dates maintained a polite separation. We retreated into the shadows of a group of trees while they passed. The midshipmen carried blue Academy blankets. From my vantage in the dark, I felt predatory and voyeuristic, and the music of the lilting female voices seemed erotic. Would any girl ever coo to me that way?

As the couples started across the footbridge to Hospital Point, I guessed what they were up to. We had heard their low, abbreviated whispers and the suggestive giggles. I watched the departing upperclassmen with envy.

"Lucky bastards!" Polk whispered fiercely. We shushed him.

We hurried across the street to the parade grounds. The intoxicating smell of newly cut grass wafted in the warm summer air. Fireflies swept the open spaces over the field. Moving stealthily in the darkest shadows of the trees, we approached officers' quarters and the wall separating the Academy from the outside world. We reached the eight-foot brick structure and surveyed along it.

"What are we looking for?" I asked.

Jeff whispered. "A safe place to come and go."

"I see," I said, not really seeing.

We crept along the wall in the dark and found two spots that were both hidden and scalable. Jubal chose one spot and looked at us.

"Give me a boost," he said. "I want to see the other side."

Placing my back against the bricks, I faced Joe and made a foothold with my hands. Ramsey put his hands on my shoulders, and boosted himself up so that he could see over the wall. His hands scraped on the bricks, brushing a rain of dust down on me. He

143

scanned the street on the other side for a minute then climbed down, which was a good thing because he was very heavy. The combination of his bulk, the extreme humidity, and the tension made me sweat profusely.

Once down, he leaned toward us. "This is a perfect spot," he whispered. "The other side is a small side street with almost no traffic."

I surveyed the wall. It would take some effort to get over, but I was sure I could make it. In Boston I had been a member of the downtown YMCA, and the indoor basketball court there occupied a space that was exactly the correct length but left no room for out of bounds at the ends. The backboards were built into the end walls. Because of this unusual circumstance, the end walls were considered in bounds, and it was possible to get into the air for a slam-dunk by planting a foot on the wall and springing upward. I could vault the Academy wall in this manner. How Jubal would manage to raise his heavy frame up that wall without assistance was another matter.

Satisfied that he had identified an escape route, Ramsey turned toward the main part of the yard. We carefully skirted the Officers' Club. What kind of punishment would be in store if you didn't stop when the Commandant yelled out a "Plebe Halt!"? I was pretty sure I could outrun that old fart Hallahan, but I didn't want to take any unnecessary risks.

We made our way cautiously among the old academic buildings. I couldn't help but feel a slight awe as I gazed at these grand old buildings. How many thousands of midshipmen had studied in these halls? What classes would I take here? How well would I do? They seemed solid, comfortable places of learning.

When we turned a corner to return toward Michelson Hall, we almost stumbled over a squad leader and his date as they nestled on a dark bench in the shadows near Mahan Hall. We froze. The couple hadn't noticed us, but we were awfully close to them.

Jubal put out a beefy arm to stop us, and waved that we should retreat. We did.

As we backed I watched the couple enviously. What a juicy kiss! I wanted one. I began to flush. It wasn't the first time in my life I ever felt horny, but I still didn't like it.

But we backed around the corner into bigger trouble. Two more sets of second-class and their dates headed our way, and they had seen us.

"Hey!" one of them yelled. "Plebe Halt!"

Shit! The chase was on! My face flushed from an instant surge of adrenaline.

We ran in the direction from which we had just come. The startled secondclassman on the bench was just emerging from his love coma when we passed. I inhaled a thick aroma of sweat and perfume. He stared at us but didn't say a word. He seemed comatose, and his date was no better off. What had they been doing? I wanted to stop and ask, but streaked passed instead.

The other squadleaders pursued.

We raced along the walk between Mahan and Michelson Halls toward the construction area. One of the pursuers yelled an almost continuous string of "Plebe Halts!"

At the back corner of Michelson we turned toward Bancroft Hall and picked up speed.

"Just like a morning workout!" Polk yelled, as we paralleled each other. Ramsey had been in the lead from the beginning, but he soon began to tire and we caught up to him.

I could hear the sounds of footsteps behind us as the squadleaders followed. I glanced back, hoping it wasn't anyone as fleet of foot as Battle. One pursuer, a tall, skinny individual, was not more than 50 yards behind. The other had stopped at the corner of Mahan Hall. That was a good sign, especially since the one still running had on civilian clothes, which included a sport coat and tie and hard street shoes that were sure to slow him down on the uneven terrain. It couldn't be easy to keep up his effort.

At the junction of the construction area, he also stopped. "I'll get you little bastards!"

We hurried to the corner of Michelson Hall, checked the open area for watchers, then ran to the side of Bancroft Hall. Within two minutes we had slipped back inside our departure door and were snug in the arms of 'Mother B.' Another five minutes found us safely in our rooms.


"Had an adventure?" Rico asked as I entered, sweaty and flushed with excitement.

"You might say that."

"Well," he said. "Battle hasn't been around yet, so you're probably safe."

I showered quickly, put on different gym clothes, and sat at my desk to recover. Recovery on a humid Maryland August night is virtually impossible, however; and I continued to sweat. Rico watched me with raised eyebrows until my breathing had slowed. I smiled but didn't offer anything. I wasn't sure if his knowing would put him in a bad position.

At 2245, Tommy Poole entered.  He grinned a very lopsided smile.  "I figured it out."

"What?" I asked.

"How to make these damn things shine.  It's science.   Let me have one of your shoes."

I hurried to my closet and removed one offending shoe gingerly.  There was so much polish on it that being in its close proximity guaranteed a black stain.  I handed it to him by a shoestring.

He took it to the sink and turned on the hot water.  Once the water was as hot as it could get, he inserted his hand into the shoe, and plunged the shoe under the near-scalding water.

Pungent Kiwi polish molecules assaulted my nose as the heat melted off all the layers I had applied.  Tommy waited until we could see the original leather, then he shook the excess water into the sink, sat in my chair, and took a cloth from his shorts pocket.  Rubbing in small circles, he began to buff the toe area.

"The heat makes the pores open and accept the polish," he said.  "Otherwise you have to work too hard to bring up a shine.  No magic - pure science."  Within a minute that shoe shined far better than it ever had after several days of my efforts.

"Where does the spit come in?" I asked.

He laughed.  "It doesn't!  That's just a myth.  A little bit of polish, a little bit of water, and small easy circles will do it."  He held my shoe up to the light.  It sparkled.  I was beginning to like this guy.

"I'll pay you ten bucks to do mine," Rico said from across the room.

"No thanks," Tommy replied.  "But I'll help you with them if you'd like."

"Great!  They're in the closet.  Just bring them back before noon meal tomorrow."

"Rico!  Tommy offered to help, not to do all the work."

Rico smiled disarmingly.  "Just kidding."

Tommy was confused.  "I will help," he offered again.

"Come back in the morning after church," Rico said, "and I'll gratefully accept."

It was considered a Class A offense to have alcohol inside Bancroft Hall. It probably still is. Class A offenses are major, meaning so many demerits that an inmate in solitary confinement in Turkish prison has more privileges. But while alcohol in the barracks was considered God-awful serious, being drunk in the barracks was not. We didn't know that.

Saturday night around midnight, Midshipman Second Class Michael Maxwell returned from liberty weaving happily along the passage, awakening most of us by singing an interesting and bawdy version of *What do you do with a Drunken Sailor?* Don't ask!

I went to the door to see what was making that awful sound. Maxwell's normally fine tenor was distorted and strained by the alcohol. Merritt stood in the opposite door.

"O'Reilly, Merritt, you douchebags!" Maxwell shouted. "Hit it for 100!"

I groaned, dropped to the deck in the doorway, and began shouting out numbers. Maxwell swayed in the middle of the passageway watching and smiling. He stunk.

As other heads poked into the dark passageway, Maxwell ordered additional pushups until more than ten of us were yelling numbers. Maxwell turned a slow, unsteady circle to watch.

By the time I had reached 50, Battle emerged from their room. His short hair was disheveled, and his robe hung loosely oven one shoulder. He looked very tired. He walked to Maxwell and put a hand on his shoulder. "Come on Maxie," he said. "Let's get you to bed." He steered his roommate awkwardly down the hall toward their room. At the doorway he paused and looked over his shoulder at us. "Knock it off and go to bed! And forget this happened!"

After the two of them disappeared into their room, my classmates and I exchanged smiles and head shakes, then returned to our own beds. The next morning a huge, stinking puddle of vomIt lay on the passageway floor near the entrance to the head.

CHAPTER 15

## *THANK GOD FOR SUNDAYS*

Tommy Poole, who was also a Catholic, and who -- more importantly -- had an operating alarm clock, woke us at 0800 for Catholic services. The uniform was Tropical Whites -- the uniform the squadleaders and officers usually wore. We had practiced how to rig the combination cap and shoulder boards, studied the proper alignment of the shirt and pants, and learned how to give ourselves a proper 'tuck.' Several days previously we had polished our belt buckles to a fine white-gold glossiness and whitened our shoes. Polishing the white shoes was as simple as dabbing liquid white stain from a polish bottle onto the nap.

It didn't take me long to get ready, and soon Rico and I joined Tommy and several companymates in the passageway for the walk to formation in T-Court. We inspected each other and agreed we looked great. I doubted Battle would have agreed, but luckily he wasn't going with us. At 0845 we left the company area and descended the ladder into the rotunda. Once there, we joined a throng of classmates headed outside.

Formation for the various services took place on one side of Tecumseh Court. A second classman stood at the bottom of the steps and directed us. He looked tired -- from last night's liberty, no doubt. Catholic formation was directed by another second classman. Nearby, smaller groups formed for their walk to services in the city. At 0850 we marched to chapel.

The main Annapolis campus is bounded by five imposing structures. On the south side toward Chesapeake Bay is enormous Bancroft Hall, its northernmost wings circling T-Court and fronting the baleful statue of Tecumseh. To the north, more than 200 yards away and separated by enormous and beautiful trees and impeccably maintained grounds, is the old and impressive library building, Mahan Hall, with its impressive clock tower. To the east toward the Severn River are identical academic buildings, Chauvenet and Michelson Halls. The jewel of the entire campus scene, however, is the chapel, which graces the western side.

The chapel at Annapolis may be the most beautiful of its kind in the nation. Possibly only Saint Patrick's in New York can rival its effect on the visitor. The chapel is shaped like a cross with the entry being at the bottom of the shaft. Entrance is through huge brass doors opening onto a wide vestibule. The chapel floor is intricately patterned terrazzo. The interior is long and wide, flanked by wooden pews leading to a circular dome more than 30 yards high which canopies the altar.

The interior stonework and dome are magnificent, and the stained glass windows that surround the upper portions of the dome have been crafted to depict four famous naval scenes. But what may lift the Academy chapel above the likes of Saint Patrick's is the music. I had to wait until the Brigade returned and midshipman structure was reestablished to appreciate it; but when the Annapolis choir sang in that chapel, it was almost like being in heaven with the angels. I've always enjoyed music, and that was the perfect place for it.

We marched into the chapel and down the main aisle to the dome. I don't remember much about my first Annapolis Mass because I spent so much time looking at everything else – Sorry, Father. Mass was not a long affair. I went to communion, said prayers for my family and my classmates, and asked God to smile on Tommy and Ronald. Outside, tourists watched and made comments about how wonderful we looked. I felt that way. It was a new feeling for me.


Sunday morning breakfast was paradise compared to meals we had recently experienced. I had time to smell the eggs and juices and taste the sweet syrup on my pancakes. There were no specific company areas. Tables were served as midshipmen arrived. The few squadleaders who were there didn't care about plebe rates or bracing and squared meals. The table where Rico, Tommy, and I sat was populated solely by plebes. We ate, chatted, and felt human again.

The company area was quiet when we returned. Many classmates were attending Protestant services -- either the main event, which followed Catholic Mass in the chapel -- or with various smaller denominations in town. We changed clothes.

Tommy Poole, dressed in gym gear, visited us several minutes later. He sat in an empty chair as I showed him how my shoes were coming along.

"Guys," Rico said, "continue talking, but I have to excuse myself. I have something important to do." With that he turned away from the open doorway, propped a book on his lap, and leaned on one arm. Pretending to read, he soon fell asleep. The ability to doze on a moment's notice and under unusual circumstances is a habit most midshipmen quickly learn. During later years I would happily walk ten minutes to my room to lie down for thirty minutes between classes.

Tommy laughed quietly. "He's quite a person."

"Yeah," I answered, "but don't tell him that. His ego's already big enough."

"Well," Tommy said, "I'm going to work out a little and see if I can get the soreness from my legs and arms. What are you going to do?"

"I don't know," I answered. "I think I'll write letters and read for a while. After lunch I'm going to try to roust out enough players for a basketball game."

Tommy looked at me closely. "I really envy your athletic abilities."

"It's nothing but practice, Tommy," I lied. Practice is important, but in most sports, you've either have the talent or you don't.

Tommy headed for Dewey Field, and I began to write a longer letter to my family.


A soft, friendly whisper tickled my ear. "O'Reilly," it said sweetly. "Wake up, dear." The voice must have coincided with a dream I was having because I smiled as I woke and stretched.

Woke! Shit! I had been sleeping! I had no idea how. I jerked my head to the left to see the perverted whisperer and I stared straight into the smiling face of the Battleaxe. My heart sank, and my face flushed. I sat upright, then stood, knocking the chair backward in the process.

"Attention on deck!" I yelled over the commotion.

It was too late. Rico already stood at attention on the other side of the room watching me, a smile on his face. Apparently Battle had caught him as well. As I pulled in my chin to brace I realized that I had slept with my head well over to one side. A tremendous cramp in my neck caused me to flinch, and prevented me from achieving full chin-dom. I groaned.

"Uncomfortable, huh?" asked Battle, feigning concern.

"Yes, sir!" I waited for the punishment to begin.

Battle chuckled. "This is wonderful," he said with sadistic gusto. "I needed two strong men to demonstrate a comearound this evening after meal. It looks like you'll be them." He headed for the door. "Comearound!" he said.

"Aye, aye, sir!" we shouted to the now empty doorway.

After the noon meal, which was also more like a brunch than a standard Academy affair, the Company split into two groupings. One group, which included Jim Merritt and John Pirelli, welded themselves to their desks and memorized plebe rates and other data. The other group searched for distractions. Some jogged. Others read books or wrote letters. Rico and Wesley sunbathed outside our window. Nikolas Papadopalas studied the academic catalog. Barton Hardesty meditated with his bible. Willy Simpson played his guitar.

I led a group of erstwhile athletes to the basketball courts for a pick-up game. I wanted Maxwell to accompany us to pick up some brownie points, but Battle met us at the door and declined for his roommate -- still hungover no doubt. Tommy Poole went along to the courts and stretched and exercised while we played. I was beginning to like that guy. He had guts -- no, actually he had *a* gut -- a large gut to be sure -- but he also had character.

We returned to our area two hours before meal. Rico was reading from *Reef Points*. If he had begun preparing for the meal maybe I should too. I showered and joined him in study.

If nothing else, 12 years of Catholic education imparts a student with one useful attribute -- the ability to memorize and recite. Even after more than 30 years, I still remember many of my altar boy responses -- in Latin.

There was an incredible amount of information to memorize, and I realized that I needed to spend more than an hour to learn everything. But I did the best I could. A half-hour before meal formation I worked on my shoes and checked my uniform. When everything was as good as I could do, I dressed, reviewed my rates, and waited nervously. The anxiety was contagious. Even Rico hustled about the room and recited in a dull murmuring voice.

Ten minutes before formation excited plebe voices shouted from four locations in the passageway, "Sir, you now have ten minutes to evening meal formation! The uniform for evening meal is Tropical Whites. The menu for evening meal is tossed green salad, grilled

New York steak, mashed potatoes and gravy, sautéed vegetables, bread, milk and butter. For dessert Apple Brown Betty. The Officers of the Watch are: The Officer of the Watch is Lieutenant Rockwell. The Assistant Officer of the Watch is Lieutenant Murphy. The Midshipman Officer of the Watch is Midshipman Second Class Eldridge. The movies in town are: At the Capitol, *True Grit;* at the Strand, *Cleopatra;* at Parole Plaza, *Easy Rider.* The days are: There are 66 days until Parent's Weekend, 68 days until the Brigade returns, and 169 days until Navy beats Army! Sir, you now have ten minutes, sir!"

Wow! Whoever stood at my end of the passageway did a pretty good job. I glanced. It was Bill Allen. He smiled as he chopped into his room. Five minutes before the appointed time the call was repeated. I stood.

"Well," I said. "This is it."

Rico nodded distractedly, still trying to memorize something.

At two minutes before formation the duty room sang out for the final time. "Sir, you now have two minutes before evening meal formation!" After reciting the meal menu they finished, " Time, tide and formation wait for no man. I am now shoving off. You have one minute sir!" The duty room members joined us in ranks.

Battle and a still-shaky Maxwell exited their room. Battle strode toward us. Maxwell sauntered slowly. Tonight was our first true uniform inspection. We opened ranks on command.

I was in the third rank. I watched the squadleaders as they proceeded down the front of the first rank and up its back and repeated the process with rank number two.

The squadleaders were serious that night. There was no smiling and no banter as they moved from plebe to plebe. Everyone received some corrective comment. A few individuals made the squadleaders angry and those classmates were asked to comearound the next evening. Maxwell pulled Barton's shirt from his pants and ordered him to return to his room for a retuck.

Maxwell purposefully scuffed the tops of Chuck Chalmer's white shoes, leaving prominent dark marks. "Your shoes look like hell," he said. "This is incentive to do better, pal."

Both stopped in front of Tommy Poole. They checked his shoes and belt and I heard him get at least two comearounds. Then they came to his hat. They puzzled for several seconds. Battle adjusted the alignment of the cap, stepped back, shook his head and tried again.

152

When the second adjustment didn't suit him, he leaned in toward Poole and said, "Your hat's on crooked, Poole!"

Tommy didn't flinch. "No, sir!"

Both Battle and Maxwell stepped back and re inspected Tommy's hat. Battleaxe looked at Max, who shrugged. "Your hat's on crooked," Battle said again.

"No sir," Tommy answered.

Battle put his face was less than an inch from Poole's. "If your hat isn't crooked, asshole, then what's the problem?"

"Sir, my head is crooked, sir!"

Battle was astounded but didn't laugh. Several of my nearby classmates did laugh, however, for which they received an instant comearound. Battle took Poole's word at face value, however, and checked the position of his eyes and ears. "Christ, I think he's right, Maxie."

He leaned in again toward Poole. "You're a freak, mister! Did you know that? You're a goddamn genetic mutation. You are also one of the damned ugliest people I have ever seen. Genius or not, you've got to go, Poole."

Suddenly it was my turn. My heart began to pound as they approached. I took a deep breath and pulled in my stomach as Battle stopped in front of me. His cologne was English Leather, sprinkled far too thickly. I could see only the top of his white cap as he bent his head to view my shoes. Slowly he raised his head to check my pants creases and lineup. "Thumbs along the seams of your trousers!" I had thought they were, but quickly adjusted. He continued to stare at my middle, so I knew he was checking something.

"Did you polish the top of your belt buckle?"

My brain whirled, considering whether I had or not. "No, sir!" I answered with the truth.

"Why the hell not, O'Reilly?"

"I'll find out, sir."

"Comearound, asshole!" Maxwell said as he and Battle moved to the next victim.

Mealtime was absolute hell, the worst meal yet. I was so busy passing food, sliding further and further out onto the edge of my seat at Maxwell's urging, and responding to repeated questions, that I didn't eat at all. I was a nervous mess the entire forty minutes. Twice I dropped my tiny morsels of food onto my lap when Maxwell questioned me.

Luckily, Ronald Steinway chose to sit next to me. I think he felt protected in my shadow. But he couldn't see that the very opposite was true. Maxwell pounced on Steinway unrelentingly. Steinway recited rates, answered innocuous questions, and must have earned 20 comearounds before the meal was over. In his desire to *train* Steinway, Maxwell even left Tommy Poole alone.

Although I responded to a thousand inane questions, the only rate I had to recite was, *"How's the cow?"*

I answered with a boisterous. . .

*"Sir! She walks, she talks, she's full of chalk, that lacteal fluid extracted from the female of the bovine species is highly prolific to the fifth degree, sir!"*

'Fifth' indicating that there were approximately five glasses of milk in the nearest container. -- Pretty stupid, huh? Then how come I enjoyed reciting it? Maybe because it was the shortest rate and the one I knew best?

Between responses I listened to Jim Merritt and John Pirelli having a virtual rate battle at the adjoining table. Every question Battle asked, they answered quickly, efficiently, and joyously. They were clearly overdoing the plebe routine, and I was a bit uneasy. Did I sound like that when I answered? Across the table Jeff Polk stared at me during one of Pirelli's enthusiastic diatribes. Jeff answered my question with a silent but resounding 'Yes!'

I felt resentful. Who the hell was Polk anyway? He wasn't my mother or my conscience. If I wanted to feel good while forcing my chin tightly against my neck and balancing myself precariously on what had to be a quarter inch of seat, while at the same time carefully and squarely lifting gram-sized bites of food to my mouth and yelling to a twenty-year-old college student about bovines and lacteal fluids, what business was it of his? Yeah, what business?

CHAPTER 16

## *COMEAROUNDS AND CONFESSIONS*

I was exhausted at the end of the meal, more so than after the morning exercises. I retreated to my room to change into gym gear for the evening's training.

"Who are my comearound guinea pigs?" Battle asked. Guevarra and I reluctantly raised our hands. So did Willy Simpson and Ronald Steinway.

"Step out here, gentlemen." We stepped.

I was beginning to feel a little better. I was sure I could outrun the group; and although Rico was stronger than I was, we had Ronald in the foursome. The shit-screen theory was going to save me again. Wrong!

"All right, everybody else back up against the bulkhead and watch! You four stand down the passageway even with the head doorway and face me."

We started chopping down the passageway.

"Move your asses!" he yelled.

We sprinted.

"When I say go I want you to sprint to the double doors. Hit the doors with both hands and sprint back. The winner does nothing. The losers do ten pushups. Ready, go!"

We sprinted. The distance between the heads and the double doors was about 50 yards and I knew the race would be between Rico and me. I beat him to the doors by a full second, and won by the same margin. This wasn't going to be so bad. I hadn't even hit full speed.

Rico dropped to the deck and had shouted out two pushups before Simpson finished. Rico was standing when Steinway crossed the line.

Maxwell ran alongside Ronald yelling in his ear. Ronald was already tired.

They didn't let Ronald do his pushups. "Save it for later," Maxwell ordered. "Line up!"

We readied ourselves for a second run, which I again won easily. But I was beginning to feel sorry for my roommate. I let Rico pull ahead at the finish of the third race, and I dropped for 10. As I stood I looked at Rico and winked secretly.

"Nice job, Guevarra," shouted Battle. "You beat the rabbit. What's the matter, O'Reilly, getting tired?"

"No, sir!"

"Lose again, asshole, and you'll do 20 pushups!" My spirits -- and Rico's -- flagged.

We ran twice more, and I won both times. Then Battle called a halt. "Okay, gentlemen," he said. "Now that you're warmed up, we're going to begin bear-crawls!"

When we didn't respond he yelled, "Down on your hands and knees!" We dropped to the hard tile deck. "Raise yourselves up on your hands and feet," he yelled.

We did.

"Now try the same race in that position. Ready, go!"

We started awkwardly forward. Within 10 yards I knew I hated bear-crawls. I could feel the slapping of my hands against the cursed deck all the way up through my shoulders. The awkward motion also made my leg muscles ache, and the friction from the tiles rubbed my hands. I really hated bear-crawls! Unfortunately for me, both Rico and Willy were ursine Olympians, and I suffered through three consecutive losses and the resulting pushups.

"Stand up!" Battle yelled.

We stood. I could have kissed him for ending the torture.

"Now we're going to do crab-crawls," he said with obvious glee.

"Sit on the deck facing away from me," he yelled.

We sat. I didn't like where this was leading.

"Lift yourselves up on hands and feet with your bellies in the air."

I lifted, but it was a very awkward position.

"Now," he said. "Same race course! Go!" We went, significantly slower. I stumbled twice on the way down the passageway and twice on the way back. It didn't matter. I was not the best crustacean in the group either. Maxwell paced me, yelling the entire three races. Pushups followed. "Stand again!" Battle yelled.

We stood, but I had trouble lifting myself off the deck.

"Back to wind sprints!"

Good! This I could do. I won the first one by several seconds, and as I watched my three companymates pushing up, I was secretly happy. To hell with bears and crabs, let's keep up this man's exercise.

"O'Reilly, are you tired?" Maxwell asked.

Shit, yes I was tired! "No, sir!"

Max turned to the Battleaxe. "Tom, this isn't fair. O'Reilly's too damned fast. He's bilging his classmates. We should adjust the course."

Battle smiled. "You're absolutely right, Tom. Steinway, come stand by me!"

Ronald hurried to Battle's position more than halfway to the double doors.

"You start from here, Ronald."

"Thank you, sir!" Ronald blurted.

Battle didn't like this answer. "What? Thank you? You douchebag! Hit it for twenty!"

Steinway collapsed on the deck and began struggling. Battle didn't say a word until Ronald finished the pushups.

After Steinway was again braced and facing the double doors, Battle stood just inches from his right ear and said. "I don't like you, Steinway. You're one of the ones who doesn't belong here. I will never intentionally do anything to help you, is that understood?"

"Yes, sir," Steinway stammered.

"Good!" Battle answered. "Remember that from now on." Battle turned to the three of us. "Simpson, stand ten meters closer to the double doors. Guevarra, stay where you are. O'Reilly, take three giant steps backwards."

"Mother, may I, sir?" Why did I say that?

Battle hesitated but didn't crack. "Give me 20, O'Reilly!"

I did. God, were my arms tired!

The race was much closer. I caught Steinway just after the double doors, and Simpson ten yards from the heads on the way back. I beat Rico with only a half yard to spare. Yes, I sprinted.

"Good job, O'Reilly!" Maxwell bellowed. "Let's try again, Tom."

We ran again, and again, and again. Each race they adjusted positions to make the outcome closer. Each time I sprinted, becoming more and more tired. I didn't win them all.

"Okay," Battle said. "Last race. The winner doesn't have to comearound in the morning and gets carry-on at breakfast. Losers do 50 pushups." They adjusted positions again. "Go!"

I was last to the double doors by a goodly margin, but I figured the others were also tired. Maybe as tired as I was. I sprinted. I could feel my system reacting to the strain. I kept it up, passing Steinway and Simpson at the ten-yard mark.

I almost caught Guevarra. Something else caught up with me, however; and immediately after the sprint I raced into the head. I made it as far as the sinks and began vomiting.

"What are you doing, O'Reilly?" asked Battle.

He couldn't hear my retching from his position down the passageway. I had made quite a mess on the floor and edge of the first sink. I turned on the water, took a deep breath, and between heaves I replied loudly, "Barfing my guts out, sir!"

"Clean up any mess you make, you pussy. And hurry up out here. We can't wait just because you get a little sick."

I was almost angry enough to say something about to last night's puke puddle, but I held my tongue in check. I used paper towels to clean up the still-warm remnants of dinner, quickly wiped my face, and hurried back to formation. I must have looked as bad as I felt because several classmates grimaced as they stared at me. Maybe it was the chunks of dinner splattered on my shirt that repulsed them. Most, however, avoided staring at me altogether.

"Sit down!" Maxwell ordered. After we had settled he addressed us, smiling slyly. "First I want to thank the volunteers for participating in tonight's practice comearound. As you can see, it takes energy, stamina, and guts to be successful in this institution. Some of you don't have those qualities and never will. Some of you need our gentle molding and encouragement. Some of you already have what it takes but need to steel your characters. Tomorrow you will all begin comearounds to Mr. Battle and me -- except for classmate Guevarra, of course. You saw what happened out there tonight. If you are not willing to give 100 percent -- even to the point of puking -- then you're not giving it all. We won't accept that. Is that understood?"

A loud, simultaneous "Yes, sir!" reverberated down the passageway.

"Is room 5410 ready for introductions tonight?" asked Battle. "Let's get to it."

Tim Richardson led off. Tim was a tall, blond, striking, athletic-looking young man. He smiled and seemed perfectly confident.

"I'm Tim Richardson," he began. "My father is in the Navy, so I moved around a lot when I was growing up, but I guess you could say that Jacksonville, Florida, is my home."

"What does your Dad do?" Maxwell interrupted.

"He's a Captain. He's Commanding Officer of the Naval Air Station in Jacksonville." Richardson smiled when he said this, knowing that he had laid a very high card on the table. I thought maybe he played it too early, unless he was holding something better in his hand.

Richardson continued. "I attended Jackson High School. I played tennis and volleyball. My mother is usually busy with Wives Club functions. I have two very pretty younger sisters. Another high card! And an older brother who plays football and is presently a First Class in Eighth Company." Trump card! Richardson wins! Smiling, he sat.

Next was a quiet boy named Aaron Rose. Aaron was an average young man, dark-haired, not particularly tall or athletic looking. "My name is Aaron Rose," he started. "My father runs a beef export business in Omaha, Nebraska. I attended B'nai B'rith school in Omaha. I played no sports, but I was a National Merit Scholar and valedictorian of my class. I have a brother who is a doctor, and two older sisters, each married."

The third classmate stepped forward. He was stocky, almost fat, and had large lips and prominently dark bushy eyebrows that clumped in the center of his forehead so that the separation between them was indistinguishable. He also had a very feminine voice that was pleasant to listen to. He could be a good public speaker. Except he couldn't seem to carry through a complete thought. He jumped nervously from topic to topic without organization.

"Ah -- I'm Steve Rogers. No sisters. I played some Pony League baseball for a while -- catcher. Born in Detroit. I have a younger brother and my Dad's an engineer with the city. Mom's dead." We stared at Steve as he regained his place.

I watched Maxwell. Behind his slanted eyes I thought I could see him mentally add Rogers to his list of maybes.

The final occupant of Room 5410 was very interesting. He approached the front of the group almost aristocratically. He was tall, blond haired, and very thin. His face was almost cadaverous, and his eyes a pale and very attractive blue. His cheekbones stood out on the sides of his face like the bony plates of a triceratops. He also had a magnificently hooked nose. I didn't envy. Being a flaming redhead I knew what a target a physical abnormality like his nose must have been for him.

"My name is Hans Rudolph," he said. Hans, what a great name. I wondered briefly if he could skate.

"My parents came to the United States from Switzerland soon after World War II." -- He probably could skate -- " I was born in Albany, New York. My father is a banker. My mother is head nurse at the VA hospital. I played tennis in high school, was ranked third in the state. I was also president of the Chess and Astronomy Clubs and the debate team. I have a sister who is one year older and another sister who is two years younger. Both are blond and very attractive." Staring at that magnificent proboscis, I had my doubts about that last statement.

After Hans sat down, Maxwell addressed us again.

"Tomorrow we will begin splitting up the comearounds. Tom will take half of you for a nice leisurely run in the morning air while I manage the fun exercises in the passageway. In the evening, exactly one hour before meal we will all meet here for a joint comearound. The following day you will change routines. Questions?"

"Sir," asked Tim Richardson. "What happens if we injure ourselves during the exercises? What do we do?"

Maxwell stared at Richardson. "Listen up, pal! If you're injured, stop whatever you are doing and tell us immediately. We'll get you to the Clinic if it's life threatening, or allow you to go to Sick Call later if it's minor."

Battle interrupted. "Why, Richardson? Are you hurt?"

"No, sir!" Tim answered confidently. "It was a hypothetical question."

Battle continued to stare.

"Dismissed!" Maxwell announced.


Inside our room, Rico turned to me. "Jesus, Kevin! I'm sorry about your being sick."

"No problem," I answered. "I just got carried away with the thought of carry-on. It was stupid. I'm never doing that again."

He looked at me all-knowingly. "Yes you will."

Although I outwardly protested his prognostication, inwardly I knew he was right again. He must be part gypsy.

When I finished my shower, Jim Merritt was sitting at my desk.

"What's up?" I asked.

"I don't know what to do," he said. "Ramsey and Polk are driving me crazy. A few minutes ago Jubal threatened to strangle Tommy if he didn't quit. He said we'll all be run to death -- kind of like you were tonight -- if Poole and Steinway and a few others don't leave the Academy soon. And Polk's constant harangue against the system is getting really old. And Tommy Poole is about as depressed as a human being can be."

"Sorry, Jim," I said. "That sounds like a load. But we'd need an army of psychologists to tackle all the problems. And Poole's an enigma. I've only been a midshipman for a week, and already I'm getting protective of the place. I'm not sure that Maxwell isn't right. Do you really think Poole will make a good officer? Maybe he *should* quit."

"Maybe he should," offered Merritt. "But it's Maxwell's and Battle's job to force him out, not ours. Poole and Steinway are our classmates, and we have to help them if we can. If we don't stick together, we're going to be in serious trouble later when it really matters."

I thought about what Merritt had said. "Maybe." I could see that Jim expected more.

"The Polk problem is easiest," I continued. "Tell him to keep his mouth shut if he can't contribute to the group."

"He's hiding something," said Rico from across the room.

"What?" I asked.

"Nobody protests that loudly unless they've got another secret somewhere. I think he's scared to death he won't cut it here, and he's setting himself up to quit. If he doesn't adjust, he'll convince himself that the place is so horrendous he has to leave to satisfy his principles."

"What about his anti-war attitude? That seems genuine enough," Merritt offered.

"Of course it is," Rico answered. "I don't know about you guys, but I don't want to die in some stinking jungle. The war doesn't make sense to me either. We all know that intuitively. But the difference between reasonable men like us and unreasonable ones like Polk is we accept the decisions we've made. If we don't want to fight, we can quit and go to Canada. So can Polk. He stays because he's really not sure and he's seeking reinforcement for his doubts. Do what I do. Ignore him. If you don't answer, he'll give up the complaining."

"Do you really think so?" Merritt asked.

"No doubt about it," Rico answered confidently.

Jim looked at me skeptically.

I smiled. "I trust Rico. The bastard hasn't been wrong about anything yet."

Merritt questioned Rico. "What about Poole and Ramsey? Can't ignore them."

Rico considered. "Listen," he said. "Tonight when Kevin here was kicking my ass in the wind sprints, he let up a bit to let me win a few so I wouldn't kill myself. No offense, but that was stupid. Maxie and Battleaxe knew what he was doing, and look what they did to poor Kevin." He adjusted himself in his seat. "I think that when we're marching or acting as a group against some other group, we've got to stick together. But when it comes to comearounds, it's every man for himself. No offense, Kevin, but there's no way I'm going to let you win, even if you're about to die. It's a matter of self-preservation."

"Fair enough," I said. I smiled. "Just don't fault me for my compassion."

Rico smiled. "You can give me all the comearound compassion you want, my friend. I'll accept it happily. I just won't give it back."

"Why the hell not?" asked an angry Merritt.

"Look, Merritt," answered Rico. "I'll tell you a little secret. I may act self-confident, but I'm not sure I can hack this place academically. You may not have listened the other evening, but my SAT scores are about the lowest in the Company. I have reservations about my longevity once the studying starts. I need every edge, and that means cutting corners and saving my energy when I can. It also means not getting noticed. I'm sorry, but that's the way it is."

I was shocked. Rico was articulate, self-confident, and wise beyond his years. He had also graduated from one of the best schools in the country. I could not believe that his SATs measured his capabilities. His statement shed new light on Midshipman Guevarra.

Merritt stared at Guevarra for a long time. Finally, he straightened. "What you say makes sense, Rico. I think I'll come to you from now on when I want philosophical advice."

I was upset. Rico had usurped my role as mentor and sounding board.

Jim turned to me. "But I'm coming to the redhead when I want action!" I felt relieved.

On the way out, Merritt pointed to my recently-stained gym shirt, which I had left on the floor by the sink cabinet. "Do something about that," he said. "It stinks."

"Spaghetti with meat sauce," I said as he left the room.

I picked up the sweat and food-stained shirt, turned on the sink water full blast and hot, and soaked the shirt. I washed out the chunks and strands and rinsed the stains from the fabric. Then I wrung the shirt and lay it outside on the windowsill to dry, although in this breeze-less humidity, the chances of it drying before August of next year were slim at best.

While I was at the window, breathing the moist air deeply, I heard the plaintive twang of a sad song Willy Simpson was plucking several rooms away. The notes seemed to hang in the thickness and oppression of the dark, moonless night. Pausing, I looked around at the evening activities framed in the bright windows that faced the inner courtyard. I felt like an outsider, peeking with hidden camera eyes into the secrets of a hundred other young men.

Plebes in other Companies were going about their lives much like we were. Some polished shoes. Some cleaned desks and floors. Others sat engaged in vibrant discussion. One other individual leaned out his window in the sixth wing two floors below. We noticed each other and waved acknowledgment. Another spy.

As I swept the dark with my secret gaze, I also saw the silhouette of Ronald Steinway. He was sitting in the deep shadows just outside his room, his backside against the slate roof panels, and his arms were wrapped around his legs. The poor kid was troubled. I thought about calling to him, thought better of it, and retreated into the room.

When I turned, I could see into the Goon Room across the passage. On the deck, practicing pushups but not looking particularly good, was Tommy Poole. He saw me and smiled. He did not see Jubal Ramsey glaring at him from the sink area. I nodded encouragement, then left him to his exercises. I said an extra prayer for Tommy and Ronald that night.

CHAPTER 17

## THE HATED POOL

I hate swimming. That may sound incongruous for a potential Naval officer, but it's an undeniable fact. Growing up in inner city Boston, I never had access to water -- at least not clean swimming water -- and the ocean off Cape Cod is so damn cold, important parts of me shrivel to the size of raisins. I think I have always been secretly afraid that if I stayed too long in the cold water off Cape Cod, my sex organ would disappearance. So I didn't swim very often, and I felt uncomfortable in any pool. Unfortunately, swimming evaluations were the second week's physical training exercise.

Now, the water off Cape Cod is God-awful cold; yet it started as the tropical and luxuriant Gulf Stream, so even way up in Massachusetts it's not icy. The water in the Academy natatorium, however, is piped directly from Antarctica.

The big toe on my right foot touched the surface of the pool briefly the first morning of swim class and I let out an involuntary yelp. I suddenly wanted to thrust that toe into a roaring fire and to follow it with the rest of my person. But, being a plebe, I couldn't flee. Instead I shivered in frosty anticipation on the tiled edge of the old pool, looking at my equally uncomfortable companymates. All of us wore identical blue-with-gold-striped Academy-issue swimming shorts. It was the first time I had seen most of them in any stage of undress.

On the positive side, George Abbott, Danny French, Mike Wojeck, and of course Wesley Lamont each looked like young Adonis. Abbott and Wojeck bulged with muscle, and French and Lamont had sculpted contours I envied. I looked down at myself. I was not impressed. I had no visible fat, but I was not developed like those guys, and I was jealous.

On the negative side, many of my classmates were flabby. It actually hurt my eyes to look at Tommy Poole. He was a corpulent nightmare. Folds of flesh hung on his middle in waves. But he wasn't the only chunker. Ramsey was no Tarzan, and Butkowski -- even though he was huge - also could have stood to lose a few hundred pounds -- or more. Nikolas Papadopalas, Douglas Goto, and Steve Rogers were not thin either. I had an instantaneous thought that it was good that Nathan Spielenberg hadn't returned. He was worse than Tommy.

We had waited only a few minutes before a very bored instructor arrived. "Good morning, gentlemen. Hot enough for you?" That line was a typical Maryland summer greeting, much like, "How do you do?" He didn't want an answer.

"This week," he began, "we'll be testing your swimming abilities. The Navy, as you can well imagine, has some strict requirements that its officers and men be able to swim. Every year you will have at least one semester of swimming instruction, culminating senior year with a one-mile swim in this pool. You will also jump from the tower above us." We looked up in awe at a shaky metal platform suspended miles above the water.

"This week," he continued, "we'll concern ourselves with your more basic abilities. Please stand at poolside. Space yourselves so you don't collide."

Hesitantly, I walked to the edge of that hateful body of water. Extending our arms to separate ourselves, we waited.

"Let's start with just a good wetting down," the instructor said. "Jump in, soak up, and return to your places here on the edge." No one moved.

"Gentlemen," the instructor chuckled. "The water won't hurt you. Jump in. Cool off."

Merritt dove cleanly out over the water and entered with a bare splash. Others followed. But some instinct for self-preservation held my feet glued to the edge. I could not jump even though I wanted to. Eventually everyone other than Simpson and I had entered the water. Several were unhappy with the frigid conditions. Willy and I saw identical fear etched on our faces.

"Jump, I said!" yelled the instructor from a position not three feet away.

As my feet came unstuck with a sucking sound, I saw Willy jump. He chose an interesting method of getting wet without getting cold. He jumped vertically outward, then turned completely around so that he faced the side of the pool on his way down. Throwing out his hands, he grabbed at the pool's edge as his feet entered the frigid water. I could see a look of agony spread over his face as his legs disappeared. Still in mid-leap I saw his arms tense on the pool's edge. As his head disappeared from view, his arms flexed mightily, and he propelled himself out of the water. The force of his desperation sent him high into the air -- so high that he stepped forward and was safely on poolside. I liked his method.

Unfortunately, I had chosen to leap out, not up. As the Arctic wet rushed up to meet me, I decided the only way to save myself would be to try to run across the pool on the near freezing surface. I bicycled my legs frantically. I swear I actually made it five steps before gravity sucked me down into the cold depths.

My toes curled against the undersides of my feet. My legs felt as if they were on frigid fire. Cape Cod raisins? Shit! My gonads disappeared. They crawled up inside my body and hid. I think they were mad at me. They stayed hidden until the swimming evaluations were finished, and then I had to coax them out gingerly.

I screamed, but the water prevented sound. And my open mouth provided a funnel for tons of icy water to enter. I sank to the bottom, ten feet below, thinking that drowning wasn't the worst way to go. But I wasn't finished yet. My curled feet, once in contact with the even-colder hard tile deck of the pool, reacted with vigor. I flexed my legs and sprang upward. I left the water, reaching into the air almost as high as Simpson. I tried to run back to the side of the pool. Two steps later I sank again.

But it wasn't all fun that morning. Eventually I entered an uneasy truce with the cold and swam a warm-up lap. I found out that I wasn't the worst swimmer. My arms and legs were long and strong enough so that I could overcome, barely, my lack of technique. The first morning we swam only a lap. The instructor timed us. If we finished within a minute, he assured us, we would pass Friday's real test. Those who did not pass would be required to spend afternoons on swimming sub-squad until they could. It was not a good prospect.

Wesley Lamont finished before I had reached the far side of the pool. Jim Merritt wasn't far behind. I finished the practice lap in slightly over a minute. Ten of us were deficient. But I was close enough to the mark that I felt I could gut out the final test. Tommy Poole, to add to his troubles, was a non-swimmer.

The instructor dismissed us with more than 15 minutes to spare, just as Maxwell returned. "How'd you do?" he asked. Most answered "Fine, sir!" but he could sense that we had trouble.

"Who didn't pass the preliminary test?" he asked. The ten of us raised our hands. He looked us over, and his eyes paused when they found me. "O'Reilly's not a swimmer, huh?"

"Tell you what," he said. "We've got some time, and I want to try a little positive leadership. We'll do the test again, just among ourselves. Anyone of you ten who passes this one has carry-on at noon meal. What do you say? Line up!"

"Okay," he said. "Swim to the other side and back in less than a minute. Christ, that's easy. Ready, go!"

I dove, trying to hit the water cleanly. I prolonged my time under the surface because my splashing, struggling surface style only seemed to slow me down. Eventually, I broke the plane of the water and struggled forward. I could hear Merritt calling out times as I flopped about, basically moving ahead.

I touched the far wall in less than thirty seconds. Instead of instantly starting for the other side, I drew my legs under my body and placed them against the wall of the pool. I thrust away from the side with thirty seconds remaining. It was going to be close. Pumping furiously I splashed across the pool. I almost collided with Tommy, who, coming the other way, had somehow gotten his trajectory misaligned and was moving sideways across the pool.

167

He saw me, stopped, adjusted himself, and continued on.

With ten yards remaining I decided not to breathe again. I took a large gulp of air, held it, and churned. In this manner I desperately splash-slapped my way to a fifty-nine second victory.

Maxwell smiled. "O'Reilly, you puke-faced bagger. You get carry-on, but if you don't beat 50 seconds on Friday, you'll have ten instant comearounds. Is that understood?"

50 seconds? Not a chance!

"Yes, sir!" I was depressed.

I couldn't lift myself out of the water. My arms were too tired. Jim Merritt nudged Hank Butkowski, and they each grabbed an arm. Butkowski was strong! He lifted me effortlessly and deposited my tired body poolside. I sat near the edge with four other non-swimming classmates, who were sitting beside me. Three more finished together as I turned to watch. Tommy Poole was more than 20 yards behind the others.

Maxwell became impatient. "God-damn it!" he yelled. Then he turned to us. "If shit-bag Poole doesn't finish within another 30 seconds, you all will have to comearound to me tonight, and I won't be as easy as Tom was yesterday."

Classmates began yelling to Tommy to hurry, but how can you hurry someone who's already doing his best?

With 20 seconds remaining, Poole was still ten yards from the edge, when he sucked some water accidentally, and his face registered panic. I wasn't the only one who noticed. Out of a corner of my eye I saw Jim Merritt explode from among the crowd and dive cleanly into the pool. Wesley Lamont wasn't far behind. Even Ramsey, who had only finished a minute ago, reacted. He plopped his substantial bulk into the pool at the water's edge, grabbed the side of the pool, and reached outward toward Tommy. That narrowed the remaining distance considerably.

Things happened quickly. Merritt and Lamont reached Poole, turned him, and kicked toward the waiting Ramsey. Within seconds Jubal had grabbed Tommy and pulled him to poolside. Hank Butkowski lifted Tommy as easily as he had me, and soon Tommy stood bent over on the side of the pool, coughing up water.

Maxwell surveyed the scene. "Okay," he said, "you guys did good. Poole was saved and so were you. Get dressed and let's get moving."

We hurried into the locker room to change.

For parade practice that afternoon Jubal Ramsey taught us how to sing, *"There's a 'skeeter on my peter,"* sung to the tune of *She'll be Coming Round the Mountain*. I was shocked. Were we expected to yell obscenities during marching drills? As it turned out, yes we were.

That evening's comearound was strenuous, but not sadistic. I lost a couple races on purpose to save classmates the pushups, but I never came close to winning a crab or bear crawl.

Room 5413 was next up. There were only three people in the room now that Big Nate had gone his chubby way. Robert James Strong was first. Robert was a light-haired, medium tall individual who spoke with intensity. He was serious about himself.

"My name is Bob Strong," he said. As he spoke, his gaze moved from classmate to classmate, spearing us with his ardor. "I grew up in San Diego, California. My father is a manager at a ship repair facility near downtown. My mother works in an insurance office. Both are active in the Church of Christ. I attended Patrick Henry School where I played soccer and baseball and surfed. I was president of my class. I have three younger brothers."

Next came Ronald Steinway. Ronald had obviously practiced his speech, because he seemed less nervous than usual. He even smiled and kept his Adam's apple under control. "Hi. I'm Ronald Steinway, but you already know that because you've heard my name yelled so often. I was born in Ontario, Canada, but my parents decided it would be better to die of heat exhaustion than frostbite, and they moved to Phoenix, Arizona when I was a baby." We laughed. He was doing well.

"I attended Santa Lucia High School in Phoenix. I was president of the Astronomy and Metallurgy Clubs, and played the trumpet in the State Champion marching band, but don't ask me to sing because I can't carry a tune. My father is a shopkeeper. My mother works for the head of Clinical Psychology at Arizona State University. I'm an only child." He smiled.

I applauded. He deserved it. Several classmates joined in.

The final occupant of the room was Willy Simpson. Willy was okay. He didn't exactly seem an ideal midshipman, but I liked him nonetheless. He was slightly taller than me but thinner, and he was exceedingly awkward, always tripping and falling over things or dropping implements or food trays. He had fair skin and a mouth full of oversized teeth so large that it seemed hard for him to bring his lips together. But he smiled so often, he seldom had reason to close his mouth.

"I'm Willy Simpson," he said in his slow, bashful, Southern style. He looked frequently at the deck and shuffled his feet. "I'm from Greenville, South Carolina. My father is Chief of Police. My mother is a housewife. I went to Blackridge High School. Didn't play any sports, although I'm pretty good at most things. I have a very pretty twin sister who is presently dating the ex-captain of our school's football team. If any of you want to steal her from her boyfriend, my Dad would be very happy. He doesn't like him very much, and neither do I."

Willy started to sit, remembered something, then burst into a broad, contagious smile. "I also play a little guitar, in case you haven't heard." We applauded.


That evening Tommy Poole visited the room.

"Hi, Tommy," I said. "Have a seat. I'd offer you a drink, but after this morning's pool incident, I'll bet you won't be thirsty again for a long time."

Tommy Poole sat cautiously in Donny Delmont's ex-chair. "I'm having big problems," he said, pausing. "Maxwell and Battle are out to get me, and I don't know if I can measure up. Do you have any ideas about how I can turn them off? Because, I'm starting to think about quitting, and I promised myself I wouldn't do that, no matter what."

I answered. "You can't do anything, Tommy. At least not until you improve yourself physically. It's their job to weed out whoever they consider misfits, and you are a perfect target. You're going to have to accept it."

"But what can I do?" he asked. "They're going to kill me and I have to stay."

"Oh, no, they're not!" said Rico. Tommy turned toward him, hope mirrored on his face.

"What do you mean?" he asked.

"They're not going to kill you, Tommy. Use that enormous head of yours. This is still America. Maxie and the Battle act like Gestapo, but they only have power if you give it to them."

Tommy was confused. "I don't understand."

"Look," Rico continued. "They can't beat you up, or imprison you, or withhold food. And all you can do in response to their demands is the best you can. If they're not happy, the worst you get are a few pushups and a good screaming in your ear. That's not so bad. What do you think they would do if you suddenly stood up and walked away from them?"

I was just as anxious as Tommy to hear Rico's answer.

"I'll tell you," he said. "Nothing! You have complete control. If you really want to make it through the summer, you can."

Tommy considered. "Maybe you're right," he said. "So you think I should defy them?"

"No, no!" Rico answered quickly. "You don't need to defy them. Just keep improving, do the best you can, and ignore the insults. They can't force you to quit. They know that, but they don't let on. Just hang in there, one day at a time like Kevin and me."

Tommy's face lit up, and he relaxed. "You know, I think you're right."

"Good," replied Rico, "because good advice is not free."

"What do you mean?" asked Tommy.

"Just remember this when I need help with my homework."

"No problem," replied Poole. "I'll be your tutor."

"It's a deal," Rico said, extending his hand.

Tommy and Rico shook hands. Tommy turned so that he could see the two of us. "You guys have a good room. I wish I lived over here."

Tuesday night, after another moderate comearound and another hectic dinner, the final plebe room introduced itself. Summer thunderstorms had rumbled all day. The wind was so bad in the morning that Battle had not taken us on the run. Instead, we did calisthenics in the passageway. That night lightning flashed outside and the rumble of thunder echoed in the passageway.

"My name is Douglas Goto," the first occupant introduced himself, emphasizing the name Douglas. I had not heard Doug say more than two words that weren't screams, except for

171

a curious incident that happened several days earlier when I introduced him as 'Doug' Goto. He told me politely that the name 'Doug' was not his name -- which was the wrong thing to say to Kevin O'Reilly. From that day forward I called him 'Doug,' sometimes 'Douggy. No matter how boisterously he protested, the nickname stuck. Eventually he adjusted. His yearbook refers to him by the nickname.

At more than six feet, Doug Goto was tall for an Japanese American. He was also muscular, and walked with an athletic grace. He had a ruddy complexion, but no trace of an accent. He also had the laughingest pair of eyes I had ever encountered. I liked Doug Goto. He always seemed ready to burst into a grin, even when things were not going well. Doug was about as American as any of us -- even more so than many.

"My grandparents came to the United States from Japan at the turn of the century and settled in Baltimore. They run a small restaurant downtown. I attended Baltimore Polytechnic Institute. I played golf and the tuba, and was in charge of the marching band. I was a National Merit Scholar and president of the Electronics Club. I have two very small -- and very pretty -- sisters named Christina and Jennifer."

Next up was B. J. Wilson. BJ was short and somewhat small framed, but very suave -- in a feminine way. He had perfect features. Eventually he would sport mounds of dark, wavy, hair. He had piercing blue eyes and incredibly white, straight teeth. I was also willing to bet that no pimple had ever dared to invade that perfect face.

"My name is William Janus Wilson," he said. "I was born in Manhattan. My father is executive producer for several television sitcoms. My mother is an ex-actress." It was his superior attitude that earned him the nickname 'BJ' -- which was not an affectionate moniker, and which stuck to him even tighter when we found out he didn't like nicknames. BJ was one of those people who somehow pissed me off in almost everything he did, even when he meant well.

"I didn't have time for any sports in high school," he continued, "and my private school offered only squash and fencing. I also have an older sister who is a fashion model."

The third roomie in 5414 came forward.

"I'm Michael Donald Wojeck," he said. Mike was a medium tall, stocky boy with a square jaw, prominent facial features, and thinning reddish hair. He was extremely easy going and reveled in social interaction, and when he smiled his light blue eyes narrowed into thin slits.

"My father is also in the Navy. He's a mustang Commander. Right now he's retired and the family is living here in Annapolis. I attended Annapolis High School. I played a little football and threw the shot put on the track team. I wasn't president of anything, but I did join quite a few organizations in school. I have a sister and a brother, both unmarried."

The final member of the room stepped forward. I didn't know much about him. He had been very quiet thus far in the summer.

"My name is Elliot Mark Zimmerman," he said in an accent that was almost British-New England. Being from Boston I immediately recognized the Beacon Hill in Elliot. He was of medium height and unmuscular, with dark brown, very intense, eyes and pleasant features. He was also soft spoken, self-assured, and probably very wealthy.

"I was born in Boston," he said, "and attended Phillips Exeter Academy in Andover Massachusetts. I played tennis. My father is an investment banker. My mother is an attorney. I have no siblings."

CHAPTER 18


*SURVIVAL AND THREATS*


Day followed day without letup.  We marched, we polished, we recited, we ran, and we coped.  And as the sweltering, grueling days plowed relentlessly one after another into deepest eastern summer, we also sweated.  It was physically and emotionally difficult, but I couldn't really complain.  Even after working off the ten comearounds to Maxwell for my 57 second swimming record that second Friday, I didn't feel particularly victimized.

Tommy Poole and Ronald Steinway were victims.  Maxwell and Battle ran the absolute piss out of them.  They couldn't recover from any group of exercises before the next batch started.  But somehow they kept plugging along.  By the end of the second week Tommy could struggle through 20 pushups, and Ronald had left the straggling runners and joined the middle pack.

I didn't eat much in the Mess Hall, but I sure fed on endorphins.  I outsprinted Battle every chance I got, and improved my strength so that I could do 71 pushups -- plus one to beat Army. Eventually I could do more than 100.  But just when I thought I had it all down pat -- about midway through the summer -- the focus of the squadleaders training shifted and I was lost again.


BJ Wilson was a smack.  He wasn't the only smack, but he was by far the worse one.  A smack is a plebe who curries obsequious favors at the expense of his classmates.  Maybe it was because BJ grew up in an "I-love-ya-baby" entertainment atmosphere, where boot licking, butt kissing, and sucking-up have distinct advantages.  Not being a fantastic athlete or the most charisma-laden individual, he may have seen smack-dom as the only way he could excel. Then again, maybe he was just a son-of-a-bitch.

One evening meal during the third week Maxwell addressed BJ. "Wilson!"

BJ's reply was sickeningly sweet.  "Yes, sir?"

"Are you serious about the tickets for the theater in October?"

"Yes, sir," answered BJ. "The Brigade will be in New Jersey on the seventeenth for the Cornell game, and the last bus won't leave for the return trip to Annapolis until midnight. Father has arranged for the limo to pick me up at the stadium and take me to the apartment for a few hours. I'll ask Alfred to drop you and your dates off at the early show and to pick me up on the way back to Cornell afterward. We should make it in plenty of time."

"How about the tickets, pal?" asked Maxwell skeptically. "Those are expensive."

"No charge," BJ offered. "My Mom can get as many as she wants for free."

"Well, okay, Wilson," Maxie replied, "but don't expect any special treatment for this."

BJ smiled. "Of course not, sir."

Polk raised his eyes heavenward. Next to him Rico's face held an enigmatic smile.

That evening Rico and I visited the Goons before lights out. Poole was visiting Battle for a special motivational comearound.

"Isn't BJ Wilson a smack?" asked Jeff Polk.

We all agreed.

"He offered the tickets to the squadleaders but not to his roommates or to any classmates!" added Polk. "And he told Doug Goto that he'll be moving to another room come academic year. He says he wants to surround himself with the up-and-comers."

Jeff looked at Merritt and said, not altogether in jest, "That probably means you, Jim."

"Shit," I said. "What an asshole."

"Up-and-comers, huh?" said Jubal Ramsey in a quiet voice from across the room. "He'll get his comeuppance all right."

"What should we do?" I asked. "Short-sheet his rack?"

Jubal and Jeff laughed like I had made an intentional joke. I hadn't. Short-sheeting was about the extent of my practical joke experience.

"No," Jubal said slowly, "I think this may call for more direct action."

"Like what?" I asked naively.

175

"The fewer people in on it the better," said Jeff. "That way if a squad leader asks, you can say you don't know anything."

Merritt spoke. "Maybe if somebody asked him to let up on the brown-nosing?"

"Wouldn't help," said Rico. "He's a born smack. Gets advantage however he can."

"Hardesty is a smack too, and so's Lamont," added Ramsey.

I spoke. "No, Joe, not Lamont. I'm sure of it."

Jubal didn't respond.

"Kevin's right, Joe," added Rico. "Lamont is like Merritt and Pirelli. They get their jollies from being the perfect plebe. Lamont's no smack. He pitches in with the best of them. Wilson never does, and Hardesty is too self-righteous. He thinks he has all the answers."

Jubal didn't answer.

I changed the subject. "Tommy is showing real improvement."

Jubal looked at me and shook his head slowly. "Poole and Steinway have got to go!"

"I don't see it, Joe," I answered. "Tommy's doing everything we are and then some. I'm rooting for him." I looked around, but support was thin. Even Merritt seemed skeptical.

"Poole won't last the summer," predicted Jubal. Rico didn't object to Joe stealing the prognostication role, so either Jubal was right or Rico wasn't sure yet about Tommy's fate.


Rico chose an interesting way to bring BJ Wilson down to size, although I'm not sure he did it intentionally. The revenge happened a weekday evening meal the third week of Plebe Summer.

The squadleaders had braced us against the bulkhead, and asked us rates interspersed with sports, political, or historical questions. Like Trivial Pursuit -- except for the pain, of course.

That evening Rico was having a terrible battle with stomach distress. We had eaten greasy -- but absolutely delicious -- pepperoni pizza for dinner. In fact, my two pieces -- gobbled in haste near the end of the meal while Maxwell's attention was elsewhere -- sat as an uncomfortable lump in my middle.  Every unintentional burp reintroduced its spicy contents.

As I stood beside Rico, I could hear his dull rumblings and grumblings of gastric turmoil.  He shifted and moaned in discomfort.  On his left side, BJ Wilson was too busy bilging classmates with volunteered answers to notice Rico's distress.

Rico finally leaned toward me when the squadleaders' attention was focused elsewhere.  "Kevin, stand by," he whispered.  "I have *got* to cut one."

I heard the strain in his voice, and I could sense that despite the delicate nature of our present predicament, Rico had reached gastronomic meltdown.

But he knew he couldn't explode for fear the noise would draw attention to himself.  Plebe survival equates with being unnoticeable.  Despite the obvious pain, Rico showed restraint and cunning.  He waited.  He nursed his innards, eased the inevitable along, and eventually something fizzed out of him.  He followed the fizz with an enormous sigh.

Relief obvious in his new stance, we waited for our next question.  But Rico had forgotten a very important fact.  The particular type of gas that now floated freely in our vicinity, when allowed to accumulate in the nether regions of the human body, will often develop a distinct and somewhat unpleasant odor.

Oh, what an odor!  The staunchest swamp dweller would have gagged.  Rico 'noticed' it first.  I inhaled the aroma an instant later.  Rico nudged me and whispered desperately.  "Move right!  Hurry!  Pass it on!"

By now I needed no encouragement.  I nudged the plebe on my right and repeated Rico's request.  The word spread, as did the smell, and everyone to my right shifted six feet until we were out of the danger zone.  There was now a gap in the ranks to Rico's left -- but his 'gift' drifted left also, and soon there were mutterings as plebes on the other side staggered.

A commotion ensued.  Several plebes muttered, "Oh, my God!"  The line shifted left.

All except BJ Wilson, who either had no olfactory sense or else had been living in New York City for too long.  He remained dutifully in his place on Rico's left, smack dab in the middle of the noxious cloud, now separated from his classmates on either side by several feet.

177

Maxwell and Battle, hearing the confusion, stopped their merriment and tromped down the line. They approached the now-isolated BJ.

"Hey, pal!" began Maxwell. "What the hell is up with you?" Then the smell hit him like a two-by-four. His eyes expanded in his head like two suddenly inflated balloons. He staggered, almost falling in the process, let out an incredibly creative curse, and backed hastily out of range. "You rotten, bilging douchebag!" he screamed. "I can't believe you did that. Hit it for 100!" His arm waved vigorously in the air as he retreated.

BJ Wilson hesitated, torn between the wrath of Midshipman Maxwell and the need to protest his innocence. He opened his mouth, obviously ready to shift the blame to someone else.

Battle didn't let him. "Did you hear what Maxie just asked you to do?" he screamed. "If you're not on the deck in less than a second, I'll see that your death is slow and painful."

Wilson dropped to the tile and began cranking out pushups, reluctantly singing out the numbers in time to his up-and-down motions.

Maxwell had backed against the far wall of the passageway and was gulping down deep, cleansing breaths to rid his lungs of the contamination. He was too overcome by the fumes to notice how many of BJ's classmates sported secret and heartfelt smiles at his predicament.

Everyone but Rico and me thought that Wilson had brought about his own fate, and we weren't about to admit otherwise. It remained our secret. Why didn't Rico confess and save his classmate the unwarranted exercise? He's not stupid, that's why!


BJ's scatological downfall was the topic of conversation that evening in the Goon Room, where there was universal lack of sympathy for Wilson the smack. Even Tommy Poole admitted that he thought Wilson was a shit-head. These were strong words from Tommy, who blushed at each of Maxwell's 'f-words.' Tommy blushed a great many times that summer. But tonight Poole was finally one of the guys. After that, he said shit-head a lot.

We discussed the major event of the week, the upcoming 'white glove' inspection on Saturday afternoon. Our rooms had been inspected by Maxwell and Battle, and most of our clothing had tumbled to the deck so many times that the floors outside our lockers were brightly polished. But this inspection was to be special for two reasons. First, it would mark the first time the squadleaders dared risk a white glove on our clean-up efforts, and second, it would be our first encounter with our Company Officer, Marine Captain Rusty 'Bull' Dillingham.

Both Maxwell and Battle had mentioned the 'Bull' during the preceding days. Maxie called him 'one crazy-assed Marine.' Battleaxe didn't appreciate Maxie's reference to 'crazy' and 'Marine' in the same sentence but did allow that Captain Dillingham was 'an interesting character.' We plebes had speculated among ourselves concerning this unknown factor in our survival, and none of us were particularly happy to be led by someone gung-ho, crazy, -- or both.

Preparations for the formation and inspection began Friday evening. Rico and I divided the room into cleaning zones. I was responsible for the sink, the shower area, and the closet. Rico would do the main area. We each were responsible for our own beds, desks, and lockers.

Dividing up the room cleaning was the wrong thing to do. Rather it was the wrong thing for *me* to agree to. Friday night after meal I attacked my zone with a vengeance. I spent an hour in the shower, scrubbing down the walls and floors, and drying everything carefully with towels. I also scrubbed the sink and faucets tirelessly, even going so far as cleaning inside the faucet spout. Jim Merritt had made a list of obscure and unlikely places to clean where the inspection team would surely elect to put the white glove, and I copied his list, intending not to forget a single cleanable spot.

While I worked my ass off, Rico read another of those damn sex novels. I could see the ridiculous spy hero on the cover, buxom blondes holding tightly to each arm, as he karate-kicked a black-clad opponent.

I became nervous about the amount of time remaining and Rico's apparent lack of concern. "Rico," I said after I finished in the shower, "don't you think you better start cleaning? It'll take at least an hour to wax the floor."

"No sweat, Kevin. I'll get it done."

A half-hour later I had finished the sink, and Rico still hadn't stirred. "Rico, when are you going to start?"

Rico put down the book and looked up at me in exasperation. "Look, Kevin. I'll get it done. If you're not satisfied with my efforts, why don't you do it yourself?"

"What?" I exclaimed. "We're supposed to be helping each other."

Rico stared at me, decided I was serious about the cleaning, then said. "Okay, you do the floor on your side of the room, and I'll do mine. Next inspection I'll do the shower and sink." He returned to his reading.

I thought about his offer. I knew the arrangement wouldn't work because of the fundamental personality differences between us. I didn't want to get into any trouble and wanted everything perfect. Rico was able to settle for the minimum. He'd never be able to do the floor to my satisfaction, and I'd worry that we would get into trouble because of it. And since a few pushups didn't bother him in the least, he'd think I was putting too much effort into the clean-up. His cost-benefit ratio was vastly different from mine.

I grunted, got out the mop and wax, and started on my side of the room. I mopped the entire floor, cleaning the mop in the shower. Next I waxed the deck according to the instructions on the bottle. An hour later I had finished the entire room. The only help Rico had given me was to lift his feet when I waxed under his desk. I watched him reading as I worked in his area. He was smiling. He knew it would come to this. Sometimes Rico's gift for understanding human nature pissed me off.

I had just sat at my desk when Ronald Steinway entered and walked haphazardly across my newly-waxed floor. "Ronald! Stop!" I yelled without thinking. I hoped that Maxwell hadn't heard that -- we were supposed to be quiet in the evenings.

Ronald saw my distress and came to a dead stop.

On stocking feet, I glided to him and checked the floor behind him for scuffs or mars. None were apparent. "Jesus, Ronald," I said. "I just waxed the floor."

Ronald looked around sheepishly. "Sorry," he said. "We're waiting until the morning. We were going to do it after morning meal and let it dry while we're at lectures."

I dropped down onto hands and knees and put my right cheek against the glistening tile. For several seconds I scrutinized the deck where Ronald had trod. It looked wonderful! I felt proud. Was I becoming my mother? I admonished Ronald. "Get those shoes off before you take another step." I was becoming my mother.

Ronald held my back for balance as he unshod. Afterward he sat at Delmont's desk and pulled a letter from his pocket. "My parents again," he said, handing it to me.

"If this is personal . . .?" I asked, holding the envelope.

"No, no. Read it," he said.

I pulled out a letter written in wonderfully sweeping strokes -- cursive was a talent I could never master despite eight years of penmanship in parochial school. This letter had come from his mother. It was dated last week.

*"Ronald,"* it said. *"So glad to hear from you. I'm happy that everything's fine. I told Professor Riggins the other day about how well you are doing, and he's offered to have you speak in his Modern Sociology class about military training and its effect on the human psyche. I hope you don't turn bloodthirsty on me (joking, love). I am so proud. You'll never know how wonderful it makes me feel. Love you always, MOM"*

I handed the letter to Ronald who was looking at me expectantly. "Shit, Ronald. Did you tell them this was a country club or something? They think you're happy here."

He stared at me for a long time. "I can't leave here, Kevin. I have to stay."

"Well, if you do, you do. But prepare yourself for more pain. It's coming, you and I both know that. Once the Brigade gets back, there'll be no let up."

Steinway nodded his head sadly. "I know. But I have no alternatives."

"There are always alternatives, Ronald."

Ronald looked up quickly. "You think I should quit, don't you?" His feelings were somehow hurt by my lack of sympathy.

"Not unless *you* want to, Ronald," I replied. "It's *your* choice. But everybody can see that you're not happy. Hell, you're depressed all the time. Why stay here and be miserable? It doesn't make any sense."

Ronald stared out the window. "You don't understand, Kevin. I have to stay. My parents are depending on me."

"Then have your Mom run the morning comearounds and your Dad do your pushups. It's not their place to put that kind of pressure on you."

Ronald stood up, not saying another word, took his shoes in hand, and departed.

After Ronald was gone, Rico looked up from his book. He had a strange look on his face. His handsome features seemed softer, almost glowing.

"Christ," he sighed. "I have got to get laid soon."

"Fat chance," I replied. "No girls until Parents' Weekend. That's still a month away."

Rico smiled wistfully. "Kevin," he said. "Come on, amigo. Don't you want to see your girlfriend naked right now? Can't you imagine yourself doing sweet things with her?"

I could tell from the way Rico talked that he wasn't bullshitting me. He was 'experienced.' I was jealous again. But I wasn't about to tell him that I had no girlfriend and that I had never seen any girl naked or done anything particularly unusual during my brief periods of clothed contact with the opposite sex.

"Yeah," I replied. "I think about all those things, but wishing isn't going to make it so."

Rico smiled devilishly. "Want to bet I get laid before Parents' Weekend?"

"No way!"

"Ten bucks says so," he said smugly. "Is it a bet?"

"How you gonna prove it?"

"Don't worry, I will."

I accepted the bet.

CHAPTER 19

## *INSPECTIONS*

We had been instructed by the squadleaders to wear a fresh set of tropical whites for the Saturday uniform inspection prior to noon meal.  Captain Dillingham was inspecting.

As I examined myself in the mirror over the sink, I was impressed.  I looked great.  Four weeks of exercise had eliminated every inch of spare body tissue and had nicely hardened and contoured what remained.  With my shirt blazingly white and tucked expertly, my brass belt buckle - top included - gleaming, and the brim of my combination cap pledged to a black brilliance, I had no doubt I was a studly young man.  Even the red stubble sprouting on my naked skull looked great.

Noon formations on the weekend were outside in Tecumseh Court, where we didn't have to chop, so after exiting the Company area, Rico and I strolled down the stairs to the Rotunda.  Awestruck crowds wandered the broad multi-patterned terrazzo floor, viewed the many 'Go-Navy' displays, and visited the sample midshipman room.  The whole setup generated admiration and support, and I could feel eyes on me as we began our strut across the Rotunda floor toward the doors.  Some of those eyes were beautiful, and some of the creatures possessing those eyes were young and nubile, and the scents of lovely perfumes made me heady.  Damn, I was horny!

But, who was I kidding?  Rico was the center of gravity for the attention focused toward us.  As we walked to the exit doors, young female bodies moved in our direction.  I swear I could hear splatters from females drooling on the terrazzo as he passed.  And Rico was really sucking it up.  He had a quality about him that was absolutely irresistible, and he knew how to use it.

I began to worry about my ten dollars.

At the moment we reached the exit doors, a flock of young lovelies blocked our path.  One blond beauty looked at Rico, and I swear he stabbed her with his gaze.  She staggered.  Rico helped her steady herself, and as he did so placed something small and paper in her hand.  He held her hand for a moment, squeezing the hand with the gift shut tightly.

"Are you okay?" he asked.  Brilliant teeth flashed in his brown face.  His Hispanic eyes sparkled.  His voice held promise.  Why couldn't I do that?  The girl smiled and Rico released her hand, and we soon passed out into Tecumseh Court.  Rico never looked back.

"What was that all about?" I asked as we strutted down the steps.

Rico reached into his pocket and pulled out another note -- one of several.  He handed it to me.  I looked around carefully and read it.

*"I've been watching you.  You are the most beautiful thing I have ever seen.  I think I'm in love.  Let's talk.  Leave a message for me at the Main Office with your name and phone number."*

It was signed Rico Guevarra, Room 5404.

I handed it back to him, and he precisely replaced it in his pocket, careful not to mar the sharp, flat outline of his pants.  "Do you think that will work?"  I asked.

Rico gave me an 'are-you-shitting-me?' look, then smiled.  "Watch and learn, redhead!"

Many of our companymates were already waiting when we arrived.  Plebes inspected each other with a desperate intensity, adjusting uniform line-ups, blowing the fuzzy dust from fellow shoulder boards, and correcting cap placement.  When Chuck Chalmers, who usually stood in front of me in the outdoor formations, turned so that I could view him from the rear, I noticed one of the dreaded 'Irish pennants' hanging from his shirt collar.  Unless I could do something quickly, this was cause for panic.

"Stand still, Chuck," I warned.  "You have an Irish pennant back here."

"Shit!" he exclaimed.  "I checked before we left the room."  I tried to get a solid grip on the small thread.  'Irish pennants' are any loose threads that extend from the fabric, and are usually found along seams or wherever any sewing took place.  You'd be surprised how many there are on a typical shirt.  I was sure Chuck had examined the shirt before he put it on, but Irish Pennants sometimes spring from the material of their own volition, particularly during the period between final checking and uniform inspection. Anyway, he missed one.

I grabbed at the thread end with the tips of my thumb and forefinger but couldn't get enough of a grip to be able to yank it out. I tried again but still could not get purchase on the damned thing.

"I can't get it, Chuck," I said. "I'll try to push it up under the ends of your collar."

"Thanks," he replied.

I worked on the thread until I had it bent over and tucked precariously under his shirt collar. It would stay -- maybe -- until the end of formation.

"Form up!" Battle ordered.

I forgot about Chuck's pennant and positioned myself so that a straight line could connect the tips of the toes of all the feet in my rank, and so that my head was precisely behind Chuck's. I also adjusted my foot placement so that exactly 90 degrees separated my feet.

Battle stood at the front of the formation and scanned each rank while Maxwell moved among us, checking our uniforms. There was no time to change anything except cap placement, and Maxie knew this. That didn't stop him from handing out comearounds for every minuscule violation of the Maxwell Uniform Code. He couldn't find anything wrong with me.

I puffed up my chest and winked at him. I got one comearound on general principles.

Before Maxwell could finish with us, there came a sudden hush. I sensed that something momentous was happening. Maxwell looked frightened as he hurried to the end of the formation to stand with Battle.

I could hear feet approaching to our rear. Battle sang out! "Midshipmen Second Class Battle and Maxwell reporting, sir! Twenty-third Company plebes are ready for inspection, sir!" From the sound of the clip-clopping, they must have been enormous feet.

The feet-sounds stopped, and a crisp, professional voice sounded out. "Very well, Mister Battle. Let's review the troops."

Battle and Maxwell followed the stranger to the front of the first rank.

Head straight, I strained to look sideways until I nearly peeked out of my ears.

I could just barely see the figures begin the inspection. Battle led. His head moved slowly up from toe to cap on the first plebe. When he finished inspecting he pivoted smartly, took a single forward step that brought him exactly in front of the second person, and pivoted again to face the next victim. Each time he pivoted he brought his heals together with a sharp click. It was very impressive.

But I said 'victim' and that isn't exactly true. I could see Battle's face from where I stood, and he wasn't concentrating on his inspection. Rather, he watched Captain Dillingham. Battle was nervous about the impression the inspection would have on the Company officer. The plebe in front of Battle could have been wearing a red shirt, yellow pants, and a baby blue hat, and I don't think he would have noticed. This was very interesting. Tommy Battle lived in awe, or in fear, of another human being. I recorded this fact in my memory for future reference.

Did I say human being? When I caught my first glimpse of the 'Bull,' I wasn't sure. The person who followed Battle was *that* different. Captain Dillingham seemed an anachronism, an obvious throwback to more primitive times. My eyes widened, and Rico, who stood next to me, grunted. He was impressed also.

Bull was enormous; at least six feet six inches, and I'll bet he weighed 230 pounds. He had somewhat Cro-Magnon features -- his facial bones and eye ridges protruded, his chin jutted forward aggressively, and his skin was pulled tightly over his face. He was also without a visible once of fat. He had no hair -- by choice. Judging from the way the sunlight reflected from the part of the taut skull that showed beneath his cap, he also polished his bald head. Even his ears were enormous. Dumbo would have been envious. But Dumbo would never have mentioned anything to the Bull about his ears. I'll bet no one did.

His lips were full and wrinkly and covered large predatory teeth, and his blue eyes inspected the uniform and personage of every plebe with a fiery intensity. Under his starched green Marine Corps uniform shirt I could see muscles ripple as he moved. His arms bulged in his sleeves. What a monster! No wonder Battle feared this guy. I almost wet myself watching him.

Bull checked each plebe. Sometimes he would bend over from lofty heights and put his face almost on top of some abnormality. He focused for nearly ten seconds on the brim of Doug Goto's hat, then passed on to the next plebe.

Maxwell whispered a quiet comearound to Doug as he passed.

Bull didn't say much. He was too busy being professional. But he became confused when he stood before Tommy Poole. He stared at Tommy's head, then adjusted Tommy's cap. Leaning back, he stared at the revised placement, frowned, and readjusted the cap. After several corrections, Bull moved on to another plebe. But before he started on the next person, he glanced back toward Tommy, started to say something, shook his caveman head in perplexity, and continued inspecting.

Maxwell gave Tommy ten crooked-head comearounds.

In less than three minutes the inspection team had finished the front of the first rank and started their march up the back side of the first rank.

It was then that I remembered Chuck Chalmer's Irish Pennant problem. I concentrated on the spot where I had hidden the thread, and I could see the bent-over end quiver in anticipation, almost as if a breeze had stirred it. But no breeze pushed the thick, summer air.

As the group approached, the thread peeked from under the collar. When Battle reached the back of Chuck's head, I swear it sprang out and tried to trip him.

In the dark recesses of the under-collar, the Irish Pennant must have sucked sustenance from surrounding material, or maybe it underwent some type of molecular mitosis at the cotton-cell level. It now waved in an imaginary breeze like a snake hanging from a tree.

Battle spotted it. He couldn't have missed it. It nearly slapped him across the face. He paused, unsure what to do. Finally, he whispered a quick couple comearounds in Chuck's ear and hurried on, hoping, I'm sure, that Bull wouldn't notice.

No such luck. Dillingham pointed to the thread, which now seemed three times its original thickness and to stretch almost to Chuck's waist. Bull frowned, shook his head, and went on to the next person. Maxwell gaped at the python-sized pennant. He grabbed and pulled. It didn't give up easily. Chalmer's head snapped back from the force of Maxwell's sudden jerk.

Maxwell tried again, but the super thread mocked him. Maxwell handed Chuck an additional ten comearounds.

Chuck moaned.

Now it was my rank's turn. I pulled my hands backward, and with my thumbnails, located the seams of my trouser legs. I placed my thumbs along those seams. I looked at my feet

187

to ensure I had not somehow lost my perfect ninety degrees. I hadn't. I squared my shoulders and pulled my head back. As Battle approached, I sucked in my gut and puffed out my chest in anticipation.

Battle glanced at me without seeing anything. His eyes, as they passed in front of me on their memorized journey from bottom to top, didn't recognize who I was. I could have crossed my eyes and stuck out my tongue and it would have had no effect. I didn't.

Battle pivoted and departed smartly -- then an enormous shadow passed across the sun. The eclipse was Bull Dillingham.

From my eyes-in-the-boat vantage point all I could see of Bull was the top of his uniform shirt which held about ten rows of multicolored ribbons. This guy was a hero! I had been taught to recognize the major awards, and on this muscular chest I could see from the tiny bronze stars on his Vietnam Service and Campaign Ribbons that Bull had been to the land of steamy jungles on four separate occasions. He had also won three Navy Achievement Awards, two Commendation Medals, three Purple Hearts, a Bronze Star, and something I thought was the Silver Star. Holy shit! It didn't matter any more to me what size he was. This guy had my respect and admiration.

Bull inspected me briefly; and because of the height disparity, I never saw his warrior's face over my cap brim. I must have met his standards, because he moved, without comment, to the next plebe, and I let out a slow sigh of relief. Soon the inspection was completed, and Dillingham marched toward Bancroft Hall to await us at our Company tables for noon meal.

Once Bull had left earshot, Battle moved to the front of the formation. "Okay, assholes," he said just quietly enough so that the civilians standing at the entryway to T-Court couldn't hear, "most of you were barely acceptable. Some of you were not and will be punished. Captain Dillingham will be joining us for meal, and at precisely 1300 we will begin room inspections."

"You had better be ready." Maxwell added.

They turned to face the summer Second-class Brigade staff which had formed at the entry to T-Court. The Midshipman Brigade Commander gave the command to come to attention and to march into Bancroft Hall to chow. We were so good the crowd cheered! -- Just kidding.

Bull chose to eat with Battle, and I was spared reciting rates for his benefit. Merritt and Pirelli were in full glory, however. Maxwell left us alone, and I was grateful for that small favor.

On the way to our rooms I accompanied Rico to the Brigade Offices where he asked confidently if he had gotten any phone or other messages. The plebe on duty sorted through the Twenty-third Company box and pulled out a note to Midshipman Rico Guevarra.

"A very pretty young blonde left this," he said jealously.

Rico took the note, glanced at it briefly, then handed it to me. Cindy Stanver had written the note and left her number. She wanted Rico to call immediately. "See you upstairs," Rico said as he headed off toward the phones.

I gave our room a once-over, recleaned the sink, and waited.

When Rico arrived, he was beaming. "I'm throbbing in anticipation," he said, "of *tonight's* rendezvous."

"Tonight?" I blurted. "How are you going to arrange that?"

"Kevin," he said seriously. "You've got no huevos, compadre."

That wasn't true. It had been two weeks since swimming evaluations, and I was just fine.

He continued. "I talked to Cindy, my dream girl, and she'll meet me this evening after lights out. We'll take a leisurely drive in her car over to Hospital Point and get acquainted there."

"How the hell are you going to get from Bancroft Hall to Hospital Point in a car with a girl without being seen, smart guy?" I asked.

Rico smiled. "Where there's a will, there's a way."

I laughed. Rico had real *balls*, mine were Natatorium-shrunk raisins.

Room inspection began exactly at 1300 as scheduled. Captain Dillingham was an absolute stickler for promptness. The three of them began on the far side of the passageway with Room 5401. I heard Hank Butkowski yell out an "Attention on Deck!" The inspection lasted two minutes. I stood in our doorway with my back pressed against the wall so they couldn't see me, and I strained to hear what discrepancies they had discovered. There was no yelling, although at one point I did hear a dull thump that could only be a chair being replaced in a desk indentation. After Room 5401, they moved down the passageway to 5403, the Goon Room.

Since 5403 was across the passageway from our room, I slipped out of sight and listened. Jubal Ramsey did the announcement honors. I could hear more, but what I heard was general banter. Bull asked the Goons questions about their backgrounds and interests while Maxie and Battle checked the room. There were no yells or thuds or thumps of any kind. 5409 was next.

Curious about the chair sound, I pulled out my chair. Gingerly I reached my hand under the desk top and felt around. I found out two things. First that the damn thing had sharp corners, but second, and more importantly, as I pulled my hand away to wipe off the now-welling wound, I saw dust and dirt mixed with the redness. Was that what they had done?

I wrapped a tissue around my finger and grabbed a dust cloth from under the sink. Going from desk to desk -- much to the delight of Midshipman Asshole Guevarra -- I fumbled under each desktop -- except Rico's -- until I had cleaned the small rim that formed the front brace of the channel-shaped support structure. Then I cleaned the tops of each drawer. Satisfied, I deposited the cloth under the sink and returned to my listening post while Rico read a technical manual in anticipation of the evening's escapade.

It was almost an hour later that the inspection team approached our room. During that period I had contacted the Goon Room by sliding a penny across the passageway floor into their room. Merritt and Ramsey came to the door. I looked at them questioningly, and they gave me a thumbs-up sign. Merritt indicated that we should check under the desks for dust bunnies, and Ramsey pointed to the top of the door. I nodded and cleaned both spots.

Rico nodded to me before the inspectors entered, indicating that I was to be the spokesman. That was fine. As Captain Dillingham's first huge foot broke the plane of the doorway I boomed out an "Attention on Deck!" aimed at deafening anyone within ten feet.

Rico and I snapped to rigidity. The three of them entered and looked around.

Bull looked at me. "Why are there only two of you?" he asked in a gentle voice.

"Sir. Our other two much-smarter classmates have left the Academy!"

"I see," he chuckled. "Who are you?"

"Midshipman Fourth-class Kevin O'Reilly, sir! And my roommate is Midshipman Fourth – class Enrique Guevarra."

Maxwell and Battle went about the room wiping white gloves across various pieces of furniture and fixtures as Bull questioned us. We remained at attention and braced throughout the process. He asked birthplaces, sports participation, and future academic and career goals.

After he had gleaned a small amount of information from each of us, Bull looked at Battle. "Everything okay?" he asked.

"So far, sir" Battle answered smartly. He went to the door and wiped his hand across the top. It was clean. Smiling slyly, he went to Delmont's desk. Pulling out the chair, he felt up inside the desktop. His hand came away clean. He smiled again and walked to my bunk. Taking the mattress by the middle with both hands, he lifted it, exposing the enclosed but previously inaccessible, area underneath. He looked inside. "You didn't clean inside here, did you, O'Reilly?" he asked, peering into the stygian depths.

"I didn't know there *was* an inside there, sir," I answered, a bit dismayed.

Dillingham laughed. "Don't despair, midshipman. This has been the best room yet. But a good Marine must be prepared. It will keep you alive when you really need it." As he said this, his eyes glazed over in obvious memory retrieval, and I knew he really meant what he said.

"Aye, aye, sir!"

The group turned to go. As Battle passed me he said, "Good job, gentlemen. Two comearounds a piece for unpreparedness."

I groaned. Later I found out that we had gotten fewer comearounds than any other room, which made me weirdly proud. Maybe I *was* becoming the smack Rico constantly implied.


That afternoon the usual group played basketball, and I had a pretty fair first game. I was beginning to think I could make the varsity team if I tried hard enough. I mean, there did seem to be a fair number of white guys here. I dribbled and passed well, but couldn't jump for shit. And maybe if I practiced more with my left hand. I decided to try only left-handed shots in the second scrimmage, but several errant shots later, gave up any hopes of being an Academy super jock.

Evening meal was a quiet affair. I think everyone, including the squadleaders, was thankful that the ordeal of the inspections was over. I intended to get to sleep early. I spent an hour in the warm early evening writing letters while sitting out on the roof deck. That night's sunset was spectacular. The reds and golds splashed across the sky in a dizzying display, and cotton ball clouds floated unhurriedly eastward.

Ronald Steinway came out on the roof from his room 30 minutes afterward. He saw me, waved, and resumed his familiar pose as night sentinel of the Company.

I left him to his reverie. I was writing a serious letter to an ex-girlfriend.

As I wrote, I considered feminine companionship and my lack thereof. I knew Merritt and Polk had serious relationships. They talked about their far away loves constantly. Even Tommy Poole had a girl back home. Listening to all that mooning, I had begun to wonder if there wasn't something seriously wrong with me. I decided to remedy the companionship situation by rekindling a relationship with a girl I had dated when I was a junior, and who I recently heard from friends might have gotten a little 'loose.'

My letter told her briefly about the hardship of being a midshipman and how I missed my friends. Then I mentioned that I had been thinking about her recently, asked if she would like to correspond, and suggested we see each other when I returned during Christmas vacation. Satisfied with what I had said, I wrote identical letters to three other girls I knew from school or other social activities. None of the girls knew each other; and I figured that if only one responded, I could satisfy the love interest requirement and maybe add excitement to my life.

At 2000 I visited the Goons to swap inspection stories. Everyone had gotten off easily except poor Tommy, who now had enough comearounds to last until Christmas leave – twenty years from now.

He pulled it out a small black vinyl notebook. On the first page at the top center in bold letters he had written the name Maxwell. Underneath he had ticked off comearounds in groups of five. He canceled out completed comearounds with a pen stroke. The list of Maxwell comearounds almost filled the page. I turned the page to see Battle's list. It was twice as long. I groaned and returned the book, mustering my most sincere look of empathy.

"I got a letter from Kate today," said Polk. "She's not happy about what goes on here. She told me to quit and come home. She says she's saving a place for me at the junior college. We can study philosophy together, protest the war, smoke grass, and make love all night. God, it's tempting."

"Go ahead and quit!" Ramsey blurted. "Join your pot-smoking anti-war friends."

"Hold on, Joe," Jeff protested. "I never participated in an anti-war rally. I have reservations about Vietnam, but if I have to go, I'll go, but I don't have to like it."

Jeff continued. "She also says that if anyone wants to come back to New Hampshire with me on vacation, she'll fix them up with a date. She knows some eligible young ladies."

"Maybe she can fit one in a box and send her down here for me," I offered. "I could use a little companionship right about now."

Merritt chided. "What's the matter, redhead, getting a little restless? Me too, but I'm saving it all up for Parent's Weekend. Lynda will be here, and my parents will give us privacy."

"So you're horny too, butt-head!" I said. "But you have a goal in mind. You don't have to develop a shallow relationship before you strike paydirt. I feel like a God-damn hermit."

When I returned to our room just prior to lights out, Rico was already gone. I checked outside the window. Ronald was still contemplating. I stood in the dark and stared outside for a long time, watching the lights go out in rooms around the courtyard. After the last room went dark, I stared at the stars for several minutes. I decided I was very lonely and that I should go to bed immediately.

I crawled into my rack, depressed but not sure why. I lay on my back, staring at the bottom of the top bunk. I had no particular fantasy in my head and my thoughts drifted. I began praying, then crying. I didn't understand why, but I knew I couldn't control what was happening. The tears rolled down the sides of my head as I shuddered in the darkness. I forced myself not to wipe them away. I felt the cold, wet drops touch my ears. Some of the liquid pooled in my ear cavities. Most dripped from my lobes to the pillow. Was this what had happened to Pirelli, I asked myself? I fell asleep, still crying, the pillow wet on either side of my head.

CHAPTER 20

## *NIGHTTIME SHENANIGANS*

About an hour later the door to the room opened silently. I woke instantly. I have always been a light sleeper. "Rico?" I whispered.

"No, it's me, Jeff. Time for some mischief. Want to come?"

"You bet," I said springing out of bed and reaching for my gym gear.

Jubal Ramsey once again perpetrated the stunt. Our goal for the evening was to get to as many Company areas as possible and 'borrow' the company guidon from its usual perch outside the squadleaders' room.

"What are we going to do with them once we have them?" I asked.

"We'll line them all up in the grassy area at the inside entrance to T-Court," Joe answered. "We'll plant them just before dawn. It'll make quite a sight to the early church formations."

Merritt and Poole accompanied us -- much to my surprise -- as well as all the occupants of 5401. The nine of us split into four groups. My 'team' consisted of Tommy Poole, Bill Allen, and myself. We were the only group of three, and I was the team leader. I was proud. We were to try for the pennants from the Thirty-first through the Thirty-sixth Companies, in the fifth wing, not far away. Jubal had drawn a rough map of where he had reconnoitered each Company guidon to be. We studied the map in silence.

"Okay," he said. "Let's not take any chances. If you can't get a flag, don't worry."

We started out at twenty-two-thirty. I led my group through our now-darkened Company area. On the way down the passageway we passed the head and startled Steve Rogers as we raced by. We didn't stop to acknowledge the puzzlement on his face.

We ran silently to avoid making any noise in our passing. I knew the best way to the fifth wing because I had traversed the same path during my romp with Jubal and Jeff.

We stopped on the landing of a small set of steps at the end of the third wing and discussed our strategy.  We decided to start on the bottom floor of the fifth wing and work our way up.  Bill and I would make the grab for the pennants since we could run and hopefully escape if challenged.  After we gathered a flag, Tommy would carry it to his room.

We sneaked down the stairs to the ground floor, and stealthily crossed the passageway connecting the third and fifth wings.  We spotted a guidon in the main passageway.  It seemed to be inviting us, daring us to try what we intended.  The dark area was very quiet.  With Tommy and Bill scouting opposite ends of the passageway, I moved down the broad passageway, hurrying but not running, my eyes alert for any sign of activity.

I approached the pennant cautiously, looked around quickly, and snatched the pole from its leaning-rest position, turned, and sprinted as silently as possible from the area.  My heart pounded so strongly I thought it would surely awaken the occupants of the rooms I passed.  I was high on adrenaline by the time I entered the ladderwell for our prearranged rendezvous.  A quick check discovered we had taken the guidon from the Thirty-sixth Company.  I handed it to Tommy and Bill and I scouted the next deck.

There was no guidon outside any room on the next deck, so we moved up one more deck, where Bill took the flag from the Thirty-fourth Company.  Tommy had returned by then, and he carried off the next flag to his room.  The next two decks went almost as easily, but we couldn't find a flag for the Thirty-first Company and decided to return to our Company.  Four flags out of six seemed like a good night to me.

We were the first group finished.  Rico still had not returned.  We waited in the Goon Room for the others.  Tommy Poole, who probably had never done an illegal thing in his life, was elated.  He giggled with delight as he recounted his trips with the guidons.  I withheld my own excitement but secretly I was also proud.

The penalties for apprehension were severe.  Jim Merritt had reminded us before we started that being out of the room after lights out was a 10-demerit offense.  Being out of the Company area without authorization was worth another 20 demerits.  And when we went outside Bancroft Hall later to plant the flags, we would be courting an additional 20 demerits.  That added up to a Class A offense -- big time punishment.  I realized that if I thought about it that way, it almost wasn't worth it.  However, I couldn't let the Company down and not participate, could I?

Most of the other groups elected to bring all the captured flags back at the end of their raid.  As the other groups returned, the number of dark lumber poles accumulated in the

195

Goon Room.  When the final group returned with its three flags, we had collected 25 of the 36 guidons.

"The last upper-class are supposed to be back in their rooms by midnight, but they'll be sneaking in until after one," Merritt said.  " I suggest we get some sleep and go out at around four in the morning to put the guidons up. Anybody that finds us at 0400 probably won't say a word about it."  We agreed to that plan and quietly returned to our rooms. Rico still was not back.

I lay down.  Excitement had released the tension from my nervous system, and I didn't feel like crying any more.  But I *was* tired.  I closed my eyes and fell asleep.

Rico returned an hour later.  I heard the door bump shut.  He hesitated, went to the sink area, and turned on the small fluorescent shaving light.

I rolled toward him and stared.

Rico had the biggest smile I have ever seen.  I knew he had been successful.

He was holding something behind his back.  "Rico's very happy," he said.

"I can tell, you rotten so-and-so."

"You wanted proof, Kevin?  Here it is!" He brought a pair of small, delicate pink panties from behind his back.

"So?" I said.  "What's that prove.  She could have brought an extra pair."

Rico laughed quietly. He hung the panties near my face.

I inhaled copious pheromones, and I knew instantly Rico wasn't lying.  "I'll pay you in the morning, you lucky bastard."

"You don't have to pay me, Kevin.  You can do me a favor instead."

"What's that?" I asked, thoughts of shoe-shining or rack-making springing into my brain.

"Cindy's got a friend," he replied.

Anyone who has ever heard those dreaded words will understand why I immediately paled.  There is a universal truth that pretty girls are always attended by not-so-pretty ones.  On the few occasions I had helped my buddies by double dating a 'friend,' I had been disappointed.  On one occasion I excused myself from chubby clutches to visit the men's room at a local drive-in during a showing of *The Creature from the Black Lagoon* -- which is one of my favorite horror movies. I climbed out the tiny back window and walked three miles home in the dark. I knew what the words "she has a friend" could mean.

Rico sensed my hesitation. "No, no, Kevin. This will be okay. I promise. Cindy can't get the car next Saturday night, but she has a friend who can. Cindy guarantees the friend is good looking and that she's a hot number."

Hold on! A hot number? My curiosity, and something else, was aroused.

"Tell me more."

"I don't know too much. But I promised to bring a good-looking stud if she could arrange another rendezvous, and she swore her friend Brenda was pretty." Rico thought I was good-looking, huh? Was he trying to scam Cindy. No, that didn't seem right. Especially when sex was on the line.

"Okay," I said. "Sounds good." I watched Rico as he went to his bed and undressed. He was humming inanely. Before climbing into the rack, he took a deep and obviously satisfying look at his trophy, tucked it under his pillow, then settled under the covers.

"The gang will be active later this morning. Want to participate?" I asked.

He hesitated. "I don't think so. I've got to recharge my precious bodily fluids."


At precisely 0400 Jim Merritt shook me awake. "Time to go. What about Rico?"

"It's a long story," I replied. "He's tired."

I hurried across the passageway to the Goon Room. On the way I noticed that the area near the head door was free from Maxwell leavings. It mustn't have been a big night for Maxie.

Merritt and I were elected scouts for the trip to T-Court. I would reconnoiter far ahead, and Jim would stay just in front of the main body while Bill Allen served as rear-guard. The twenty-five guidons were divided among the remainder of the group. We discussed the plan, intending not to say a word the entire trip out or back unless we ran into an emergency.

Our path would take us through the rotunda, practically under the noses of the watch staff. I descended the stairs to the main deck and peered around the corner at the office area. There were several plebes and a second-classman on duty inside but no activity whatsoever. I motioned to Merritt that it was okay to come forward, and I scurried to the main outside doorway. From the dark recesses of the big brass doors, I checked the surroundings. Every room that fronted T-Court was dark. No sounds disturbed the scene except normal night noises and quiet music from a radio in the Main Office. Everything seemed perfect.

Cautiously I exited Bancroft Hall, moving stealthily onto the wide landing at the top of the steps. No one in the Main Office could see me without coming to the window and leaning out. By now Merritt and the group were waiting near the doors. I motioned them outside as I descended the steps and transited T-Court, my eyes on the Main Office during the entire passage.

I stopped in the grassy area and ducked down behind the short architectural wall. No one was anywhere nearby. I stood and motioned to the group, who now waited on the landing for my signal. The first flag carrier started forward. It was Hank Butkowski carrying the first five poles in his two hands. Each person carried consecutive numbers. He hardly made a sound as he ran across the stones. I indicated the place where he was to stick the flags into the soft earth, and he began planting. While he worked, I checked everything again and signaled for the next runner.

Jeff Polk brought four guidons. He and Hank carefully spaced each flag exactly two Hank-steps apart. I signaled the next runner as Jeff moved out onto the campus and positioned himself near an enormous tree, where he could be the long-distance sentry.

Tim Butler brought four more flags. Three of those we planted on the west side with the others; the other began the flag formation on the east side of T-Court. Jubal brought four more without incident, as did George Abbott. The last flag carrier was Tommy Poole. I signaled. He started down the steps, tripped, and sprawled on the hard granite steps. Everyone gasped.

Tommy had enough sense to hold onto the poles, but the noise of the wooden shafts striking the steps seemed incredibly loud in the dark, still, silence. Jim Merritt sprang down the steps and grabbed both Tommy and the poles, pulling him out of sight. Bill Allen ducked inside Bancroft Hall, to warn us if someone from the Main Office came to investigate the noise. We flag planters dropped to the ground behind various bushes and shrubs

Tommy lay still for several seconds. I could see him clearly. He shook his head groggily while Jim held him steady. His head-down position was precarious, and he was still in some danger of tumbling further. I could also see the window to the Main Office. The noise had alerted someone. A second-classman stood framed in brightness, staring out into T-Court. I adjusted my position to minimize any chance of being seen. The figure in the window continued to stare, his gaze shifting up and down the Court for nearly a half minute. Eventually he turned and disappeared from view.

I signaled Jim.

Jim and Tommy got to their feet, careful not to make any noise with the poles. They each carried two poles each. A full minute passed. Finally Bill Allen emerged from the doorway and signaled that all was well. I stared at the bright window for another ten seconds and signaled them to come across. Tommy went first and Jim followed him closely. Ramsey glared at Tommy when they arrived. He snatched the poles from Tommy's hands and handed them to Hank. Within two minutes they were embedded in formation with the others. Our prank looked great.

 We assembled in the grassy area, and I signaled Bill Allen. Bill indicated that all was well, and Tommy sprinted across the courtyard. The others followed until Jeff and I remained. I waved to Jeff, and he started toward me backpedaling, his attention on the campus area. As he neared the grass he stopped and a look of horror on his face as he stared in the direction of the Severn River.

I heard a voice. "What are you staring at, you miserable ass licking plebe?"

I was horrified. We had been discovered. But how had someone gotten so close without our seeing him? Taking a chance, I slipped closer to Jeff and looked at where his gaze had frozen. At first I didn't see anything, then I saw movement in the dark, almost at ground level.

A second-classman sat sprawled against a tree. One leg was drawn up against his chest; the other stretched in front of him. He had been drinking. He had been drunk. He had been sick. I knew this because of the smell of alcohol that clung to him like a cheap perfume. I also knew it because of the dark stain on his shirt front and lap where he had vomited, too incapacitated to turn his head.

He tried to smooth his shirt front, but instead smeared the vomitous mess. Pausing, he stared at his now-moist hand uncomprehendingly, and wiped it on the red brick walkway. He tried to stand but fell over on his side.

"Do you need help, sir?" I asked.  My voice startled him.

"Shit, no!" he answered.  "Do you think I'm helpless?"

"No, sir," I answered.  The squadleader struggled to his feet and wavered unsteadily as Jeff moved beside me.

"Say," he said.  "What are you guys up to anyway?"  He stared, eventually saw the poles behind us, and looked up.  His eyes traveled down the line of poles.  He chuckled.

"How many?"

"Twenty-five," I answered.

"That's just great!" he said.  "Did you get Thirty-third Company?"

"Yes, sir!"  I had gotten that one myself.

"Well, lemme have it," he said.  Jeff started toward that pennant.

On a hunch I blurted, "Sir, that would mess up the formation."

The squad leader pondered.  Somewhere in the dark recesses of his alcohol-soaked brain he saw the very fuzzy logic of this.  "You're right," he slurred.  "Leave it for prosperity."

I think he wanted to say 'posterity' but I wasn't about to correct him.

Gripping the end of the wall, he turned toward Tecumseh Court and staggered forward.

I reached across the wall and grabbed his arm.  "Sir, if you go that way someone is sure to catch you.  Better to go the back way."  I pointed toward Dewey Field.

He pondered again.  "You're absolutely right," he said, too loudly.

Jeff and I quickly glanced toward the Main Office.  When nobody showed a head for several seconds, I signaled Jeff to go.  He sprinted.  By now the others knew something was wrong and had disappeared into the building.

 "Do you need any help getting back?" I asked the now departing midshipman as he began wavering down the walk.

Shit, no, plebe," he replied.  Then he stopped and stared again at the flags.  "I wish my asshole plebes had balls like this."  He staggered down the dark walk.  I hoped he made it back.

I watched the departing figure for several seconds, then turned toward Bancroft Hall. There was no activity in the Main Office window. I began my sprint. Ten steps out into the open, a white-uniformed figure appeared in the bright window. He saw me! The figure was about to turn and say something. I waved my arms violently, palms outward, in a gesture to wait. The figure paused. It was a fellow plebe. Relieved, I reached the steps I put my index finger to my mouth in a signal for silence and sprinted up the granite stairs. Inside Bancroft Hall I paused. If the plebe had given an alarm, the watch squad would soon pour from the office and cut me off before I could make the stairs. I counted to ten slowly. Nothing happened.

Deciding I was safe, I hurried to the stairs and ascended. I didn't realize until I had gotten to the next floor that I had been holding my breath. I exhaled a stress-relieving sigh and continued upward toward safety. Pausing outside the Company area to ensure no one was watching the passageway, I silently opened the door and slipped inside.

Instead of going to my room, I stuck my head in the Goon Room. Polk and Merritt were still up, talking at a desk in the dark. Ramsey and Poole must have been in their racks.

"All's well," I whispered. It felt like I got absolutely zero sleep in the time between when I lay down and when, two hours later, it was time to get ready for mass.


I was tired when I finally dragged myself out to Catholic formation. Even the sight of the 25 pennants hanging limply in the humid morning air did nothing to perk me up -- not until a group of watch squad plebes rushed down the steps toward our flag formation. I chuckled and nudged Tommy Poole who smiled in return. We had a secret. Under the direction of the second-class watch officer, the guidons were removed from the loose earth and carried to Bancroft Hall for later distribution. Soon we headed off to chat with our Maker.

I would never normally consider intentionally sleeping during mass. In parochial school the nuns instilled a sense of reverence and respect in me that prevents even the thought of such a thing. At Annapolis, however, three factors temporarily changed my attitude about slumber and sacrilege. This change had nothing to do with the church setting, which was awe inspiring. Nor was it related to the priests who said mass in the chapel. They were always dynamic leaders and captivating speakers. And I loved the choir and the organ music.

My attitude wavered because of three disparate factors that completely overrode the music, the venue, and the environment.  First, I was God-awful tired the entire four years I was a midshipman.  The academic, physical, emotional, and social schedules were overwhelming; and any reprieve from the pressure found me automatically dozing off.  Second, attendance at church was mandatory, and I never liked to be told what to do.  The third reason, was 'Sleepy Hollow.'

The chapel dome has a wide balcony along a portion of both sides.  Midshipmen always sit in the forward-most sections downstairs.  Guests sit in the main aisle and the balconies.  The areas under the front balcony have several long side-facing rows of pews affectionately called 'Sleepy Hollow' by midshipmen.

Our squad leader that Sunday was a very tired second-class.  His eyes were bleary and his voice gravelly.  He trudged us to chapel rather than marched.  After he ensured that we were properly seated, he went to the area under the balcony and selected a position in the middle of one of the back rows.  Because those seats faced sideward, I initially thought he sat there to watch us plebes better.  However, after the introductory portion of the mass I noticed his head disappear from view.

 At first I thought he was tying his shoe or adjusting his kneeler, but five minutes later while we were standing for the gospel, he still hadn't emerged.  I knew something portentous was happening.   Deductive reasoning, coupled with the fact that if I listened hard enough I could hear the sound of deep steady breathing coming from his vicinity, led me to decide that he was either lying prostrate on the kneelers praising the lord in a rumbling nasal chant - or else he was asleep.

I was disgusted.  How could anyone come to church specifically to sleep?  Didn't he know this was the house of God?  Why didn't someone turn him in?  What kind of place was this anyway?  I was still indignant several minutes later when the plebe on my left side -- who luckily happened to be Tommy Poole -- nudged me awake.  My head had fallen over so far to the left that it rested on his shoulder.  I wondered briefly if he thought I was being fresh.  I shuddered awake, straightened, and looked around.  No one had noticed my siesta.  Most of the plebes were themselves in snoozeville, although none had been so bold as to use his neighbor as a pillow.

I glanced in the direction of Sleepy Hollow.  It was still noisy, but seemingly devoid of population.  It wouldn't always be so.  During academic year Sleepy Hollow was a very popular place for slumber seekers.  Some first-class would bring plebes along to act as lookouts, which would be fine if the plebes themselves weren't droned to sleep by the sound of so much snoring.   Sleepy Hollow would be populated in a classic plebe big-space, plebe big-space, plebe big-space arrangement all midshipmen recognized.

However, in the face of all the hypocrisy and negative motivation to the contrary, I can honestly say that I never intentionally slept during chapel.  The operative word here is 'intentionally.'  I said extra Hail Marys as a penance for my earlier slumber.

But I sure needed sleep that morning.  I ate my breakfast in a daze, and crawled into my rack for a two-hour nap before noon meal.

CHAPTER 21

## *RONALD'S DECEPTION*

On Monday morning, Battle let the better runners scamper ahead while he ran alongside Poole, taunting him mercilessly. The things he said were creative and incredibly disgusting, and I could hear them all the way from my position near the front of the pack. Tommy responded with renewed effort. He ran strongly -- if not quickly -- through most of the race. I watched from the finish line as he approached, and spurred by the urgings of Battle, began to sprint. I cheered as he gutted along, but I was almost alone in my encouragement.

Tommy faltered as he neared us. His face radiated agony, and his breath huffed in labored gasps. His legs pumped wobbly, the new thigh muscles straining to keep up the pace. Battle stopped his harassment to watch the gutsy effort.

"Keep it up, Tommy!" I yelled. "You're doing great!"

Twenty yards from the finish, a surprised look spread oven Tommy's face. His pace dropped to a quivering plod and his eyebrows arched. He opened his mouth, gasped, then wretched noisily, and almost immediately collapsed, vomit gushing from his mouth as he fell.

On the way down he reached out a stubby arm to push himself away from a grassy nose-dive. Unfortunately for Tommy, that arm landed in the very center of the mess. His arm slipped along the grass. He tried valiantly to pump his legs and regain verticality, but he couldn't. Instead he sprawled forward and landed with a plop on his stomach. I could hear the wind whoosh from his lungs, and see small globs of undigested stuff spit outward onto the nearby grass.

I doubt in all his life that Tommy Poole had ever had the wind knocked out of him. He didn't know what to do. He panicked as he desperately sought to return air to his lungs. His ample weight, pressing on those very lungs, made that task difficult.

A shrill wheezing sound emerged from his widely-opened mouth. His expression became desperate. His eyes bugged outward.

Remembering Merritt and the pool, I reacted. I ran to Tommy and turned him over. I looked into his frightened eyes. I think he must have decided he was going to die and wanted no part of it. He reached upward toward me, wide-eyed, almost like a sinner on Judgment Day. His look said, "Please, Kevin. It's not my time yet. I still owe Maxwell a million comearounds."

"Easy, Tommy," I said. "You're only winded. Relax and it will be okay." Taking his two legs, I lifted them into the air. After a few panicked seconds, his lungs opened and the air rushed back inside. He sucked down several grateful gulps, relief visible on his face.

Satisfied that he was recovering, I reached down. "It's okay Tommy," I said. "You'll live. Let's get up." I helped him to his feet. He staggered as his now-exhausted frame tried to support his weight. I put an arm around his shoulder, and began helping him to the finish line. No one else had come forward. When I looked up, I could see why.

Every plebe face was turned toward Battle. He was livid. His face had turned deep red, and the veins stuck out on his nearly-bald forehead. He stared at the two of us, speechless for the first time this summer. I realized I was in big trouble, but I wasn't sure why. Tommy and I crossed the line, and I let go of Tommy. He bent over at the waist to regain his composure. I looked up. Nothing happened for several long seconds.

I stared at Battle. He wasn't watching Tommy. His madman's eyes bored double searing holes into my skull. I held my own unblinking gaze until my eyes began to water. I had seen this look before on the basketball court, and for a moment I thought he was going to start a fistfight. I quickly sized up the encounter. I was bigger and maybe stronger, but he had better endurance and was a crazy bastard, which could mean a lot in a fight. But I had been in fistfights with crazy bastards before. Hell, I had even been knocked unconscious once by a punch I didn't see coming, so I knew what could happen if we mixed it up. I decided I wasn't afraid of this puke-faced shit-head at all. And I told myself that what Midshipman Tommy Battle didn't know was that when I get angry I get really mean. And just staring at him was starting to rile me. Shit, I might just go after him myself right now. I sure would feel good if I did. I decided to kick his ass all the way back to the Company area, and maybe beyond. I began to step forward.

Mike Wojeck stuck out his foot before I could complete the first step and then pretended that I had collided with him. He fell in front of me, blocking my path. "Watch it, Kevin!"

"Huh?" I said, emerging from my warlike trance. I looked at Mike. His face was hidden from Battle's view. His eyes entreated me to calm down.

I suddenly realized what I had been about to do. Holy shit! I must be crazy. I helped Mike to his feet. "Sorry. I must have lost my balance." I straightened and looked up. Battle's back was now turned toward me, and he seemed to be staring down Dewey Field toward the old Severn River Bridge. "O'Reilly," he said calmly without turning. "Give me 50."

I dropped to the grass and began screaming out the push-up count.

Battle stared into the distance until I had finished. "Stay in leaning rest, O'Reilly."

Battle addressed the group. "O'Reilly screwed up, and I'll bet no one knows why."

"Because he helped Poole, sir?" volunteered BJ Wilson.

Battle momentarily renewed his anger. He snapped. "Do you know what a rhetorical question is, Wilson?"

"Yes, sir," BJ answered tentatively.

"Well, smack, the question I posed was just that. Rhetorical! I didn't ask for an answer. I didn't want an answer. I don't even like your answer. Give me 20 for being a bilge."

Wilson dropped to the grass, his feelings hurt by Battle's anger.

I was still at leaning rest, my arms beginning to weaken.

"Gentlemen, O'Reilly's heroism in Midshipman Poole's behalf was out of place." He looked at Tommy. "Poole, front and center!"

Tommy scurried wearily to a position in front of Battle.

"Your good buddy, O'Reilly, is in trouble because he didn't let you suffer, Poole, you miserable twit. Does that sound crazy to you, Poole?"

Tommy didn't answer. He was probably as confused as I was.

It sounded crazy to me. I waited for enlightenment, my arms straining.

Battle continued. "You've never puked like that before, have you, Poole?"

"No, sir."

"You've never lost your wind before, have you, Poole?"

"No, sir."

Battle stared into the distance at some point above Tommy's head. "This is a tough life, Poole. But people in the military are expected to overcome severe challenges. More than most civilians can ever dream of." He paused, still staring far away.

"Sometimes we die in the service of this country. Nobody wants that, but it's a fact. The military is the most hazardous occupation in the world. Did you know that?"

Before the now-rising Wilson could volunteer, Battle interjected, pointing at Wilson. "That's another rhetorical question, asshole." BJ wisely remained quiet. Battle continued. "You joined the world's most dangerous profession." He turned to the rest of us.

"If you graduate -- a fact which is in question for some of you -- you will return to your tenth reunion to find that several of your classmates are already dead. By the time you retire the number of deceased will be significant. The chances are good that one of your Twenty-third Companymates will not live to retire."

"To gain the best chance for survival in this very dangerous business," he continued, "you have to learn to test and exceed your limits. The only way to do that is to experience the edge, to live on it, to relish it." He stared into Tommy's eyes.

"You didn't just face the edge, Poole. You ran smack into it head-on. And you didn't like what you saw there. I could read that all over your face. In combat there won't be any Mommy to help you out and dry your tears, and there may not be any O'Reilly to get you back on your feet. You have to learn to do it all on your own, because *you* are the only person you can count on."

Battle turned to me.

By now my arms vibrated, ready to collapse. My stomach sagged uncontrollably almost to the grass. I hunched and jiggled my shoulders to relieve the pressure. It didn't help.

"You've got to learn not to be such a good classmate, O'Reilly. I intend to run Poole's ass until he quits, and if I can't do it this summer, then God help him when the Brigade gets back, because the 'Tigers' will. I don't want any more interference from you or your classmates in my handling of Mr. Poole. Do nothing to assist him unless his life is in danger; otherwise, I'll run your ass out along with his. Understood, O'Reilly?"

The pain in my arms was so intense I would have agreed that my mother had once been Queen of England -- although if my Irish Mom knew I would have considered associating her with anything British, she would have made me feel far worse than a little leaning-rest. "Yes, sir!"

"Good," he said, a sadistic gleam in his eyes. "Now get up so we can return to Bancroft Hall in time for formation."

I rose unsteadily and shook out my arms to restore circulation. I could see Tommy Poole staring at me from 20 feet away. I winked to let him know I was fine, although, to tell the truth, my arms and I were beginning to have doubts about the wisdom of helping out classmate Poole.

Battle led us back to Mother Bancroft at a slow jog. He was very quiet. I took that as a good omen. Maybe he was considering my actions in a different light and his conscience was beginning to hurt him. I hoped so, but somehow I doubted it.


That evening Battle had a special comearound for Poole, Steinway, Hardesty, Rogers, and me. He positioned the five of us at varying distances along the passageway, with me always farthest from the finish line. Then he gathered the others to watch. Before each race he had my classmates place push-up bets on the winners. If they picked correctly, no penalty. For further incentive, anyone who picked ten winners would get carry-on at evening meal.

We runners could get carry-on by winning ten events. The competition was intense. I wasn't sure about the others, but I would just about kill for carry-on. I had no intention of losing if I could help it. Most of the early betting was on me, and the crazed screams from my classmates as I sprinted up and down the passageway were almost deafening.

It was certainly unnerving to be the center of so much attention and pressure, and I was angry the entire evening about being the performing monkey -- but I really wanted that carry-on.

I glided to three easy victories before the squadleaders adjusted the spacing to the point where I didn't think I could catch the front runner. Before every race Rico looked at me, and I would indicate with a nod or a shake whether I thought I could win. The Puerto Rican Rasputin carried on.

I didn't like listening to my classmates as they rooted for someone else to beat me. I knew this didn't make sense. They wanted a chance to relax as much as I did. But it still pissed me off. I vowed to show the bastards who could run, but the distances between the other runners and myself were daunting. I didn't win as often as I wanted.

Midway through the 'entertainment,' Maxwell upped the stakes and lengthened the course, which was to my advantage. I won twice more for a total of five victories. Hardesty and Rogers had accumulated three apiece, and Poole and Steinway had two. At the same time he announced that as an added incentive, anyone who lost would now get an extra comearound. I signaled Rico that I couldn't win the next two races, and I didn't. Tommy Poole did.

Then Ronald Steinway did something that sealed his future as a midshipman. During the third-to-last run, as I sprinted on the return leg, trying desperately to catch the leaders, I saw Ronald, ten yards ahead of me, wobble on his thin legs. He moaned and slowed up just as I evened with him, then he dropped in a heap as I passed. I didn't pause. I caught and passed the leader, Steve Rogers, at the finish line -- my eighth victory.

As I turned and headed toward the starting line, I noticed that, something significant was up. I stared at a scene that has been indelibly etched on my subconscious ever since.

The squadleaders yelled insanely, but the crowd noise was gone. Ronald Steinway lay sprawled on the tile floor on his belly. His legs, slightly parted, pointed down the passageway toward the double doors. One arm stretched in front of him, hiding his face from view. The other lay underneath his body. He didn't move except for the rasping breaths that wracked his frame.

Maxwell knelt on one side of Steinway, Battle on the other. They were not there to help Ronald to Sick Bay.

"Steinway, you pussy!" yelled Maxwell. "That was the most pathetic feint I have ever seen. Get up and get ready for the next run!"

"So help me God, Steinway!," added Battle. "If you're not on your feet in three seconds, you're as good as dead!"

I watched amazed. I hadn't seen Ronald fall, but he looked out of it to me.

His two tormentors didn't let up. The abuse and promises of torture continued for several seconds, increasing in volume and escalating in scope.

I hoped Ronald had the sense to stay on the deck. Now that he was there, it was the only logical thing to do.

Then Battle pulled a dirty trick on poor Ronald. "Steinway," he said in a calm voice. "You can't fool me. I know you're faking to get out of exercising. That's a form of deceit, you know? And that makes what you're doing an honor violation. If you don't get up this instant, I'll haul you before the Honor Committee, and you'll be out of here in a week. Time's running out, Steinway."

Steinway stirred.

Jesus, Ronald! I almost shouted for him to stay on the deck. Battle couldn't prove Ronald was faking, and there was no honor violation without proof. But if he got up, he would be admitting that he tried to deceive the squadleaders. In my brain I yelled repeated 'Stay downs!'

He didn't hear me. His arm moved under his chest. He slowly pushed himself up off the tiles, shaking his head groggily. But even from my distant vantage, I could see that Ronald *was* pretending. He looked like a really bad actor playing an exhausted human. He was too dramatic, and his scene was too *staged*. Despite his pretenses of confusion and swoon, his eyes, which darted from side-to-side in his typical nervous mannerism, were alive and frightened. He knew he had been caught. He stood, pretended to recover, and jogged unsteadily to his starting place.

Every eye was on Battle. Neither he nor Maxie said anything when Steinway got to his feet. Now they both stared at Ronald malevolently

I realized in that instant that any chance Ronald had of making his parents happy had ended. The squadleaders were going to kill Steinway.

The lull in the racing was to my advantage. I kept warm by jiggling my thigh muscles and swinging my arms. I also think that the Steinway incident took the fight out of the other competitors. I won the last two races easily. The monkey had gotten his banana.

CHAPTER 22

## *LUST WILL OUT*

My big rendezvous with a supposed nymph named Brenda was fast approaching. As the days passed, my thoughts focused on the upcoming event and on girls in general. It will come as no surprise when I say that female companionship and sexuality were prime plebe topics of conversation. For most of my classmates, getting good sex would have been infinitely preferable to getting good grades. Many got neither.

In that regard I suppose that midshipmen are like other red-blooded males when it comes to relationships. However, monastic isolation infuses an intensity in the midshipman dating process that can be and often is overwhelming. Few midshipmen survive the four years of sociological turmoil and remain faithful to their girl back home. Most lose their virginity as students at Annapolis, either on the wet grass at Hospital Point, in a bedroom at a June Week cottage, or in a house of ill repute during summer cruise. The temptations are too all-powerful, the needs too all-consuming, and the uniform and its associated mystique too empowering.

Some of my classmates recognized the sexual energy they exuded and wielded it in a fun-loving way, never promising their partners anything more than companionship and intense physical contact. Rico was foremost among them. He was the best 'swordsman' I have ever known, and I never once heard any of his conquests complain about a second's worth of time they spend in his arms. But there were others, like Danny French, for whom the uniform and the power were means to a not-so-glorious end.

In other respects, Danny French was an ordinary midshipman who participated in the process as energetically as any of the rest of us. But when it came to dealing with women, he was immature, scheming, insincere -- and worse yet -- a braggart. Danny, being handsome and athletic and having a father who was a City Councilman, already knew how to wield power, both politically and sexually. Being all of the above plus a midshipman made him dangerous to any female who happened to come within the range of his charm.

To borrow a pre-World War II phrase, Danny French was a cad. He wasn't the only cad among us, but he was the most blatant and unrepentant. Danny bragged about how he and four friends formed a club in High School, the sole purpose of which was to deflower unsuspecting young ladies. According to Danny, he was club president and head deflowerer. Six virgins already had fallen for his charms, and according to Danny, his parents were bringing another unsuspecting victim to Parents' Weekend, when he was certain to add another girl to his trophy case. With Danny, sex was never a question of feelings.

But while Danny's lack of sexual conscience was the epitome of crass manipulation, none of us except George Abbott seemed immune to the temptations of sex. Big George had met his sweetie pie, Diane, during their freshman year in high school, and the two of them instantly knew they were made for each other. George carried her picture in his hat, had her portrait on his desk, and kept another photo in his shirt pocket next to his heart. As for sex, despite four years of dating, George bragged that he and Di had never had sex, and had vowed they would wait until they were married. I admired George's restraint.

The only glimmer of weakness George even admitted was that he once peeked down Di's blouse as she was bending over to pick up a book she had dropped. He shamefully confessed this immoral act to Diane immediately, but rather than chain him to a pew and beat him with a catechism -- an act I'll bet Big George secretly would have enjoyed -- she forgave him and took to wearing turtlenecks. I guess she didn't want to tempt the demons within poor George. At the time we thought George was naively. George must have thought us all heathens.

I say all this because in the preparation for the big night, I had no plane of reference to compare what I wanted to happen with what I fantasized might happen. I found myself stuck between Danny and George. On the one hand, the thought of seeing this girl solely for the purpose of getting her skirt off appalled me. On the other hand, I sure wanted to see what was inside that mythical skirt.

I was in a quandary as to what to do about preparing for the encounter. Rico and I had agreed not to say a word about our plans. You never know when a classmate will turn screw, particularly if a little carry-on is on the line. So I couldn't just ask for advice, and I also couldn't let on to Rico the extent of my inexperience. I didn't want to disappoint him. So I did the next best thing. I borrowed one of Rico's 'training manuals.'

He understood immediately. "Getting yourself revved up, huh?" he asked. I agreed.

212

It was not a difficult book. Of course, I only skimmed the dialog, deciding it would be meaningless except to provide me with a good base from which to develop my sexual vocabulary. I was wrong about that. How many times in your life can you find the opportunity to use a phrase like 'throbbing love muscle' in casual conversation? Besides, I discovered that in the heat of passion I usually become incoherent.

I decided to study the steamier scenes intensely -- from a purely technical standpoint of course. I finished the book in under an hour, amazed that two people could do the things suggested on those pages. I also noticed that a great deal of my blood seemed to be concentrated in one particular area. No wonder Rico didn't want to be disturbed when he was reading one of these things. If he reacted like me, a standing Rico would surely have fainted from the volume of the blood collected in his throbbing love muscle. - What do you know? I did use that phrase.

Armed with the information imparted from that one book, I felt ready for my encounter with Brenda. Of course, there wasn't much blood left in my brain at the time, so I suppose any thoughts of sexual prowess should be forgiven.


That Saturday was significant for two reasons other than the impending date with sexual destiny. For one thing, Patrick Mulvaney got a 'Care Package' from home. Most of us from time to time received boxes of goodies, which usually included a few cookies, maybe a piece of a sibling's birthday cake, and a copy of a local newspaper. But when Pat received a package, several grown men had to carry it.

Living on a farm with ten other people, I suppose the Mulvaneys learned to do things in a bigger way that most of us. But this was bigger than big. Mrs. Mulvaney must have enlisted all the sisters and several neighbors full time to bake the prodigious amounts of cookies that came Pat's way. His favorite, we soon found out, were of the chocolate chip variety.

Just after noon meal, while I was trying to decide if I should read another 'technical manual' in case I had missed some subtle points, I had a sudden, almost uncontrollable urge to visit Room 5409. Maybe the sound of tearing paper and ripping cardboard gave me a clue. Maybe the smell of chocolate wafting down the passageway perked my senses. Maybe it was the sight of the long line of classmates forming up outside Pat's room that alerted me. I just knew that I had to visit my old friend Pat -- with whom I hadn't had more than five minutes' conversation in the last six weeks. As a matter of fact, except for showing up like a vagrant at a soup kitchen whenever he got a package, I'm not sure Pat and I ever had a conversation that didn't include the word 'cookies.'

The second and far more momentous event was a surreptitious visit by three first-class midshipmen who would all too soon become our Company leaders. It happened just after evening meal while the fried chicken and baked potato dinner still sat undigested in our young stomachs.

A gruff and unfamiliar voice sounded from the passageway. "Plebe Ho!"

I had removed my shirt and shoes and was in the process of taking off my pants when the voice called out. At first I was startled. I reacted slowly, unsure whether to go into the passageway in this stage of undress lest it be an officer who had called us forth. I wasn't sure yet about the protocol with officers.

But I could hear other classmates scampering, and I decided that hesitation might hurt me worse than indiscretion. I braced myself along the bulkhead just outside the room and yelled out my identity simultaneously with my other companymates.

In the confusing moments between my exit and my bracing, I noticed three individuals in civilian clothes standing in the center of the passageway. They looked us over as we surged forth.

"Well, well. What do we have here?" said one of the group after we had all assumed our positions. "Our new plebes. Aren't they cute?"

"Give us 20 pushups, all of you!" said another harsh voice.

We dropped to the deck and started singing numbers. During the pushups I glanced at the newcomers to see who they were. I had no idea, and neither Maxie nor Battle was in attendance, which also confused me.

"All right, pussies, on your feet," the tallest one yelled.

"At ease!" the first one snapped.

The first speaker, the shortest, sported a Marine Corps close-cropped haircut. He took the lead. His clothes weren't half bad looking. -- He should give Battle lessons on how to dress.

"My name is Sidney Littleton," he said from his parade rest position. "I will be Tiger Company Commander for the second set this coming winter. Since I happened to be in

214

the area between summer cruise and vacation, I thought I would stop by and introduce myself and let you know what you can expect from my classmates come September." He indicated the tall, dark-haired individual to his left. "This gentleman is Dale Micklewski."

Micklewski smiled sardonically but said nothing. He seemed to be sizing us up. I didn't like his look at all, and I shuddered. Several of us did.

Littleton sensed our reaction and laughed. "On my other side is my good friend and roommate Peter 'Wild-man' Kopciak. He's another pussy cat."

I stared at the 'Wild-man.' Something told me Sidney was lying.

He chuckled again.

I decided I didn't like Sidney. There was something about him, besides his stupid name that was at the same time both arrogant and unredeeming. Maybe the Academy crucible had ground the humanity from him, and all that remained was his baser side.

He turned slowly, keeping his hands precisely positioned behind his back, which seemed very affectatious in civilian clothes. "You are going to be part of the Twenty Third Company Tigers," he said with some pride. "We are the meanest, toughest, most gung-ho Company in the Brigade, and we're proud of it."

He snorted, then indicated his companions with a nod of his head. "*We* had a Plebe Year. You can count on that. None of this sissy stuff you've experienced so far, and a whole lot worse than the worst we can do to you and stay within the rules."

He stopped and stared wistfully at us before continuing. "I wish we could show you a real Plebe Year. By not having one, you will miss out on the greatest challenge in the military." He paused. "It's too bad."

"But," Littleton continued, perking up a bit, "we fully intend to give you the best Plebe Year we can within the limits the Academy sets. It's the least we can do for you and for this institution. So don't worry. You'll have a Plebe Year. You just won't have a real Plebe Year." There was no question in my mind about his seriousness. I began to worry. Up to that point I didn't really believe that the return of the Brigade would be so bad. I mean, everybody had to study, didn't they?

"I suppose 'Big Jim' Daly is the worst of us," he continued. "Pray you don't get in his squad. But Wildman here is also a plebe killer. He gets pretty intense sometimes."

215

Wildman smiled broadly, and Littleton continued.   "And I also have a reputation. It's completely deserved, believe me; but if you survive, you'll one day thank me for my attention."

He and his companions had turned so that they were facing away from us.  I looked at the Goon Room.  Polk shook his head in disbelief.  Ramsey stared at the backs of the three first-classmen, sizing them up.  Poole looked terrified.  Merritt seemed angry.

I found myself a bit angry too.  How dare they insinuate that what we had experienced thus far wasn't a Plebe Year.  It sure felt like a Plebe Year to me.  Besides, I bet I could outrun any of them.  I also bet myself that I could handle anything they could dish out -- although I really wanted to avoid the dishing.

My irritation was broken when Maxwell and Battle entered the area through the double doors. They stopped and stared.  Maxwell was openmouthed.  Battle narrowed his gaze at the trio.

"Where the hell have you been?" asked Littleton gruffly.

 "We stopped by the Main Office to pick up a note for midshipman Maxwell," Battle replied boldly.  "While we were there we talked to the duty section about scheduled activities."

"You know you're not supposed to leave the plebes alone!" snapped Littleton.

"We were in the Main Office," answered Battle evenly.

"That's no excuse," said Littleton officiously.  "Put yourselves on report for not following correct procedures, and you can bet I'm going to let Rock Stone know about this."

I was shocked.  Littleton was putting our squadleaders on report.  Hell, none of us plebes had received any demerits as yet.  This was incredible.

To his credit, Battle didn't flinch.

"May I remind you, Sidney," he said slowly, "that you are not allowed to be in this area. This wing is strictly set aside for plebe training, and that means only the second-class assigned to the plebe detail.  Shouldn't you put *yourself* on report for not following correct procedures?"

Littleton stared at Battle, then smiled, nodding his head slowly and regarding Battle with open malevolence.  That same look radiated from Micklewski's and Kopciak's ugly faces.

"Touché, Midshipman Second-class Battle," Littleton said. "We'll be going now."
Littleton spun a quick circle and laughed, "See you guys in September!"

The three amigos disappeared around the corner and down an unused passageway.

Battle and Maxwell exchanged glances, then Maxie spoke. "All right, everyone. The fun's over. Back to your rooms."

As the squadleaders hurried to their room. I could hear them whispering furiously.

I said to Rico, "What did you think of that?"

"All crap," he said.

"You think he wasn't serious?" I asked.

"Oh, no! Littleton was serious. But he spouted shit."

"What about the thing with Battle?" I asked.

"Battleaxe just went up a notch in my estimation from asshole to just plain ass," replied Rico. "Come on, Kevin, lighten up. We've got better things to think about."

Rico was right as usual, but before I completely calmed, I decided to visit the Goons.

The goons became silent when I entered. They had obviously been discussing something they didn't want an outsider to hear. The question was, did they consider me an outsider?

"What's up?" I asked.

"Plenty!" answered Polk.

Jim Merritt looked at his roommates before speaking. "We're discussing our future," he said. "Tonight's incident throws new light on everything."

"How so?" I asked.

Ramsey spoke fiercely. "Are you shitting me, O'Reilly! We just met the midshipman from hell, and you ask what's changed? Maybe you didn't see that gleam in Micklewski's eyes, but I did. The guy is insane."

I looked at the others, and I could tell from their expressions that they agreed.

"Let's not panic yet," I said. "It could be that the whole thing was staged to scare us."

217

"Well, it worked," said Polk. "And besides, that little confrontation between Battle and Littleton was not staged. They hate each other. And all three of them hate plebes. This is going to be one miserable year, my friend. Is it worth it?"

I thought he was asking himself that question, so I didn't answer. Tommy Poole had been quiet to this point, and I watched him as he stared out the window, deep in thought.

"Look, fellas," I said, trying my best to sound reasonable, "let's take this one day at a time and see where it all leads. Besides, look at Tommy here." When he heard his name, Poole turned toward me. I don't think he even knew I was in the room until that instant.

"Nobody has caught more shit than Tommy, and he's doing just fine. No way can what they do to us come academic year be any worse. By God, if Tommy can hack it, so can I."

Tommy's eyes narrowed and he stared at me for a long second before speaking. "Tommy's not doing so well," he said sadly. "Tommy's tired. Tommy's in constant pain. And Tommy's sick of the humiliation." Poole turned back toward the window.

"That's what we were discussing when you entered," offered Jim Merritt. "Tommy said he's thinking about quitting, and some of us are trying to talk him out of it."

"And some of us think it's a great idea!" added Ramsey with more vigor than necessary.

I watched the four of them for a second. Whoever assigned roommates could not have put four more disparate personalities into the same small space. This was a perfect microcosm of opinions, and a great laboratory to watch how the pressure changed people, and brought out the best -- and the worst -- in all of us.

"Tommy! Listen!" I said. "You can't quit. If you do, you acknowledge everything Maxwell and Battle said. You *will* be a pussy. And how's is it going to affect you? After you leave, are you going to start believing that crap they spouted. That decision could affect your future in ways you can't know. I'll say a prayer for you Tommy. My Mom always prays to Saint Jude. He's the Patron Saint of Lost Causes. It can't hurt."

"Y'all are so full of shit, your eyes should be deep brown," said Ramsey leaning back in his chair. "Where did y'all get your psychology degree, and what makes you think you know everything? Come down to earth, redhead, and stop living in your fantasy."

"Maybe you're right Jubal," I replied a little angrily. "Maybe I *am* the biggest bullshitter in this Academy. Christ knows my mother accuses me of that often enough. But I'll tell you something. Tommy Poole has more heart and guts than the best of us. I hope that if it ever gets too hard for me, I can remember what he's had to suffer. He's a hero in my opinion. I'll say a prayer for you too!"

Tommy eyed me skeptically, then turned his head back toward the darkening window. "I'm going to discuss everything with my family and make a decision during Parents' Weekend," he said sadly. "I don't want to quit, but God, this is the hardest thing I've even done."

No one said a word for a long time. I could sense that their private moment with Kevin O'Reilly was ended. I was an outsider again. I turned toward the door, and discovered that the excitement had made me horny. "Well, guys, the redhead has better things to do. See you later."


Rico was brushing his teeth in anticipation when I entered. "Hustle, Kevin," he said. "They'll be here in 30 minutes."

"No problem," I answered. "I'll take a quick shower; then it's just another uniform race."

I turned on the water. While it warmed, I went to the window and gazed outside. The night was humid and moonless and no breeze stirred the dark masses of trees. But life went on in the courtyard windows around me. The myriad fluorescent rectangles seemed unusually bright in contrast to the darkness that gripped the Academy. Or maybe my mood made it seem that way.

The visit by the 'Tigers' must have had a profound effect on the entire Company. No music issued forth from Simpson's guitar, and the usual subdued but intense grab-ass and banter were also missing. I turned toward Simpson's room, fully expecting to see Ronald Steinway perched on his favorite spot. He was. I was about to shout a word or two of encouragement, but I could hear soft sobs drifting my way on the still air. I ducked my head inside.

I finished my shower, shaved, brushed my teeth, and got dressed in fresh gym gear.

Rico checked us out before we departed.

"Follow me," I whispered as we exited the room toward the heads. "I know some secret ways to the outside."

We jogged stealthily along dark unused passageways and down narrow stairways until we came to the exit door I had used with Ramsey and Polk several weeks previously. Once

219

outside, we rigged the door for later entrance, crept in the darkness toward the parking lot of the Midshipman's Store, and waited hunched over in the shadow of a bush.

We didn't wait long. Five minutes later, a dark, late model, automobile pulled around the corner from the direction of the yacht basin and turned into the parking lot. It stopped in front of us, and its headlights went out. I saw two shadows inside.

The shadow in the front passenger seat turned, knelt on the seat, and stretched to open the door behind her. The lights came on inside the car. A very pretty blond girl -- Rico's Cindy -- knelt on the passenger seat, looking in our direction.

I strained to see the driver, but Cindy's body blocked my view.

Rico nudged me. "Let's go," he said.

We crept from behind the bushes and sprinted for the back seat. Rico piled in first. I was close behind.

Cindy shut the door, and it bumped my backside as it closed.

"Get down in the wheel-well and cover yourselves with the blanket," she said.

A large dark blanket lay in the back seat. Rico reached for it as we slid down.

"Wait," said the driver, "let me get a look at my date first." She snapped on the overhead light, turned around, and faced me.

Hunched over on all fours on the floor of an automobile was not exactly the position I would have chosen for an introduction. We stared at each other. I felt like that monkey again. I caught a glimpse of a hard but pleasant face, dark eyes, no obvious deformities or scars, and an enormous head of hair, piled up on her head in a beehive. She was also chewing gum furiously. Not exactly the type of girl I would have picked for myself, but I was not complaining. Besides I wasn't even sure what my type of girl was yet. This was the time for experimentation.

"Hi! My name's Brenda."

"I'm Kevin."

Brenda turned toward Cindy, smiling. "He's cute! He'll do!"

The girls tittered.

It's possible to get from Bancroft Hall to Hospital Point and not leave the grounds.  Going through the gates with a dark, covered lump in the back seat might have posed a problem.  At least I thought so at the time.  That was before I got to know the civilian gate guards, who we affectionately referred to as 'Jimmy-legs.'

Being mostly older gentlemen and Federal government employees, they lacked any type of military zeal.  I believe their standing orders were to keep outsiders out rather than escaping midshipmen in.

During my second-class year, when it was 'illegal' to have a car, I struck up a friendship with a friendly black guard who stood weekend duty on Gate Number Three.  His name, oddly enough, was Jimmy.

Jimmy didn't care what time I crept in, what clothing I had on, or what condition I was in.  And he always addressed me as 'Admiral' O'Reilly.  I would enter through Jimmy's gate.  During first-class year Jimmy let me smuggle my brother Sean -- who was as big as some of my classmates by then -- onto the campus late the night before the Army-Navy game so he could spend the night with me and get a taste for military life.  I even 'borrowed' a uniform from a plebe about his size and snuck him on the bus so that he could participate in the march-on and the hat trick.  Without any practice, he still marched better than some of my plebes -- who did *not* have a Plebe Year like mine, by the way.


We drove slowly through the dark campus, Cindy giving directions.  I felt silly hiding under a blanket in the rear of a car.  But Rico was also huddled in the identical predicament, and misery loves company.  And the potential rewards?

The ride to Hospital Point took ten minutes.  Brenda stopped the car along the road adjacent to the Academy cemetery.

"Stay down while we check the area," Cindy said.

She and Brenda shifted in their seats as they looked in all directions.

"I think it's all clear," she announced.

Rico straightened and opened his door.

Cindy and Brenda exited their own doors, and I slid out the same side Rico had used.

"Bring both blankets," Cindy offered.

Rico already had one.  I grabbed the other.

Cindy clutched Rico's arm as they turned toward the hillside.

"Let's move uphill away from the car," I suggested, "in case someone checks nearby."

"Good idea," Rico replied.

Brenda held my arm with her hands.  She squeezed my biceps and I flexed in response.


The grassy hill leading to the cemetery is steep in places, but there are level plateaus where trees, decorative bushes, and a few departed naval officers are planted.  Rico and Cindy selected a spot under a spreading tree whose drooping branches hid any view of the road.  Brenda and I picked a similar location twenty yards away in the 'shadow' of a large granite headstone.  Light filtering from a streetlight down the hill revealed that we were near the resting-place of Captain Benjamin Fromme.  I hesitated, shuddering slightly.  After further consideration, however, I assumed that Fromme, who must have once been a midshipman himself, would have no objections to my dallying nearby; in fact, he might even approve.

I spread the blanket and Brenda sat in the dark, holding her knees with her arms and watching me.  She had on a pair of tight short pants, and in the dappled dimness that filtered into our niche from a streetlight 30 yards away, I could see she had good, strong-looking legs.  I sat next to her and put an arm around her shoulders.  She leaned in toward me and rested her head against my chest.

"Nice night," I whispered, not knowing what else to say.

"Uh, huh," she replied quietly.  We sat in the dark for several long seconds.

"Is anything wrong?" I asked.

"No," she answered.  "Just a little nervous about this."

About what, I wondered?  Was she assuming something was going to happen?  I hoped so.  "How come?" I asked.

"I don't know.  You seem nice enough.  But I don't really know you at all."

"We could talk," I said. "Get to know each other a bit."

She thought for a minute. "Kevin?" she said. "Would you think badly of me if I didn't want to talk -- if I just wanted you to kiss me."

Was she crazy? I was instantly excited.

"That would be fine," I stammered.

She turned toward me and pushed me down onto the blanket. Then she climbed on top of me and settled herself against me.

"Oooohhh, Kevin," she said. She pressed herself against my chest and kissed me.

The kiss lasted more than a minute, our passions compounding all the while. I was in danger of losing control. She saved the day.

Moaning, she straightened, sat on my chest, and began removing her clothing.

Afterward I was never completely sure what happened. Every bit of it was new and intense and I had nothing to compare it to. It was like riding a runaway train and knowing another was racing inevitably toward me. I knew vaguely we were going to crash, but I didn't care. Hell, I welcomed the explosions. I urged it on. I wanted to feel the flames and taste the finality of it.

In whatever universe I temporarily occupied, time did not exist. There was only a period of 'nowness' that did not change while we two trains raced headlong toward each other. I saw her approaching. A light, white, as intense as the sun that shattered against me. Suddenly there were sounds! Roaring. Moaning. Squealing. Laughing. And the now-ness changed to instants, and the intensity subsided until I was back in reality. What had happened?

At first I thought the explosion had injured me. Where had I been?

Brenda moaned, waking me completely. Her head had settled on my shoulder, facing away from Rico and Cindy. Unfortunately, her beehive -- which had the consistency of thirty-day concrete -- pressed against my nose and mouth and distracted me from the afterglow.

"Hey, stud," whispered Rico from his blanket, "time to go."

Brenda straightened, patted me on the head, then reached for her garments.

I did the same.  As she was about to slip into her undies, I said, "Brenda, could I keep your panties as a remembrance?"

She hesitated.  "Kinky, huh?"

"Sort of."  She looked at the dainty, lacy object in her hand, almost as if seeing it for the first time.  It was so dark I couldn't see her expression.  She handed me the panties.

In the parking lot we uncovered, sat up, and looked around.  All was quiet.  Before we departed, Cindy grabbed Rico's arm.  "I love you," she said sweetly.

Rico was taken aback.  "Me too.  I'll call you."

Solemnly I reached up front-ward and touched Brenda's massive hairdo.  "And I love you, Brenda," I said tenderly.

She gawked.

Every eye in the car watched as I continued to pat her rigid coif.  Then I smiled and gave her an exaggerated wink.

We returned to our place in the bushes.  After the car turned the corner, we made our way stealthily toward the waiting door.  When we passed under an exterior light I stopped to examine my shirt.  It was wrinkled and moist from exertion.

Rico watched closely.

I broke into an enormous grin and displayed my pink, frilly, trophy.

Rico slapped me on the back and laughed.  "O'Reilly, my man.  You're a true stud."

CHAPTER 23

## *RONALD'S DEMISE*

Back in the Company area I sensed something was wrong. Instead of deathly quiet, I could hear mumbling noises from several plebe rooms. I looked at Rico, who only shrugged.

No sooner had we entered our room than the door of the Goon Room flew open. Merritt sprinted across the passageway.

"Steinway has disappeared!"

"What do you mean?" I asked.

"He isn't in his room. Simpson said Ronald was sitting at his desk writing a letter home when he left to go to the head. Strong was asleep. Anyway, when Simpson returned, Steinway was gone. Simpson checked the head and the other company rooms but no Ronald."

I spoke. "He seemed sad after dinner; maybe he went for a long walk to clear his mind?"

"Simpson doesn't think he'd leave the area. He's scared to death of any attention."

I went to the window and checked outside. I didn't see Ronald, but I also didn't have a good view of the entire roof. "Let me check something." I climbed out onto the dark roof.

"Where are you going?" asked Merritt.

"Ronald liked to sit out on the roof and meditate. I'll check around out here."

"Be careful," Merritt warned. "It's awfully dark."

I stood and began walking with my feet placed one in front of the other in the copper gutter and one hand on the tilted roof, leaning in an exaggerated angle away from the edge. It *was* precarious in the dark, and I've always been a bit acrophobic -- some condition for a future jet pilot, huh? In this shaky manner I moved toward Ronald's room, checking the roof as I went. I couldn't see anything.

I arrived at Ronald's room and peeked inside. Merritt and Rico were there, along with several other classmates.

Merritt turned to me. "Should we wake Maxwell? There was trouble for not reporting Spielenberg's absence."

"Let's develop a plan," I said. "We should conduct our own search first. Maybe he's got a bad case of diarrhea  and he's been in a stall all this time."

"I already checked," said Willy.

"I'll gather the others." Merritt departed.

I stayed on the roof, looked out into the dark, and tried to think. Where would I go if I were Ronald Steinway? -- I wouldn't go anywhere! After all, I had my lonely perch if I wanted solitude, so there was no reason for meandering around Mother Bancroft -- that would only invite trouble I wanted desperately to avoid. I was a prime target for the squadleaders, and the interruption by Littleton and his cohorts promised more trouble. But I couldn't quit because my parents were counting on me, and I couldn't disappoint them because they were so proud. But I couldn't stand this place another minute, and I was desperate, so I had to do something. . . .

I suppose the solution to Ronald's problems had been with me the entire time, poised just beyond my consciousness. I hadn't chosen to recognize it because it frightened me. I had pushed it away and tried to avoid it. But my brain reached the inevitable conclusion, and I decided there was only one true possibility of escape for poor Ronald.

I sighed. It wouldn't get any easier the longer I waited. I slid on my rear down into the gutter. Placing one hand on the roof, and the other firmly gripping the edge of the gutter, I leaned over the black void.

I became disoriented and frightened beyond comprehension. The shadows swirled wildly beneath me. I yelped and pulled back. But in that instant of swimming vision I saw an indistinct lighter blob among the dark plant shadows four floors below. That blob seemed deathly still.

I whirled away from the roof's edge and sprawled on the tile facing the window. For an instant I thought I was falling over the edge, and I reached with open hands and gripped the roof tightly. I became lightheaded. I moaned loudly, my left cheek pressed against the roof tiles.

"Ooooohhhhhh, Jesus! Mother of God! No!" I began to hyperventilate.

Bob Strong came to the window. He looked at me and saw the distress on my face. He turned pale. He didn't say a word, but his eyes asked the question.

I nodded quickly, gulping air.

"Oh, no, Ronald, no!" he said with a shrillness that sent chills down my already weakened spine. I grabbed harder at the tile and I could feel the fingernail of my right ring finger peel back painfully. I didn't let go.

Jim Merritt jumped out the window and scampered over me to the edge of the roof.

I watched as he peered over. He wasn't afraid of heights, and I was irrationally angry.

He stared for less than three seconds then hurried inside the room. He even said, "Excuse me," when he bumped against my hand on his way past.

"Strong," he asserted, taking charge, "you and Simpson race down to the Main Office and get an ambulance over here immediately. Tell them someone has fallen from the roof. Ronald's directly below your room in the bushes. Pirelli, you and Ramsey find Ronald and see if you can help."

"What, from four floors up?" asked Jubal sarcastically. "We won't be any help at all."

"Maybe the bushes broke his fall?" offered Simpson.

"Yeah, and pigs can fly," offered Ramsey.

"Hurry, Jubal!" said Merritt. Ramsey didn't object further, and he and Pirelli followed Strong and Simpson out the door.

"Rico, you and I had better wake Maxwell."

"Let's get Kevin first!"

Silence followed. Rico came slowly to the window. He stared at me, then touched my hand gently, much as I had touched Ronald's shoe several weeks ago.

I shuddered.

"You okay, Kevin?" he asked softly.

I stared at his hand, suddenly frightened. "Ohhhh God!" I jerked my hand away from the contact and moaned again, much louder than previously. Loud enough to wake the dead -- maybe that was the reason. The sound of my cry echoed in the courtyard eerily and sent renewed shivers down my spine. I'm sure I woke every plebe whose room bordered the courtyard.

I began to cry uncontrollably. My body racked with convulsions. I shook my head to stop the tears. They immediately ceased and I became lightheaded again, then incredibly angry. Almost instantaneously, however, I calmed.

Rico reached out. "Come on, Kevin. It's not safe out there, and you've had a shock."

I felt suddenly drunk. "That's two shocks in one night," I said, now laughing uncontrollably. "One was good, but this is not so good, Rico. Ronald's dead."

"I know, Kevin. Come on in. We've got to report this." He grabbed my arm in a firm grip, and began pulling me in.

I took a deep breath, and my senses cleared. I felt the tension wash from my body in a gushing turbulence that left me feeling strangely renewed.

I leaned toward the edge and Rico jerked me quickly back toward the room. I looked at him calmly. "I'm okay now, Rico. I have to look one more time. I'm afraid if I don't, I won't ever be the same again."

Rico looked at me skeptically. He must have decided that I was okay, because he let go.

I leaned over the edge and looked down into infinity -- poor Ronald's Infinity. Jubal was right. Ronald didn't survive the fall; I could see that from here. Ronald was broken. No doctors were going to help him, and all the King's horses and all the King's men couldn't help.

Sighing, I turned toward Rico and nodded. I crawled away from the edge and back into the relative safety of the room -- Ronald's ex-room.

Jim Merritt was waiting at the doorway. A crowd of plebes had gathered in the passageway. They had heard but had not believed the words. The three of us walked to Maxwell's door. We looked at each other.

I decided to take the lead. I knocked. There was no answer. I knocked again, louder, but still no one acknowledged us. Looking at Merritt, I pushed the door open and turned on the overhead lights. Merritt and Guevarra followed me inside.

My first reaction was, 'What a pigpen!' In fairness to the squadleaders there was almost no clutter or dirt in the room, but a few things were strewn around near the sink where Battle had prepared for his departure on liberty, and one of the desks was covered with an open newspaper and several novels. We plebes could never get away with this. I glanced around the second-class inner sanctum. One rack was made-up but empty. In the other, a form under the covers stirred slowly. Maxwell must have been a very heavy sleeper.

I calmly walked over and shook him. "Sir!" I said. "Get up. Something's happened."

Maxwell stirred, then turned groggily. He focused on me with great difficulty. I thought at first he had been drinking.

"What the hell do you want, O'Reilly? You had better have a good reason for this!"

"Yes, sir!" I said. "There's been a bad accident. Ronald Steinway may have been killed."

"What!" Maxwell leapt from his bed. "What happened? When? Where?"

He donned his robe and raced past Merritt and Guevarra into the passageway. Pausing, he looked up and down for Steinway.

"Where is he?" he asked.

"Sir," Jim said. "He fell from the roof outside his room, but we don't exactly know when. We've sent for an ambulance, and two classmates are down there with him now."

Maxwell brushed Jim aside and ran into Steinway's room. "Shit! Let me see!"

We watched as he went to the window leaned out, then crawled slowly, to the roof's edge. "Don't touch him!" he yelled to someone below. "You might injure him further." He continued staring for almost a minute, then pulled back inside and came into the passageway. "I'm going down to check," he said. "You people stay here."

"What about Mister Battle?" I offered.

Maxwell stared at me. He hurried into his room and returned with a slip of paper. He scribbled on the paper, and looked up. "Pirelli!" he yelled.

John Pirelli came forward.

Maxwell handed him the note. "Call this number. Ask for Tom Battle. Tell him about Steinway and to get back here ASAP. If you can't reach him, put on gym gear and go to that address. Knock until he answers. Carry your ID. Run like hell. If you get stopped, tell the gate guard there's been an emergency and that the Duty Office authorized your trip."

Pirelli started to speak. "Don't ask questions, damn it! Get going!"

After Maxwell had hurried out the double doors, the rest of the company crowded around to hear what we had to say. I let Jim and Rico tell the story. I was beginning to get the shakes again. I trudged to the nearest bulkhead and sat down, hunching my knees to my chest. After a minute, the loud noise of an ambulance sounded shrilly in the T-Court area, and the entire plebe Brigade came awake. Excited shouts and loud questions seemed to emanate from all directions.

I stood and walked through the double doors to the balcony overlooking the rotunda. I watched the frantic activity below. Plebes in rooms across the way saw me and did the same. Soon the balconies filled with classmates and second classmen, everyone wondering about the commotion.

It didn't take long for the ambulance crew to get what was left of Ronald loaded onto a gurney and rushed through the rotunda into the waiting jaws of the ambulance. They seemed in an awful hurry for a lost cause. Soon only the murmur of excited voices echoed in the rotunda.

A midshipman watch officer came out into the center of the rotunda and shouted. "It's all over. Get back to your rooms immediately."

"What happened, Phil?" asked a second-class from across the way.

"Not sure yet," the watch officer answered. "But a pretty severe accident."

While we stood on the balcony, Maxwell came up the stairs flanked by an officer in crisp tropical whites. It was Lieutenant Large again!

We began snapping to attention and yelling but he cut us short. "None of that bullshit tonight, okay?" he said. He looked at us, then said. "Let's go inside the Company area." He herded us through the double doors. Once isolated from the rotunda he said, "Okay, everybody relax. Sit on the floor, please."

"Guys," he said, speaking to us as equals -- something that hadn't happened thus far this summer -- "I'm really sorry to inform you that your classmate and friend, Ronald Steinway, is dead.  There'll be an investigation to determine what happened and to prevent future accidents of this sort, but from what we can tell he was crawling along the roof in the dark and slipped.  He broke his neck in the fall, and his death, thankfully, was instantaneous."

Lieutenant Large stared at the deck and twirled his hat nervously in his hands.  "Who were his roommates?" he asked.

Strong and Simpson raised their hands.

"Who was with him at any time this evening?"

Patrick Mulvaney raised his hand.

"Who discovered the body?"

I raised my hand.

"Okay," the officer said.  "Get some sleep if you can.  Tomorrow morning sometime before noon I want anyone who might have information that could shed light on this tragedy, to come by the Main Office and give a statement.  That should be about all. Again, I am truly sorry for this unexpected sadness."  With that, he turned and walked slowly out the double doors.

Maxwell stood.  "When you give your statements tomorrow, tell the absolute truth."

He was troubled by something, however, and I knew what it was.  "What about Littleton's visit?" I asked.

He became irritated.  "What about it?"

"Well," I said, "I'm sure it doesn't relate to what happened to Ronald, but if the visit became general knowledge, it could mean trouble to all of us."

I had lied about the relationship between tonight's visit and Ronald's leap to destiny.  I did think the visit might have been the final straw for Ronald.  I didn't for a second think Ronald had fallen from the roof.  But I couldn't prove anything, and besides, what purpose would voicing my opinion on that matter serve.  No one could do anything now to save Ronald, and a fall was certainly a more noble death than a suicide -- that is, if any death can be noble.  There didn't seem to be any sense in bringing it up if we could avoid it.

Maxwell thought about the situation, then addressed the group.  "Okay," he said.  "Tell the absolute truth in your statements, but do not mention the visit by Littleton *unless . . .*" He emphasized the word strongly.  "you feel it has a direct bearing on the accident. Getting Littleton in trouble, despite the fact that he is an asshole, will not do a thing to help Ronald, and will only cause complications for you later.  I say again, I am *not* ordering you to say nothing about Mr. Littleton, just use discretion and common sense."

 "Okay," he said reassuming his squadleader guise.  "Get to your rooms and get to sleep – if you can!"  The Company began wandering toward their respective rooms.

"I said now!" Maxwell exploded.

Some of my classmates immediately braced and chopped.  Others did not react.

"Mulvaney! Goto!  Give me 20!"

Both were confused.  Neither reacted.

"Now!" Maxwell screamed.

I don't know why, but I grabbed Maxwell firmly by the arm.  I then turned him around so he was facing away from the rest of my classmates.

 "Maxie," I said in a fierce hush.  "Jesus man!  One of our classmates is dead!  We're all shocked.  This is no time to pull the squad leader bullshit.  Take it easy.  Show some compassion."

Maxwell stared at my hand on his arm, considering.  Then he shook my hand away and toward the Company.  "I have been reminded that the events of this evening have been a shock to us all.  That's true for me too.  I'm sorry.  You all have carry-on until further notice.  Now please get some sleep if you can." Maxwell went to his room.

I found myself very tired.

Jim Merritt stood in front of me.  He raised his eyebrows.  "Maxie?" he asked quietly.

I smiled.  *"He who will not risk, cannot win,"* I said, quoting Reef Points.  "It worked."

Rico was also hovering nearby.  "You got huevos the size of cannonballs, amigo," he said. As I came closer Jim wrinkled up his nose questioningly.  "You also smell funny, O'Reilly."

I smiled and lifted the front of my shirt to my nose and breathed deeply. "I do, don't I?"

Rico laughed.

Jim was confused, but I provided no enlightenment.


The next morning after chapel I gave my statement to the Officer of the Day and then said good-by to Aaron Rose and Bill Allen, both of whom had decided to depart Annapolis for greener, and hopefully less dangerous, pastures. I bought Bill Allen's nicely polished shoes even though they were a half-size too small.

CHAPTER 24

## *AFTERMATH*

For the next week things were quiet in the Twenty-third Company.  We attended lectures, practiced on the rifle range, and marched as usual.  We even participated in the plebe Company marching competition and came in ninth.  There must have been some very inept plebes in the Class of 1971, because I thought we stunk.  But Maxie and Battle had forgotten we were plebes.  We endured no comearounds, no early morning runs, and no bracing at meals.  It was almost heaven.  So why did I felt cheated?

I reported to the Main Office on Sunday and gave my report.  I avoided mentioning the visit by Littleton and my escapade on Hospital Point.  Apparently everybody left out the part about Littleton, because nothing ever came from the incident.

The Academy's Accident Investigation Report declared that Steinway's death was an accident caused by a misstep on a dark evening in a place he should not have been.  To avoid any repetition of the same event, the Superintendent issued a memo forbidding any excursions onto the roof.  That was fine with me.  For the rest of that year I could not look outside at night and not expect to see troubled Ronald sitting in the dark, contemplating his future.  If ever a spot were likely to be haunted, it would be that lonely stretch of roof outside Room 5413.  But I didn't intend to verify my ghostly suspicions.

Monday evening, the entire Brigade of plebes attended a special memorial service in the chapel.  Twenty-third Company sat up front, just behind Ronald's parents, who were flown in from Phoenix to meet with the Superintendent and bring Ronald home to rest.  It was a wonderful ceremony.  Rear Admiral Conrad's speech was emotional and uplifting.  Ronald's mother wept the entire service, and his father comforted her stoically.

The military has had a great deal of practice over the years in honoring its fallen heroes, and Ronald certainly left the Academy in style.  I'm sure it made his parents proud.  At the end of the service when the congregation sang the Navy Hymn -- which is one of the most touching and beautiful tunes ever written -- and we sang the part about *"those in peril on the sea,"* I cried too, and I wasn't the only classmate in tears.  Ronald was certainly in peril.  I just wish he could have chosen a different escape, God rest his troubled soul.

We lost three classmates that unfortunate week, which was very depressing. Ronald, of course, was first. Aaron Rose was next. Aaron had been a borderline midshipman, struggling with his place in the military system. I was certain he only wanted a good excuse to depart, so his leaving didn't particularly surprise me.

I did regret Bill Allen's decision, however. I considered him one of the best in the Company. With all the posturing and pretense it was hard to tell who was being himself. I never had that problem with Bill. I liked his smile. I liked his sense of humor. And I especially liked his ability to see through the baloney and view the system in comfortable perspective. I hardly knew him, but I was sure we would have become good friends.


It was Jubal Ramsey who crashed us through the impenetrable barrier that Steinway's death erected and brought us back into Plebe Summer where we belonged. It happened on the Friday after Ronald's demise, one of the hottest and most humid days of that long summer.

We had remained depressed, including Maxwell and Battle, with no sign of let-up. The squadleaders led us to events but without any vigor. They inspected us but missed discrepancies that would have meant major punishment only days earlier. Meals were dormitory affairs with no questions asked and no three-chews-and-a-swallow hassles. It was good for us, but it was also not good for us at the same time. There was no fun -- or pain -- any more.

On Friday morning we had attended a final academic lecture in Sampson Hall, where we selected majors, chose classes, and received our tentative schedules for the first semester. On the return march toward Bancroft Hall, a lethargic Battle, noticing that a flock of lovelies hovered expectantly along the walk, perked, turned toward us, and said over his shoulder in a very uncommanding voice.

"Ramsey, how about leading us in a song?"

"Aye, aye, sir! There's a skeeter on my . . ."

Before Ramsey could belt out the next word, a surprised Battle spun around, tripping and almost falling to the bricks in the process. He yelled. "Ramsey! Knock it off!" Straightening, and continuing to march backward, Battle eyed Ramsey for several seconds, his eyes wide as basketball hoops. Then he smiled.

I had never seen Tommy Battle smile before.  It wasn't a bad smile; and, best of all, it was a genuine smile.  He followed the genuine smile with a genuine laugh, which we all imitated.

It felt good to laugh after so long in the doldrums.  That laugh drove away the last residue of Ronald's death.  We were plebes again, and Battle and Maxie were our squadleaders.  In that instant I loved those guys -- but I must admit I was a bit caught up in the emotions of the Moment.

"Ramsey!" Battle yelled, still smiling.  "Give us a song.  But make it appropriate or I'll personally boil you in oil."

"Aye, aye, sir!" Jubal immediately began a stirring but not so tuneful rendition of *She Wore a Yellow Ribbon* for the girls.  They loved it.

The Saturday afternoon after Ronald's death we had a meeting with Captain Dillingham.  The squadleaders wouldn't tell us what it was to be about.  Bull braced us up against the passageway wall, while he conducted the meeting.  I decided this was a sign that Plebe Summer would continue.

"Gentlemen," Dillingham began, "in three weeks the Brigade returns, and things will be very different around here.  I want to make sure that you are prepared, and I have discussed your individual progress with Midshipmen Maxwell and Battle.  There's good and bad news to report."

"The good news is that every one of you qualified with both rifle and pistol.  Seven of you were double experts.  That's excellent.  You also finished ninth in the Marching Competition, which is good considering the recent tragedy.  I also thought you did a good job on your rooms and uniforms for the last inspection.  Keep up the good work."

 "But," Bull continued, slapping one hand palm up on the other to emphasize his points, "I am disappointed with some other results of your training thus far."  I could see him as he approached my position, and I noticed how much his enormous biceps muscle bulged as he slapped.  I figured this was an intentional show of prowess designed to intimidate us.  It did me.

"First," he continued, "the squadleaders have given me their evaluations of your individual performance, and only a very few of you reached the highest category.  Work harder.  There's room for improvement.

"Second, I have noticed that several of you still do not carry yourselves like potential officers in the Unites States military. Some of you remain disgustingly fat, slovenly, and in far from perfect condition. That must also improve.

"Third and most important, I had a long talk with your squadleaders this morning, and I discovered that several of you continue to hold back the development of your classmates despite ample evidence that you are not suited for this institution." He paused and his eyes narrowed. "I don't like that at all." Bull's voice, normally gentle, rose in volume. "I told Midshipmen Battle and Maxwell that I want my Company lean and mean, and I asked them to work harder to weed out the non-performers. If you fall into that category, please do your duty and go home."

Bull stopped in the center of the passageway midway down the line, and turned smartly toward us. "One final point, gentlemen. Your peer evaluations must be given to the squadleaders by evening meal today. Fill out the evals privately. Do not consult among yourselves. I expect we will be able to draw some interesting conclusions from this first evaluation." I wasn't sure what he meant, but I dutifully retreated to my room after he dismissed us and filled out the evaluation form. I ranked myself an honest number three, behind Merritt and Wojeck. Rico was my number four.

Comearounds returned with a vengeance the next week. Battle and Maxwell redoubled their efforts to steel our characters and to remove Tommy Poole and the bottom dwellers from our ranks. It was not a pretty experience.

"God-damn you, Poole!" Battle yelled. "You're a pussy! You're bagging it! I know you can move faster than that. If you don't beat Butler this next time, every plebe in the Company does 50 pushups." He also set an impossible task for Tommy, who lost the race as expected, and dropped to the deck for pushups.

"No, Poole!" yelled Maxwell. "You relax, Just like you've been doing during comearounds. Your classmates will do the work for you." Tommy stood in the passageway while the rest of us yelled out the 50 numbers, plus one to Beat Army and one for Ronald Steinway. Tommy was embarrassed and angry, and so were several of my classmates.

I was also angry, but more with Battle than Tommy. Besides, pushups were nothing! At least the first time. Two minutes later after Poole lost the next impossible race, it was harder to crank out 50. The third time they were damn hard and very irritating. The fourth time they were almost impossible. Most people could not finish. The fifth time my arms gave out after ten, and only Rico, French, and Lamont finished. The sixth time I hardly lifted myself from the cold deck, and even Lamont strained. There was no seventh time -- at least not that day.

The push-up punishment continued over the next two weeks. Anger accumulated.

"Son of a bitch!" I announced to Rico and Merritt later that week during an evening visit in our room. "This push-up shit is pissing me off."

"Better to be pissed off than pissed on," replied Rico, not at all acknowledging the seriousness of the matter.

"Come on, Rico," I said. "What Tommy is doing to us is pretty bad."

"Poole isn't doing anything to you, Kevin," Rico answered.

"Then what do you call these aching arms that I can hardly lift?" I asked.

"Come on, redhead," Rico said sarcastically. "Even you can see that your aching arms are part of a little game Battle and Maxie are playing to put peer pressure on Tommy and some others. It's not Poole who's the villain here; it's our glorious squadleaders."

I hesitated. At heart I knew what he said was correct, but it seemed that no matter who was the actual culprit, my arms would not be aching so much if Tommy were not still a midshipman.

"What you say may be true, Rico," I answered. "But even *you* must admit that Poole doesn't belong here."

Jim Merritt sidled up next to me when I said this to lend support to my statement.

"Jesus, Kevin!" Rico said, startled. "Listen to yourself. Just two weeks ago you were calling Tommy Poole the biggest hero since Audie Murphy. Now he's suddenly a worthless douchebag who doesn't measure up to *your* standards. What's happened to you?"

"I don't know," I replied smugly. "Maybe I'm just seeing the light."

Rico shook his head sadly. "I liked the old Kevin better than 'greaser' Kevin." he said. "I hope you see your error soon."

"Wait a minute, Rico," added Merritt. "I like Tommy. But his staying slows the rest of us down and prevents us from moving ahead."

I smiled. Good old Merritt. That was a good point. Tommy *was* hindering our progress.

"Moving ahead?" asked Rico incredulously. "To what? Better rack-making? Straighter formations? Shinier shoes? Give me a break. I personally would not choose Tommy Poole for a close friend, but he's not my enemy either, and I for one am focusing my resentment where it belongs -- right on the heads of two assholes who are supposed to be leaders but who are really children playing silly games with people's lives."

Neither Jim nor I had a reply to this argument -- probably because we both knew Rico was right. I wasn't yet ready to admit it, however, and I lapsed into a funk that lasted an entire day. I didn't like being forced to take a moral stand on the issue I had considered settled in my mind. I began to consider and reconsider other issues.


Plebe Summer had a strange effect on me. Like a quiet evening rainstorm, the Academy sneaked up on me and thoroughly drenched me with its outpouring. And once the traditions and ceremonies soaked in, I found I could not and would not separate myself willingly.

One bright, hot morning nearly at the end of Plebe Summer I awoke and discovered that I was no longer a civilian proto-plebe. Suddenly -- and surprisingly -- I found myself a full-fledged, heart-and-soul, into-the-breach, damn-the-torpedoes member of the Brigade of Midshipmen. Kevin O'Reilly had joined the fleet.

With that change, however, came certain responsibilities and certain fundamental shifts in my logic process. During the first part of the summer it didn't really matter who made it through the torture and who didn't. We were, after all, companions in confusion, partners in pain, teammates in torture. We were equals in the same miserable boat. But as the summer wore on, my young body firmed, my shoes achieved a mirror finish, and my marching became crisp and precise, I began, not to adapt, but rather to adopt. It became *my* Academy rather than *the* Academy.

I began to esteem the place and accept it as a bastion of brave and honorable history, an institute of noble and august tradition, a school of the highest moral and ethical standards. And I charged myself with its protection. I didn't want the image -- *my* image -- tarnished in any way.

But that admission of reverence and adoption had a darker side. Its very exclusivity meant that not everyone could be worthy. And I began to wonder things -- like what was

Barton Hardesty still doing here? He was far too religious. And Doug Goto studied too much. And Jeff Polk was a rabble-rouser. Those people were different -- maybe too different. They didn't fit the Academy image.

And Tommy Poole? What made him think he would ever make a good naval officer? He looked terrible in his uniform, he couldn't march for shit, and he didn't know the winner of the last World Series. He didn't even care. Why *was* he staying? Maybe Bull Dillingham was correct, and it would be better for the Academy if he and some others quit.

My intolerance for Tommy and the other 'marginal' plebes seemed to rise almost in lock step with the intensity of the physical exertion we underwent, which is why Rico's admonition troubled me. Just when I thought I had it all figured out, he confused me.

But my resentment focused not only on the "misfits," wishing them uncomfortably away, it also elevated itself to the Plebe greasers who had settled themselves smugly at the other end of the social and leadership spectrum. Grease was also the name of the rating system used to evaluate an individual's adaptability to the military and the Academy. Every midshipman receives a semester grease grade from his superiors and peers that reflects his 'Annapolis-ness.'

Having superiors evaluate performance and aptitude is a necessary part of life, inescapable except for the out-of-work or self-employed. I could accept that. But at Annapolis we also evaluated the grease of our own Company classmates, rating them by name from first to last. I never liked the peer review process; it always seemed somewhat Nazi to think that my classmates were tallying mental points for and against me to use in their secret evaluations.

The results of the first peer review -- the one Dillingham wanted finished so badly -- were posted outside the squadleaders' room on the Monday following Bull's pep talk. Wojeck and Merritt were first and second -- just as I had predicted. I came out number 10, and Rico was 15. Someone obviously made a mistake in the ranking or the calculations.

It wasn't that 10 was a bad number. I just felt I would rank better among my classmates. After all, I was a fairly nice guy. I avoided controversy. I did more than my share of work. And I considered myself well-liked. Apparently I wasn't as good as I had thought. I wondered why.

I studied the names of the classmates who made the top to determine what it was that put them there. And I suppose I also secretly wondered what I could do to join them. I expect the Academy wanted me to do exactly that, but as it turned out, it didn't work that way with me. Surprisingly, when I applied my own patented O'Reilly logic to the process, I found that I didn't particularly like what floated at the top any more than what groveled at the bottom.

John Pirelli was far too intense and unpersonable for my liking. Tim Richardson was much too self-assured and arrogant. Bob Strong had a single-mindedness that scared me. Mike Wojeck was the nicest of the greasers, but he was too gruff and unpolished. Even Jim Merritt, who to my way of thinking had the best leadership qualities, showed a certain eagerness to please that begged belief. And how the hell did BJ Wilson out-grease me? And why did I even care?

I don't want to be second best. It's human nature. But I'm also an Irish realist, and I have always tried to be aware of my many shortcomings. It helps me keep life in perspective. I quickly accepted the truth that, despite their faults, the best in the company were better than me. I was never going to be able even to hold the door open for the Chief of Naval Operations, much less lead the Company through a parade. I wasn't a born leader. I didn't have the inherent charisma. That was that. Case closed. Time to move on to other pursuits.

CHAPTER 25

## *MUTINY IN THE RANKS*

On the evening after posting the grease results, the squadleaders called a surprise general meeting.  Rico and I chopped to the assembly area across the passageway from the squadleaders' room and waited, braced against the wall.  Maxie and Battle emerged together.

"Carry-on, gentlemen," Maxie said in his mischievous voice.  "Have a seat."  We sat on the tile deck and waited.  Ever since the resumption of hazing, I had developed a dislike for the way the two of them were treating us.  It seemed as if they were being childish and petty.  I watched as they conferred quietly.

Maxwell walked to the bulletin board, and pointed to the grease list.  "Has everyone seen this listing?" he asked.  Of course everyone had.  It had been *the* topic of discussion all day.

"Well," Maxwell continued, examining the list with feigned interest, "it does indicate some very interesting things about you guys.  Let's see."  He looked more closely, then settled his gaze on the bottom of the list.  He pointed to the names and called them out.

"Poole? No surprise there.  Butler? Ditto.  Hardesty? Agreed.  Rogers? Yes there too.  Chalmers? Sure thing.  Simpson?  Maybe so.  And Polk?  Now that's a surprise.  I wonder what he did to piss off his classmates."  He then straightened up and turned toward us.

"Okay.  Let's have those gentlemen out here, front and center, please," he said.

The aforementioned plebes trotted reluctantly to the fore.

"Face your classmates, gentlemen," Maxwell said in his most sarcastic whine.  "Let them get a good look at you."  They turned.

All except Tommy Poole were plainly embarrassed.  Poole stared at us defiantly.  He caught my eye.  I winked at him.  He smiled briefly.  I also tried to signal reassurance to Jeff Polk, but he stared resolutely at the deck as he shifted nervously from foot to foot.

"This is the bottom of the barrel, gentlemen," continued Maxwell. "These are the lowest of the low. They are the dregs. The waste. The scum."

Some of us murmured uncomfortably and Maxwell stopped. "Don't be angry at me," he said in mock indignation. "It's not my list -- even though I might agree with it. You guys developed it yourselves." Maxie strolled in front of the group, shaking his head and pointing to the unfortunate selectees with a raised palm as he walked.

"These are the classmates you feel are not adapting to the Academy system. These are the classmates you believe are not coping with the pressures. These are the classmates you say are not leaders." Maxwell paused and turned toward the group. "I can't say as I blame you. They are a very depressing collection of misfits, whiners, and non-performers."

He again turned toward us. "For the rest of the summer I will refer to these people as *The Magnificent Seven*. They don't belong here, we all know that. We'll be counting on the more responsible members of your group to help us convince the misfits to hit the road. Hopefully, by the time the Brigade returns, there'll be no more *Magnificent Seven* for any of us to worry about."

"Now," Maxwell continued. "I want you *Magnificent Seven* to look at your classmates. Can you see the disgust on their faces? Can you see the disappointment in their eyes? Your classmates think you suck, guys. Isn't that reason enough to quit? Why not make it easy for everyone and get out now. Don't waste our time.

Maxwell looked at us.

I was offended. This was degrading.

"I want you to wave good-bye to the *Magnificent Seven*. Help them on their way, gentlemen."

Some of my classmates began waving at the unfortunate group. Others stared in disbelief. A few openly refused to participate.

"Wave good-bye! All of you!" Maxwell screamed. Many more classmates began waving. Maxwell caught my eye. My hand wasn't yet in the air, but it was creeping upward.

"One, sir! Two, sir! Three, sir!" Jubal Ramsey began counting out pushups.

"Ramsey," shouted Maxwell. "What the hell are you doing?"

243

"Pushups, sir!"

"Why, Ramsey?"

"Because ah'm not going to wave like you want, and I thought I'd just start my punishment without being asked, sir." The passageway became quiet except for the sound of Ramsey's counting.

Maxwell was enraged. His face reddened, his eyes bugged, and I could see him ball both hands into tight fists.

I looked at Ramsey and caught Merritt's eye. He nodded to me. I knew what he wanted. I nodded in return. He and I began pushups. Within a few seconds, every plebe who had been seated on the deck was shouting push-up numbers.

Maxwell screamed. "Stop immediately!"

We didn't.

Maxwell was still too emotional to utter more than a croak of frustration.

Battle stepped forward calmly.

"Stop this disobedience or you are all on report." he announced.

Several plebes paused, but the majority continued.

"That's 5 demerits." No one stopped. "That's 10 demerits." No one stopped.

Polk and Poole dropped to the deck and also began pushups. The other five former standers followed suit. Soon the entire Company was shouting.

"15 demerits!" said Battle. "20!" Still no one stopped.

"If you don't stop immediately, you can forget about Parent's Weekend," added Maxwell, who had calmed sufficiently to be coherent. Most of the plebes paused. The suddenly stuttering voices of twenty-five plebes, caught between doing what was right and losing what was important, added a disharmony to the previously boisterous cacophony.

Feelings of primal elation fled and I became enraged. I wasn't the only angry plebe.

Tim Richardson stopped his pushups. His face was flushed with ire. He stood, brushed dust from his hands, and turned toward the squadleaders.

"No way are you going to take Parents' Weekend away!" he said defiantly.

"Who gave you permission to speak, asshole?" asked Maxwell.

"I gave myself permission, asshole!" We all stopped to observe and listen.

"What did you say!" screamed Maxwell.

"I said you're an asshole!"

"Not only did you just lose Parent's Weekend, mister, but you just committed a Class A offense. You won't have any liberty for two months."

"I don't think so," said Richardson, calmly.

"Oh, really? Why?" asked Battle.

"Because you're way out of line, and you know it. If I have to call my father and tell him to cancel his leave from Jax because I won't be able to see him and Mom, he's going to want to know why. And when I tell him how you violated the regulations, then punished us for refusing to cooperate, he's going to want to have a heart-to-heart talk with his classmate, the Superintendent. After I explain to them what's been going on, I'll bet there will be two second classmen who won't be on liberty for a long time either."

"Are you threatening me, you son-of-a-bitch?" asked Maxwell, advancing on Richardson. Tim braced himself. Ramsey and Butkowski jumped in front of Richardson and prevented him from moving any closer to Maxwell.

Battle stopped the confrontation by restraining Maxwell with an outstretched arm.

Maxwell paused, staring hard at Richardson, who mirrored his gaze.

"Okay," said Battle. "Everybody sit down so we can settle this."

We paused, shocked, as we realized what had almost happened. I could hear several long and exaggerated outflows of breath from classmates who had stopped breathing during the confrontation. Ramsey and Butkowski helped Richardson sit, and Battle let go of Maxwell.

Battle then stepped forward. "There seems to be a misunderstanding." he said. "The peer grease list on the wall is important for several reasons. It tells the senior midshipmen how well the plebes are performing among themselves. It gives each of you an opportunity to see what your peers think of you. It also gives everyone a chance to improve. Most important, however, it should open up your minds to the thought that some of you may be wasting your time and ours. There are certain qualities a good naval officer must possess in order to succeed. Some of it can be trained. Some of it can be learned. The rest is natural. -- You either have it or you don't." He paused, and his quiet voice took on a questioning tone.

"Why would anyone want to stay here knowing that they won't be successful in the fleet? It doesn't make sense." Battle paused again and turned toward the *Magnificent Seven*.

"Some of you will not -- cannot -- be good officers. That's just the way it is. You might as well accept it. Maxie and I love this place. We don't want to see anyone unhappy, but we are also committed to doing the best we can this summer, and that means training you for your responsibilities once the Brigade returns. That also includes motivating the poor performers into giving up a senseless dream.

"About tonight," he continued. "It's possible that we may have gotten a bit overzealous, and we apologize for that. But we cannot allow any of you to get away with open defiance of our authority. Your classmate issued a threat to us this evening. He may be serious about what he says he will do, but so are we about what we do. If it means doing some extra restriction to see that discipline is maintained, we're ready for that challenge. However, what I suggest is that you forget about what might be considered inappropriate treatment of your classmates, and we will reduce the demerits you receive to 10 . . ."

There was a general grumbling at this statement, and Battle held up his hand. ". . . which we will hold in abeyance until the return of the Brigade. If there are no repetitions of tonight's mutiny, then we'll forget about the demerits. Fair enough? Good, that's settled. Get back to your rooms and get ready for lights out."

I returned to the room. Rico flopped at his desk and laughed. "Richardson sure put out Maxwell's fire, didn't he?"

"I'll say," I replied. "I was obviously wrong about Tim."

Rico laughed. "No, you weren't, Kevin. Richardson's didn't act out of concern for his fellow plebes. He could give a shit. He's too arrogant and self-interested, and he thinks his Dad and big brother will protect him when the chips are down. I think he's wrong. He played a big card tonight, and he won. But his victory's only temporary. He's a marked man from now on."

"What do you think Max and Battle will do come September, swami?"

"They'll forget the whole thing happened if we do."

"What about Richardson?" I asked. "Do you think he will?"

"I'll bet he was scared shitless. He'll forget."

"How did Polk get on the bottom part of the grease list?" I asked, changing the subject. "I didn't vote him there."

"Well, Kevin," Rico replied. "I think most of our classmates are tired of listening to the complaints. He'll have to keep his negative comments to himself."

"But criticism is healthy."

"Sure -- for you and me, but not for some of our classmates. They're too insecure as it is, and they don't want to hear any of Jeff's cryptic sarcasm. His ranking is a signal to knock it off for a while. I'll bet it won't matter next year. We'll be youngsters, and our enemy won't be physical exercises or the squadleaders; it'll be the system. We'll all be complaining among ourselves next year just like Jeff, wait and see."

"I guess so," I answered skeptically.

The squadleaders had upset me with their humiliation of Poole and the others, and with the added physical attention we all were getting. I didn't cooperate with my usual gusto for the next three days.

The two most important books in a plebe's reference library are his *Reef Points*, and a copy of the latest version of *The Guinness Book of World Records*. The first contains every bit of information a plebe must know to survive the grilling that goes on during meals and comearounds. The second book is important because upperclassmen expect their plebes to be a portable version of *Guinness*.

"How many medals did Jessie Owens win in the 1938 Olympics, Merritt?"

"Sir, Owens won three medals at the Berlin Olympics. A gold in the 100 meters, another gold in the mile relay, and a gold in the long jump. And the year was 1936, sir, not 1938."

"Nice work, Merritt. How are the Saint Louis Cardinals doing in the pennant race, Lamont?" He picked Saint Louis because he was a native of that fair city. To survive as a plebe, you had to know these things and anticipate.

"Sir, Saint Louis is presently in second place with a critical series coming up in Pittsburgh this weekend."

"Good.  Hardesty, who is Johnny Unitas?"

Barton paused, considering, and when he could not find the name under his mental files, said, "I'll find out, sir!"

"Comearound, Hardesty!"

Being a consummate Red Sox and Celtics fan, I already knew a great deal of sports data, and having had a memorization fanatic named Sister Dorinda as my eighth grade principal, I could learn almost anything instantly.  I also enjoyed the mealtime newspaper debates.

CHAPTER 26

## *WAR AND PEACES*

Every plebe read the newspaper before morning formation -- usually the Washington Post or the Baltimore Sun -- and had to be ready to speak about any topic. Squadleaders would ask, "What's going on in Europe?" or "When's the next NASA launch?" or "Who won the mayoral election in Atlanta?' and the designee would give a brief report. I was never so informed on the status of the world as when I was a midshipman.

Battle was in a pensive mood. He always seemed to get this way when the morning discussions concerned the topic of the war in Southeast Asia. The summer of 1967 was a grim and thought provoking period.

"Papadopolas, what's the latest body count?"

Nick answered. "As of this morning, 31,000 brave young Americans have paid the ultimate price, sir." It was a question Battle asked most often, and this was the only acceptable way to answer.

Battle, being a potential Marine Corps officer, was interested in strategy and body counts. "What's the enemy body count?"

"Sir, as of today the enemy has lost 250,000 brave young men."

"Goto, what's your analysis of the situation?"

Douglas Goto, the most analytical of us all, seemed to recognize aspects of any situation that we had overlooked. "Sir, if we accept Westmoreland's theory that a kill ratio of 10:1 is necessary to successfully defeat a guerrilla opponent, then we are short of that goal. However, the enemy efforts are presently stalled in the northern jungles, and we have made recent progress in several areas."

"Wojeck, what do you think we should do?"

Mike Wojeck was the Company hawk.  He had a voice that was as forceful as his personality, and he almost seemed out of place among his more-refined classmates.  "Sir, the war has drug on for too long, and the death toll is too high.  I think we should nuke 'em into the Bronze Age."

"That's God-damn drastic, Wojeck.  It was already suggested and denied in Korea.  How do you think the rest of the world will respond?"

"Sir, who cares?  We made a commitment.  Either we do it 100 percent, or there's no sense in being there."

"So you think we should either destroy the enemy or get out?"

"Sir, if we're not going to fight to win, than what's the use in fighting at all?"

"How would you win the war, Polk?"

Jeff Polk struggled.  "Sir, I wouldn't.  I don't see any sense in being in Vietnam.  There's nothing to gain.  Our allies are repressive and backward and no different from the communists.  We have no reason to be there.  I say get out now."

"What about dominoes, Mr. Polk?" asked Battle.

"Sir, the Domino Theory is wrong," Jeff said.  "Nations become communist not because of military intervention and suppression but rather for economic reasons."

"You think the communist system is better than ours?" asked a skeptical Battle.

"Of course not, sir.  But we are a developed nation.  Hardly anybody here has to worry about their next meal – except, of course, for plebes."

Battle didn't laugh.  "What are you going to do if you get sent to Vietnam, Polk?"

"I'll go where they send me, and do what I have to do."  Jeff drew the silent attention of Tom Battle for a full ten seconds.  This kind of answer did not endear Jeff to Battle or to any of the other potential Marines -- many of whom were totally committed to the support of the president and the nation, and understood the grim possibility that the course of the duty they selected may add their own names to the body count.

"How do you feel about the protesting going on at home, Wilson?"

I didn't like anything about BJ, so naturally, anything he said I would disagree with.  "It's everyone's right to protest, sir.  This is a democracy."

"What about when the protests could cause serious harm to our troops?"

"If you're asking about the Jane Fonda thing, sir, I think she's got to follow her own convictions."

Battle didn't like that answer. "What if her actions give aid and comfort to the enemy?"

"Sir, if that's what she believes, then more power to her."

"Wojeck? What do you think?"

"Wilson is full of shit, sir!" Most of the plebes at the table agreed with Wojeck, and even from a braced-up position we nodded assent or grumbled support.

"How about you, O'Reilly? What's on your mind about this?"

I wished he hadn't called on me. "Sir," I said. "It's all very confusing to me, and I hate the thought of the slaughter on both sides. I also think communism is totally wrong, and Jane Fonda and friends can kiss my ass. My intuition tells me that my leaders have made the best decisions they can, considering the circumstances."

Battle was quiet for a long time. "Carry-on, everyone, and look at me."

We turned.

Battle folded his hands in front of him. "Time for another lecture. This one is vital.

"The three most important words you will learn here at Annapolis are the ones that the Academy code is based upon -- duty, honor, and loyalty. This institution is an arm of the military of the Unites States, and you are potential officers in that military. Wherever duty calls, you must go. Wherever you go, your service must be with the utmost honor. *And* you must follow the orders of your superiors implicitly.

"But this is not Nazi Germany, gentlemen. You are not required to follow an immoral or illegal order. In fact, you are forbidden to do so. We don't kill prisoners or shoot civilians. If you are ever asked to do immoral things, you must refuse. But you may indeed be asked to kill the enemy. That's what war is all about. You cannot refuse that order, because by doing so, you will endanger your comrades.

"You also can't refuse to fight and call it an immoral war. The issue of whether a war is valid is one that the government and the population must decide. You are all soldiers of our nation. If you want to protest the war, do so with your ballot. You will be punished if you do not support the will of your president.

"So let me make myself clear on this. You can talk all you want. Your opinion is valid, no matter how misguided. But what you feel must stay an opinion. No overt action or protests are allowed. If you can't live with that, resign now. I promise you'll get even less sympathy when the Brigade returns. A great many of the midshipmen come from military families or have relatives who have served in combat or who are in Vietnam now. You will be in trouble if you don't watch what you say on this issue. Is that clear?"

He didn't wait for an answer. " Brace up! Hardesty, who's Mickey Mantle?"

"I'll find out sir!"

"Comearound, Barton, you pussy!"


I returned to the room that morning after breakfast full of thoughts about war and death and honor. I wished I could be sure about things like Wojeck and Polk, but I kept coming up against ideas that seemed too profound and too complicated for me to grasp. Vietnam was one of those issues.

I found a note on my desk that said I had a message waiting in the Main Office. I hurried downstairs to pick it up. The message was a baby blue letter-sized envelope that had been hand-delivered this morning. It smelled good, and I could see that the plebe on duty was jealous. I smiled knowingly at him and hurried to my room to savor the experience. My first love letter.

As soon as I opened it, I saw Brenda's signature in neat cursive at the bottom. I smiled in anticipation. The note was a single page. It was a single paragraph. It was almost a single sentence, and not a very good one at that.


*"Dear Kevin,"* it said, *"I had a wonderful time last Saturday, but we can't meet anymore because I'm married. My husband is a union carpenter and I have two wonderful children that I don't want to disappoint, so I'm sorry. You were a great lover, and it was fun.*

That was it? I had been kissed off, dumped, jilted, and abandoned by my first love interest. One part of me was devastated. It had been a thoroughly enjoyable experience that I really wanted to repeat. The second part of me was shocked. Holy shit! I did my first big act with a married woman. Christ, I could've gotten into serious trouble! Goddamn labor unions. Then there was a third part of me that was proud. Great lover, huh?

I put the note down on my desk and noticed Rico staring at me.

He raised an eyebrow.

"Brenda says I'm a great lover."

"That's nice," replied Rico, obviously waiting for the rest.

"Okay, Rico," I said. "What do you know?"

"About Brenda's children or about her being unavailable for further poking?"

"Both," I answered.

"I found out about her family two nights ago when I was talking to Cindy. As a matter of fact I urged Cindy to convince Brenda to knock it off with you."

"What?" I blurted. "How could you?"

"Kevin, Kevin," he replied, "stop thinking between your legs, amigo. The consequences of seeing a married woman are too great to consider. She was using you, and I probably just saved your life. But don't worry. Cindy's got other friends."

I was content with the bone Rico offered, and I said nothing further. I tacked the letter to my bulletin board, displaying it like a badge of honor, and I gained a bit of Company notoriety for being the first classmate to get a "Dear John."

My message was simple. "See, Kevin O'Reilly is human enough to be hurt, but man enough to make light of it."


Another week passed, and Maxwell and Battle continued focusing their unmerciful harassment on the *Magnificent Seven* with each of the rest of us serving as secondary characters in the drama. I was a very tired secondary character. The rest of us began to wager on the outcome. Barton Hardesty was the reluctant front runner in the betting race on the next classmate to exit the rotunda doors. He didn't help himself with his unworldliness.

Battle was pissed at Barton. "Hardesty, you fart-sniffing puke. Don't you know anything?"

I had sprinted past the retching Willy Simpson that morning to earn carry-on at breakfast, and Hardesty now sat across from me. I had a front row seat, so to speak, for the morning's demoralizing entertainment.

A frustrated look passed across Barton's face as he answered. "No, sir."

"Did your God-damn high school offer any sports, asshole?"

"No, sir."

"Did you ever watch news or sports on television, you shit-for-brains?"

"No, sir."

"Where did you go to school, anyway, numb-nuts?"

"I went to Memphis Christian Academy," Hardesty answered.

"Well, you may be smart, Hardesty. But your education leaves a Goddamn lot to be desired. You don't know shit about anything important."

"Request permission to speak freely, sir?" Hardesty had been increasingly uncomfortable under the grilling, and I could see him preparing to make a statement of some kind.

Battle considered the audacious request. "Okay, pal. Speak up!"

"Sir," Hardesty said. "I am deeply offended by your language. It is not Christian to take the Lord's name in vain. It troubles me. Please stop."

I watched Battle. He winked at me. Why? I don't know.

Then Battle shouted to Maxwell's table, "Tom, Hardesty here says my language offends him and I should stop using bad words. We've hurt his feelings. Should we respect his wishes?"

Maxwell pretended to think. He stared up at the ceiling for several long seconds, then looked at Battle. "Fuck, no!" he replied loudly.

Several of my classmates tittered.

I was shocked at the amount of off-color language flung about. I could never get away with even thinking some of those words around my mother, and my father -- even though he worked in a very rough environment -- rarely cursed. I suppose when you're that big you don't need colorful language to get attention. But I also hadn't been sheltered from the nastier elements of the English language. I certainly heard my share of colorful epithets on the basketball court and on the neighborhood streets, and technical manuals like Rico's had many interesting words and phrases. But I had always been uncomfortable using them. I still am. But I was also smart enough to know when to protest and when to bite the bullet.

Battle looked at Hardesty and smiled wickedly.

"Sorry, pal. This ain't the Boy Scouts. Salty language is part of the fleet. You'll have to train your shit-stained ass to put up with it."

Hardesty winced. He must have realized that it would be a lot worse for him, language-wise, from now on.

Tommy Poole still caught the worst of it, although his performance was improving. He could sometimes beat Rogers and Butler in the morning runs, and he equaled Chalmers and Butler in pushups. I've never seen anyone retch as often as Tommy, so I knew that his efforts must have been quite a strain.

Two weeks before Parent's Weekend, after watching him pass out during an evening comearound -- this was a legitimate feint because I could see his head strike the tile floor as he fell -- I began to admire Tommy again. I realized how silly my superior attitude had been.

CHAPTER 27


## *PREPARATIONS FOR THE PARENTS*


The week before Parents' Weekend we selected roommates for the upcoming academic year. We would be moving to the first deck of the fourth wing for the academic year, and we had to consolidate. I hadn't realized that Rico and I would have to acquire new roomies, but plebes don't live two-to-a-room, and the departure of seven classmates made a few gaps in the Company ranks.

This presented a problem. I didn't want another roommate. Rico and I were getting along just fine, and I'm more the hermit than the socializer. The thought of putting up with another set or two of problems was too much to consider.

On the morning of the room selections Jim Merritt chopped into our room just prior to morning formation. "Guys," he said. "Have you decided on your new room additions?"

"No," I answered. "Not yet."

"Can I join you two?"

I looked at Rico. We both liked Merritt, so I didn't see it as a problem.

"What about the rest of the goons?" asked Rico.

"Tommy Poole wants to move in with Butler, Butkowski, and Abbott. They said it would be okay. Polk wants to room with Simpson, and Strong wants to stay with Willy. So either Jubal or I have to go. I decided it would be me."

"It's fine with me," I said. Rico nodded concurrence.

Then Merritt hit us with the kicker. "BJ wants to room with us too. Is that okay?"

No, it wasn't! Not for me anyway. "Well . . . ," I began.

Rico answered for the two of us "Yea, it'll be fine."

I felt betrayed. I turned to look at Rico.

He smiled and nodded encouragement.  His look said, "Trust me, Kevin; you'll see."

"I guess so," I said reluctantly.  What else could I do?

The approach of Parent's Weekend brought up another problem for me.  While everyone else was dreaming about seeing their favorite girl from back home, I still had not been able to arrange for anyone feminine to tag along with my family.  None of the girls I had written to had replied favorably to my letters.  One didn't remember me at all -- that hurt.  Two were already connected to someone 'wonderful,' and I could tell by the tone of their letters, they had marriage plans swimming around in their empty heads.  The last one wrote me a nice note informing me she was preparing for college and didn't have time for a relationship.  I seemed to be the only plebe with no plans for wanton sexuality that weekend.  I missed Brenda.

My mother, bless her misguided heart, sensed my frustration -- probably because I whined so much about being companionless.  In a letter a month prior to the big event she informed me that she had asked several of the neighbors if their daughters would like to come on the trip to keep me company.  Particularly she was focusing of Sarah Connelly, a girl I had known since parochial school.

The instant I read that statement I threw the letter unfinished down and hurried to a phone.  Jesus, what was my mother trying to do to me?  If in the heat of passion I had tried to touch one of the neighborhood colleens, I would be persona non grata in South Boston for the rest of my life.  I had to squelch any ideas she had about any neighbor's daughter and me.

Luckily, she hadn't completed plans for Sarah Connelly to accompany them.  I was relieved.  Sarah was kind of cute, but she had the personality of a rock and had an older brother Patrick who was big as a truck.  Rather than have Mom's detective work go to waste, I asked her to accumulate a list of potential dates for when I returned at Christmas time.  She agreed.  I think she and Dad must have been talking about his own boot camp frustrations.  But not with Sarah, Mom!  I had to have a heart-to-heart talk with Big Kevin real soon, and since I would be alone Parents' Weekend, I decided that would be the best time.

I was surprised to find out that Rico wasn't going to see Cindy that weekend.  His parents were bringing down a 'friend' named Rosa from Brooklyn.  "It was arranged long ago,

Kevin. I told Cindy I wanted to spend the time with my family, which is the truth, sort of. She understands."

"Does Rosa have any friends?"

Rico laughed but didn't offer any help.

The incident of the Company guidons had become a topic of conversation among the squadleaders. Battle and Maxwell mused about what group of brave young men had the gonads to pull that off -- certainly not us. Afterward, the Companies took to hiding their banners in a select plebe room overnight. If the flag turned up stolen, God help the plebes whose responsibility it was to guard it.

The guidon incident ignited a rash of evening sorties. Some nights there were more plebes running around campus than asleep in their racks, and a constant thunder of young footsteps echoed along the night passageways on the remaining weekends.

One Sunday morning we woke to find that someone had painted the statue of Tecumseh blue on one side and gold on the other. I liked it that way. It gave the beaked-nosed Indian a certain character lacking in his bronze motif. Another time one of the display fighter aircraft -- which must have weighed several tons -- was moved nearly a quarter mile to T-Court.

The late night activity was not without its risks. As the big weekend approached, plebe antics became more pronounced. Several groups were caught in the act of mischief, and only the direct action of the Superintendent prevented them from losing all privileges. In an act of unusual kindness and understanding, he postponed the punishment of anyone apprehended in an unauthorized evening's event until after Parent's Weekend.


On Wednesday night prior to Parent's Weekend, I visited the Goon Room to ask their plans. Several of us had discussed the possibility of getting all our families together for a dinner out in town on Saturday night. When I arrived, their room was dark. Only Merritt and Ramsey were awake, and they were each reading by the light of their desk tensor lamps. Polk was snoring loudly, and Poole was curled up in a lump against the opposite wall.

"Have you guys thought about the Saturday night dinner idea?" I whispered.

"Yes," Merritt answered. "My parents think it's a great idea."

"My Momma's still considering," Joe answered cautiously. "I'll let you know."

"What about Jeff and Tommy?" I asked.

"Don't know about Tommy yet," Jim answered, "but Jeff said his parents might want to spend a quiet evening with him, and he had plans with Kate."

"I'll bet," I tried to keep the jealousy from my voice. "What about you and Lynda?"

Merritt smiled. "We'll work something out. Don't worry."

"Attention on deck!" The sound exploded from somewhere nearby. We sprang to attention in the dark and braced in anticipation. Jubal almost tipped over his chair in the process. Jeff Polk snapped awake and dropped his covers on the floor as he leaped down from his rack. Within two seconds we stood alertly, waiting.

Nothing happened for several additional seconds, and the room became deathly quiet. Then I realized that I hadn't heard the door open. I twisted my head in the direction of the doorway and found the room empty except for four braced plebes and one still-sleeping classmate. I relaxed and began to laugh quietly. At first the others didn't realize what was funny.

"Tommy just had a comearound dream," I said. "Poor guy. He can't escape the system even when he's zonked out."

We sat down again and Joe outlined what was to be our last bit of mischief before the Brigade returned. Battle and Maxie expected something. They had threatened us with bodily harm if we did anything to them before the Brigade returned; but they became more and more nervous as the final days approached.

Tired of the unrelenting discipline of the past months, I needed rebellion. We decided the act would take place on the Friday night before the beginning of Parent's Weekend. That way, the squadleaders would have no time to react. The following Monday their harassment would end, and the "Tigers" reign of terror would began. Friday I went to bed at lights out; the excitement of the impending activity churned in my mind.


At 0200 a soft tap at our door announced that the company was assembling in the passageway. Rico and I dressed in shorts and gray sweats, pulling hoods down over our faces for disguise. We congregated outside the squadleaders' room. The passageway was just dark enough that I could not recognize the majority of my classmates in their hooded garb, but I could sense they were ready for action.

At Jubal's signal, we stormed into the room, divided into two equal groups, and raced for the beds. Battle and Maxwell didn't have a chance. What followed was less than 60 seconds of confusion, muffled cries, and struggling bodies. We subdued them, and hoisted them into the air, several on each arm and leg. Battle, dressed in skivvies, took it calmly. Maxie, in shorts and Saint Louis Cardinals T-shirt, struggled and tried to yell.

We gagged Maxwell with a washcloth. I could almost taste the adrenaline that pumped throughout my system as I carried my part of the burden -- which happened to be a lower piece of Maxwell's' left leg.

Companymates stood watch at key intersections. We stormed the dark passageways and ladders, and proceeded outside into T-Court.

The night was moonless, deathly still, and humid beyond belief. Not slowing a step, we moved like two racing amoebas pushed out by frantic struggles and pressed back by our own momentum. The Severn River and the dark Yacht Basin beckoned.

As Maxie sensed our destination and our probable purpose, his struggles increased. We almost tripped and went down. I thought to myself that it was pretty stupid for Maxwell to struggle so much, particularly when if he did get loose, he would land painfully on the hard ground. But he didn't escape, and I don't think anything could have stopped us that evening. We had taken control of our own destinies in a mini-mutiny and had united in a common purpose. Maxwell be damned! We surged on.

We arrived at the Yacht Basin within minutes. We were far enough from Bancroft Hall to ungag our prey and savor the 'conversation.' The expletives rushing from Maxie's mouth were exquisite. We laughed. Maxwell struggled as he yelled, while Battle calmly accepted his fate. Maxie wasn't being a good sport.

One of us checked the water for obstructions; but since it was pitch black, the surveillance was cursory at best. Battle was first to meet his fate.

"Any last words?" someone asked.

"No," he replied. "Hurry up so I can get back to sleep."

The first group stood back from the edge of the pier, swinging Tommy Battle by his arms and legs. "One! Two! Threeeeeeee!"

He sailed into the humid blackness, limbs flailing. After a short pause we heard a loud splash.  Someone checked to ensure he came up for air.

"Y'all better go grunt!"  Jubal yelled.  "'Cause ya'll sure can't fly!"

We readied the angry Maxwell.

Back and forth he went, still struggling and yelling and cursing at us.  He was acting stupidly considering how we were now in control of his fate.

I looked at Hank Butkowski and nodded rearward.  We backed away.

Maxwell yelled louder.

"One!"

He jerked.

 "Two!"

He wiggled.

"THREEEEEEEE!"

He pulled and pushed and . . . was airborne.  Maybe it was his struggling at the exact instant of our toss; perhaps we had too much confidence in Hank Butkowski's strength; or maybe the frustrations and angers of plebe summer made us all want to punish Maxie a bit.

Maxwell flew along the wooden pier, facing the starry night, screaming and waving his arms and legs as if he could climb back to earth.  As I watched, I suspected that his trajectory was not exactly what we had hoped.  He disappeared in a blur of motion. Then we heard. "Bump . . . Bump . . . Kerploosh!"

"Shit," I said too loudly.  "I hope we didn't kill him!"

We waited in the dark, holding our collective breaths.  We didn't kill him.  We didn't even slow him up.

Within seconds he sputtered to the surface, yelling louder than ever, and the spell of remorse shattered.  We raced for the safety of Mother Bancroft, and feigned sleep.

Battle and Maxie returned several minutes later, sloshing down the passageway.  "You almost broke my ass, you miserable bastards!"

I imagined I could hear a limp in the wet sounds.

"The Brigade's almost back and you still can't do anything right!"  Battle added.

I caught a slight hint of amusement in his voice.

"I'm going to murder every one of you!" Maxwell yelled just before he closed his door.


Maxwell didn't murder us on Saturday morning.  Instead he gave us a final desperate passageway running that made me very tired.  That morning we prepared for the return of the Brigade.  We moved our things from Room 5404 to Room 4024 -- Twenty-third Company's assigned area.  Our new room faced an enclosed alcove of T-Court.  Directly across the wide passageway was Room 4025, which housed Ramsey, Polk, Strong, and Simpson.

Rooms with windows opening on the outside world had a deep moat-like trench directly below them.  This moat prevented excursions through the windows.  We plebes would have to sneak out by the doors -- if we could sneak out at all with an additional 3,000 eyes watching.

These rooms were so large that each of us had a rack mounted on the deck -- a vast improvement over bunk beds.  Rico and I were first in the door, and we selected opposing racks on the starboard side of the room, Merritt and Wilson took the port side.  I still wasn't happy about rooming with BJ, but he probably wasn't happy with me either.

After stowing the gear, we marched to the Midshipmen's Store for book and study equipment issue.  Each midshipman receives a monthly salary of one-half an ensign's pay, which is pretty good money for a cloistered novitiate.  From this, the Academy deducts charges for laundry, books, and meals, and anything we bought in the Midshipmen's store could be charged to our personal account.  What remained at the end of the month wasn't much, but it provided spending money.

Actually it was more cash than I had ever had in my possession.  I let most of it accumulate in a home town bank account, only cashing 20 dollars a month for various and sundry items. I bought a clock radio and a desk tensor lamp.

CHAPTER 28

## *FAMILIES*

Parents' Weekend began at precisely 1300 hours on Saturday, immediately after noon meal. The formation for meal was as loose as any we had ever had. Every one of us was anxious to get away from the bosom of Mother B and be human again. Mom had called me from the hotel and left a message that they had arrived and would be waiting by Tecumseh for me.

I was excited. It had been only three months since I last saw them, but those three months amounted to a universe of emotional distance. I wasn't the same Kevin O'Reilly they left at the Field House, and I was anxious to share my metamorphosis. I think my parents suspected great changes but were a bit afraid of who might meet them beneath the stoic statue.

Hundreds of people witnessed the noon meal formation that day. Most were parents, relatives, and friends of the Plebe Brigade. We turned crisply and marched tall. The spectators applauded, and it made us all feel very special.

Meal was a hurried carry-on affair. Maxwell and Battle were as anxious to be rid of us as we were to get away. They also had plans. We would be allowed to ride in cars during liberty hours, and there would be no evening meal formation. Liberty expired at midnight -- an early night for a typical eighteen and nineteen-year-old. But to a plebe who has just spent three months forced to turn lights out at 2100 or face the consequences, it was daring and mature.

But we would have to wear our uniforms in public. After three months of nothing but uniforms, I would rather have worn civilian clothes. But a later poll of the mothers present at the company dinner revealed that uniforms were their clothing of choice. I suppose I could understand that. We did look damn good.

We talked excitedly during noon meal and made final arrangements for the evening congregation. Jim Merritt had called an Italian restaurant in town and made reservations for 25 at 1800. At the last minute, Jeff Polk had decided to be included. BJ Wilson, whose parents had to stay in New York to make preparations for the upcoming television season, would tag along as a solo.

At precisely 1300, doors in all parts of Bancroft Hall opened with identical whooshes, and ecstatic plebes rushed the hot August afternoon. The sight of hundreds of startlingly white uniforms hurtling down outside stairs and charging headlong across the tile courts was nearly overwhelming. The smiles on those excited faces rivaled the sun that blazed overhead. My smile was foremost among them. Tecumseh Court was alive with excitement, and even the usually sullen bronze gaze from Tecumseh himself seemed to have developed a knowing and enigmatic twinkle.

There is nothing more warm and secure than a mother's hug. Mom's hug was great. Even Big Kevin's bear-like grip was satisfying.

"It's good to see you guys!" I pulled back from them, trying to see how much they had changed since I last saw them. I saw with some surprise that they hadn't changed, not a bit – or had they? On further examination I noticed that Big Kevin and Sean were different somehow. Why? They both waited, smiling. I looked more closely.

"Your hair!" I exclaimed.

They had both gotten their hair cut very short -- almost as short as mine. Why? I must have looked puzzled.

Dad spoke. "We wanted you to feel more at home with your own short hair, Kevin." This was an unexpected surprise. Being surrounded by a thousand identically shorn young men, I hadn't given my hair a single though since the first day. Apparently my family thought the short hair was a big deal to me. It was very touching.

I pointed to Sean's head. "You let Dad talk you into that?"

"It wasn't easy," Big Kevin answered.

They examined me critically. I must have seemed completely different -- but not bad different. Mom was near tears -- good tears. And I had never seen Big Kevin's massive chest swell the way it seemed to that afternoon. They liked what they saw, and I was glad.

"We sure missed you, big brother," Sean burst out.

"Yeah. I missed you too."

"Well, there's a lot to catch up on," Mom offered. "What would you like to do?"

"How about a quick tour. Then we can go to the hotel for a swim in a real pool."

"Real pool?" asked Sean, frowning.

I laughed. "I'll tell you all about it later."

"The tour sounds great, son," said Big Kevin, putting two huge hands tenderly on my shoulders and squeezing slightly. I had never seen him so outwardly affectionate since I was very small. Smiling, he drew away, somewhat surprised at himself.

"Sorry, Kevin. We're just so very proud of you."

"No, Dad," I answered. "It's okay. Touching parents is allowed. We're not supposed to show any public affection with unrelated females."

"You mean like that?" asked Sean laughing. He was pointing to a classmate, partially hidden behind a huge poplar tree. The plebe was engaged in a passionate kiss with a person obviously not a relative; or else their family had a different idea about closeness than mine.

"Probably a 'cousin' from Tennessee," joked Dad.

"We could have brought Sarah Connelly to keep you company," Mom offered when she saw how my glance quickly became a stare.

"Mom," I said laughing. "Can you picture Sarah and me doing something like that? I wouldn't want to melt the ice queen, and if I did I wouldn't want Patrick to kill me either."

Mom didn't seem convinced. "I don't think Sarah's cold at all. She's grown up quite a bit. She's become very popular. You just have to get to know her better. She's really very nice."

"I'm sure she is, Mom. But you can't tell me that her brother has suddenly become docile." Patrick Connelly had been an linebacker on his high school football team, and he had also been outstanding at breaking furniture and people when he was angry. And Patrick was very protective of his baby sister.

Mom laughed. "No, Kevin, Patrick's still a problem for poor Mrs. Connelly."

We started toward the chapel, walking slowly on the wide brick walkway. Sunlight piercing the thick foliage made the white uniforms flash. It was a warm and humid day --

the radio had predicted a record -- and I could see that Big Kevin, who was a furious sweater, would suffer if we stayed outside too long. I gave them the abbreviated tour.

We walked first to the chapel, and I showed the family where I usually sat and explained the protocol of Sunday mass at Annapolis. I didn't mention Sleepy Hollow. My parents were suitably awed. Afterward we viewed the tomb of John Paul Jones and listened with a hundred other visitors as the civilian guide explained about John Paul and his importance.

Like every attraction at Annapolis, the crypt and its accompanying display cases were meticulously maintained and professionally presented. Everything the Academy does, is with style and aplomb, except maybe Plebe Year, where gusto and intensity are essential.

After the chapel, we visited the Academy Museum and strolled the grounds between Mahan and Bancroft Halls.

Sean quizzed me on the significance of every statue and memorial, most of which I could remember from my study of *Reef Points.* Sean was impressed. Finally we went into Bancroft Hall and saw the displays and sample room. The entire tour took about an hour. Mom, the family shutterbug, took seven rolls of Instamatic pictures.

"Well, how about a dip in the pool?" I asked as we walked down the steps leading from the Memorial Hall in the rear of the rotunda. "Dad looks as if he could use one."

Big Kevin was very damp by this time, and he grunted affirmation.

On the way down the broad stairs we passed Maxie and his date going up. Our eyes met, and he halted. "Midshipman O'Reilly," he said pleasantly. "Are these your parents?"

"Yes, sir," I said. "This is my Mom and Dad and my brother Sean. And this is Midshipman Second-class Maxwell, one of our cream puff squadleaders."

Maxwell laughed. "This is my friend, Rebecca," Maxwell said indicating a petite blond who stood admiringly at his side. Then he noticed Big Kevin and was suitably impressed.

"You have a good son, Mr. and Mrs. O'Reilly -- but his sense of humor is a bit bizarre."

"Thank you. We think he's great."

"Has Kevin given you a tour?"

"Yes, he has," Mom answered. "It's a wonderful campus."

"We like to think so." Maxie swelled with pride. I thought he was going to cry.

"Well, sir," I said, "we're off to where I can immerse myself in a pool without icebergs."

Maxwell laughed again. "You think the natatorium is cold, huh? Well, to tell the truth, so do I. It makes me shiver just thinking of it. I hate swimming."

Wow, Maxwell had a human side. Maybe he wasn't so bad after all? I decided to reserve judgment on Maxie.

The drive to the Holiday Inn on Ritchie Highway took more than 30 minutes. "I know the hotel is far from Annapolis," my Mom, "but it was the closest one we could afford."

"Did you know that the ones in town wanted to charge almost 100 dollars for one night?" Big Kevin asked.

I whistled. "God, Dad, that's incredible."

"Yeah," he said, "even *this* hotel costs more than a day's take-home. Plus the gas for the drives down and back, plus meals and souvenirs. It can really add up."

Dad worked outdoors at a backbreaking job for a few hundred dollars a week. I knew he was worried about money. But Sean and I never had to worry about toys or sports equipment. Dad always provided, even if Mom had to wait an extra year for the new electric range or if we all suffered an additional winter with a furnace that rumbled.

Annapolis must have been a godsend for Big Kevin. He and Mom had always been determined that I would get an education; and if I had elected to go to a local college and hadn't gotten a scholarship, they would somehow have found the money, but it would have meant deep sacrifices. Now all they had to worry about affording was an occasional trip to Annapolis to visit. I was contributing, and I felt good about that.


It took me less than five minutes to shed my uniform and get poolside. There must have been other parents that shared my Dad's view about costs because several plebes were already in the water. Some of those plebes had sisters. Some of those sisters were cute. I strutted to the edge of the pool and surveyed the area coolly. I noticed the stares of some of the sisters, and I stuck out my bulging chest and pulled in my washboard stomach. Then the mood shattered.

267

Preoccupied with the choreography of my entrance, I had forgotten about Sean, who came up behind me and shoved me headlong into the water. I yelled, terrified, forgetting for an instant where I was, and preparing myself for glacial immersion. I landed with an undignified splash. My terror disappeared, replaced by a feeling of comfort and release.

I rose from the water, at first intending to deal with my brother in a physical way, but titters from the girls around the pool calmed me. Instead, I splashed water in Sean's direction.

"Nice dive, big brother!" he yelled from the relative safety of my parents' doorway.


Fifteen minutes later my parents emerged from the room and selected a place at a nearby table. My mother, always uncomfortable about the dangers of sunburn on her freckled and sensitive skin, immediately slathered lotion on her extremities. Afterward she did the same to Big Kevin. As she spread the white liquid on Dad's back I noticed with some surprise that he was carrying a bit of extra weight.

Apparently when I wasn't looking my father had lost his muscle tone and had become somewhat -- perish the thought -- fat. And Mom, who was never the skinniest of women, seemed more matronly. Could it be that my parents were getting old? How old were they anyway? I discovered I hadn't the faintest idea. I didn't even know their birth dates. That upset me. I should have known those things.

Sean, an even worse swimmer than I, leaped into the pool over my head and swam splashing and flailing to my side.

"How's the water, big brother?"

"It's wonderful. A big change from the Academy pool. The water there is too cold."

"Shrivels your pecker, huh?" Sean asked.

I did a double take. "Where'd you hear that?"

"Hey," he replied soothingly, "I'm almost 11. I know more than you think."

"Maybe so," I said. "I hope you don't say things like that around Mom and Dad."

"Are you kidding?" Sean asked. "Mom would die, and Dad would kill me."

As I watched the activity in and around the pool, I noticed a young lady in a black bikini staring at me. She was lounging on a reclined deck chair on her belly with her head facing the pool. She lifted herself to get a drink from a Coke on a table next to her. Oh, my!

Sean hit me on the arm. "Great tits, huh?" he whispered.

"Hey, knock it off!" I said, staring at the girl.

"No time for girls, big brother."

"There's always time for girls, Sean," I replied, laughing. I decided to handle this the way Rico would. "Check this out."

I took a deep breath and ducked under the water. Bending my knees, I pushed off in the her direction. I made the distance in one breath, and surfaced just in front of her.

"Hi," I said as I put my arms on the pool deck in front of her. I flexed my biceps slightly, hoping she would notice.

She did. "Hi," she replied.

"My name's Kevin," I said. "I'm a plebe at Annapolis."

"I'm Kathy." She had a Midwestern accent. "My brother is also a plebe. We came from Omaha to visit."

"Where's your brother?"

"He and my parents went out to buy some groceries. They'll be back any minute. Then we're going to visit Annapolis and have dinner."

"We have almost the same plans," I said. "I'll be back here about nine."

"Kathy!" A plump woman called from the second floor balcony. "Time to go, dear!"

"Okay, Mom!" Kathy rose from her lounger.

I almost choked.

She looked down at me and smiled smugly. "See you later, Kevin?"

I thought quickly. "How about 21:30. Sorry, 9:30 this evening right here?" I hoped the drool wasn't showing.

She smiled. "Okay, 9:30. See you then."

I stared as she went.  She knew I was watching.  I could tell by the way she walked.

I swam back to Sean.

He looked at me disapprovingly.  "Still driving the girls away, huh?" he said.

I laughed.  "I have a date with that young lady for later."

"With her?  No way!"

"Yes way, Sean.  Your big brother's growing up too."


Sean and I roughhoused in the pool for about fifteen minutes; then my Mom called to us.  "You boys better get over here and put some lotion on.  You'll burn for sure."

I was exasperated.  She was right, but I wished she wasn't such a Mom sometimes.

We sat at the white metal table.  Mom handed us the *Sea and Ski*, and I applied a light coat.  Sean followed suit.

Dad emerged from the room carrying a six pack of *National Bohemian Beer*.  He plunked the beer on the table.  The beer had been iced in a chest they had brought along for the trip.  It looked deliciously cold. Dad sighed as he popped the tabs from his and Mom's cans.

He and Mom were both beer drinkers.  Dad was a straight-from-the-can kind of guy; Mom used a glass and ice.  She was the only person I ever knew who drank beer on ice.  Dad hesitated then pushed the now four-pack toward me.  "Have a beer, Kevin?"

Wow!  This was the first time he had ever offered to share alcoholic with me -- except for the traditional Christmas toast of flavored brandy.  He knew I had experimented with drinking during high school.  I had even been sick inside his old '57 Chevy one terrible night -- which hadn't exactly made him happy.  But this was a coming-out for the two of us.  He was accepting my near adulthood and offering a sudsy toast to acknowledge my new status.

I accepted!  The first taste was like heaven.  National Bo was now my favorite beer.  It had a texture and smoothness like no other brand of beer I had ever tasted -- both of them.

In fact, I had no idea whether the beer was good or not. My sole reason for drinking previously had been to get loaded and act silly. But this beer met two critical criteria: it was cold, and it was wet. I took a second big swallow.

"Take it easy, Kevin," said Dad. "You're not used to it."

"Sure Dad," I put the beer on the table. "This is great!"

"Glad to be away from the Academy?" asked Mom.

"You can't imagine," I replied.

"Want to talk about it?" asked Dad seriously. "I've been asking around down on the waterfront and I've heard that these places can be hard."

"You don't know the half of it, Dad."

"If you want to leave, Kevin," said Mom. "It's okay. We don't care if you stay or not." I knew she was fibbing, but she obviously didn't understand what the challenge.

"Mom, don't worry about me. I can hack it. You're going to meet a guy tonight who's had it ten times harder than me."

"Have they treated you badly, Son?"

"No worse than anyone else, Mom. I'm okay, really."

Dad changed the subject. "Well, you've filled out nicely."

"That's from about a million pushups and two million miles of running,"

"It looks good on you," Mom said.

I glanced at Sean. "I'll bet you never thought you'd have a muscle man brother, did you?" I raised my arms and flexed my biceps. The stark sunlight exaggerated the bulges.

Sean reached up and grabbed my right biceps and squeezed. "Wow!"

"When do classes start?" Dad asked.

"Monday. I have all the typical freshman courses in the engineering curriculum, except I'll be in advanced math and chemistry. I also decided to take German as a language, plus an additional environmental science course. I'll be carrying eighteen credits."

"Good," Dad said, getting serious. "Now how do you like it there?"

That seemed a strange question. I had always thought you went to college to get an education, and that being happy was secondary. I answered cautiously. "It's great! I wasn't sure at first if I would enjoy the military, but I fit in pretty well; and some of the discipline and tradition is kind of fun. I feel almost at home."

Mom didn't like that answer. "You still have a home, Kevin, and lots of friends who are asking about you."

"Like Sarah Connelly?"

Mom ignored me. "If you ever get tired of this, you'll always be welcome."

"Do you have the hots for Sarah Connelly?" asked Sean incredulously.

"Sean!" Mom interrupted. "Kevin doesn't have 'the hots' for anybody, and Sarah is a nice girl." She looked at Big Kevin and continued, "Where does he get those ideas?"

Dad chuckled. "Don't know, hon." He enjoyed Sean's blurtings.

"Kevin has a date," Sean said. "For tonight. With a girl he met at the pool just now."

"With the one I just saw you talking to?" asked Mom disapprovingly. Big Kevin, however, did not disapprove.

"Yeah. For around nine-thirty. We'll talk and exchange addresses."

"You gonna kiss her?" asked Sean.

"Sean," I said, faking moral outrage, "how could you insinuate that I would do such a thing?" Then I leaned in closer to him and whispered, just loud enough for my parents to hear. "If she'll let me, you're damned right!"

Mom said. "You don't have any time to be serious! Studies come first!"

"Not even Sarah Connelly?" I asked half sarcastically. "You've been pushing Sarah at me. Are you sure you wouldn't like me to start dating her?"

"You can date her, but I don't want you getting serious," she said with finality.

"Tell Mrs. Connelly that I'll be writing to sweet Sarah, and maybe we'll have a date or two when I'm back for Christmas leave."

For the next hour we traded small talk about life at Annapolis, happenings in the old neighborhood, and the Red Sox, who as usual were blowing a late season lead to the nearby team from Baltimore. Mom and Dad liked my bragging about our late night escapades. I did *not* mention my trip to Hospital Point. Mom never would have understood, and I think even Dad might have been a bit shocked to discover the nature of my first sexual experience.

"Is there anything you need from home that we can send you?" Mom asked.

"You know what? I've been thinking about that very thing," I answered. "If you could make be a batch of your Christmas cookies and send them in late November, I think it would really endear me to the upper-class."

My Mom made the best Christmas cookies in the world. I had tasted neighbors' cookies, and relatives' cookies, and friend's' mothers' cookies, and store-bought cookies; and my Mom's were absolutely the best. They were something to die for, and I didn't see how anyone could do better. I knew that if my squad mates ever got a taste, I'd be in good with them forever. They'd be begging me to ask Mom for more. Mom's oven would blaze in sugary glory, and her cookies could be the ticket to my Plebe Year salvation.

Years later, after she passed away while I was stationed overseas, Sean and I searched the house trying to find her recipes. But they were missing from her kitchen recipe collection, and from the reams of other documents and mementos she kept in a thousand places all over the house. With her death, the most wonderful cookies ever baked would never again grace any holiday table, and Christmas would never be the same.

"Of course, Kevin," she said. "I can do that. But why?"

"Because your cookies are the best in the world," I answered incredulously.

"You've never said that before," she said.

"I haven't?" I hadn't? Why not? "They are, trust me!"

"Then you'll have them," she said.

I could see my statement pleased her, but I wondered why I hadn't ever said that I adored her cookies. My God, I usually ate a thousand every holiday. Then I wondered what other similar gaps I had left in my home life.

"How many dozen do you want?"

"Several."

I watched her make mental preparations for the cookie barrage she would send.

I smiled.  If the upper-class didn't like them, I'd eat every one.

"What are your plans this year?" I asked Sean, who was going into his seventh grade at Our Lady of Good Counsel Catholic School.

I'm gonna play soccer again," he said, "and try to hide from the nuns."

I could understand his attitude.  I'm too hyperactive.  Nuns and I didn't get along very well, as my still-aching knuckles and backside would attest.  Actually, the brothers at St. Catherine's High School weren't much better, just more devious in their tortures.

I had played a bit of soccer in grade school -- most East Coast parochial school boys do -- and my skills were fair, but Sean was an outstanding player.  He had a natural talent for the game, and already several high schools in the Boston area were recruiting him.  I secretly hoped he would choose St. Catherine's, but the better soccer players went to Saint Henry's across town.

"That's great," I said.  "Did you play in the summer league?"

"Of course," he said proudly.  "I was scoring champion again."

"Any other news from the home front?" I asked the three of them.

"Sarah Connelly says 'hi'," Dad offered.

Mom wasn't amused.  "Okay, Kevins.  That's enough about Sarah."

Sensing the finality of her remark, we shut up.  It's not wise to mess with Mom after she says a subject is closed.

CHAPTER 29

## *FESTIVITIES*

At 1700 we went inside to dress for the meal.  Mom put on nice church clothes and Dad wore a coat and tie -- something he rarely did except for weddings and funerals.  Despite vigorous protests to the contrary, Sean also put on a sport coat and tie.

I told him he looked good, which was a big mistake.  He turned toward Mom.  "It's too hot for this, Mom."

I looked at Big Kevin, who I could see completely agreed with Sean about the attire, but who also knew better than to argue with Mom when she had her mind made up.  "Stop complaining, Sean," he said, running a finger along his shirt collar to ease the tension.  "If I have to suffer, so do you."

Mom gave Big Kevin an exasperated look but said nothing.

I showered.  They gaped at how quickly I was ready.

"You sure look good," Mom said, her eyes sparkling with tears.


The drive to Annapolis was uneventful.  The section of Ritchie Highway leading in to Annapolis is lined with deep deciduous forest and scenic rolling hills.  I spent a few quiet minutes gazing out the open window and soaking in the peacefulness.  It was quite an emotional change from the hectic activity inside and around Bancroft Hall.

We exited at the convergence of Route 50 and Ritchie Highway where the sign indicated Annapolis lay 5 miles ahead, and stopped for a few minutes at the scenic lookout just east of the Academy across the Severn River.  In the early evening, with the sun just descending toward the western horizon almost exactly behind the big dome of the Academy chapel and the river sparkling a soft rippling orange, it was a stirring sight.

I looked at Dad, who leaned his two big arms on the stone railing to enjoy the view "Pretty impressive, huh Dad?" I asked quietly.

275

He grunted affirmation, which was usually as enthusiastic as he got.

While the rest of us admired the view, Mom took pictures of everything. I often wondered if Mom ever saw any of the sights we visited: she was so busy recording events. But she enjoyed the photography, even if the quality of her old Kodak Instamatic left a lot to be desired. A new camera was another of the expenses Big Kevin and she had decided to forego.

Mom arranged us for pictures along the stone wall with the Academy in the background. I didn't have the heart to tell her that at this distance it would be very difficult for anyone to recognize the buildings in her pictures. I posed -- standing at attention, standing at parade rest, saluting, cap on, cap off, and sitting on the stone wall. She loved it and I didn't complain.


*La Tratoria* was a somewhat dingy three-story brick-faced building in the middle of a row of similar structures on Main Street. Only a hand-painted sign in the small dark window indicated that this was the place we sought. From the street it looked hardly big enough to seat our party.

We paused. We were ten minutes early, and I didn't see anyone else I recognized among the throngs that strolled the narrow cobblestone street.

We had found a parking space about a quarter mile away, and the walk in the humid near-evening had already caused Big Kevin to sweat profusely. He was uncomfortable. Sean whined through the entire walk. Only Mom held up stoically -- that was her nature.

Sensing that action was required, I pushed open the glass door and held it for my family. The interior seemed dark, particularly after the evening brightness on the street. It was also warm inside, and heavy with the pleasant smells of cooking. An elderly, dark-haired woman approached, holding several menus to her bosom.

She had a trace of an accent. Italian? "Welcome! How many in your party?"

"Jim Merritt made reservations for us," I told her. "There should be about 20."

"Oh, yes," she said, "the Merritt party. This way please."

She led us through the narrow restaurant toward a back section. Most of the tables were set for four, and each was covered with a red and white checked tablecloth. Candles in

276

red glass containers burned on every table, and every table held a tiny bud vase with a single red rose.

I liked this place. I smiled at my parents. We didn't eat out very much at home. And I had 50 dollars in my pocket to pay for their meal. I was going to do this right.

The restaurant was nearly empty. A young civilian couple sat in a corner by the window. One other plebe family sat at a table against the wall. I smiled at him as we passed, but he was focused on his father, who was lecturing him on the latest events in Little Rock, Arkansas. I swear I heard the father say "Them there Razorbacks" in the brief period when we passed.

The matron led us through an arch into another part of the restaurant. Without the bulk of the kitchen to take up space, this back area was much wider. And the back was all ours. Jim Merritt and his family were there. Of course he would get here early.

He rose, as did his father. "Kevin," Jim said warmly, "glad you could make it."

"This is my father and mother, Mr. and Mrs. Michael Merritt, and this is Lynda, my 'sister'." He winked at me. Lynda was very pretty. Jim and his parents laughed.

Lynda feigned indignance. "I am *not* his sister."

I introduced my family.

Mr. Merritt stared at Big Kevin. "Everybody calls me 'Happy'," he said. "My God, you are a biggun. Ever play football?"

Dad laughed. "I've always been large. And yes, I did play football for the Army team in the Pacific during the war. I was a fullback."

Mr. Merritt stared at Dad. "And then some," he said.

I stared open mouthed at Dad. He had never said he played football for the Army or for anyone. That was interesting. I had to start talking to him more.

"Are you comfortable dressed like that?" Happy Merritt asked my Dad. Mr. Merritt had loosened his tie, and draped his jacket over the back of his chair. "Come on. Get comfortable. We're all friends here." Dad looked at Mom, who indicated approval with a nod of her head. Quickly, he and Sean were coatless and open-collared. They both looked more at ease.

Mr. Merritt was a slightly rotund, older gentleman, who had a jovial and entertaining personality. Soon he was regaling Dad with stories of Texas and the oil industry. Mrs. Merritt, who had obviously heard the stories several times before, began a quiet conversation with my Mom. I couldn't hear what they were saying, but they glanced at Jim and me and smiled.

I watched Jim and Lynda.

Lynda noticed me staring and smiled.

"I'm jealous," I said.

She looked puzzled. "Of what?"

"Of Jim. You're much too attractive and nice for this country clod. Are there any more at home like you?"

"Kevin doesn't have a girlfriend," Jim said.

"That's too bad," Lynda answered, "because you're a good looking man." Man? I liked this girl. "But I'm sorry," she continued. "No sisters."

"How about your mother?" I asked.

They laughed, as did Sean, who was listening from his seat next to mine.

"She's married," Lynda said.

"Happily?" I asked questioningly. They laughed again.

"Kevin is the Company jokester," Jim said.

"I can see that."

A few minutes Jubal Ramsey and his family entered, and introductions were made again. Jubal was right. His sisters *were* big, and the oldest kept staring at me. But Jubal's Mom was the star of the show. She was a dark-haired and wonderfully articulate woman who had lived in several exotic places around the world, and she could tell a story beautifully. I could see where Joe got his personality. She was also very pretty -- a trait that had apparently skipped Jubal. And she wasn't married. -- I stopped that train of thought immediately.

The Pooles and Polks arrived simultaneously. I exchanged small talk with the Polks for a minute, but even surrounded by so much enthusiasm and good spirits, I was feeling lonely and sorry for myself. Then Rico showed up.

Rico was by far the handsomest man in the room, and in the restaurant, and probably on the planet. He shone like a brilliant sun in his white uniform and his parents hovered proudly nearby like attendant planets. The Guevarras were happy, fun loving, and garrulous.

And Rosa was the most beautiful creature I had ever seen. She had long, lustrous black hair, so straight and shiny it sparkled. Her complexion was pale and flawless, and her eyes dark and smoldering. She had full red lips, a perfect nose, and shapely breasts.

In her dark miniskirt, were the most perfect set of long legs I had ever seen. Conversation stopped when Rico introduced his family and Rosa. Christ, no wonder Rico had decided to forgo Cindy's pleasures. I would be satisfied just staring at Rosa, much less doing some of the things Rico had in mind.

And Rosa sat next to me, ha, ha! I held out her chair before Rico had the chance to offer.

He looked at me from behind Rosa's back, his eyes alive and mischievous. He smiled, totally sure of himself. What a guy! Rico took the seat at the end of the table so that he faced Jubal. Maybe he wanted to watch Rosa and make sure I stayed a gentleman?

I soon discovered that Rosa had one glaring flaw. When she opened her mouth to talk and words began to flow past those perfect teeth and lips, she had the most thick and grating Brooklyn accent I had ever heard. I had expected to hear Katherine Hepburn, but instead out came the Bowery Boys. But she was as boisterous as the Guevarras, and I soon forgot her speech idiosyncrasies and fell victim to her charm. Rosa also liked to touch, and when she rested her hand on my arm to emphasize a point, it was electric. I would have done anything for this woman.


BJ Wilson showed up ten minutes later, just as we were about to order.

"Sorry I'm late," he said with his usual charm. "I had a phone call from Dad, and he and Mom wanted me to tell you how much they wished they could be here. Dad's feverishly working on the *Bonanza* editing for next week's season opener."

"*Bonanza?*" asked Mr. Merritt.

"Yes. My Dad is the producer for the series, and my Mom runs a fashion studio in Manhattan. This is a very hectic time of year for both of them."

"I'm sure they wanted very much to be here, dear," said Mrs. Poole.

BJ smiled at her. "Yes, ma'am. They did."

Everybody on Jim Merritt's side of the table adjusted seats so that BJ could sit between Lynda and Kate. Poor Lynda and Kate. They'd have to listen to BJ's insufferable stories. He immediately focused on Rosa, however.

I looked at Rico.

He smiled. He wasn't worried. But *I* was a bit peeved because I had been doing a pretty good job of occupying lovely Rosa. Now, with BJ spouting stories of Broadway and Hollywood, I was outclassed. I quieted and engaged in conversation with Kate and Lynda.

We ordered our food, and the meals had arrived with such a clamor of warmth and garlic and cheese smells that I was overwhelmed. I had become so used to Academy food – which, as I said, is very good -- that I had forgotten other tastes existed. My lasagna was delicious.

Except for some wonderfully told stories from Mrs. Ramsey -- I wonder how old she is anyway? - and some interesting oil tidbits from Mr. Merritt, the meal was comfortably quiet.

At one point, a laughing Rosa leaned against me. When she leaned, she exposed a great deal of delicious pale cleavage inches from my widened eyes.

Always the bon vivant, I sputtered and snapped my head so quickly to the opposite side that I cricked my neck. I could feel my face redden. I looked at my Mom, but her stare was disapproving. My Dad could hardly control his chuckling. BJ and Jeff roared laughter in my direction. Feeling like a voyeur for glimpsing Rosa's forbidden treasures, I glanced at Rico.

The bastard winked at me.

I put my arm around Rosa's milky white shoulder, and sneered at Rico. "Do you have any sisters, Rosa?"

By the time the meal ended and our desert plates were cleared, we had consumed enough food to feed a small army. It was such a pleasant unhurried affair, so different from the slam-bam Academy meals, that I was overcome with respect for my classmates and admiration for their families and friends. I leaned backward in my chair and boomed a contented sigh.

Jim and Lynda looked up from their muted conversation and smiled at me. I smiled at them. Then I winked at Jeff and Kate. Then I grinned at Rico. I even tried to peek surreptitiously down Rosa's blouse, but Rico caught me and laughed. I didn't care. Life was great, and everybody, including the normally obnoxious BJ Wilson, was getting along famously.

I listened in on surrounding conversations, almost out-of-body. Mr. Guevarra was telling Mr. Polk about the grocery business, emphasizing a point with his unused dessert spoon. Mrs. Ramsey was telling my Mom and Mrs. Poole about life in China before the war. -- She couldn't be any more than forty years old. Jubal's sister, Becky, was watching me. I smiled at her. She smiled in return. She had a nice smile.

Big Kevin was telling Mr. Merritt about how he almost invested in a mahogany farm in the Philippines after the War. Mahogany? The Philippines? I really had to talk to Dad. He had had a secret life I knew nothing about. Near the end of the meal BJ excused himself. He returned a few minutes later just as several of the ladies excused themselves to 'powder their noses.'

Our parents exchanged addresses and promises to write and send Christmas cards. We also exchanged mutual invitations of visitation rights.

Finally Mr. Merritt said. "Well, it's about time for the checks."

"No need," BJ Wilson said with a charm and a flourish I envied. He stood. "Ladies and gentlemen," he began. "You will be pleased to know that although my Dad could not be here, he sends his greetings -- and his Diner's Club Card number." BJ laughed. "The dinner is on him. He says he hopes you enjoy it and that he and Mom have already made plans to be here June Week when we scale the Herndon Monument. He waved to someone just out of sight of the room entrance. Immediately two waiters entered carrying trays with champagne.

Jim Merritt seemed uncomfortable. BJ continued. "I know it's not legal to drink within the seven-mile limit, but we Tigers have been known to take a few risks, and this is the perfect occasion for a toast."

The waiters offered glasses to each of us, including Sean. I intercepted his.

BJ raised his glass. "To the Class of 1971!" he said.

We drank. It was good!

Jim Merritt spoke next. "BJ," he said. "Please tell your parents thank you from all of us. It was a very pleasant meal and I enjoyed all your company. To the Twenty-third Company!"

We drank again.

Jubal raised his glass. "To the Brigade of Midshipmen!"

Rico was next. "To our wonderful parents!"

Jeff stared at Kate. "To our sweet and lovely companions."

Tommy Poole was next. "To Ronald Steinway!" he said sadly.

We drank a solemn toast.

Everyone looked at me. In my contented stupor I didn't realize that my classmates had alternated toasts. It was my turn! My brain fumbled. My buddies seemed to have covered everything possible. I paused, trying to be dramatic, but in reality searching desperately for something to say.

I raised my glass. "Three months ago, the seven of us fresh-faced and innocent young men began an adventure." I liked what I had said so far. Now what? "The adventure has not been without its pain." I raised my glass to Tommy. "And its losses." I lowered my head and paused. I continued. "But we made it, despite the odds, despite the stress, despite the fact that it would have been far easier to be somewhere else. There are heroes in the making at this table, and I'm damned proud to be counted among them. To us!"

Everyone raised glasses with me. I finished my wine with a flourish. I thought briefly of throwing the glass against the brick wall but decided that I had been dramatic enough. I sat. Everybody smiled at me.

Rosa gave me a 'special' look.

I winked at Rico.


Dinner broke up soon afterward, and we were in great spirits as we exited the restaurant into the warm moonless night. Overhead, stars blazed, and I felt as if I were blazing just as brightly. Mom held my arm as we strolled the quiet cobblestones toward our car.

"That was a nice speech, dear," Mom said.

"Did you practice it?" Sean asked.

"I made the whole thing up as I went," I boasted.

Sean looked at me skeptically.


As we drove away from the city I glanced at my watch. It was 2030, an hour until my rendezvous with Kathy of the marvelous body. Feeling invincible, I smiled. What a hero! What a stud! Maybe things would be more satisfying later?


In the room, Dad removed a fresh six-pack of my old friend National Bo from the cooler, and we sat around a small round table to talk.

 "What's this about football in the Army, and mahogany in the Philippines?" I asked.

Mom answered. "Don't listen to that crazy talk. Your Dad was bragging nonsense."

"That's okay," I said. "I want to listen."

"It's nothing really, son," Dad said. "I played a little football for the Army team during the war. A scout for the University of California even talked to me about a scholarship. But I'm not a California person, and I had to get back to work after the war because my family needed the money. And the mahogany thing was an idea several unit comrades and I discussed. We even calculated how much we would each need to invest to make it work. But too many of us dropped out of the venture when the war ended, and we forgot about it."

Wow, my Dad was almost a college football star and an entrepreneur. I was impressed.

"Those were very nice people we met this evening," Mom said.

"Yeah they were, weren't they?"

"I had a nice time," she continued.  "How about you, Kevin?" she asked Dad.

"It was fun," he said.

"Sean?"

"Me too.  Wasn't that Rosa lady beautiful?"

"I'll say," I answered.

"She was hanging all over you, Kevin," Sean observed, nudging me.

"I wish!" I said.  "But she wasn't at all interested in me.  She's Rico's girl."

"He's a handsome young man," Mom said, "but not as handsome as you, dear."

I looked at her disbelievingly.  Moms, don't we love them?

We talked until almost 2130 when Mom yawned.  "Go on your date, Kevin.  I'm tired.  I'll get ready for bed.  Dad will drive you back."

"Okay.  I'll see you tomorrow."  I kissed her on the cheek and hurried into the bathroom where I changed into my swimsuit and a T-shirt.  Then I started for the door.

"Be back at exactly 1115," Dad admonished as I departed.

I acknowledged him with a wink and grabbed two beers from the table.

CHAPTER 30

## *LOVES LABOR CROSSED*

There were a few young children at the pool when I opened the short fence and went inside the pool area. I selected a pair of lounge chairs and pulled them out of sight of my parents' room. Then I settled back and waited. I could see Kathy's room from where I sat. The curtain opened just a bit and someone peeked out.

In moments she exited the room, waved at me, and came down the stairs. She had on her bathing suit, but over her top she wore a T-shirt with a Mickey Mouse logo on it.

I indicated the chair next to me. She looked up at her room.

"Can we move them over some more?" she asked. "I don't want my parents spying."

I pulled the chairs side-by-side in a far corner of the pool area.

I popped a beer for her and she took a deep drink.

Then she rolled onto her side and said. "Tell me about yourself, Kevin."

I outlined the life of Kevin O'Reilly in about sixty seconds. I was still feeling the influence of the champagne and the beer, and I was amorous. I brushed a strand of hair from her face.

"There," I said. "Perfect."

"Do you think so?" she asked demurely.

"Absolutely," I answered.

"Thank you."

I took her hand and brought it to my mouth and kissed it.

"That's nice," she said.

I leaned in to kiss her, but she pulled away and turned over onto her back.

I moved after her but she held up a hand.  "Not here," she said.  "Too many people."

"Where can we go?" I asked.

She considered.  "Let's move over some, so we're completely out of sight, Okay."

I saw some chairs in the corner behind a bin used to store pool equipment.  "Over there," I said.

Once we were settled on a plastic lounge chair, she slid over next to me and held my arm.

I flexed for her.

"There," I said, turning toward her, "now we're alone."

She reached a hand to my face, slid her hand behind my head and pulled me toward her. We kissed, at first tentatively, then with greater passion.  She was a good kisser.

I pulled her toward me.  I could feel her ample chest against me, and it felt good, and my passion mounted.

After five minutes I was incredibly excited.  I slid my right hand up until it settled comfortably on her bikini top.  She didn't resist.  So far so good.

"I really like you, Kevin."  Ah ha!  That was something to start with.

"I like you too, Kathy," I said, and touched her again.

She looked at me but didn't do anything to stop me. But she didn't respond either, and I was confused.  I tried to smile at her.  "Is something the matter?"

Still, she didn't say anything, and I noticed in the dim light that a glimmer of a tear had formed in the corner of one eye.  I suddenly felt like a real ass.  My God, what was wrong with me?  I was being Danny French -- the guy I ridiculed.  I removed my hand and stared at it.  I felt bad about myself.  My passion had died.

I turned and faced the night sky.  "I'm really sorry."

She didn't answer.  I could hear her crying gently, and I felt even worse.

I put a hand gently on her cheek.  "What's wrong?"

She continued crying.  "I didn't want you to do that," she finally said.

"I didn't know," I said apologetically.  "I'm sorry."

"I'm sorry too," she said. "I'd better get home."

I tried to kiss her but she avoided any contact.

I was confused and a bit angry. I didn't really do anything, did I? It wasn't like we had sex or anything like that. Why was she so hurt?

Gently, I turned her face toward mine and kissed her. She responded, then broke contact. "I have to go."

"Will I see you tomorrow at the pool?" I asked.

"We'll be out all day."

"Will you write me?" I asked. "Please? I'll leave a note under your door later."

She smiled. "Okay," she said. Then she kissed me again.

"Stay here," she said. "I'll go on ahead alone." She turned and put her arms around my waist and hugged me. "Good-bye, Kevin," she said.

I didn't like the finality of that statement.

She hurried down the walkway to the stairwell.

I remained where I was for more than a minute, then walked to my parents' room and entered quietly. Dad and Sean were waiting inside. Mom was asleep in the bed farthest from the door. I could see from the look on Dad's face that he was surprised that I had gotten back so early.

"Did you get kissed?" asked Sean.

"Maybe," I answered.

"Get anything else?" he asked tittering.

"Wouldn't you like to know?" I think my deceptive smile indicated more than actually happened, but I didn't correct his perceptual error. I dressed in my uniform, and the three of us left the hotel for Annapolis. Traffic was light, and we arrived ten minutes early. I hugged Sean and Dad in the parking lot of the Midshipman's Store and told them about the Yacht Basin incident. They enjoyed the story. Then I raced up the steps and through T-Court.

I arrived two minutes early. Merritt and Wilson were there.

"How was your evening, Kevin?" Jim asked.

"Interesting.  How about yours?"

"Great.  We took BJ with us to the hotel and sat talking by the pool all evening."

"What about Lynda?" I asked.

Jim looked confused.  "She was there."

"I mean," I continued.  "What about you and Lynda and . . . being together?"

Jim laughed.  "O'Reilly, you poor sad thing.  There's more to life than sex.  It was wonderful to see her and touch her.  I'm perfectly satisfied."

"Merritt, you're not shitting anyone!"  Rico had arrived.  "Rosa and I had steamy, exhausting sex for two hours this evening while my parents were in Annapolis shopping for souvenirs.  It was great, and I'll bet she won't walk straight for a week.  No way is just looking as good."  Rico turned to me.  "Rosa says hi, by the way.  I'm going to have to keep an eye on you from now on.  I think she was interested in you.  It must be your tragic Irish charm."

"When you finish with her, let me know," I said.  "I'll gladly take seconds."

Rico laughed.  "I don't know when I'll finish," he said.  "She almost wore me out."

Because this was a special night, Maxwell and Battle held a muster in the passageway at precisely 0030.  We braced while they called the roll.  We weren't all there.  Both Richardson and Mulvaney were missing.  Mulvaney arrived during the muster, Richardson showed up an hour later.  Both of them were written up for their tardiness, and now faced weeks of Restriction musters to work off their 25 demerits.

After the muster we went to bed.  Liberty would start on Sunday after a special 1300 parade for the parents.  As we prepared for sleep I remarked to the room, "I had a great time tonight at the dinner.  All the families were wonderful people."


My family came to the chapel for mass.  They watched as we marched up the chapel steps and into the church, and they repeated the greeting as we departed.  Mom took a thousand photos.  That morning after mass and meal I straightened my things in preparation for the Brigade's official return that evening.  The Brigade would be assembled at the 1800 meal formation. I began to feel apprehension. I didn't want to go through the plebe shit again. I had completed Plebe Summer, hadn't I? Shouldn't that be enough?

The day was sunny, hot, and humid -- Surprise! Surprise! Luckily, our parade for the parents was an abbreviated affair. The 36 companies marched out onto the field and halted in precise locations indicated by markers set into the grass. We did the manual-of-arms, and the Superintendent spoke about how proud he was of us, and told our parents about the adventure we had ahead. Within 30 minutes we marched the pass-in-review for the dignitaries, and our parents.

As we marched along the street toward Bancroft Hall, I heard Rico remark, "Look at those tits!" All heads swiveled toward Rico's side of the formation, which happened to be mine as well. Ahead, a girl and her family watched the groups pass. The girl was extremely well developed and attractive. It was Kathy.

She was scanning the companies and looking at the guidons. She was looking for me. She knew what Company I was in from my note. As we neared, I leaned outward to get her attention. The red hair shining from under my cap was a beacon. She saw me, smiled, and raised her arm slightly to wave. She didn't want her Mom and Dad to see. Maybe they were protective.

"She knows you, Kevin?" asked Rico incredulously from his position behind me.

"It's Kathy," I said. "I met her yesterday."

"And already she's giving you that look? You lucky bastard. Did you . . . ?"

"Not saying." I answered.

"Holy shit!" he exclaimed. "You stud! I'm not letting you within a mile Rosa!"

Naturally I didn't let on.

I was dressed in my tropical whites and out the door in ten minutes. My family waited in the parking lot for me. We repeated the hugged greetings, and headed to the hotel.

My family and I relaxed at the pool for an hour. I shared their beer with an unaccustomed gusto. We were pals. As the beer mellowed me, I began to relate some of the more unusual experiences of the summer. For the first time I talked about Ronald Steinway and Tommy Poole. When I recounted Ronald's last moments, I felt tears forming in my eyes. I finished the story, teary but not weeping.

Mom, however, was crying. "That poor dear," she said. "I feel so sorry for his parents."

"I feel sorry for his classmates," said Dad.

What a strange thing to say. "What do you mean?" I asked.

"You're the ones who have to cope with what happened. He's out of it now."

I hadn't thought of it quite like that, but I could see that Dad was right. Ronald would be a cloud that hung over us for a long time to come.

"It was like that during the war," he continued. "Every time we lost a buddy it was really hard to go back into combat again. But you do what you have to do, Kevin."

We made plans for Christmas and I informed Mom that I would indeed be writing to Sarah Connelly -- Patrick Connelly be damned. Mom seemed pleased. All too soon it was time to leave. I hadn't even caught a glimpse of Kathy the entire afternoon, and I was disappointed; but I'd write her and make things better.

The drive to Annapolis was silent. We said tearful good-byes in the parking lot and my parents promised to watch for me during the evening meal formation. I hurried inside -- and confronted utter bedlam.

CHAPTER 31

## *THE BRIDGADE*

The previously deserted passageways teemed with strangers, everyone a potential enemy. I didn't like the look of most of them. Gear was being stowed, and loud greetings exchanged. The clamor of so many people rushing to prepare for formation was overwhelming. I was frightened. I could imagine how poor Tommy Poole must be feeling. The fun was only starting for him. I wondered how his conversation with his family went.

I chopped to my room, chins tight against my neck and my eyes unwaveringly in the boat. I didn't want any trouble just yet. I was first one back. There were 15 minutes to formation. Merritt and Wilson showed up almost immediately after me, and Rico followed them by five minutes. As we prepared, Tommy Poole appeared in the doorway.

"Talked it over with my family," he said, his voice assuming a steely quality I hadn't heard before. "I'm staying!"

We each congratulated Tommy, and he hurried to his room. I began to worry about how prepared I was for this. "I don't even know which platoon we're in," I stated.

"It must be posted," said Merritt. "Who wants to check?" No one volunteered. The flow of human tide outside the room was frenzied. I didn't want to be caught up in it.

"Kevin," Rico said, "you deal with these people better than we do. You go."

Where did he get that idea?

Maybe the beer still had me emboldened. I accepted the challenge. I hurried outside and chopped to the Company bulletin board outside the Company Office. There was a crowd checking the Company information. I inserted myself into the group and scanned the list hurriedly. So far no one had noticed a plebe in their midst. I found our names: second platoon, first squad.

I turned to go, and almost collided with Midshipman First-class 'Rock' Stone, our Company Commander. I almost wet myself. He knew I was a plebe: he could smell my fear. "What the hell are you doing here, plebe?" he said.

"Checking the formation listings, sir!" I yelled.

"You should have done that about two hours ago when they were posted. You're blocking the view of the upper-class. Give me a 100 -- but over there out of the way."

"Aye, aye, sir!" I chopped to a position against a far bulkhead and started cranking out pushups. At 100 I leaped to my feet and hurried down the passageway. I was not amused.

"So much for my ability to deal with people," I announced. "That trip cost me 100."

"Sorry, Kevin," Rico said, not at all repentant. "So what platoon and squad?"

"Two and one."


Evening meal formation was a confusing game of hunt-your-place, and there was no time for any special attention for any of the plebes, which was good. The meal was a similar affair since the upper class attention was more for their classmates than on us plebes. We returned to our rooms without incident. God, was I relieved. I didn't want to be doing this; I wasn't prepared.

We began to ready our things for the start of academics in the morning. I had turned toward the window dividing my books into stacks when a voice announced from the doorway.

"Excuse me. Which one of you is Kevin O'Reilly?"

I turned. A strange plebe stood in the doorway.

"I am," I replied. He looked me over as I walked toward him. Relieved that the visitor had nothing to do with them, the others went about their business. "What can I do for you?"

"You can stay away from my sister!" he said loudly. "She told me about last night. She's only 16 years old, you know!"

I started to speak. Sixteen? But she had said that she had graduated from high school, hadn't she?

"Listen . . . ," I began. It was the last thing I said clearly for several days.

I saw him move, and I saw a glimpse of something fist-sized coming quickly at my head. I was unprepared. Everything went black.

I awoke on the floor of the room. My mouth was full of blood. By probing my tongue, I could feel that my two front teeth were loose and that my lip was split on the left side.

Rico stood in the doorway staring down the passageway. Merritt knelt beside me. Wilson sat still at his desk, eyes wide.

"Are you okay, Kevin?" Jim asked. I tried to answer, but my mouth was full of blood and my lip was quickly swelling. I mumbled and tried to sit up. Jim went to the sink, got a washcloth from the rack, and soaked it in cold water. He brought it to me. I wiped my face, but I still had the blood in my mouth. Jim and Rico helped me to my feet. I spit an enormous quantity of blood into the sink. It splashed the entire sink and mirror with bright red dots.

I rinsed my mouth for a minute until the bleeding stopped.

Rico and Jim hovered nearby. "Do you want us to help you go to Sick Bay?" Jim asked, and for some reason I became angry.

I mumbled loudly. "Naaaaaa, Ah don won ta goh ta Sk By!"  That's what came past my injured and swollen lips.

Jim and Rico jumped back as flecks of bloody spit sprayed from my mouth in all directions along with the incoherent words.

 Rico understood.  He laughed and Jim looked at him as if he were insane.

"Sixteen, huh?" Rico said. "Christ, O'Rellly, you really run the gamut, don't you? Do you know any women your own age?"

I tried to smile but it hurt. It was funny. It had to do something about the Irish curse that seemed to follow me.

I staggered to my desk and tried to clean myself. I had experienced split lips before from during basketball games, so this wasn't a new experience. It still hurt though.

Jim Merritt sat in his chair.  For the first time I could see a taint of strain on his normally stoic face.  I could also see that BJ Wilson was definitely regretting being roomies with Kevin O'Reilly the wondermid.  Only Rico was unperturbed.  He enjoyed this.

"Christ, Kevin," Jim said.  "What next?"


Almost immediately a stranger entered the room.  We snapped to attention.

He came to my desk and put a pair of grubby black shoes down in front of me.  "Okay, Howdy Doody!  I need these shoes looking good before morning meal."  He turned and departed.

I stared at my roommates.  Jim and BJ seemed discouraged.

Rico was still smiling.  "I guess now we know that the Brigade's back," he said.

"Ye weh dah," I said.

Made in the USA
Columbia, SC
07 June 2021